MICHAEL SIEMSEN

WITHDRAWN

THE
OPAL

Fantome

Copyright © 2012 by Michael Siemsen

All rights reserved, including the right to reproduce
this book or portions thereof.

First Fantome trade paperback edition October 2012

FANTOME and logo are trademarks of Fantome Publishing,
LLC, the publisher of this work.

Manufactured in the United States of America

1 3 5 7 9 10 8 6 4 2

ISBN: 098344692X

ISBN 13: 978-0-9834469-2-7

Connect with the author:
facebook.com/mcsiemsen
www.michaelsiemsen.com
mail@michaelsiemsen.com
twitter: @michaelsiemsen

**This book is dedicated to Darian,
Christina, and Erik**

THE OPAL

ONE

If Tuni's best friend ever asked what she and Matt had done for their six-month anniversary, she would have to lie about the most important part. "I gave him a rock" sounded, well, odd, and she wouldn't really be able to go into further detail.

She felt the stone's smooth weight in her hand as they walked along the well-worn trail, shaded by lush tropical foliage. Colorful birds flitted about them, adding their haunting, musical calls to the white noise of an unseen watercourse. She finished the "note" and tucked the rock into a fold of her sarong.

The trail widened, and Matt paused for her to catch up and walk beside him. Oblivious to her plan, he took her hand in his, and a look passed between them that they had shared often lately. He wasn't great with the whole *words* part of the relationship, but they could and did talk about things, and she didn't feel the lack of intimacy that had finally sent her running from each of her previous boyfriends.

Like the others, he told her she was beautiful, but somehow, from his lips, it didn't sound the same. And she believed his corny declaration that he liked her even more without makeup, in her comfy clothes, and white athletic socks.

"Matthew," she said in her London accent tinged with Anglo-South African. Of all the people he had ever met, she alone put the emphasis on the end: "maTYEW."

She tugged on his gloved hand, but he was already stopping. She followed his gaze through the gap in the trees to the view of the lagoon: a breath-slowing

THE OPAL

panorama on an idyllic Bora Bora afternoon. Miles away, over the ocean, dark clouds volleyed silent bolts of lightning.

"Yeah?" he said without turning.

"Thank you again for bringing me here," she said.

Now he turned, smiling brightly, and leaned in—carefully—for a kiss.

Running her fingers over the bump the rock made in her sarong, she decided to give it to him later, when they were back in the suite. It would be more comfortable for him to read it there, anyway. Conditions there would be optimal for a real kiss, too. She had learned there were certain . . . *logistics* involved when it came to physical intimacy with Matthew, but it seldom bothered her. They started down the hill.

Her head buzzed with excitement about her gift. He always maintained that he wasn't a telepath, couldn't read minds. But that was only *technically* true. Because he could read people's imprints on objects—feel their emotions, experience their thoughts, see through their eyes—it was really only an issue of timing. If, right now, she were to make him sit down and take off his glove, and placed the rock in his hand, he would be reading her thoughts of a few moments ago. To her, the difference was merely semantic. She had the opportunity to share her feelings about who he was to her, in a way that no one else on earth could do for another. True, this was the honeymoon period of their relationship, and the intensity of their feelings might well diminish over time. *No, not diminish,* she realized. Rather, their feelings would become something they both could savor, as opposed to wolfing them down in desperate gulps. Whatever the future held for them, he would always have the rock, and with it, he could experience this snapshot in time whenever he wished. And unlike a written message, its power and meaning could never fade.

They reached the bottom of the hill, back on the resort's grounds, where the wild jungle growth gave way to manicured plumeria, ginger blossoms, and bird-of-paradise. Other couples roamed the paths, some with that intent pace that bespoke a clear destination, but most with the happy aimlessness of lovers lost in each other.

Tuni noticed the odd single soul standing alone by one of the bungalows. Attractive, sharp suit, hair in a tight ponytail. She made eye contact with the stranger for an instant before both broke off to look elsewhere.

She and Matt followed the orchid-lined path around the end of the building, toward the grand lobby.

"You ever feel like we're being watched here?" Matthew asked.

"You noticed her, too?" Tuni whispered.

2

"Who?" he mock-whispered back.

"The woman in the suit back there. I thought you said that because—"

"Oh, no, I was being ironic." He gestured at his decidedly untropical attire of cargo pants, turtleneck, gloves, shoes with socks. "Since you mention it, though, I did see a woman in a suit yesterday, but it looked like the resort workers' uniform. Was it gold?"

"Yup. She's an employee; it's the same suit." She pointed at the concierge as they passed his mahogany lectern. "Let's hurry up and fetch our booze before I turn into a bloody paranoiac. I need a shower, too."

✷ ✷ ✷

Tessa Hollander pinched the button on her earbud wire. "Looks like they're headed for the lobby. Should I follow or post?"

The path the couple was on would lead them right past her. This would be the closest they had been since Tessa began—

Oh, shit! The female subject had looked directly at her, made eye contact. Major screw-up. She should have had her shades on, at least. Definitely not going to report that little detail. The couple disappeared down the path. She heard the tinny sound from her dangling earbud and popped it back in, then activated the mic again, "Sorry, Garza, I didn't catch that."

"I said post in sight of their cottage and let me know as soon as they're back. We move on your word."

"Got it."

He sounded pissy. Still sore from last night's rejection, no doubt, but rules were rules, and he was married, besides. Tessa pulled off her gold Noa Noa Resort coat and turned it inside out, folding it over her arm as she walked back down the path to the overwater bungalows. Based on this pair's habits over the past few days, they'd likely be back soon.

The male, Matthew Turner—Caucasian, 26 years old—was the millionaire. About five-eleven with light-brown hair, he looked thicker than the agency's file photo of a gaunt, pale kid. He must have packed on a good fifteen to twenty pounds in the gym since the picture was taken. Odd thing with this one, though: he was always overdressed for the weather. Yesterday, through binocs, she had seen him on a boat, in a full-body wet suit. The warm water made a wet suit unnecessary, but if he insisted on it, why not the cooler short-sleeved Farmer John style? And same thing today—who went hiking in cargo pants and a turtleneck when it was ninety degrees? Strangest of all—and she had missed this the first couple of times—he always had on these thin flesh-colored gloves. At first, she had thought him a burn victim, or maybe he was covered with swastika prison tats, until she saw him on the deck of their bungalow in just shorts. He was pale as a ghost but didn't seem to have anything to hide. Maybe he was one of those germaphobes.

And Turner's file was missing a page. The bottom of each sheet read *1 of 4, 2 of 4, 3 of 4*, but she didn't have *4*. Her boss, Garza, in his usual macho fashion, had just said, "Don't worry about it."

The female, Tuni St. James (South African-born, joint UK and U.S. citizenship, 32 years old), looked like a runway model, though she had the unconcerned walk of someone more studious than social. Privately, Tessa thought it the walk of a bitch, but she had to allow that a D cup size, along with five inches over her own height, may have colored her thinking about the woman. Tessa was accustomed to being the eye magnet in the room, and anyone who shifted the attention from her was apt to get on her bad side.

Both subjects were associated with a museum in New York City. And both were about to have their vacation rudely interrupted.

Tessa grabbed a beach chair from the row atop the grassy ledge and dragged it onto the sand. A young couple with an excitable Chihuahua strolled alongside the placid turquoise lagoon that led to the bungalows. Other couples—it seemed everyone on this side of the island came in pairs—walked without purpose, as if intoxicated by cloying, nauseating, undying romantic love.

Tessa kicked her sandals off and slid her slacks down to her ankles, revealing the bottom half of her purple bikini. Her blouse joined the jacket and slacks on the sand, and she sat down, intentionally slowly, temporarily interrupting the honeymoon bliss of more than one nearby couple. She pulled her shades down from the top of her head and shifted her eyes left, pretending not to notice a wife's reproachful glare at her man's wandering attention. Tessa smiled inside and turned her focus to the bungalow of interest.

"In position," she murmured.

✶ ✶ ✶

Matt slid the key card through the slot and swung the door wide for Tuni. "After you," he said theatrically.

Inside, the cool air felt good, but he knew she would soon be too cold. He turned the thermostat up a few degrees on his way into the bedroom. The bed was still in sweet disarray. *No maid service needed here,* he mused. No surprise imprints to smack into when removing his gloves for a quick face washing. Let the housekeeping staff "dirty" the place all they liked—after he and Tuni were done with it.

He dropped his gloves and peeled off the sweaty turtleneck, tossing it into one of the closets, then grabbed a washcloth and used it to turn on the water. *You've touched this faucet before,* he chided himself. He scrubbed his face and turned off the water with his bare hand—no issues.

Tuni called from the other room, "What are we doing right now? I still have to shower."

"I was going to lie out on the balcony—get a few more rays before sunset." He looked himself over in the mirror and said, "I don't think I'm even *white* yet!"

He kicked off his cargo pants on top of the turtleneck and slid on some long swim trunks.

Tuni leaned in the bathroom doorway, threw her sarong atop the growing pile, and laughed. "I don't mind you transparent, you know."

He smiled and grabbed her wrist in passing, leading her through the living room to the sliding glass door. He reached for the handle, then hesitated, his hand hanging in the air as if frozen.

"Crap, have I . . . ?"

"Twice now, yes."

"Sorry," he said with a sigh. "This will never stop being weird."

He forced himself to clutch the handle, exhaled when nothing happened, and slid the door open.

"See?" Tuni said. "This is what you *paid* for. Everything new from the resort's expansion. I know you asked for twenty-four-seven 'do not disturb,' but the housekeeping staff wear gloves all the time—I've seen them." Now she took him by the hand out onto the patio. On the glass-topped wicker table between their two cushioned deck chairs were two sweating glasses of spiked cola. Beyond a low guard rail, the lagoon reflected the sinking sun. "Remember," she said, "it's not worth a bloody nickel if you can't enjoy it."

Matt sat down on the chair nearer the door as Tuni walked back inside. He stretched out, well aware of his bare legs, back, neck, elbows, and heels, all rubbing against foreign objects of unknown provenance. He picked up the glass beside him and sipped. His lips touching strange glass.

* * *

Tuni grabbed the rock from her purse and took a deep breath. She walked back outside onto the balcony and climbed on top of Matthew, careful to keep her bikini bottom touching only his long shorts, and not letting her top get too close to him. He looked up at her and smiled with elation.

"How daft is all this?" she said.

"How's that? Which part?"

"*'Which part?'* Look at you! Bloody wearing shorts? Not even a T-shirt?"

He smiled, stroking her arms. "Get what you pay for, right?"

She gave him a quick kiss on the mouth and carefully stood up, peering out at the sky. She had the stone palmed at her side. *No better time than now* . . .

"You are so frickin' beautiful, it's scary," he said.

She turned, one brow aloft. "Odd compliment, dear. Let's stow that one away permanently, shall we?"

One of her exes had always said something similar. Matthew couldn't possibly know. He was just being immature—an attempt at cuteness. But the memory had blemished the moment, so she decided to give him the rock *after* dinner.

"Sorry . . ." He suddenly leaned up. "Oh, shit! What time is it?"

She glanced at the wall clock inside the room. "Half past six, why?"

He started to get up. "Our reservation! For some reason, I thought we had more time . . ."

"Relax, Mr. Punctual. They're not going to give our table away if we're five minutes late. I'm still all sandy anyway—gonna take a quick shower. Enjoy the view for a few before you get dressed, okay?"

She walked inside, leaving the sliding glass door open behind her. The room felt a bit cold, so she flicked off the thermostat on her way past. The wall jets in the shower sprayed from three sides, and she tossed her bikini top and bottom onto the growing mound of clothes and stepped in.

* * *

Matt closed his eyes and leaned his head back on the deck chair cushion. *Everything new,* he reflected. Four thousand a night was a small price to pay for a week like this. He still worried, still hesitated before letting his skin touch anything, but that wasn't really a habit he *wanted* to break. For the sake of the vacation, he had to find a happy medium. If he touched something with an imprint, Tuni would be stuck with the consequences. Though they had seemed to fall into a good rhythm on avoiding hazards, he couldn't have his ability dominate their budding relationship. That had happened to him before, and it didn't work. Tuni was the best thing in his very weird life, and he wasn't about to make the same mistakes with her.

"Hello, Mr. Turner," an English-accented man's voice said from above his head.

Snapping his head back quickly, Matt saw the last face he had ever expected to see again. Dr. Garrett Rheese, one of the few people who knew of Matt's ability—and the only one who could set off the alarm now shrieking away in Matt's head. Rheese's middle-aged face sagged oddly from looking down on him, but the triumphant smile was unmistakable. Two tall men with buzz cuts flanked him as he held out a big, thick book.

"I'm going to need your help tracking down a little something," he said. "Thank you in advance."

The book dropped onto Matt's stomach. His body fell limp on the chair, and the familiar rushing sound sucked into his ears as his body shifted into a fetal position. But it wasn't *his* body he was feeling.

I am Heinrich Strauss. I am thirty-four years old. I live in a mansion in Salzburg, Austria. The year is 1917. I'm crying, curled up in my bed. My wife has left me for a poor dancing man from Vienna. I pray on this Bible that I may find the strength to go on.

TWO

He spoke in a sympathetic tone, his brow furrowed with concern. "Little cuts—only little ones, dear." His manner was that of a pediatrician about to give a shot. "They hurt a teensy bit at first. Then, unfortunately, you will begin to anticipate the next one, and the next, until, in your head, they become the most painful thing you could ever imagine. And they feel surprisingly hot. Once the cuts are halfway up your arm or leg, the entire area feels this heat. But I'm going to start you off at the ankles today, okay? That is okay, isn't it? You look angry. That's okay. Just be sure to stay still; otherwise, a little cut becomes a big cut, and there's only so much I can do for those."

He rested the scalpel on her thigh as he took a pair of latex gloves from a bulk supply box and pulled them on. Then, using a cotton ball, he rubbed alcohol on both her ankles. With the blue gloves and protective glasses, he could pass for a real doctor—or a nurse, perhaps. He picked up the scalpel again and gave her an apologetic smile. He could tell that, like the others, she wondered if he might actually be either.

She held her head up, feeling the drugs, and watched with dizzy, shifting focus as he inspected the shiny blade. It was the kind that real doctors used.

The sharp edge touched her skin.

For a moment, she couldn't look away—she would watch it happen. But at the last second, she let her head drop back and squeezed her eyes shut. He made the first incision, and if not for the slight sting of the alcohol in the cut, she might have thought he was just drawing a line on her skin with a ballpoint pen. She tilted her head up from the table again and looked. Now he wore a big, disturbing smile and appeared to be short of breath. The inside of her pale ankle had a thin red line about two inches long. He dabbed at the trickle of blood with a stack of gauze squares.

"See? Not so bad, right?" he said, flipping the gauze over and dabbing some more. His small eyes held hers. "It's because they are so sharp—much sharper than a razor blade. That's so folks can get stitched up all nice and neat and without much scarring. Now, the next . . ."

Against her better judgment, she watched him slice into the other ankle. He was going deep. Had he cut this deep last time? It probably didn't hurt any worse, but her terror had multiplied, and she screamed into the gag. Her body seized beneath the chest and waist restraints, and she pulled wildly at the leather wrist and ankle straps.

He rolled back on his little stool and watched impassively.

"Oops, you must have peeked," he said, but she didn't hear. "Never a good idea—although I do, um, *appreciate* it." Inhaling slowly and deeply, he waited. He reveled in the tingle that crawled up the back of his neck and spread over his shoulders. He felt himself stir and tighten down there, and then came the numbness at the tips of all his fingers and toes.

She let out another small scream—more a growl of frustration than a shriek—and her body went limp. In all the frenzy, her thin hospital gown had climbed up her thighs, and she saw that he was looking. His little mouse eyes crossed just a bit.

Standing up, he laid the cool scalpel on her thigh, pinched the hem of the gown with both hands, and pulled it down to cover her. He smiled kindly, his eyebrows scrunched like those of a wise old nanny. "That was quite a big tantrum for such little cuts!"

She glared at him with seething rage. She wanted to trade places with him. She wanted to cut him into little pieces. She would make it last . . .

"You should try to relax," he said. "This is a long process, and I've got to keep you healthy until . . . Well, let's get that second cut taken care of, hmmm?"

She closed her eyes and felt him lift the cool metal off her leg.

She opened her eyes, and the light was different. There were people around her. Policemen, one in a suit, the other in uniform, both staring at her. The uniformed one sipped from a coffee mug.

"Report, Matty." The suited man clapped his hands together and snapped his fingers next to her ear. The man's face was blurry. "C'mon back, boy. It wasn't even that long. Matty!"

They found me . . . I'm alive . . .

"Give him a minute, Rog," the other policeman said.

Him? Boy? Rog . . . Roger Turner—Dad . . . Uncle J . . . I'm me.

She . . . she's already dead . . . Where's the . . . ?

The little boy's eyes rolled around the room until they found the scalpel. It lay on a plastic tray beside him. Dark, dry blood on it, tiny flakes on the tray beneath it. *Her* blood. From the "little cuts" that eventually went all the way up her legs and arms to other places he shouldn't be thinking about. The bad man had done it before, many times. He was thinking about those other times while sitting there watching her flop around. He was thinking about everything he planned to do to her. It made the bad man buzz inside.

"Matty, c'mon, now!" his dad said. "Everyone's waiting on you."

"Um . . ." Matty Turner choked a little. "I saw his face as her . . . and, um . . . I know what the room looks like."

"*Him,* boy! You weren't him at all?" Dad was getting frustrated.

"Rog," Jess Canter—Uncle J to Matty—said as he laid a hand on his partner's shoulder.

"I was," Matty sniffed. "Like, back and forth, between them . . . He . . . he's done it a bunch of times, too. He killed her, right? She's already dead?"

Roger's nostrils flared as he inhaled. "We need a name, Matty. Name, age, place. Name, age, place. That's how we do it, right? First priority. So do you have it? Name, age, place?

Matty's eyes turned up as he searched the ceiling for the answer. He didn't know it—had been too distracted by what he saw and felt. He thought of a name that sounded right.

"I . . . I think maybe . . . Gary?"

"*Gary,* Matthew?" Dad wasn't holding in his frustration any longer. "The *cat's* name? C'mon, boy, this is bull! These are people's *lives.* You can't just make stuff up!"

"Can . . . can I have some water? She was real thirsty."

"Exactly, Matty. *She* was thirsty, not you. *She* got hurt, not you. You have to do better, kid. Take control of it. Tell it what you want. It's not a movie, right? We practiced this how many times now?"

"Uh, a bunch?" Matty sat up and rubbed the insides of his ankles. His dad brushed his hands away.

"Yeah, a bunch. Now, we gotta get you back in there, okay? Five more minutes."

"Uh, Rog, I don't think that's a good idea just yet," Jess said. Other people could be heard chatting outside the closed door.

"He's *my* son, J," Roger said. "I know what he can handle."

Matty felt the panic coming on, saw the scalpel lifted from the tray. More tiny flakes of blood fell from it, drifting down like dark little snowflakes of rust. He swallowed, shook his head, and defiantly tucked his bare hands into his armpits.

"Stop messing around, boy. We don't have time for this nonsense. Gimme your hand."

His father's body bent over him, the scalpel in one hand.

"I don't want to, Daddy. Please. Just . . . just give me a minute!" All at once, Matty became aware of every bit of exposed skin: his neck, cheeks, ears, the little bit of unprotected wrist in front of his armpits. His socks came up past his calves, but he felt as if his ankles were out in the open, too. "No, please, Daddy. No . . ."

Uncle J cupped a hand in front of his eyes as he turned away.

His dad spoke softly. "Just a few more minutes, Matty. You need to be tougher than this, though. Lotta people depending on you. Name, age, place, yeah?"

Matty's dad pulled one of his son's hands free, held it open, and brought the scalpel to the palm.

"Little cuts, dear . . ."

Matty woke up in the back of his father's car. He felt the hum of the road, the cushioned bounce of overrun potholes. He opened his eyes and saw the back of the driver's headrest. It was fine, brown leather.

Not Dad's car. Just a dream. One of the investigations. "Dr. Hoboken," the news called him. How old was I—eleven? Whoa, woozy head. This is how she felt. Altitude . . .

Twenty-six-year-old Matthew Turner looked around him. But he wasn't in a car. It was his own plane, the Gulfstream G150 that he bought just a few months ago—well, half bought. He would pay it off within a year. He had wanted to pay cash in one transaction, but he didn't have fifteen million available to spend just yet, and he couldn't abide the thought of a used plane, with all those imprints. "New or nothing"—that was his mantra.

He peered out the window and saw puffs of cloud, with ocean peeking through between.

How the hell did I get here? His memory was foggy, and his eyes had trouble staying focused. He felt an odd sensation in the back of his head, near the neck. It reminded him of the muddled high of some of the stronger pain meds he had taken during physical therapy. Yeah, this was a very druggy feeling.

The seat in front of him rocked back a little. Someone was in front of him, and someone next to him. He glanced right and saw the glow of a tablet screen in somebody's lap. Nubby, wrinkled fingers, Cambridge ring, canvas coat, bald head. Dr. Rheese, the man behind his two-month coma last year. The doctor had since grown a thick, gray mustache and a paunch.

Shit! Rheese . . . right. Oh, God . . . Tuni!

"Where's Tuni?" Matt demanded, sitting up. But his gloved hands were behind his back, the cuffs around the seatbelt coupling.

Rheese didn't turn or look up from the screen in his lap.

"Your lanky black tart is fine, Turner. Just relax." The familiar aristocratic British accent. "Much travel lies ahead."

Matt peered down at the iPad in his captor's lap. A map filled the screen. Rheese was dragging the image of the map across the surface, waiting for more segments to load in the vacant areas. The device was protected within a navy blue suede case. *Matt's* navy blue suede case. Matt's iPad, connected to Matt's enormously expensive satellite-based in-flight Wi-Fi. Rheese glanced at him, frowned, and turned the screen away.

"Mind your manners, lad. You'll know what you need to know, when you need to know it."

"Tell me where she is—now!"

"You want me to knock his ass out again, Doc?" the man in front of Matt said without turning around. He had a faint Hispanic accent. "We got more of that juice."

Matt leaned into the aisle and saw a thick, tan neck and a black buzz cut.

Rheese considered a moment, then simply passed the question on to Matt with a raise of his eyebrow and a smug smile. Matt shook his head and turned away in silence.

"Not necessary, it seems," Rheese replied.

Matt squeezed his eyes shut and tried to remember what had happened. He and Tuni were in Tahiti at the resort. She had gone in to take a shower. That's when he had heard that obnoxious, pompous voice behind him. The shock of that moment had felt like a bucket of ice water being dumped on him. He had looked up to see Rheese and two other guys—one of whom, presumably, now sat in front of him—and he was out before he could do anything.

He must have put some artifact on me. Where was I in the imprint? Right, Austria! Rich guy pissing and moaning about his wife taking off. Curled up in his bed with a giant, fancy Bible, talking to himself for hours. The Bible—that's what he dropped on my stomach! But I didn't come out of it when the imprint went to dark space, or when they took the thing off me . . . The "juice" that guy talked about—that must be why I was dreaming about . . .

Matt looked out the window again, noting that the sun was behind them and had either just risen or was about to set. They had drugged him, clearly. But how did they manage to get him on the plane? He had worn only swim trunks on the hotel room balcony, so someone had to have dressed him. All these thoughts put a sour twist in his stomach, and he repressed a panic attack with self-soothing thoughts that those things had already happened. It was done. His skin was appropriately covered.

Since discovering his "specialness" (as Mom called it) at age nine, Matt had obsessively protected his bare skin from contact with foreign objects. Turtleneck shirts, high socks under long pants, gloves, and knit beanies remained a daily necessity. Not *every* object or surface in the world possessed emotional imprints from other people, but most did, and he never knew which would or wouldn't. A brand-new jacket, ordered over the Internet and shipped inside plastic wrapping? Most likely safe. A door handle at the local coffee shop? Guaranteed imprints—some of them scary. And as a child, he learned that bare skin touching imprinted object meant instant sleepy time—his head went fuzzy, his eyes rolled back, his legs gave out, and his face said hello to the ground.

To others, it looked like some chronic form of narcolepsy: he was just falling asleep at random times and locations. But in Matt's head, he was reliving the experience of someone (or many someones) who had, at some point, touched that same object, whether two centuries or two hours ago. The order in which he experienced the imprints depended on the power of the imprinters' emotions at the time of contact. Door handles were more an embarrassment than a real threat, since he would typically break skin contact as he fell— sometimes even catching himself before any real damage was done. But even just sitting down on a subway seat, your shirt could sometimes ride up and expose the small of your back . . .

Matt had once ended up riding the train for seven hours, trapped in an endless loop of misery and joy unknowingly deposited over the years into a shiny orange plastic seat back: a teenage girl just dumped by her boyfriend, a drunken stockbroker having the night of his life, a schizophrenic homeless man dreaming of suited men hiding inside old metal garbage cans to spy on him, a baby with a full diaper wailing up at a blurry ceiling as Mom tried repeatedly to shove the pacifier back in its screaming mouth. To passersby, the young guy slouched by the window appeared to be just another sleeping student. He wasn't freed until a custodian came through and, fearing he had "another cold one," pushed over the comatose passenger, breaking the contact between Matt's skin and the seat.

Outside the plane's window, he could see the clouds growing paler. That meant the sun was rising, which told him they were headed west. West of Tahiti, so Asia . . . or Europe, or back to his favorite: Africa. Not that it mattered, but knowing that he was getting farther from home rather than closer just sank him deeper into despair.

"That's the Pacific," Rheese said. "We're headed to Australia, where we'll transfer to a commercial aircraft, then off to Ukraine."

Rheese had opened the door to further dialogue.

"Why are we going to Ukraine, and where is Tuni?"

Rheese sighed. "She's still in Tahiti, still in the hotel room where last you saw her. She will remain there—under supervision, of course—until I'm done with you."

"*Done* with me? Who the hell do you think you are?"

Rheese gave a weary sigh. "Yes, done with you. I spent a bit of time investigating your background this past year. Little of interest to find at first glance, however . . ." He paused and tilted his head toward Matt, ". . . I must say that if *I* possessed an ability such as yours, I would probably avoid the public eye when using it for financial gain."

Matt chided himself. *The goddamn newspaper!* He had operated under the radar for seven years while working for the museum. Only a few select people there knew of his talent, and—in everyone's interest—they kept quiet his role in artifact tracing. Since they couldn't very well disclose Matt's findings, they primarily used the information as a guide or fact-checker for existing theories and measurements. He had started with the museum at 17, referred there by his Uncle J on the theory that he needed something that would keep him busy and use his talent for something positive. "It can't be that *everything* out there has a traumatic story, right?" Uncle J had said. *Well, maybe.*

They had paid him well for his age. Not having much of a social life, he could save most of his wages, and got himself a car after a year and a half. A VW Jetta. Not new, as he would have preferred, but the previous owner hadn't left any imprints lying around, so he was happy with it. No more subway, no more crowded sidewalks. Four years later, he got an idea. And within two short years after that, he was a multimillionaire. The Jetta now sat in his driveway, parked in front of the gleaming Porsche and gathering layers of dust.

"You traced a single piece of Spanish silver to the scuttled galleon where the rest had lain for over three hundred years," Rheese said in a slightly bewildered tone. "That company C-Trex—they must adore you. I was actually tickled as I read the article and saw your smiling face among all those elated men and women. Sixteen tons of silver—good Lord! Personally, I think they took you to the bank on the profit sharing there, but I suppose you could work out a better deal next time, eh?"

"I wouldn't have been able to do it without them."

"Nor they without you," Rheese smirked. "And you could have worked with anyone, but there is only one Matthew Turner. We may work out a similar arrangement, you and I."

Yeah, that's gonna happen, asshole.

"As for Ukraine, well, I suppose I should have you get started on that. But first, let us discuss airport protocol and interactions with officials."

"Yeah, whatever—I get it. Alert anyone that I'm a hostage, and Tuni *gets it*, right? I still have trouble believing just what a steaming heap of shit you are."

Rheese didn't bat an eye. "A classic dramaturgical arrangement, I'm aware, but no less effective for it. The difference here is that I am not some archetypal villain, nor are you the hero. On the contrary, I was smeared and robbed—admittedly indirectly—by you and am simply recouping losses. I'm not threatening your life or limbs, nor is the colored lass in any danger. That said, to ensure that things remain so, you are to behave like a good little boy."

"Uh, let me see—what part of that *wasn't* a threat just then?"

"Interpret it as you will," Rheese said breezily. "Will you conduct yourself with some decorum, or do we need to have a different conversation?"

"I don't know what 'decorum' means, but I'll act normal. How long will this take?"

"We'll be there tomorrow morning," Rheese replied. "Our meeting shouldn't last beyond noon, local time."

"Uh-huh, and then what?"

"Oh, right. Well, we'll have to see how it goes, I suppose. Assume you'll be back on vacation within a few short days."

"Oh, *only* a few days? Is that all? And Tuni? She's a *hostage*! Do you even get that? What about my pilots? Are they up there? I . . . I'm not doing anything until I talk to Tuni."

"Hey, kid," the man seated in front of him said, his voice soft yet menacing. "Shut yer whinin' little punk mouth before I stuff my sweaty sock in there and duct-tape it. You'll do just what yer told, or I'll tear yer goddamn throat open and rip out yer tongue." As he spoke, he leaned out and partially turned so that Matt got a first look at his face: dark skin, cheap shades, goatee, a silver-capped canine tooth, acne-scarred cheeks. He had the hulking, round, neckless shoulders of a body-builder. "We call it a *corbata colombiana*—Colombian necktie. Shit's agony, and definitely calls for a closed-casket funeral."

"That's enough," Rheese interrupted. "We're not threatening anyone here, remember? Don't make me speak to your boss about it."

The man muttered a few Spanish vulgarities and settled back into his seat, out of sight.

"I will allow you a quick word with your lady friend when it's convenient," Rheese continued. "That was already planned. Your pilot is in the cockpit, where he belongs. I fired only the copilot (on your behalf), replacing him with this charming fellow's partner. The pilot knows he'll be set free in Australia. And by the way, he's already activated the jet's emergency distress beacon, in case you were wondering."

Matt studied Rheese's face, wondering what was so amusing about that. He could practically hear the drumroll as the man waited for his reaction, but Matt gave him only stone-faced silence.

Unable to hold out any longer, Rheese said, "Fortunately for us, my aide-de-camp is quite knowledgeable about such things—he secretly disabled it before the pilot stepped aboard."

"You're so pleased with yourself," Matt said.

"True, I suppose," Rheese admitted, returning his attention to the screen on his lap, "although genius is a heavy burden nonetheless."

THREE

The Gulfstream landed at Brisbane International Airport in the early evening and taxied toward the private aircraft zone, where it passed a line of three other small jets waiting to unload. Pounding rain drummed on the roof and streamed down the windows. Matt watched out the window as a ground guide in rain gear and a reflective vest waved his conical red flashlights at the cockpit, trying to steer them into the line, then gave up as they continued taxiing toward some hangars at the end of the tarmac.

There the jet swung left and stopped between a hangar and a large stucco building. The man who had threatened Matt got up and stuck his head in the cockpit to talk to someone. A minute later, Matt's new "copilot" came out of the cockpit. Also Latino, he had the same buzz-cut hair, broad shoulders, and ripped physique. But this one had the sort of bad-boy good looks that incited shallow women to leave their nice-guy boyfriends. Both men struck Matt as military types, right down to their lace-up commando boots.

Their introduction was less than ceremonious: "You gonna behave?" the handsome one asked Matt.

"Yeah, I'll be good," Matt said.

"You sure? 'Cause we could always just *ship* you there. Wouldn't have to interact with anybody at all."

"I'm sure."

"Good. Let's go, then. Doctor, you got everything?"

"I believe so, Mr. G." Rheese said it with an air of childish delight.

"Just 'G,' Doctor. And he's just 'Z.' Now, let's get moving before security gets here." He glanced at his watch. "We're running a little late, too."

Matt half expected Rheese to ask if he could have a code name, too.

Duffel bags and packs were pulled out of the storage areas. Matt's pilot, Vin Chiu, his wrist cuffed to the yoke, gave him a concerned good-luck nod from the cockpit. Walking down the steps, Matt hunched beneath the oppressive rain.

"Here," Z yelled, giving Matt his rolling suitcase. Matt took the handle and followed Rheese and G along the walkway between the stucco building and the hangar. Z walked behind him, with a duffel slung over each shoulder. Lightning struck somewhere nearby, its flinch-inducing crack echoing between the buildings.

G stopped at a door, pulled a card from his hip pocket, and swiped it through the reader by the door handle. The lock clicked, and he held the door open as the other three walked in.

Inside, G handed Matt a stack of papers and a passport just before they reached security. Matt flipped open the passport to discover that he was, apparently, one Albert Apedaile, from New Orleans. They made it through without any problems or special attention from the affable Aussie guards. The gate attendant smiled, said "G'day," tore off her piece of each ticket, and hurried them down the Jetway to their plane, which was almost done boarding.

"I'll take your bag there, mate," a young baggage handler said, reaching for Matt's suitcase. "Have yourself a good time in Brizzy, didja?"

"Uh . . . yeah," Matt replied, handing off the suitcase. "It was a blast."

"Lovely town," the handler said with a grin, and took the bag down the stairway to the cargo section.

G and Z took their seats in front of Matt and Rheese. Matt looked at his row and paused.

"Hurry in, Turner," Rheese snapped. "You're backing up the queue."

Matt swallowed. He imagined the hundreds of people who had sat in this seat before him: people phobic about flying, colicky babies, businessmen in the throes of financial disaster, people flying home for an unexpected family funeral. He calmed himself with a deep breath and with the mental exercises he had been working on for the past year. *Stick to the mechanics,* he said to himself as he retucked his undershirt and pulled his wet sweater down over his jeans. Then he pulled up the collar of his turtleneck and tugged the knit cap down over it in back.

From the next row, Z hissed at him in the hushed but menacing tone of an angry parent in a public place. "Get in yer damned seat."

Matt was ready, and he slid into the window seat as Rheese plopped down beside him to let the line of glaring passengers behind him proceed.

"I need to use the bathroom," Matt said, and Rheese groaned.

Z's nose suddenly appeared in the space between the seats. "If it can't wait till we're in the air, you'll just have to piss yerself right there."

Rheese murmured, "He'll do no such thing, Sol—er, Z. You . . . you just worry about yourself. Now, is it urgent, Turner, or can it wait until after takeoff?"

"I guess it can wait."

Rheese leaned forward and snapped at Z, "See? How hard was that—a small measure of civility?" He turned back to Matt. "Now, then, lad, after everyone is seated, I'll need you to get to work on this artifact of mine."

"What's the artifact?"

Rheese glanced around. Behind them sat a small child and a woman wearing earbuds. Across the aisle to Rheese's left, two long-haired, sporty-looking lads laughed and discussed something loudly in another language, presumably Ukrainian. No one else was close enough to hear what Rheese had to say, and the young men's noisy banter would help ensure privacy. He turned back to Matt and spoke quietly.

"Well, you've already made its acquaintance. It's a Bible. I need everything it's been through."

Matt frowned. "What Bible? The one you dropped on me? There wasn't really anything of value in the imprints I got—just the usual Bible stuff."

Rheese's eyes fell to half-mast. "Indulge my ignorance."

"People praying . . . So-and-so is sick, so-and-so didn't return when they were supposed to, guilt, pleading, mourning, crying. *Bible* stuff. Trust me, if that thing is more than a hundred years old, it's probably got a year or more of useless imprints—in *reading* time, that is."

"I need to know when and where it was separated from its companion volume, and to whom the other volume went."

The jet pushed back from the gate as flight attendants patrolled the aisles, inspecting seat backs, tray tables, and lap belts.

"Look, Rheese—sorry, *Doctor* Rheese—you let me talk to Tuni and I'll help you with whatever, but you have to understand that I *know* all about these things. This is what I've done for over fifteen years, and I can tell you, there would be so much time involved in reading this thing that it could never be worth it. Even on the tiny off-chance that I found some magical clue that tells you these other books are mortared into this wall in such-and-such castle, blah blah blah, how much could a *book* possibly be worth?"

"Twenty-five million American dollars."

Matt turned and gaped.

"What I have is volume two of a Gutenberg Bible. You do know what that is."

"Like a Jewish Bible?"

"Please do not clarify whether that was a joke, as I will assume that it was and move on. They are the rarest, most valuable books in the world. Fifteenth century, the first books ever printed on a printing press with movable type. Very few were produced, and every complete copy is accounted for—every orphaned volume, every individual leaf. A single page can fetch a hundred thousand at auction."

"So why don't you just sell the part you have? Wouldn't that alone be worth millions?"

"It isn't mine, you buffoon. Of course I would sell it. I need you to trace it back to when it was separated from its sibling volume. Volume two's generous owner has offered me a whopping sum for finding its other half. I informed him that for me to deliver on this deal, I would need his copy for a week."

"So you dropped an ancient, fabulously expensive book on my stomach?"

"It is not ancient, technically, and it was the only item I had that I knew for certain would have history in it. I can't exactly *check* these things, you know."

"And then you drugged me."

Matt noticed that in front of them, Z was repeatedly stretching his neck and rotating his shoulders.

Rheese sighed. "To be honest, I thought that the most humane method. But if you wish to have your ability and yourself abused further, do let me know."

"I see. So you were doing me a favor."

Z suddenly turned around again. "Doc, for the love of God, just let me take this punk to the bathroom and . . ."

Rheese put up a hand, turned to Matt, and said, "Are you *refusing* to read the Bible . . . so to speak?"

"No, I'm just—"

"Lovely, then we have an accord!" Rheese leaned over and opened the attaché case between his feet.

"Well, I guess it's a long flight," Matt said. "But I can't just go all the way through! Don't make me do that. I need my timer."

"The armband gadget? Certainly. Where is it?"

Matt groaned. "It was in my suitcase."

"No problem. I'll be your timer. How long would you like to go for?"

"Oh, uh . . . I don't know. Maybe twenty, thirty minutes at the most."

Rheese glanced at his knockoff Rolex. "Sure, let's call it an even hour for simplicity's sake. (We do have a fourteen-hour flight ahead of us)."

"Well, I still have to take a leak. Seriously."

Rheese sighed. "Fine, thirty minutes for the first round!"

He pulled a heavy volume from its thick protective bag and placed it gingerly in his lap. It was bound in leather that had once been black, with a ribbed spine and brass adornments at the corners. Rheese unfolded an airline blanket and draped it over the book, holding it as if he were a magician about to reveal a platter full of doves.

"We need to be discreet with this, and *you* need to be careful with it. Do not touch the pages, do not hold it by only one cover, do not touch the print on the spine, do not—"

"What if I accidentally piss myself while it's in my lap?"

Rheese frowned and returned the book to its soft vellum wrap, careful to avoid rubbing any edge or surface.

"I was half-joking," Matt said.

"Yes, I recall you being quite the comic in Kenya." He always pronounced it *KEEN-yuh.* "You can reach into the bag. Try to touch only the brass corner. I must stress that this *cannot* be returned in any condition other than the one in which it left home."

"You weren't this paranoid when you were plopping it onto my stomach—and it was heavy."

Rheese redraped the book with the blanket and handed it carefully over.

Matt said, "Thirty minutes."

"Yes, yes, thirty minutes. Carry on."

The jet's engines revved up to their takeoff-level wail, and the craft hurtled down the runway. Matt let the g-force nestle him into his seat, set his elbows on the padded armrests, and let his beanie-covered head sink back against the headrest. Sliding off his right glove, he wedged it between his legs so as not to lose it while unconscious.

"What time is it?" he asked.

"It is . . . nine twenty-two."

"So at nine fifty-two you pull my hand off, yeah?"

"For certain."

Matt didn't trust Rheese to do what he said, but the threat of Matt urinating on himself—or, God forbid, on the book—should be leverage enough. Besides, he had already read the first twenty or thirty minutes of this book's imprint, and there was nothing there that would traumatize him. If it turned bad, he could always rewind back to the beginning and re-experience the Austrian guy blubbering about his unfaithful wife. And he was beginning to feel the need to pee, so it wasn't a complete lie. He let his hand drop onto the corner of the book.

✳ ✳ ✳

"Turner?" Rheese said.

Matt's eyelids were shut, but Rheese could see his eyeballs quivering behind them. His chest moved up and down at a slow, even pace. Rheese poked him in the ribs, to no avail.

"Can he hear us like that?" G said through the space in the seats.

"No," Rheese replied. "It's practically a coma. His mind and senses essentially shut down, replaced by those of another person.

"Then I have to tell you," G went on, "you are far too good of a liar. The whole thing with the book? Makes me wonder about *our* past conversations."

"I've been forthright in all our dealings, Garza. You just do your part, keep a leash on Solorzano there, and everyone will walk away from this rich and happy."

"Right," Garza said.

"What about the one back at Turner's resort, with the woman?" Rheese asked. "Will he keep it together?"

Solorzano's face appeared over the top of his seat back. "That's my brother. You don't need to worry about him."

"If you say so. He appeared a bit twitchy."

Garza and Solorzano shared a glance. Garza's look said *keep cool.*

"Did you receive any more info on our transportation from Zaporizhzhya once we land?" Rheese asked.

"Yeah, he's sending a car. We don't need to worry about it."

Rheese chewed his lower lip. "That might be rather a worry—not having our own vehicle when it comes time to depart. You'll understand what I mean when you meet him. However you might imagine a Ukrainian billionaire to behave, take that and multiply it by ten."

FOUR

After hanging her keys on the hook by the door, Beth Turner picked up the mail from the floor and started flipping through it on her way to the kitchen. *Bill, junk, junk, bill, junk . . . Oh! And a postcard from Matty!*

Before reading very far, she turned it over to the picture side. A glossy photograph shot from up high—probably from a helicopter—of a moon-shaped island surrounded by a ring of white sand, in the middle of a perfect turquoise ocean. At the top, in a very island-vacation typeface, it read, *"Bons baisers de Bora Bora."*

"Rog, hon?" she called, then heard him come in from the garage.

"In here," Roger answered before appearing in the kitchen. "How was it?"

She stepped over to him and they exchanged a quick kiss.

"Enh, nothing to report. The usual white-elephant gift exchange."

"You get anything good this time?"

Beth lit up, "Oh, yes! I was shocked somebody gave this away. Have a look!"

She pulled a carved wooden sculpture of a fish from a gift bag and set it on the counter. Roger looked at it and nodded in silence.

"Isn't it beautiful?" she asked. "I'm thinking the master bath."

"Mmm-hmm," Roger said. "Maybe the guest bath . . ."

"Well, I like it." She rotated it ninety degrees, thinking he just hadn't seen it from the right angle. "Anyway, there was no booze this time, because of Carolyne, and therefore no embarrassing outbursts from Vandersbock."

Roger grabbed a diet soda from the fridge, popped it open, and slurped down a third of it. "Which one is that? The fat balding guy?"

"No, that was Perry." She shook her head in good-humored exasperation. "His funeral was last year." She dropped the other mail on the counter. "Oh, yes, a postcard from Matty! 'Something-something Bora Bora.' I thought he was going to Tahiti."

"I think that's part of it." He tried to grab it from her, but she pulled it back out of reach.

"Hang on, Mr. Grabbyhands. I wanted us to read it together."

"Just read it," he growled. "What's it say? Did *he* write it, or did she?"

She flipped it over and glanced at the writing, "It's Tuni's writing, but I'm sure they wrote it together."

"Uh-huh."

"'Dear Mom and Dad, Tahiti is the most beautiful place we've ever seen on Earth. The water is warm, people friendly, and everything'—'everything' is all in caps—'is relaxing. You simply must holiday here together some time!'"

"Oh, yeah, that's got the boy written all over it," Roger said drily.

"Quiet, Roger. Oh . . . there's a little sideways note here, too." She turned the postcard ninety degrees. "'R and B, you will appreciate pics of M in shorts. —T.'"

Beth's hand went to her mouth, and she looked up at her husband. He stared at nothing and nodded.

"Good for him," he said, sounding as though he meant it. "That's . . . that's real good for him."

"Oh, my God," she said. "I'm actually tearing up here, hon."

They adjourned to the den and sat on their respective favorite couches. Framed pictures covered every wall but the window side. The candids: 6-year-old Matt and 2-year-old Iris in Mom's arms, preteen Iris with braces, 8-year-old Matt with Mom. Grandpa Luke fishing with a younger, thinner Roger. Every school picture the kids ever had taken. The photos of Iris followed her through middle and high school, but Matt's school pictures stopped at age 10. A current shot of smiling Beth and Roger on vacation in Nassau. The most recent picture of Matt was his newspaper shot, framed in oak.

Beth dabbed her eyes with a tissue and chuckled. "I mean, it's not as though we're the parents of a paraplegic who just took his first steps, but it's *kind* of like that, you know?"

Roger swallowed and nodded, deep in thought. His gaze drifted across the photos above him.

She continued, "You just want him to be normal . . . *feel* normal, you know?"

He didn't say anything.

"What do you think, hon? I can never read your faces."

Roger shrugged. "It's good, yeah. I think it's real good."

Beth sighed. "Okay, Mr. Robot. I'm calling your daughter. Maybe she and I can have a nice little cry together." She put a hand on his shoulder in passing and left the room.

Roger stretched an arm out from his couch and picked the postcard up from the coffee table. He sounded out the message, *"Bons baisers de Bora Bora,"* and gazed at the image on the back.

"Good for him."

FIVE

The Ukrainian customs officers appeared to be preoccupied with drug trafficking, and their muzzled German shepherds and shorthaired pointers nosed each person who passed. The uniforms of the officers reminded Matt of old Cold War spy movies.

After claiming their bags, he and his three captors walked outside the automatic glass doors. Stinging cold slapped their faces. Of the four, Matt was the closest to appropriately dressed. Z, in a short-sleeved button-down and cargo pants, swore and tilted his head to the wind. Snow covered the ground and lay piled in high berms on either side of the plowed road.

They found a row of cars with drivers holding signs. Most of the signs were in Cyrillic letters, but G spotted one that read "CHURCH" and waved to the driver.

"Misters Church?" the driver said in a thick Slavic accent. He wore a tight long-sleeved thermal shirt under a fleece vest, dark blue jeans, and ushanka hat. His vehicle was a brand-new limousine version of a Mercedes R-class crossover.

He loaded the bags into the trunk as Z opened the door and everyone piled in. The interior was warm and nice, without the gauche overdone luxury Matt had expected. The rear seats were of fine leather, with six body-cradling seats in two facing rows. They had enough space to stretch their legs out without inadvertently playing footsie. Bottled waters awaited them in underlit cup holders, and the armrests boasted more switches and knobs than those in the airplane they were just on.

Z found a small, shiny black electronic tablet on one of the seats. He turned it over in his hands, inspecting it, when a voice came through the vehicle's speakers.

"Do no touch, please. Put it where, please."

Z looked through the clear glass panel at the back of the driver's head. The driver glanced back through the rearview mirror but said nothing more.

G gestured for him to put the thing back. "Stop messing with stuff," he said. You break one thing in here, it probably costs more than your whole truck."

Scowling, Z put it down.

"Where are we going?" Matt asked.

"We are meeting someone at his home," Rheese said. "A very wealthy someone. All you need to know is that you're staying in the car unless called upon. And *if* called upon, you will only answer what is asked of you. Answer honestly and succinctly, with no cheeky nonsense, understand?"

"What will I be asked about? Is this for the Bible, 'cause I told you I didn't learn anything more than a few Psalms and my way around a cathedral in Vienna."

"We have a nearly two-hour drive ahead of us. My hope is that you come upon something a bit more concrete before our arrival."

"Not likely. When do I get to talk to Tuni?"

Rheese seemed to ponder this for a moment and then said, "Let us see if we can't use the landline where we're going. None of our mobiles work in this country anyway. Acceptable?"

Matt shrugged. "I don't see much of a choice. Gimme the damned book. I'm telling you, though, this is a complete wild-goose chase."

As Rheese dug in his attaché case, Matt looked at the men he knew as G and Z. Both were staring at him with the voyeuristic curiosity that reminded him of yokels at a carnival freak show. He was used to this, but there was something else, too. Ill-concealed fascination was normal, but this was something he hadn't previously seen in observers. It might just be indifference, but he couldn't put his finger on it. It was more like they were watching a documentary on how shipping containers are made: you don't really care, but there's nothing else on. Or maybe they didn't believe it was real—also a typical reaction.

Rheese carefully handed him the book, in its wrapping, and Matt laid it on his lap. He took another look at his audience and felt a sinking, helpless sensation. His thoughts drifted to movie scenes, the ones where someone is made to drink the potion from an unlabeled vial. They must be voluntarily sedated—rendering themselves defenseless or, worse, poisoning themselves—on the assertion that it is the only way to free their kidnapped loved one or get to the bad guy's lair. The parallels lingered in his mind as he removed his glove. Of course, he would be no more vulnerable now than during the time between the hotel and waking up on his jet. But now he was on the other side of the planet, on his way to who-knew-where.

"Wait," he said. "My timer—it's still in the suitcase."

"I'll wake you, lad," Rheese said with a sigh. "Stop stalling. Time is of the essence here."

And with that, Rheese slapped Matt's bare hand down onto the ornate book cover. Matt's head lolled back as if his power switch had been flipped to the off position.

* * *

He felt the usual rushing sensation in his head, like being shot through a progressively narrowing pipe and squeezed into a long, skinny noodle at tremendous speed. It never lasted but for a couple of seconds before he was squirted out of the tube like toothpaste, reformed into the shape of someone else's body. At least, that was the best analogy he could muster when describing the experience to others. It was typically a very quick process—these days he needed maybe ten seconds to acclimate to the new environment. All senses turned on in the usual succession—vision, hearing, touch, smell, taste—and nebulous thought forms gelled and clarified into a comprehensible format.

In this case, the thoughts were of the same man he had met twice before: Heinrich Strauss, a 34-year-old landowner in Salzburg, Austria. He had been away only a week in Venice. She had no idea of his philandering while away, and yet, upon his return, he got a sickening note—a note that made him want to be dead. He lay on his side in a luxurious four-poster bed, rocking himself as he cradled his most prized possession. God would not ease his suffering. God would not bring her back or make her see that this dancer she'd run off with could never keep her the way Heinrich did. God was punishing him, but for what, he could not imagine. He had to die. He could see no other way to escape the feeling, the physical pain in his stomach, the nausea. *Fast-forward.* Matt couldn't stand this guy.

The next imprint was a German cardinal, caressing the book, delicately turning the pages, reading the Latin Psalms like poetry. As he runs his fingers along its edges, despite its being the Vulgate and not the King James version, he considers himself closer to God than ever. It is 1951.

Fast-forward. Next . . . next . . . Yes, past the sermon in Turin . . . and here we are. Chambéry in Savoy, 1684. Big wedding coming up. Matt had only just begun to touch on this imprint at the end of the last session.

The priest, Emil, walks along the pews with the book tucked under one arm, smoke wafting from the incense in the swinging four-chain thurible. His back aches; his gouty left foot is on fire. On the far side of the nave, Deacon Simon does his best to walk in step with Emil's limp as they proceed up the aisles toward the altar. *Simon is a pest,* thinks the priest, glancing across the pews. He is perturbed by the notion that this red-haired imbecile will one day replace him.

Perhaps sooner rather than later, Emil thinks, and a memory from earlier in the day pops into his head. He had one of the sisters, Olivie, splayed across a table in the convent's crypt. She was fighting him but not in any meaning-ful way. Another few minutes, and she would have succumbed, but Monsieur Simon decided at that supremely inopportune moment that he must fetch a bottle of wine for the sacristy. Emil cannot shake the image of his judging, admonishing, freckle-ridden face.

Is he so ambitious that he would report the encounter to one of the bish-ops? And if so, would he know which ones might be receptive and which would chide him for such talk, as they hark back to their own misdeeds?

The names of transgressors known to him flash through Emil's mind.

At the altar, Deacon Simon places his book down on the lectern and steps back.

"I am only reading from Matthew and Corinthians," Emil says. "The arch-bishop will inform you of his requirements upon his arrival at the castle."

Simon stares at him blankly for a second before his face lights up with recognition and he grabs the book back with a quiet apology. He places it atop its stand toward the rear of the altar as Emil finds the pages he had earlier selected.

"Fetch me a couple of marks, please," Emil says. It would look good to be able to flip to the right page without a tassel hanging out, as if one's fingers were divinely guided, but too many would be watching, and it was more crucial that things run smoothly. Royalty from all over would be present. "Also, make note that the castle will have considerably more pews."

Simon nods.

That's right, nothing happened, you lout.

"I think we are fine for now. We will practice with the others this afternoon. I already know my sermon."

He closes the book.

He opens the book.

It is the next day. The Bible has been brought to another place: the castle he spoke of. Hundreds of people in lavish gowns and elaborate uniforms are staring at him. Cough, sniff, murmurs . . . A duchess brought an infant, and everyone in attendance disapproves. Archbishop Bertrand swapped readings and inserted two songs . . . Everything is in disarray . . . sniff, baby crying, cough, sneeze, the smell of unwashed bodies . . . chuckles . . .

✱ ✱ ✱

"Get it together, Turner. We're almost there," Rheese said.

Matt stretched his back and neck. Sometimes, after a reading, it felt like waking up in the backseat of Mom and Dad's car after a late-night function. *We're home, buster. Let's go inside and get you in your P.J.'s . . .*

One time, when Matt was 10, he pretended to be asleep so his dad would carry him to bed, as he used to. It had worked, but his cheek ended up on his father's shoulder. The leather jacket had an imprint of an angry argument with Mom. He never pretended to be asleep again.

Matt opened his eyes to see G and Z hunched over and peering out the big side windows. Matt turned and looked out, too. It was still morning, but the world had turned white. Snow fell at a hard angle. They had just passed some sort of entry gate and were approaching a huge field with snow-laden spruce trees planted equidistantly apart. It looked like a field of green chess pawns with icing.

As the car curved right, a building came into view on the left. The outside walls were of a shiny white material, broken up by enormous glass panels.

It appeared nothing like a house, more like a modern office building or art museum. Stone accents and unexpected angles, as well as the lush landscaping, broke up the cold lines.

The car circled the building and pulled up in a spacious porte cochere. There were several luxury vehicles: the predictable million-dollar sports car, a stretch luxury sedan, and an oversize SUV. The one out-of-place car was a rusty old 1980s Porsche, faded red, with a broken taillight and several gray, Bondo-filled dents.

A slim, well-dressed man stepped out from an automatic sliding door. He appeared to be in his mid to late twenties, with perfect black hair, pale, flawless skin, and large eyes. He walked with confidence, ignoring the single-digit temperature. The driver opened the passenger doors, and Rheese stepped out.

"You are Dr. Rheese?" the man said with what sounded to Matt like a Russian accent.

"Indeed I am, good sir." He held out his hand and they shook.

The man hunched over a little to look inside the car. "I am Markus, the house manager." His eyes scanned the faces inside.

Z slid out of his seat and stepped onto the cobblestones.

"And who are you?" Markus respectfully asked.

Z shivered, hugging himself. "Can we go over this shit inside? God *damn*!"

Markus stood patiently and smiled.

"Security, all right?" Z answered.

"Then you will remain here."

Z frowned. "Oh, hell no!" he said, but then fell silent when Rheese put up a cautioning hand.

"And who are you?" Markus said to Matt.

"Oh, I'm just waiting in the car," Matt said, stuffing his hand back into his glove. Markus's eyebrows rose, and his curt smile informed Matt that an answer was still due. "I'm, uh, Matt . . ." He looked to Rheese for help.

"The young man is my researcher on the business matter. He can wait here while I conduct my business with Mr. Ostrovsky."

"No, he will come inside." Markus said. His tone was matter-of-fact but still gracious. He held out a hand and helped Matt out of the car.

G followed Matt out and stood beside Rheese.

"And who are you?"

"Business partner." G mirrored Markus's thin smile.

Markus regarded him for a brief second before saying, "Ah, yes, I believe we spoke on the telephone. Very well, let us proceed to check-in." He walked briskly, his shiny black shoes clicking on the paving stones of the porte cochere. "None of you have any items on your persons that would raise concerns, I trust?"

"No," replied G.

The glass doors parted ahead of them, and out walked two fur-clad young women with disheveled hair and smeared makeup. Each carried a large purse and held an envelope. They looked a bit shaken as they hurried past, stiletto heels clicking arrhythmically on the stones. Matt glanced back and saw them climb into the old Porsche.

The glass doors slid apart, and Rheese, G, and Matt followed Markus into an anteroom of sorts, with doors labeled in several languages, the third of which was English: "Office," "Receiving," "Security," and "Check-in." Security also had a floor-to-ceiling window. A uniformed woman sat inside, looking at a bank of video monitors. The place had the feel and decor of an office building, down to the thin, rugged carpet and the potted ficus trees in the corners. Markus opened the door marked "Check-in" and held it wide.

"English," Markus said to the man awaiting them. "Everyone, this is Dmitri. He will guide you through the check-in process, which should take no more than ten minutes. Assuming all goes well, I will meet you inside the main hall. Thank you for your patience."

Markus turned and left, and the door clicked shut behind him.

"This is everyone first time visit to the house, it is?" Dmitri said. All three nodded. "This is very good. The check-in process is simple one, and is here in place to protect both the property, its employee, and guest such as the yourself. There is no individual that may occupy the house or its outlying structure without first processing through check-in. Any of you has question or concern?"

Matt raised his hand.

Rheese murmured out the side of his mouth, "Put it down, Turner."

"Yes, you, sir, have question?"

"Will we be required to remove our clothing for this?"

Dmitri nodded understanding and cocked his head sideways with a confidential smile. "Only if you no pass part one, or if you are looking-good lady visitor." He snickered. "I only joke. You have not to worry for this." He stepped over to a big metal table with a stack of white plastic bins on it. Handing each of them a bin, he said, "Please empty all pocket into this and proceed to door."

Rheese and G filled their bins with coins, keys, papers; Matt had only an airline ticket stub and a bit of lint. The next room had the familiar-looking airport metal-detecting archway and an X-ray conveyer, manned by three people in security uniforms. The husky man at the conveyer waved Rheese over and gestured for him to place his briefcase on the belt.

"Sorry, but this cannot go through there," Rheese said as Matt and then G were being waved through the archway.

The X-ray operator said something in Ukrainian to Dmitri, and they exchanged a few words.

"Apologize," Dmitri said. "You must pass case through."

"I will do no such thing," Rheese said. "Fetch your boss and he will agree with me."

"Just a moment, sir," Dmitri said, smiling with only his mouth. He stepped into the other room and spoke into a radio. He returned a moment later to the quiet little room, where everyone else stood in awkward silence, avoiding eye contact. "You will need to remove content and pass case through."

"Very well," Rheese said, and taking out the Gutenberg Bible, he placed the empty briefcase on the conveyer. Curious eyes passed over the book as they waited.

The X-ray man nodded as the case appeared out the other end of the machine, and Rheese replaced the book inside it.

"Now, the arch," Dmitri said.

With a sigh, Rheese handed the case to Matt and stepped through the archway without setting off any alarms.

"Brilliant," Rheese said. "Now, are we done?"

"With this part, yes. Please take seat here while we step into interview room with just one."

Rheese looked at Matt, and G looked at Rheese. Matt looked at both of them.

"Does it have to be only one?" Rheese asked. "We are a bit pressed for time."

Dmitri smiled and recited the applicable line from the appropriate policies and procedures manual: "If individual wish not to comply with established rule and procedure of check-in process, they may be escorted off property and added to permanent no-entry list."

"This one"—Rheese pointed his thumb at Matt—"wasn't even supposed to be in here. He was going to wait in the car. Your friend Markus *asked* for him to come in!"

"I understand, sir," Dmitri calmly replied. "Do you wish to return to vehicle, or do you wish to proceed with check-in?"

Rheese's face flushed red, and he growled, "Proceed."

"Wonderful. You will go first." He nodded to G and opened the plain white door for him.

While G followed Dmitri to the interview room, Rheese and Matt sat down on the hard bench by the wall. Rheese leaned toward Matt and whispered, "You will behave yourself in this interrogation. Do not forget that I have your—"

"I haven't forgotten anything, Rheese," Matt muttered. "So you can stop with the stupid threats."

A few minutes later, the door reopened, and a smiling Dmitri gestured for Rheese to enter.

"You now."

The door closed behind him.

Matt waited, feeling self-conscious under the lingering glances of the security personnel. The only sound in the room was the hum of the equipment and someone's wheezy breathing. Finally, it was Matt's turn, and he walked into a room furnished with a single metal table and two chairs.

"Have a seat, sir," Dmitri said as he grabbed a clipboard from a hanging bin on the wall.

Matt sat down.

"Why do you wear glove and this snow hat inside?" Dmitri asked, his tone as pleasant as ever.

"Is that one of the questions?"

"No, I am only curious. Plus, I need glove remove for test."

"Why do you need 'glove remove'?" Matt asked.

"I have finger contacts for you. This is lie detector test."

Matt nodded and glanced around the room, "Do you know what a germaphobe is? Someone who is afraid that if they touch anything, they'll get sick and die?"

"I have sister-in-law like this, yes. Very annoying."

"Well, that's what I am. Will your things work through latex gloves? You know, like doctor gloves. Do you even have any of those?"

Dmitri considered this, studied Matt's face for a second, and said, "I think this work. Let me get you glove."

He left Matt alone in the room, listening to the air whistle through the single vent in the ceiling. His thoughts drifted back to Tuni. She had always protected him in situations like this. Even using the germaphobe story, she accomplished whatever was needed in a given environment without raising any eyebrows. She had even wangled them a private balcony at the Coldplay concert a few months back. And she never made him feel like a freak. He hoped she wasn't too scared right now.

Dmitri came back in and dropped a pair of beige latex gloves on the table. Matt hoped they weren't used. He pulled off his gloves and replaced them with the beige ones. No imprints. Dmitri crouched down under the metal desk and pulled out two sets of wires with finger clamps. After sticking these on Matt's index fingertips, he took the seat across from Matt.

Clipboard in hand, he said, "Full name?"

"Matthew Turner."

"Spell for me, please."

Matt spelled it.

"Age?"

"Twenty-six."

"And where you live? America, right?" Dmitri smiled knowingly.

"Yes, America."

"Good, now . . ." Dmitri leaned forward and looked Matt directly in the eyes. "Do you have any negative feeling for Mr. Vitaliy Ostrovsky?"

"I've never heard of him."

Dmitri appeared shocked by this and glanced up at the wall behind Matt. Matt turned around and saw only a single lightbulb. It was off. Dmitri shrugged.

"Do you wish to do harm in any way to Mr. Vitaliy Ostrovsky, his property, or his business?"

"No. Like I said, I don't even know who he is."

Another quick glance over Matt's head.

"Last question. Is there any secret pertaining to your visit today that Mr. Vitaliy Ostrovsky, myself, or his security personnel would be interested to know?"

Matt took a deep breath and pondered. If he said no, it would surely be detected as a lie. If he spoke the truth, it could set off a chain of events he couldn't possibly control. It could go either way. What he said next could get Tuni freed, or it could get her hurt or killed.

"Yes."

Dmitri looked up from the clipboard. *"Yes?"*

"Yes."

"And what this might be?"

"I don't want to be here."

"You do not? Why is that?"

"I would rather be in Tahiti, on vacation."

"Ah, yes. So would I." He smiled and made a note on the clipboard. "Good, then let us join you your friend."

He took the sensors from Matt's fingertips and escorted him to the door. Rheese's expectant face greeted them as he shot looks from Matt to Dmitri and back to Matt.

"Are we quite done?" Rheese said.

"Yes, done," Dmitri replied.

Markus thanked Dmitri and said, "Follow me, please."

They followed him down a long, curving hallway with ceilings fifty feet high. Giant tapestries and artwork hung on the smooth white walls. One wall changed to glass, looking into a skylit tropical courtyard with dark green foliage, palm trees, and a realistic-looking rocky cliff face covering one side. A small river ran through the miniature jungle and out the other side, disappearing beneath the floor.

The glass wall ended as they passed by the courtyard, and eventually, they came to a large, arched opening and an expansive sitting room. This was broken up into several smaller areas, each with a different style of matching couch, chairs, and coffee table. A row of billiard tables filled the far end of the room, and rectangular windows high above let in eight slanting bars of sunlight. At the ground level, the windowless walls were lined with bookshelves, artwork, tapestries, and a flat-screen TV the size of a billboard. Modern chandeliers hung from the ceiling, and a ten-foot-high marble fireplace revealed another large room behind it.

G went to the nearest couch and was about to sit down when Markus said, "Ah, Mr. Ostrovsky has invited you to join him at his breakfast table. Right this way, please."

They crossed the large room to a set of intricately worked bronze doors which appeared to catch Rheese's attention.

As Markus slid the doors back into their wall pockets, Rheese said, "Byzantine . . . remarkable."

Markus nodded approvingly. "Eleventh century, newly installed just this year. Mr. Ostrovsky has impeccable taste."

"Ah, Doctor Rheese!" a voice said from across the room. "We meet again!" A silver-haired man with olive skin stood up from a big table, his arms outstretched. He wore a thick white robe, untied and hanging open, leaving his hairy chest and belly, and all the rest, in full view. He looked fit for a man his age.

They walked up, and he came round the table. Rheese pretended not to notice Ostrovsky's lack of trousers or undergarments, and Matt followed his lead, though he wondered if the man simply didn't realize his robe was hanging open. Whatever the reason, his visitors got a full view of Vitaliy Ostrovsky.

"Welcome, welcome! I hope the drive was not too onerous in this weather. Hello, hi—you are this business partner?"

G shook his hand. "Yes, pleased to meet you, sir. You have an impressive home."

"What, this old dump? Ha ha . . . no, I know. That is the idea, right? Build what you love, and whether others approve or not, it will leave an impression. And you are this Matthew?"

"Yes, sir."

"Well, thank you for coming to my home, one and all. Please, have a seat. I hope none of you have eaten just yet. No? Good, because you are in for a treat."

They took seats in luxurious high-backed chairs, at a table that appeared to be pure concrete. An enormous silver chandelier hung over the table. Before them were settings of silver chargers and black plates with white saucers. On the saucers, napkins had been formed into hummingbirds suspended atop tripods formed of two forks and a butter knife. Long dishes of mixed fruits and berries divided the table down the middle.

A woman in what appeared to be housekeeping livery mixed with a nurse's uniform walked in, holding the hand of a little girl in a big, fluffy pink dress.

"Taty!" the girl screamed, and ran to Ostrovsky. He leaned over his chair's armrest and raised her high over his head.

"My little Veronikitty! We are speaking in English today, all right?"

The little girl pouted and looked accusingly at the others present.

"*Nee!*" she said, and her face told them that meant "no."

"Veronika . . . " Ostrovsky said in a warning tone. A bell chimed from another room. "Roza, take this little monster from me. Feed her whatever she wants."

The nanny nodded and took Veronika in her arms. As they left the room, the little girl started making demands in Ukrainian.

"She is a spoiled one, no?" Ostrovsky said. He spoke as if to old friends. "I do it on purpose, though, you see. I'll have two more in the next five years. Little girls. They will love me like no other in the world, and girls who love their daddy never go away. Boys? They feel competition. As teenagers, they

42

get bold and try to test you. That's what I did. And I never went back. Screw them, you know? And if they don't leave, it's because they want to take over, take your money. That's why I want only girls. And I tell you what, I am ruining them for any little punks who want to come sniffing around for diamond vaginas. If they want to get married someday, I might allow it, but if I've done my job right, the little bastards are going to be miserable!" He laughed and pounded the table. "They'll be like servants to my little princesses."

"What if you have a boy?" Matt asked.

Ostrovsky turned to him, his smile dipping a little. "I won't."

Matt swallowed, fearing that he knew what that meant.

A tall older woman in a white chef's smock and toque emerged from a swinging door. Three men in tailcoats followed her, all holding covered platters. They arrived behind each guest and, setting the saucers with napkins aside, removed the chargers and plates and set down a platter in their place. They lifted the ceramic covers away in choreographed synchronicity, revealing a meal that came as a surprise to all but Ostrovsky. The servants left, but the chef remained, standing a short distance back from their host.

Each of the platters exhibited a hamburger-shaped item hidden inside a thin paper wrapping. Beside this was a patty of hash brown potatoes, half-wrapped in the same thin off-white paper. It looked like a generic McDonald's breakfast. The servants returned and placed a glass of orange juice and a cup of coffee in front of each guest.

"Surprised, eh?" Ostrovsky said. "Open them up and take a look."

They cautiously peeled away the wrappings, unveiling sandwiches made with an English muffin, a circular egg, sausage, and cheese. G leaned in and inhaled the scent.

"Looks just like a Sausage McMuffin, no?" Ostrovsky said with undisguised exuberance. "I've been having her work on this for the past year. First try: unacceptable! Some kind of lamb sausage, perfectly toasted muffin, aged reserve Hungarian cheese, duck egg. I tell this bitch, 'Look, I am not asking for some gourmet shit that vaguely resembles a Sausage McMuffin! I want a goddamn Sausage McMuffin!' She was very hurt. They take this shit personally because it is their art, but I don't give a shit. I have more money than most nations, so my goddamn cook should be able to replicate whatever food I want. If someone else can make it and sell it for two goddamn dollars, I can have it made for me at home, no?" He leaned out and glanced back at the chef, then returned his attention to his guests, snickering as he thumbed behind him. "She tried again a month later—better, I suppose, but it still wasn't right. I made her go to McDonald's every morning for two months and have one. She's been getting very close since then. The hash brown? Perfect. She nailed it last year after I told her, 'Yes, that is more salt than you would put in an entire meal, but that is how they make it!' Go ahead, taste the hash brown first. Tell me it is not spot-on. The right oil, perfect crisp on the outside . . ."

They each took a bite, Rheese a little less enthusiastically than G and Matt.

"Goddamn right!" G said with astonishment. "That is a Mickey D's hash brown for sure."

"Yeah, I can't tell the difference," Matt agreed.

Rheese smiled and nodded in silence.

"Okay, now, let us *all* try the McMuffin," Ostrovsky said, carefully picking his up from the paper, sniffing it, inspecting the color. He squeezed the sandwich gently and glanced back to the chef. "Well done with presentation, Irochka. The extra-fine cornmeal on the top and bottom provides excellent hand feel." He turned back to the table. "Last time it was the grainy sort, like regular English muffin. Inexcusable."

She curtsied subtly, raising her chin in anticipation of the next test: taste.

They all chewed, deep in concentration. Their eyes hung on Ostrovsky, apparently shifting the food from one side of his mouth to the other. He swallowed and took another bite, Matt and G following suit while Rheese returned his to its platter and drank some juice. Ostrovsky smacked his lips.

"Well? What do you think? I am very interested to hear from Americans on this."

"I thought it was good," Matt said.

"Yeah, it's really good," G concurred. "Seems right to me."

Rheese shrugged. "I don't really eat this sort of thing, so hard to say."

"Matthew, you look an honest young man. Tell me the truth. Is it the same as the hash brown? Can you tell the difference?"

Matt looked apologetically to the chef, still standing behind Ostrovsky. Her wrinkled lips seemed capable only of pursing.

"It's . . . it's not the same," Matt admitted. "Sorry, but it's real close. I think it's mainly the sausage. Also, the English muffin is too normal. Theirs are softer, squishier . . . something about them that makes them seem forever fresh. But like I said, it's still very good!"

"No, no, you don't have to apologize, my friend. This is her fucking job, and she gets paid a fortune to take my abuse. You are correct; it is not the same.

A hundred times closer than the first one, I tell you that, but not the same. Irochka," he said, and she stepped forward. "Another failure. I'll give you my scores later."

She curtsied and returned to the kitchen without a word. Ostrovsky wolfed down the rest of his sausage and muffin sandwich and hash brown. With his mouth stuffed, he said, "I know that bitch is crying in there right now. So sensitive."

G and Matt ate some more of theirs while Rheese sipped at his coffee.

"What do you think of that coffee?" Ostrovsky asked him.

"Mmm, delicious," Rheese said.

Ostrovsky shook his head, "Tell the truth, now, Doctor. Matthew here went out on the limb and spoke his mind—a laudable deed."

"Honestly . . ." Rheese looked down at his cup. "It's terrible."

"Right!" Ostrovsky blurted with a grin. "She perfected it around the same time as the hash brown! Now, if you all don't mind, let us adjourn to the sitting room to talk business."

Just as they left the table, the big bronze doors rolled open with a soft rumble. Markus greeted them with a pleasant smile and waved them into the room. Rock music played from unseen speakers. The vocals were in Ukrainian, Russian, or some other Slavic language.

"There are tea and pastries, sir."

"Thank you, Markus. Tell Denys to prepare downstairs for later."

Markus bowed his head, crossed the great room, and left up the main hall. Ostrovsky strode to one of the sitting areas, his silky robe flowing behind him like a cape and allowing peekaboo views of his pale, hairy backside. Behind his back, G made a gesture and shook his head, mouthing, "What the hell?" to Rheese.

"Have a seat, please. Let us talk about this business. I have about twenty more minutes to devote to this matter before I must bid you all farewell."

Rheese opened his attaché case and carefully extracted the book. The table in front of him had a plush-covered board on it, obviously placed there for this purpose. G slid it in front of Rheese, who carefully placed the book on it. Ostrovsky sat down in the lounge chair next to Rheese, flipping the sides of his robe away so he could sit.

Ostrovsky produced a pair of silky white gloves from under the table. He slid them on, opened the cover, and peered at the first page, running his fingers over the text and colorful embellishments. He leaned forward and held his nose close to the paper, inhaling deeply and noisily.

"Smells good," he said with a smile. He had the excited look of a drug addict about to score the best stuff ever. He flipped the book over and felt the spine and the brass adornments. Reopening it to a random page, he scanned it, flipped to the next, then turned several more pages, searching for something. Matt could see Rheese cringing at the fast, careless page turns. Ostrovsky poked a page, said "Ah!" and then read aloud: "Quod fuit ab initio quod audivimus quod vidimus oculis nostris quod perspeximus et manus nostrae temptaverunt de verbo vitae." He looked up at Matt. "You know what this means?"

Matt nodded, "Yes."

Rheese's head popped up and turned to Matt, "Wait . . . really? You speak *Latin*?"

Matt shrugged.

"Tell me what it means, Matthew," Ostrovsky whispered, as if asking a poet to recite his work.

"Well, it's not complete. That's just the first part, right?"

"Shh," Ostrovsky wagged two fingers at him and nodded to the book. "Just the passage."

"All right," Matt said, leaning forward. "Um . . . just paraphrasing . . . it says, 'That which was from the beginning, which we have heard, which we have seen, which we have looked upon and touched with our hands, of the word of life . . .'"

"Very good, Matthew! Very good indeed. That section alone—forget that it goes on—by itself, does it have any special meaning for you?"

"I don't know . . . not really," Matt lied.

"Nothing?"

"Nope," Matt said.

"Hm. I would have thought otherwise." Ostrovsky rested back in the chair, swirled a finger around in his chest hair. "Hmm . . . disappointing."

"Anyway," Rheese interrupted, "as you can see, it is in impeccable condition. Every page present. Likely among the best-preserved of the surviving copies. It is uncataloged, so you would be free to display publicly, hide away, sell, or what have you. But the story—"

"Tell me, Matthew," Ostrovsky said, ignoring Rheese. "Had you ever heard of me?"

"Nope."

"That's good. And now? Do you know who I am now?"

"Not really. Some rich guy, I guess. A *really* rich guy." Matt gestured around the room.

"Ha ha, yes, of course. Don't worry, this pleases me. I have no desire to be a household name. There is comfort in being number forty-three on *Forbes*'s list. This is intentional, you see? There are thousands of bank accounts, trusts, investment accounts, properties all over the world, attached to different names, estates. You add them all together, connect them to a single person. Perhaps that person is higher on a list than previously suspected. But you know what? I stay here, in my country. Unlike these sissy millionaires flocking to England—dual citizenship, and all that." Ostrovsky appeared to have wandered away from his subject. He searched around the room, scratched his undraped privates, and resumed. "Matthew, tell me about this Bible."

"Well, Doctor Rheese is really the—"

"No, no, go ahead, Turner," Rheese insisted.

"Oh, well . . . I know some of the people who have used it—you know, where they were and when . . . stuff like that . . ."

Markus appeared behind Ostrovsky, leaned close, and whispered something in his ear. Ostrovsky's face did not change. He nodded, and Markus walked away.

Matt was still speaking, ". . . I believe the separation of the two volumes may have occurred sometime after—"

"Hold on," Ostrovsky interrupted, then grabbed a remote from the end table and turned up the music. He rocked his head with the beat. "I love this part!" He performed an air drum solo while biting his lower lip, eyes closed. "Okean Elzy. You know them?" He looked at Matt.

Matt shook his head.

"What, no? One of the biggest bands in the world! They are like Ukrainian equivalent to America's U-two."

"U-two are from Ireland," Matt said matter-of-factly.

Ostrovsky looked at him, still smiling but almost with a sneer. "Well, what do you think? Could you get into this, or do you have to understand lyrics to like a song?"

"It's all right, I guess."

Shocked, Ostrovsky shot looks at Rheese and G. "I don't understand Americans! You probably listen to bullshit, whiny music. Who is your favorite American band?"

"I don't know . . . I listen to a lot of different stuff. Look, do you want to hear about the Bible or what? The first volume—"

"Turner, knock it off," Rheese said. "We are guests. Vitaliy . . . Mr. Ostrovsky, Turner can tell you essentially the entire history of this book. He has made great headway in tracing it to the matching volume one, as well."

Ostrovsky again slumped back in his chair, frowning, with his legs spread wide. He squinted reproachfully at Matt as his head bobbed. He picked up the remote and turned off the music.

"Markus!" he shouted. Then he turned to Rheese. "I will give you one hundred thousand for the book. No negotiation."

"One hundred . . ." Rheese blurted. "Just the . . . are you bloody *joking*? You haven't even . . ."

Markus reappeared from the hallway, "Yes, sir?"

"Our guests are leaving. If Dr. Rheese wishes to sell, pay him one hundred thousand for the book."

"One hundred thousand!" Rheese muttered. "That's not even a fraction! No one would . . ."

G stood up. "Mr. Ostrovsky, sir, I think there's been a misunderstanding. See, we were looking to sell—"

"Yes, yes," Ostrovsky interrupted. "Deal or no deal, like the television game show. Thank you for visiting." He stood up and walked away. He said to Markus in passing, "Tell Denys never mind," and disappeared around the corner.

Rheese was in a daze, unable to grasp what had gone wrong. He carried on a conversation with himself under his breath, gesturing at the book and at himself.

"Gentlemen, if you will follow me," Markus said.

"This is your fault, Turner," G said, jabbing a finger into Matt's chest.

"What? Because I told him U-two are Irish?"

"You screwed it up with your shitty attitude. You're going to pay for this."

"Sorry if I have an attitude about being kidnapped! I'll try to look on the bright side!"

G looked as if he was going to hit him for sure, but he took several deep breaths and pushed him forward.

They followed Markus back down the curving hallway, past the little indoor jungle, and through a door at the far end. It was a small office, with a nice wooden desk with two guest chairs. Markus walked behind it and sat down. He unlocked a drawer in the desk with his key and pulled out a check-book and ledger.

"So, Dr. Rheese, do you wish to go through with the proposed modified transaction?"

Rheese was still in shock. "I . . . I can't . . ."

G interrupted and said, "Look, do you mind if I confer with my business partner here in the hall?"

"Not at all," Markus replied.

G escorted Rheese out the door and closed it behind them. Markus gazed at Matt, who watched the wall clock's second hand tick away.

"So," Markus said to Matt. "Do you use this germaphobe excuse often?"

"What?"

"When people ask about your gloves and such."

"Oh . . . um, yeah, I guess." *Is this guy fishing, or does he know?*

Markus reached into another drawer in his desk and produced a business card. He handed it across the desk to Matt. "It is English on the other side. If you are still . . . *in the market,* as it were, give me a call in six months if you are interested in work. He will have forgotten this interaction by then and will pay you extremely well, as I suppose you can imagine. Just don't involve these other two, hmm?"

Don't ask. "Yeah, all right. Thanks."

Rheese and G came back in.

"We'll take the hundred thousand," G said.

Rheese pulled out the book, stared wistfully at it, and then slid it onto the desk. Markus picked it up, rolled his chair to a cherry cabinet, and placed the book in a safe, locking it afterward.

"To whom do I write the check?"

G and Rheese looked at each other, and G said, "We require cash. U.S."

Unfazed, Markus slid the checkbook into his desk drawer, opened another drawer, and took out a lockbox. He opened it and withdrew four stacks of perfectly crisp bills. G stuffed them into Rheese's case, and the three of them followed Markus outside. He left them at the door with a pleasant smile and wave.

"Thank you for your visit."

When they appeared, the limo door opened and Z popped out. He stretched his arms out, palms up, apparently aware that something had gone wrong.

"Later," G said as they got in.

SIX

The staring bothered her the most. He would just stand in the doorway, mouth open a little, and his sunken eyes would slowly pan across her body as if filming a landscape in a nature documentary. She didn't want to think about what his pocketed hands might be doing. Her own hands were cuffed for most of each day. She got to stretch and breathe once in the morning and once at night during meals, not counting loo breaks. Her captor would mark it off on a clipboard of tasks and then send a text message from his phone. She supposed it was good that he reported to *someone,* even though she didn't know to whom.

When she had emerged from the shower three days ago, he was standing there in the bathroom in a button-down khaki shirt and black cargo pants. She had the towel in front of her, but he had seen everything before she screamed and covered up. She had planned her moves, expecting him to attack, but he simply stood there, staring, and said, "Get dressed. Quickly." Then he had walked out, closing the bathroom door behind him. She had raced to lock the door and then grabbed the wall-mounted phone beside the bidet, but the cord was gone from the base and the wall jack. Her purse, too, had been taken from the counter, so no mobile phone. She had thrown on her clothes but was afraid to leave the bathroom. He knocked.

"Hurry up. You have thirty seconds."

She knew the shoddy door lock would do nothing. She knew that he knew that; it was why he walked out and closed the door.

When she came out, he was right there. He grabbed her arms, spun her around, clasped handcuffs on her, and tossed her onto the bed. And there she had remained. Others had already taken Matthew. It was only the two of them in the bungalow now.

He stopped staring at her for the time being and turned back to the suite's living room.

"When do I get to leave?" she asked. She had said it before and received no satisfactory answers.

He looked silently back at her for several seconds before saying, "Do you want to shower?"

She let her head fall back onto the bed. He left her and flopped noisily down onto the leather couch in the living room. His phone sounded with artificial button clicks as he composed another text message. Her mind was a confusion of half-baked escape scenarios and defeatist naysaying. The over-water bungalow was interconnected to others via branching pier walkways, but too far away for anyone to hear her. If she screamed when food was delivered, he might just kill the delivery person. If she were willing to be that heartless, it might actually bring others looking for them, but there remained the fact that Matthew was also a captive. Anything she did to get free might well endanger him.

So I lie here shiftless like a bloody dosser.

She heard his mobile phone ring in the other room, heard his muffled "Yeah?" Silence.

"Okay, hold on a second."

He walked into the bedroom and held the phone to her ear.

"Say something," he said.

"Um, hello?" she said.

"Miss St. James . . ." The voice made her grimace. She knew it immediately.

"Rheese," she replied. "What are you bloody thinking? How dare you—"

"Tuni?"

"Matthew!" she said.

Rheese's voice returned. "Put Raúl back on."

Raúl. She had a first name now. That was something, anyway. And Matthew was alive, at least. He took the phone away from her ear and listened as he left the bedroom.

"Understood. Yes. Can . . . can I speak with Fernando? Oh, fine, but tell him he needs to call me. I keep trying . . . hello? *¡Ai, pinche cabrón!*" The phone clacked down onto a table.

★ ★ ★

A couple of hours passed with Tuni shifting from her side to her back, to her other side. She cried off and on, as she had since it all began. What were they doing with Matthew? Where was he? Was he equally worried about her? It sounded that way. Where was the rock she had prepared so specially for him? She had left it on the kitchen counter. Anyway, it was completely irrelevant now. *Bloody Rheese.* The man was vile. The phone call was obviously to have Matthew hear her voice, to prove she was still alive.

How would this end? Her guard, "Raúl," had made no attempt to conceal his face. He was of Latino descent, though he spoke with only the hint of an accent. His cheeks were pocked from acne. He was tall and strongly built, hair cropped short. She could see him in a military uniform. He was at least disciplined enough to keep his hands off her—so far, anyway. If he wasn't worried about being identified later, did that mean he was going to disappear abroad—or that she wouldn't be left alive to identify him?

The only hotel telephone still plugged in rang in the kitchen. She heard him stride over to it without picking it up. It rang three more times and fell silent. He tapped away at his phone screen. Another text message. "The room phone rang," she imagined him writing to Rheese. "What should I do?"

His phone sounded off that it had received a reply. He wrote back. It went on in this way for several minutes, until Tuni heard a loud crash and a gunshot.

SEVEN

"So how big was it?" Z asked.

The car merged onto the highway heading south, back toward Zaporizhzhya. The windshield wipers swung at full speed. Though it was not yet noon, the sky had gone dark beneath a heavy layer of charcoal clouds. Cars and trucks zoomed by, sloshing through the muddy snow.

"Never mind that," Rheese said. "Thanks to Turner's poor manner and Ostrovsky's eccentric petulance, we are quite short on revenue."

"It is so not my fault," Matt said.

"Shut up, punk," Z snapped.

Rheese continued, "Fortunately, we did not walk away empty-handed. Gar—er, G here—had a splendid idea that will hopefully bear fruit. Unfortunately for Mr. Turner, this will extend his stay with us for some time."

"What? What are you talking about? And what about Tuni? I didn't get to talk to her, and you said—"

"Yes, yes, lad. The meeting did not end as expected—on many levels." Rheese and G shared a look. "We will get you in touch with her as soon as possible, but for now I'm afraid that is low priority. I do need to get to a phone and contact some chaps I know. I'll give it a shot at the airport. Perhaps we'll have a moment for you to exchange a word or two with her. The good news is, the funds received for the Gutenberg will further bankroll our pursuits."

"Yeah, what about that?" Matt said. "You said the Bible was someone else's that you had to return. Why did I even bother reading it all that time if you were just going to sell it to that guy?"

"There was a change of plans before we arrived at the estate. There was no time to fill you in. Its original owner will not be the happiest, but when all is said and done, he will be rewarded handsomely."

"And he's just going to accept that? Who is this saintly mystery person?"

"That's none of your concern. Besides, if he has any issue with receiving fair market value for it, I will refer him straight to Vitaliy Ostrovsky and have them work it between themselves. I feel somewhat bad, but we have larger affairs now."

"The adults need to talk now," G said. "We got anything for him to read or whatever?"

"I'll cover my ears."

Rheese looked around and said, "Hmm, well, not really . . ."

Matt thought of a hundred things in the car with them that would surely have imprints, but he remained stoic. He did not want to be forced into another session. Fortunately, Rheese seemed preoccupied with ancient artifacts as the sole source of imprints.

"Do you have any more of that chemical you used back on the island?" Rheese asked.

Uh–oh . . .

"Had to leave it on his plane," G replied. "Could have been a problem at airport security."

Rheese glared at Matt. "This could all be over if you had held your bloody tongue, you know that? Yes, the damned thing tasted right! Yes, the music was sublime—a soul-satisfying delight, in fact!"

"Look, I'm not very good at talking to people," Matt replied. "Blame it on homeschooling."

Rheese sighed and peered at his watch, "Well, it's another hour to the airport. Everyone just keep quiet. I'm going to attempt a quick catnap." He picked up the little leather pillow from between himself and Matt, placed it between his cheek and the window, and wriggled down in his seat.

Matt glanced at G and Z. Both wore their displeasure with him openly. As if that weren't enough, Z mimed lifting his own chin, slid a finger across his throat, pulled an invisible tongue from the invisible gash, and adjusted it at his collar as if tightening a tie.

And in that moment, Matt realized he was more frightened of these two than he could ever be of Rheese.

★ ★ ★

"Funny you should mention that, Professor," Jimmy Moon's voice said through the pay phone. "I got a lead yesterday on something that might fit that description. Price was way out of my range, but if you've got the bankroll, you could probably flip it for a tasty profit."

Rheese smiled and clenched his fist. Things were looking up. He peered through the window into the departures terminal. More airport police with dogs were patrolling the area where Garza and Solorzano were sitting inside with Turner. They let the dogs do a quick sniff as they passed, but continued on their way. Another opportunity to alert the authorities, which Turner had passed up. At least that part of the plan was working.

"Tell me more," Rheese said.

"Hang on a sec—I've got a picture here . . ." Jimmy, Rheese's old assistant, described the item, shown on a table lit by a desk lamp, with a square ruler beside it for scale. He went on to provide what little further information he had, and offered to put in some research hours for a fee and get back to him. Luckily, Jimmy knew the general area where Rheese needed to go, and the contact information for the source, so they didn't have to spend another night in Ukraine.

Rheese signaled to Garza to bring Turner to the phone. Best to get the call to his woman out of the way. It surely wouldn't muzzle his relentless blathering, but it had been a part of the deal, and it would remind the lad who was in charge. He considered giving them a minute to exchange whatever teary-eyed drivel they felt was necessary, but it was six bloody degrees outside.

"That was bullshit, Rheese!" Matt complained as they reentered the terminal.

"You heard each other's voices. Leave it, or you wait until it's all over before speaking with her again."

Garza held Matt back as Rheese went off to the counter.

Rheese bought their tickets, opting for a stop in the Philippines to avoid potential detainment in Australia. Though Jimmy hadn't been able to dig up any news, it was a safe bet that Turner's pilot had been discovered and had told his tale to the authorities. Rheese and company's fake passports would allow them to evade detection only so long.

EIGHT

Tuni's shoulders rose up with a jolt, as if trying to cover her ears since her hands could not. She hadn't heard a real gunshot since she was a small child, but that had to be the sound which came from the living room of the hotel bungalow. Before that, a double crash: something striking the entry door, and then the door smashing into the wall.

She kept her face buried in the bed's soft comforter, telling herself to look, to get up. But she argued with herself that she had to be silent, that everything would be okay if she was silent. People would forget she was here. *Right.* In the seeming eternity before she heard another sound, she tried to imagine what had happened. Certainly not police, because there were no words, no "Hands up!" shouted before firing. And was the gunshot from her guard, Raúl, or from whoever kicked in the door?

"Miss St. James?" said a deep male voice with an accent. *Arabic, perhaps?*

"Are you awake?"

Tuni turned on her side and looked down past her feet to the doorway. A tall, light-brown-skinned man stood there, wearing a concerned expression. His hair was trimmed short, and his features looked North African or Arabic.

"Are you okay, ma'am?"

"Who are you?" It was the only thing she could think of to say.

"My name is Abel Turay. I'm with Interpol." He flashed a badge. "May I remove your handcuffs?"

She didn't know why, but she hesitated before answering, "Yes."

THE OPAL

He disappeared behind her. She felt the cuffs jostle. One came off, then the other. He helped her up by the elbow, but she didn't want to be touched—certainly not by some stranger who had just shot someone.

"He's . . ." She nodded toward the living room. "He's dead?"

"Oh, no, no, ma'am. Beanbag gun, to the forehead. He's knocked out right now, but not for long."

"What?" She stood up off the bed but felt light-headed and sat back down to steady herself. "So he's . . . he can—"

"I took his gun, ma'am. You are in shock, I think. We should get you out of here right away."

Tuni stood up again, holding her hands out for balance as if walking a tightrope. She looked at his face, her eyes poring over it as if trying to understand it, to decipher its features. It was a kind face, almost cherubic, with pale gray-green eyes. "Interpol? That's police, right? Why wouldn't you just arrest him? Are you . . . are you alone?"

"Ah, no jurisdiction here, Miss St. James. And no, I have two men with me. One is covering us outside to ensure no one else comes. The other is watching your captor out there. I will explain everything to you, but I insist we leave right now. Is there anything I can carry for you?"

Tuni's head began to clear. Things were making slightly more sense. She looked around the room and down the hall into the luxurious master bathroom.

"My phone," she said. "I need my phone . . . my charger. Can I . . . do I have time to grab my clothes and things?"

"Quickly, please. We already retrieved your phone and charger from the kitchen."

She ran to the mirrored closet door, slid it open, grabbed her suitcase, and saw that Matt's was gone. She filled her suitcase from the dresser, then rolled it, half-open, into the bathroom, where she scooped the entire counter of makeup and toiletries into it with one arm.

"Let's go," she said.

He walked to the doorway ahead of her, stopped, and poked his head out.

"Still clear, Isaiah?" he said.

A voice from the other room replied, "Still clear."

"Abel, is it?" Tuni said.

"Yes, ma'am," he replied as they hurried across the room to where the splintered front door lay on the entryway floor.

Tuni peered back and saw the other officer standing by the couch, gun in hand. On the floor, jutting from behind the couch, she could see Raúl's limp legs sticking out.

"Is Matthew safe?" she asked. "Did you guys get him yet?"

"No, ma'am, not yet. Sorry, ma'am. We will talk about all these things. Let's go."

"But this arsehole probably knows where he is. You aren't going to interrogate him?"

Abel Turay stopped outside the doorless entryway, beside another man—also with a gun, and wearing a sport coat and khaki pants. Abel sighed. "Miss St. James, I understand you have a lot of questions, you are worried about your boyfriend, and have been afraid for your life these many days. But we *have* to leave this place now, and you have to trust me that everything will be answered and that we're going to do our best to save Matthew."

"And I *have* to go with you?" Tuni asked with an air of suspicion.

"Absolutely not," he replied. "As I said, we have no jurisdiction here. My men and I will go on our way and continue our tasks, but if you do not wish to accompany me, I strongly encourage you to leave this hotel altogether and go straight to the airport. U.S. Customs can help you from there. I'll give you my card so that I can answer your questions when you're ready."

He searched his coat pocket.

"Bollocks to that," Tuni said. "Let's go." She stepped onto the smashed door and stopped. "Wait!" She released her suitcase handle and turned to run back in. The officer behind her held up his hands to stop her, but she cut left into the kitchen and saw the smooth gray stone atop the marble countertop where she had left it. She reached for it, paused, scanned the area, and grabbed a cloth napkin. After wrapping it up in the napkin, she tucked the rock into her front pocket and continued through the door.

Obviously relieved, Abel took her suitcase handle and strode up the wooden pier to the orchid-lined path, with Tuni at his heels and his two men close behind her.

In the living room of the suite, behind a leather couch, Raúl Solorzano lay bleeding on the brand-new carpet installed only three weeks ago. His blood trickled from the bullet's entry wound above his left eyebrow as his glassy eyes stared across the darkening carpet.

NINE

Matt shifted restlessly in the SUV's backseat. His neck and back hurt like hell. He had a ripping headache, his wrists were chafed and his hands cramping from the handcuffs, his eyes burned, his throat was dry, and his stomach cried out for a real meal. How much of the past few days had he spent on airplanes? He'd managed perhaps five hours' sleep out of the past seventy-two. Desperation had begun to set in. At least he'd gotten to hear Tuni's voice. She sounded more worried about him than about herself, so that was good, he supposed. He needed to hear more. See her face. Smell her . . . touch her skin . . . taste her mouth. She was truly perfect in every way. If all this were to end right now, she would have him fed, medicated, hydrated, and sleeping in a warm bed inside thirty minutes.

Rheese and his two bruisers were standing outside, lingering around the remote Petrobras gas station's pay phone. Matt watched as the local passersby gawked at them. He supposed that this part of Medellín, Colombia, was a bit off the beaten tourist paths. Then again, was there *any* part of this country that got many tourists? The streets weren't as dirty as he had expected, and the people weren't walking around in rags, but it was very foreign, and Matt just wanted to be home. The one thing that made him feel better was that he knew a lot more Spanish than Ukrainian.

The muffled ring of a telephone made it through the closed windows, and G grabbed the pay phone's receiver. Matt could hear nothing of the ensuing conversation.

★ ★ ★

Garza answered. *"¿Sí? Él está conmigo. Voy a traducir."*

"What's happening?" Rheese demanded. "What's he saying?"

"Just relax, Doctor," Garza said. "He asked if you were here; I told him I would translate for you. We just talked about this. *¿Qué le dijiste?* He wants to know how much we can pay him today."

"Ninety thousand," Rheese said. "Just tell him the ninety thousand."

Z interrupted. "You don't want to start lower? Let him talk you up?"

Rheese brushed him off and gestured for Garza to say it.

"Noventa mil dólares estadunidenses . . . He says that's not enough. *Es todo lo que tenemos hoy en día.* I told him it's all we have."

"Tell him we can get him another fifty in the near future," Rheese said.

"Podemos pagar otros cincuenta mil en un par de semanas . . . ¿Sí? . . . We have a deal. Hang on. He's telling me where we need to go."

Garza jotted down the directions as Rheese rubbed his hands together. They walked back to the SUV and got in.

★ ★ ★

"We have about thirty minutes to kill," G said to the group. "Anyone else hungry? I saw a burger place down the street."

With his proposal unanimously accepted, the four of them ate quickly and got back on the road. Matt felt a bit better physically, though he still longed for painkillers and sleep.

An hour later, Z stopped the SUV at the end of a washboarded, potholed road. An old chain-link fence blocked off a large, patchy grass field with weeded-over basketball courts and boarded-up buildings that clearly had once been a school. Beyond the field, a forested hill rose up and melded into the mountain range that encircled the valley of Medellín. All four sat in the vehicle, surveying the scene.

"This shit is dangerous," Z said. "Who says this ain't a cartel setup?"

"This man has nothing to with any of that nonsense," Rheese said. "He's only here on a brief business trip and heads back to Cuba this evening. What possible connection would he have to the drug cartels?"

"You don't know nothin' 'bout this stuff, Doctor," Z said. "In jolly old England you ain't gotta worry about yer family gettin' snatched, what you say to who, who's friends with what guy. It's real life out here, homes."

"He's right to be concerned, Doctor," G said. "We have no weapons, no surveillance, and a single exit path. It's odd for a visiting businessman to propose this kind of spot for a sale."

"Rubbish! It's precisely *because* he's a businessman and doesn't want to be seen engaging in a large transaction such as this! I would want to go somewhere discreet as well."

Z leaned over to G and said, "Look at that hill, bro. That shit could be crawlin' with snipers, guerrillas—you name it. He say to actually come *onto* the field?"

"Yeah. He said part of the fence would be open."

"Right over there," Matt said, pointing to a spot where, indeed, the chain-link fencing had been cut and spread wide enough for a vehicle to drive through. Multiple tire tracks marked the pathway.

"This is bullshit, man," Z said. Then he perked up. "Hey, Doctor, if yer so confident this shit's all cool, why don't you walk out there on yer own, do the deal, and come back?"

"Well, I suppose I could—it's just, the Spanish, you know . . ."

G interrupted. "Hold on. He doesn't have to do that." He gave Z a stern look. "We're all getting out. I'll go with you, Doctor, to do the deal. Matthew, you'll stay behind that line of trees at the east end of the field. Fan—um, Z—you're our spotter. I want you on the west end, concealed in one of those buildings. From there, you can watch the hill and the car."

"Why the car?" Rheese asked.

"Nothing for you to worry about," G said. "Just don't want anyone hanging around it. We're in Medellín—cars have a strange habit of blowing up if you don't keep an eye on them."

Rheese opened up the plastic shopping bag and transferred the cash from his attaché case.

"What if he didn't come alone?" Z asked. "He say he was comin' alone?"

"He didn't say. But if he has one or two people with him for protection, it's understandable. This is a lot of money and an expensive item we're talking about."

They got out of the vehicle, and Z lifted open the hatch, grabbed a pair of binoculars from a backpack, and casually walked off down the road. Rheese,

Matt, and G walked along the fence to the opening and stepped through. They continued along the inside of the fence until it ended at the line of tall trees and shrubs that bordered the former schoolyard. G led Matt into the overgrown vegetation, stopping at a short palm tree with long, spreading fronds that hung almost to the ground. G tried to break off one of the spiky fronds, but it was too strong.

"Turn around," he said, and Matt complied. Unlocking one of the handcuffs, G pulled Matt to the palm and recuffed his hands in front of him, around the base of the frond. He took another look at the sharp spikes and, apparently, decided there was no way Matt could rip his way free without skewering his arms, chest, and probably his face in the process.

"Sit tight and keep quiet," he said. "Oh, and if you see anybody coming from *that* way"—he nodded toward the deepening woods to the east—"it's probably in your best interest to scream like hell for us to come running." G trotted off.

Matt looked into the thick growth where G had pointed, and wondered if someone might actually come sneaking up from there. The whole scene had a quality of unreality: he was a witness to some kind of shady deal in the middle of Colombia, in danger of being kidnapped from his kidnappers. He'd heard all sorts of stories about people being snatched and held for ransom, or just showing up headless a few days or years later. He didn't appreciate Z's Colombian necktie business, but he liked it even less standing in the middle of Colombia!

He watched as G and Rheese walked deeper into the field and then stopped. G pointed to something outside Matt's field of vision, and a second later came the sound of an approaching engine. From the other side of the field, an old, weathered Honda sedan appeared. It stopped a short distance from Rheese and G, and as Rheese took a few cautious steps back, four men got out. One, shorter and better dressed than the others, hung back by the car while his companions approached Rheese and G, spoke for a minute, then patted them both down. One of the men motioned for the short one to come forward.

Matt leaned out from the palm to try to see where Z had gone, but he could see only part of the old school buildings through the nearby trees. He tried to bend the frond to get a better view and felt something prick his wrist through his shirtsleeve. It was one of the long spikes jutting in a row, like sawfish teeth, from the base of the frond. He rotated his arms around and pinched the spike to see if he could break it. It was too hard to do with his fingers, but he got one into a link of the handcuff chain, twisted, and snapped it right off.

He glanced out and saw Rheese talking to the short, well-dressed man. He decided to break off some more spikes around where his wrists were, to avoid further pokes, and within a couple of minutes, he had broken off all the spikes on one whole side of the frond. He took another look out at the field. Rheese was looking closely at something in his hand. G leaned over and was inspecting it, too. Rheese nodded, and G handed the plastic bag of cash to the short guy, who reached in and made a cursory count, waved, and turned to go.

Suddenly, a loud whistle came from the buildings. G turned around toward the sound, then spun all the way around to scan the area. He grabbed Rheese, tucking him under his arm, and rushed him back toward the fence. The short man and his friends also lit out running, and jumped into their car.

Matt couldn't tell what was happening, only that it couldn't be good. He searched all around him for anything suspicious, keeping a keen eye on the woods to his right. His shoes crunched the dead foliage beneath him. He couldn't see Rheese or G anymore, and there was no sign of Z. The Honda had disappeared from sight, its revving engine fading in the distance. Matt turned back to the palm frond. He needed to get himself free. He continued twisting with the chain links until he had the whole shaft free of spikes. Now there was just the broad, leafy end—still sharp at the edges, but nothing that would hurt too much. Opening his arms as wide as the cuffs would permit, he eased his way along the frond, turning his face aside so that the turtleneck took the brunt of the scratching from the rigid leaves. He made it past the widest part, took another couple of steps, and felt the feathery tip pull through as the frond shot back up to its normal position. He was free—from the palm, at least.

He pushed deeper into the wooded area, toward the neighborhood they had driven through on the way in. As he walked, he could see slivers of backyards and houses between the trees. Behind him, he could see or hear no pursuers. He continued until the wild area ended and he found himself behind a row of run-down houses. Children played in a backyard, laughing and throwing green guavas at each other.

With no idea what he was doing, where he might go, or whom to ask for help, Matt began to wonder whether he had made a terrible mistake. But now that he was free, he couldn't imagine surrendering himself. No, he needed to find a phone so he could call the police in Tahiti and tell them about Tuni. But what if she ended up in a standoff, her guard's arm around her neck, and a gun to her head? Could he trust the cops on a French tourist island to know how to handle that kind of situation?

THE OPAL

✶ ✶ ✶

Solorzano ran through the jungle, dodging around spiny palms and vaulting rotting logs. He had clearly seen the reflection from the hill. His first thought: a sniper—perhaps accompanied by a whole squad of guerrillas. But standing hidden inside the school's gardening shed, he had peered through a ventilation grate with the binoculars and spotted the actual source of the flash: one black man holding a big camera with a telephoto lens. Solorzano had whistled to alert Garza before taking off into the woods.

Hurdling another downed tree and rounding a thicket of low growth, he caught a glimpse of Garza and Rheese running back out through the broken fence, toward the rental SUV. The engine whine of the seller's vehicle had already disappeared back up the forest road.

Solorzano spotted the photographer and broke into a full sprint. The man heard him coming, but too late. With a look of alarm and confusion, he dropped the camera and reached for the gun in his waistband. Solorzano jumped, smashing into the man's midsection with his shoulder, knocking the wind out of him, and probably cracking a rib or two. They landed on the slope and rolled several turns down the hill. When they came to a stop, the man was trying to suck in air, but Solorzano rose up and came down with a powerful punch to the solar plexus. The man gagged and bile bubbled up from his mouth before he passed out.

"I'll take that," Solorzano said, picking the gun up from the dirt. It was an untarnished new-looking .40-caliber Glock. Then he got up and went back to retrieve the camera.

After some fumbling about with the buttons, he found the camera's power switch. The last photo taken popped up automatically: a close-up of Garza with a piece of Rheese's ear in the frame. He pressed the left arrow button: another shot of Garza, zoomed back a little. Back, back, back, and he found a shot of Garza with the punk Turner heading into the trees on the other side of the field. Then one of his own back as he was walking away from them. Then the SUV, when they first pulled up.

"You don't look like a cop, homes," he muttered. "What's yer deal?"

He went through the man's pockets and found a set of keys, a money clip with a stack of Colombian bills, a pack of cigarettes, and a lighter. No passport or other ID. He checked the guy's pulse and, finding one, started walking back across the field.

Garza held a questioning hand out the SUV's window. Solorzano waved the all clear, and Garza and Rheese got back out. They met at the gap in the fence.

"Nice camera," Garza said.

"Yeah, check out the pics. Some good ones of yer pretty mug."

He handed the camera to Garza.

"You find someone?" Rheese asked.

"Yeah. Black dude. He's knocked out back there, but we should head out. I also got a new toy." He pulled the pistol from behind his back.

"Hmm, law enforcement?" Rheese asked.

"Doubt it. No ID or nothin'. Should I go get Turner?"

Garza looked up from the camera. "Yeah. You got your key? He's cuffed to a tree."

"Yeah. Be right back."

Solorzano crunched over the dead branches, leaves, and palm fronds. He could have sworn this was where he saw Garza go in.

"Turner!" he yelled. "Hey, where the hell are you, you skinny little shit?"

He walked back out to the field and called to Rheese and Garza. Both of them looked up. Solorzano spread his arms out, palms up.

"He's right there!" Garza shouted. Solorzano shook his head. "God damn it!" Garza slapped his forehead.

"He got away?" Rheese blurted. "He bloody *escaped*? How? You . . . you said he was cuffed!"

"I know. Shit! He can't be far."

"I'm right here," Matt said from behind them. Garza and Rheese spun around. "When you guys ran off, I thought you were ditching me. I got away from that stupid tree, went through the houses to the street, and came right here. Are we safe?"

Garza glared at him accusingly. "Thought twice, did you?"

"Huh? No! I told you, I just—"

Garza interrupted, "You just keep thinking about your girlfriend whenever that crafty shit starts popping into your head. You made the right choice this time."

"I came right here! I . . ."

Solorzano joined them, giving Matt the stink-eye as they put him in the SUV, and then walked to the front bumper.

"Take a look at this," Garza said to Solorzano.

Rheese pulled a roundish object out of a velvet drawstring bag and held it out in his palm. It was the biggest gemstone Solorzano had ever seen. Bluish, with speckles of turquoise, orange, and red—a dozen hues glinting in the sun as Rheese turned it ever so slightly. It was cut with facets, like a diamond.

"That's some sick shit," Solorzano said with a grin. "Is it real?"

"Of course it's bloody real!" Rheese snapped. "And the stone itself is just the start of it!"

"Yeah, but look at this," Garza said to Solorzano as Rheese dropped the jewel back in its bag. He turned the camera back on and clicked through several shots.

There was the stone, sitting on a table beneath the light of a desk lamp. Beside it lay a square ruler showing its dimensions.

"And . . . " Garza said, clicking to the preceding photo—also of the stone, but from a different angle.

Click, another angle; *click,* close-up; *click, click, click*—eleven shots in all.

Garza said, "The time stamps on these pictures are from yesterday."

Solorzano frowned and shook his head. He gazed out to the other end of the field, where the photographer was probably regaining consciousness.

"So what's this mean, bro? Why they wanna take pictures of who they're sellin' to? Some kind of setup? Entrapment?"

"Don't know, but we need to get the hell out of this country ASAP," G said. "We gotta scope out the airport before we all go in, though. Fando, get rid of that gun. We'll dump the camera, too, but I'm keeping the memory card."

"We're going to Cuba, gentlemen," Rheese said. "To wrap up this adventure and collect the prizes. We need to get to a phone, though. I must speak with my assistant to find out what else he has discovered about our new treasure."

"Shit," Solorzano said. "That thing ain't enough of a prize?"

Garza shook his head, "It's worth a lot, but nowhere near what we planned to make off this—not when we split up the cuts. Think about it: the agency gets a small share, plus we got two ops in Tahiti and two wrapping up in North Carolina. Shares start looking pretty insignificant—know what I'm saying?"

Solorzano glanced at Rheese, saw he wasn't looking, gave a questioning look to Garza, then cut his eyes down toward the velvet bag. Garza shook his head. *No, we're not taking it for ourselves.*

"All right. So what's in Cuba?" Solorzano asked.

TEN

"It's an opal," Rheese said, holding up the enormous faceted gemstone in his palm. "Thirty-one millimeters in diameter, twenty-one-millimeter depth. Near-perfect roundness. Seventy-six-point-six-five carats. One of a kind in all the world. Specs alone, it would be worth about two hundred and thirty thousand dollars, or . . ." He looked at Matt with a sly smile. ". . . ninety and an IOU, as the case may be."

Outside Rheese's window, Matt watched a road sign streak by: *Velocidad controlada por radar.*

"It's very pretty, Doctor," Matt said in a bored tone. "Where's it from?"

"Ah, but that's always the question, isn't it? It's the *story,* lad. That's the key—especially at auctions. The fact that a single sheet of paper can sell for a hundred thousand dollars? Rubbish, if you ask me. Conversation pieces for bored elites—bragging rights at private card tables and in the locker rooms of ten-thousand-quid-a-month fitness centers. Regardless, this slightly weathered marvel is worth far more as a guide in *your* gifted hands than as a cleavage centerpiece. You see . . ." He pinched it and held it close to Matt's face. "It's a tiny piece of a much greater prize."

Matt felt guilty to find himself actually interested in Rheese's discourse, even if it was only a small voice behind the constant noise of peril. He remained far more concerned with Tuni's predicament and his own. The SUV slowed, and both of them looked forward.

"Fando—checkpoint," G said. "Reach back and get his cuffs off, quick."

Z quickly leaned back and keyed off the cuffs, dropping them to the backseat floor.

"Thanks, *Fando,*" Matt said.

Z looked back at him with surprise and then scowled at G. "Dumbass," he growled.

"Don't worry about it," G replied. His sunglasses stared back from the rearview mirror. "Turner, this is your chance to redeem yourself. You get asked any questions, I better see an Oscar-worthy performance, *comprendes?*"

Matt nodded, and he meant it.

A soldier with a slung rifle spoke with G as another walked around the vehicle, cupping his eyes to see in the various windows.

"I need passports," G said, and Rheese handed him two.

Rheese pinched and pulled at the coarse hairs of his moustache as he watched the soldiers. A gold ring clinked three times on Matt's window. Matt looked out at the soldier holding up his passport. Three more clinks, harder and faster.

"Roll down the window, idiot," Fando said. "It's tinted."

Matt found the switch and brought the window down halfway. The soldier compared his face to that of his photo, then did the same with Rheese, who flashed the same goofy smile displayed in the passport. A cursory glance around the backseat, and the soldier snapped a nod to his superior.

"*Está bien,*" the first soldier said as he handed G all the documents. He waved them along and whistled to the next vehicle.

Rheese reached forward for his passport and Matt's, but G dropped them in the cup holder beside him and said, "Might as well hold on to them. More checkpoints along the way. Cuff him back up, will you?"

Rheese leaned back in his seat and gave Matt a sideways glance. "I don't think that's necessary," he said. "The lad understands the stakes here and won't be trying any more reckless stunts. Turner?"

"Right . . . yeah. I'm not going anywhere. I told you."

Rheese replied, "Well, you're going where we take you, but I understand your meaning. Let's get back to it, shall we? Where was I?"

He dropped the gemstone out of its black velvet bag and held it between his thick fingers.

"It's a tiny piece of a bigger puzzle," Matt said.

"Yes, it is," Rheese said in a low, almost suggestive voice. He was clearly giddy about this new expedition, and Matt was all for keeping him in a positive mind-set. "You see, a stone like this gets marked and cataloged and tracked. Do you see this engraving here? That's Arabic and reads '*Inshallah*'—essentially,

'If God wants.' And this little swirly swoop is the signature of the jeweler who cut it: 'Bin Husain'—quite certainly not his whole name. The rest of the stone around it has, unfortunately, degraded over time or was chipped away, but this was more than enough to identify it."

"So it's Arab," Matt said with a hint of *let's get on with it* in his tone.

"*Cut* by an Arab, yes. But the stone itself goes back further than that. It was likely mined in Egypt and used in various royal jewelry or adornments until, perhaps, being buried with a pharaoh, high priest, or other important person. Based on its condition—minimal wearing—the stone was likely entombed for a couple of thousand years before being taken by grave robbers sometime in the tenth century AD, arriving in the possession of someone in the Fatimid dynasty—the leaders of the Arab world at the time—who then commissioned it to be cut with the facets you see here. It was then that it was dubbed *Ruh Allah*—the Spirit of God. This is all well documented, mind you, and, although not strictly relevant to our mission, wonderfully fascinating history. Besides, you may be lucky enough to see some of this business firsthand. As I was saying, the caliph, a gent called al-Ḥākim, had the finest blacksmith in the world—his name has been lost to history—craft a sword for his son,' Alī az-Ẓāhir, the seventh caliph of the Fatimids. Are you following all this?"

"Opal from Egypt, cut by Arabs, caliph guy makes a sword for his son."

"Good enough," Rheese said. "The Arabs had a metallurgical expertise that no one else had. They forged weapons and other items from Damascus steel—with materials and technique lost for a millennium and only recently synthesized. This sword in particular, called *Sayf Allah*—"

"Sword of God?" Matt ventured.

"You're paying attention—how refreshing. Yes. So . . . the Sword of God was adorned with numerous precious metals—gold, silver, hundreds of tiny diamonds—and capped with the spiritually significant stones: turquoise, hematite, carnelian, and . . ." Rheese raised his eyebrows.

"Opals."

"Opal. Yes, precisely. Such stones were said to be in the rings worn by Ali himself, cousin and son-in-law of Muhammad. You know who Muhammad is, I pray?"

"The Muslim prophet, yeah."

"Indeed. Al-Ḥākim's goal was to create the ultimate Muslim sword for his son. The red carnelian was embedded in one end of the cross-guard, the turquoise in the other, and hematite inlaid as a line down the grip. The opal—*this* opal—was the centerpiece, enclosed in the pommel. That's the sort of ball tip at the end of the hilt. Keeps the whole thing from slipping out of your hand but also serves as a counterbalance to the heavy blade. *Sayf Allah* is said to have been the most perfectly crafted sword of its day: exceptionally light, brilliantly balanced, and—if ever actually used as a weapon—wholly functional. I am certain it was made with an equally stunning scabbard to match, but history has no record of it."

"So you want to find this sword."

Rheese brushed this off with a lazy wave and noisily gulped down some water from a bottle.

"Think you've said enough, Doctor?" G said, his sunglasses filling the rearview mirror.

"Fret not. He needs to know what he's *not* looking for as much as what he *should* be. The more background he has, the less time we waste." Rheese rolled his eyes at G's back, shook off his irritation, and turned back to Matt. "Now, then, the sword: yes . . . and no. If otherwise intact, *Sayf Allah* would be a *monster* of a find, and it may be out there somewhere in the world. But I am much more interested in what accompanied this opal when it was hidden, sometime around the late seventeenth century."

"And what's that? Diamonds?"

Rheese regarded him for a beat, as if unsure whether this was meant as a slight. He said, "Possibly, but silver is much more likely. You see, the Spanish were very busy seafarers during the period I'm about to get to. Their silver was essentially the world's dollar. They were minting coins in Peru, where they had natives slaving away in mines, and shipping it across the Atlantic on a weekly basis."

"I'm familiar with all this, Doctor," Matt said, trying not to show his weariness at Rheese's rapt enjoyment of his own voice.

"Of course you are," Rheese said. "What with all your seafaring with treasure hunters, you must be only a couple of units short of a doctorate! Well, what you may *not* have known is that two centuries before your Spanish-Confederate loot hit the ocean floor, Spain *owned* the Caribbean, and pirates, privateers, British, French—*everyone*—was sniffing around Cuba and the other islands, taking ships, attacking harbors. It was like the Wild West on the high seas. And while the freebooters usually lost to the superior Spanish ships, they sometimes won. Most often, though, the thieves sailed away crippled, painfully aware that they would be sunk if they had to fight again. This is where the hidden treasure map stories come from. Go ashore and hide the treasure somewhere no one will find it, until you can come back with a more seaworthy vessel, or perhaps under the guise of an innocent trade ship."

Matt forced himself not to yawn.

"Smaller islands could be convenient, but it would look highly suspicious to be anchored off one. Better to make port in an unimportant bay and send a small party into the jungle.

"*This* opal—not just a beautiful gemstone with impressive specs, but a known historical object with an exceptional story—was found . . . are you ready for this? . . . alone, sealed off from the world within a small cavity *inside* a bloody strangler fig tree! Like a pearl in an oyster! Better yet, like a pearl in a bloody *rock*! This strangler fig is a tree that grows around a host tree—a palm or a mahogany, for instance—until the host tree dies and there stands in its place this massive, gnarled behemoth. The tree in question was logged out last year in fifty or more thick slices. To the shock and delight of some poor lumber worker at a mill, one of those slices birthed this gem before his very eyes. A gift from God, he no doubt thought. But the little guy doesn't get to strike it lucky in Cuba, no sir. Long story short, upper management got hold of it, and here we are, eight months later. They sent it along with their business development manager on a scheduled trip to Colombia. You saw him—the squat fellow in the suit."

Rheese plopped the stone back into its velvet sack and pulled the draw-string tight before replacing it in the satchel at his feet.

"And what makes you think there is more to find?" Matt asked and glanced outside the window, noticing the warm rays of sunlight had suddenly disappeared. Still on a main highway, the SUV had entered a deep canyon with steep walls.

"Because when you plunder a Spanish ship and take the time to go and hide your booty deep in the jungle, you do not go there to hide a single jewel. My research has the whole thing worked out. Not for you to worry about."

"What about the other slices of that tree?" Matt asked.

"Sawdust."

"Oh, right, of course. Do they know where it was cut down?"

"Yes, we do. The entire area has been deforested. It's a landscape of brush and weeds and sapling palmettos until about a hundred meters in. That's where the protected rain forest begins. And before you ask if the rest of the area's trees have been checked, the answer is, *of course*. Imbecilic executives thought they might have themselves a forest full of expensive jewelry. Personally, I would not have wasted my time. The opal was more likely left as a marker to something *buried* nearby, not embedded in another tree. That's what you will tell me for certain after you do your magic with it."

"And what if there's nothing else? What if I read it and it turns out some tricky pirate ran off with it and hid it for himself? Seems a little premature to fly all the way to Cuba without even knowing. Besides, are Americans even allowed to go there?"

"The government doesn't look twice at educators and their research assistants, as long as they stir up no trouble." Rheese's face hardened. "And as for the former question, there most certainly is *more*. So if you report otherwise, I'll know you're lying."

"Okay, yeah, I get that," Matt said. "You *would* suspect something like that. But what if there *really is* nothing more? I mean, is that just so impossible for you to accept that you think there's *zero* chance of it?"

Fando, in the front passenger seat, glanced over at G. G was paying attention, too, glancing at the rearview mirror as he drove, apparently awaiting Rheese's answer.

"Trust me," Matt continued. "I didn't hit pay dirt on the first try. I went through quite a few source objects before I found the one that had what I needed."

"I have no such concerns," Rheese said, pulling out Matt's iPad.

"I don't think you quite understand how my ability works, either. I don't get the whole story on an artifact. It's not only limited to when it was in physical, skin-on-skin contact, imprints only stick when the person feels *strong* emotions, good or bad."

Rheese put the tablet aside and began digging around in his bag.

Matt went on. "There's the very real possibility that essential clues are missing from the thing. Because the person had it in a sack, or they were just walking along and indifferent to the world and, therefore, not imprinting, or it was in their pocket, or . . . really, any number of other possibilities. The odds are never in my favor."

Rheese sat up with the opal in his hand. "Well, lad, only one way to find out, eh? We've still a bit of a drive."

Matt sighed. "Do you just have me read things to shut me up when we're traveling?"

"That's just an added bonus. Your silence when unconscious is indeed golden."

ELEVEN

I am female. It's my twentieth year. My name is Tadinanefer, daughter of Bes of Swenet. I'm running. I reach the edge of the city, turn. Must run . . . he said I have to. I stop and crouch in between a tree and the city wall. The City of Amun. My chest burns. I'm out of breath. My chest *stings*—I'm jabbing the enormous stone against bone. I pull it away, look at it again. It changes everything.

She thinks she'll be caught any second, Matt observes. *Two voices shouting in her head.*

One of the voices says, "You did what you were told," and images of elaborately gowned officials flash in her head. Names whiz by with associated faces. They don't look worried but have a definite sense of urgency.

The other voice says, "This doesn't happen without a price." And she sees angry guards tearing through her father's things, beating him, beating her little sister. But these images are illusory, whereas the previous ones are real memories. The face of the man who pried the gem from the golden crown and thrust it into her hands. His name is Sen-mes.

"Take it! Sell it in Tyre or farther north. Let no one in this city see it!"

A thought consisting only of words repeats in her head: How did this happen?

It's meditation for her. We are . . . she is *rocking back and forth as she thinks it. At the very least, the motion centers her.*

It's late, and the moon not yet risen. The city is quiet but for the distant sound of striking stones. *Tok . . . tok . . . . tok . . . tok . . .*

THE OPAL

She wipes her eyes because the tears sting. She knows what they are doing. The memories of less than an hour ago are vivid in her head: men scaling statues with ropes pulled by others on the ground. They chisel away the faces. She had run past the old temple, where a man sat on the shoulders of another, who, in turn, sat upon another's. The one on top was scraping away the last bits of a name. They shifted to the next carvings of the name and began chiseling these away, as well. *Tik . . . tik . . . tik . . .*

This girl knows it's the name of Hatshepsut—the symbol for her name— and her statues, all being defaced. Hatshepsut used to be the pharaoh. Why is she being erased *all over the city? She's been dead a long time. Why the sudden destruction of her legacy? Who ordered it? Tadinanefer wonders the same thing; she doesn't know why.*

Her eyes dart right and left, still fearful that someone will see her, demand to know what she's doing: "And what have you got there?" But no one is about. She looks down at the perfect gem, a stone that only a living god could possess. She rubs her index finger over its surface in circles, thinking this could be the last time she gets to touch it before someone takes it away from her, back to where it belongs or to others who are allowed to possess things of such beauty. That may be the best outcome. She thinks of throwing it away from her, kicking dirt over it, but what if the officials change their mind and come looking for it?

"I got rid of it . . . I threw it away . . ." They would never believe her. Her father's imagined beating returns to the foreground of her thoughts. More tears flow. She glances around again, inhales deeply. She gets up, hops a bush, and breaks into a run again. Several houses farther, she remembers the jewel in her fist and places it in the draping linen under her arm, twisting it before tucking the mass into her waist belt. This was the worst thing that could ever have happened to her family.

She thinks, *We're going home. Father will be livid . . .*

Dark space. We're still in the car. Rheese's heavy breathing beside me. I can feel my body again. The opal's in my hand.

Matt called the space between imprints "dark space." It always felt the same. The previous imprint faded away, including not only the view through the eyes of the imprinter but also the thoughts and the sensations of the imprinter's physical body. Usually, a few seconds later, he could feel his own body again. Matt didn't understand exactly why he couldn't feel both sets, but his father theorized that his nervous system couldn't handle the input overload from four arms, four eyes, twenty toes, and so on. But Dad had always believed the boy could do more—break the rules that, to Matt, seemed carved in stone. And in the beginning, Dad was right; Matt's skill improved at a fairly consistent rate. But at a certain point, the new discoveries ended, and his understanding and control over the experiences hadn't changed much in years. It didn't matter. Dad would tell him, almost shouting, "Take control of it, boy. Don't let *it* control *you*."

As if I had a damned choice, Matt thought, hearing his father's words in his head.

The next strongest imprint would arrive any second now. He had no idea how long it would last, and he didn't have his timer on. Without dark space, he was completely dependent on Rheese to take the opal away. But he didn't think Rheese knew about the dark space. It could work to his advantage at some point.

Matt risked a quick peek through his right eye. Rheese was playing Angry Birds on the iPad. Poorly. But at least he appeared to be enthralled. Matt decided to shimmy the opal off his hand—pretend it fell off while he was under. Since his hand lay hidden between his legs, it proved fairly easy, and he made a good show of groggily waking up.

"Wha . . . " he moaned, blinking rapidly.

"What the . . . ?" Rheese leaned over to grab the stone.

A fantasy action plan entered Matt's head: grab Rheese by the ear, yank back, get him in a headlock, snatch the opal, roll down the window, toss it out, and let it smash all to hell when it hit the asphalt at sixty miles per hour.

Rheese had already sat up, opal in hand. He quickly examined it as if in fear that it had been damaged. His eyes snapped to Matt. "Well?"

"I . . . uh, it's Egyptian."

Rheese's shoulders slumped. "Well . . ." He scratched his freckled pate and smiled. "A revelatory breakthrough, indeed. Perhaps a more thorough retelling would be prudent. Pretend I'm your Amazon tart, seated across an RV table."

That stung. Matt feigned indifference, but Tuni was very much on his mind.

"A young peasant woman has it. It was given to her by an Egyptian official. All through the city, people are defacing statues of the previous pharaoh—chiseling her name off monuments and whatnot."

Rheese's eyes widened. "Hatshepsut," he said in a tone almost of reverence.

"Yeah, her. Somebody ordered it. So this girl is hiding with it . . . doesn't know what to do, worries about what will happen to her, her family, et cetera."

Rheese nodded. "Go on . . ."

"That's . . . that's it. Then, you know, I came out of it. She was hiding for a while, then ran again before tucking it away."

Rheese sat back, deep in thought. He sighed, though perhaps more in wonder than in frustration.

Matt went on. "This is usually how it goes. It's a lot different from what you're thinking, the way imprints work. Sometimes I spend weeks with an artifact before I get anything more than a date out of it."

"The date!" Rheese blurted. "What was it?"

"It was . . ." Matt thought back. She was roughly aware of a day, but not a year. That far back, few cultures were, but there had often been other markers that he was able to give the museum, which enabled them to piece things together. "Does '*ipip*' help at all? She was aware it was the middle of *ipip*—summertime, I guess? Didn't really have a firm date in her head."

Rheese's head swayed side to side, as if he were recalling a long-forgotten tune. "Of course, of course—how would she? It's irrelevant, anyway. Doesn't help us here. Is there more from her, though?"

"I don't know," Matt said. "She was heading home."

"Hatshepsut—just *imagine*," Rheese said again under his breath. He turned back to Matt with excited eyes, spoke quickly. "That's one of the great mysteries of Egypt, you know. Why someone tried to erase her from history. The *power* that you hold—it's . . ."

"It can come in handy, yeah . . ."

"Bloody shame it's wasted on you, is what I was going to say. But it's neither here nor there. Not my field any longer."

Matt shrugged. Probably best not to respond.

"Hmm, right. Well . . ." Rheese turned the opal over in his palm, then looked to the front of the car. "How much longer to the airport?"

Garza glanced down at the seat beside him, then back at the road. "Twenty or thirty minutes."

Rheese looked back at Matt. "Have any trouble sleeping on planes?"

"Nuh-uh, not this time. You need to understand that reading an imprint doesn't count as sleeping. I'm frickin' exhausted."

"It's a five-hour flight, Turner. You want to waste the entire time sleeping?"

"'Waste' . . ." Matt said. *He just doesn't get it. No, that's not it—he just doesn't care.* "Look, I really need to sleep, Rheese. Maybe just a quick one before we're in the air."

Rheese smiled. "Of course, lad! Whatever you like. Just know that the longer it takes for you to find what we seek, the longer we stay in the jungle."

Was the man ever interested in anything that was *not* in a jungle?

✶ ✶ ✶

Matt fast-forwarded past Tadinanefer's imprint and found himself in someone new: a Norwegian man . . . lying atop of a pile of dead bodies.

TWELVE

eth Turner reached over to the end table and answered the phone on the second ring. "Hello?"

"Beth, this is Tuni."

Beth stiffened. Tuni's tone was ominous, her voice shaky. "Oh, God, tell me, hon. What is it? Just say it."

"It's Matt. He's . . . he's been taken. It's Dr. Rheese, Beth. He's the one from—"

"I know who he is. Is my Matty okay, though? Do you know if he's okay?"

"I got to hear his voice on the phone earlier today. I'm sure Rheese won't hurt him. You know, he wants to use him to find something, is my best guess. I'm with some officers from Inter—what's that? . . . Why the bloody hell not? Well, I need to let—"

"Rog!" Beth cupped a hand over the phone as she yelled toward the garage door.

Tuni was still arguing with a muffled male voice. "Well, that sounds bloody asinine," she said. "But okay, whatever. Beth, I'm at the airport right now. We're going to try to find him and bring him home safe. I'll update you constantly, okay?"

Roger came in from the garage, saw Beth on the phone, and yelled, "What happened?"

"Tuni, hold on. Roger's here. Tell him everything you know. It's Matty, hon! That son of a bitch Rheese has him somewhere!"

"What?" He snatched the phone out of her hand.

"Tuni, tell me everything. And speak slowly." He motioned to Beth to grab him a pen and notepad.

"I'm so sorry, Roger, I have to go through security—need to put my phone in the thing. I'll . . . I'll call you back."

He held the phone at his side and began pacing.

"What happened?" Beth asked.

"I guess she's at an airport. Said she has to go through security. Calling back. What did she tell you?"

Beth relayed what little was said. Roger's neck muscles pulsed, and his nostrils flared.

"Jesus Christ!" he shouted at the silent phone. "How long does it take to go through security?"

"Call her back!"

"She'll call. Who'd she say she was with, again?"

"She said officers with something, but then someone cut her off. It sounded like they didn't want her to say."

"What? That makes no sense. There's no police force that would do that. What did she say, *exactly,* before she was interrupted?"

"I don't know—that's it!"

"That's *not* it! You're giving me bullshit paraphrasing! Say the goddamned *words*!"

Beth scowled as the tears streamed. "I . . . told . . . you . . . already."

Roger growled and hit the cordless phone's callback button.

"Hello, I'm afraid you've reached Tuni's voice mail. Be a dear and leave an actual message if you need me. Cheers!"

"Tuni, call us back, please," Roger said. "Do not go anywhere with anyone until you speak with me. You might be in danger."

✱ ✱ ✱

"Where's my phone?" Tuni asked the short, round security agent as she balanced on one foot to put on her other shoe. "My passport was with it, too."

He glanced around lazily and shrugged. Her purse waited at the end of the conveyer, but there was no little blue basket with her things. She looked around and spotted Abel Turay and his fellow officers behind a clear plastic panel. He was waving to her and pointed at his other hand, which held her phone and passport. She grabbed her purse and walked to them.

"Sorry," Abel said as he handed them to her. "They were just sitting there while you were stuck behind that woman."

Tuni waved off the apology as she powered the phone back on. "Which gate are we?"

"This way," he said. "Number three."

She walked behind them as her phone booted up. It seemed to take an especially long time, or perhaps it was just her impatience. When it reached the home screen, though, she had no signal, and a message popped up: "INSERT SIM."

"Damn it! Why now?"

Abel glanced back as they walked. "Problem?"

"My stupid phone won't work. How do I check the SIM card?"

"Uh-oh. Hopefully, the X-ray didn't mess it up. I've heard of that happening before. Try taking out the battery and putting it back in."

"That didn't happen on the way here," she said as she slid open the back and popped the battery out with a fingernail. "Or with the thirty some-odd other scanners it's been through."

She spotted the SIM card and slid it out, looked it over, and fitted it securely back into its slot before reinserting the battery. The phone again began the booting process.

"We are boarding, miss," Abel said, gently guiding her to the ticket taker. "Please, take your ticket."

"Just hang on," she said as the home screen appeared once more.

"INSERT SIM."

"Bloody heap of shit!"

She looked around for a pay phone and caught a nearby woman turning her child away and shooting Tuni a dirty look.

"Don't know if it was your intent, ma'am," Tuni said with saccharine tone and a smile to match, "but that face makes you look like a bat."

"Ms. St. James," Abel said sternly, "please hand in your ticket and come."

Tuni huffed, dropped her phone into her purse, and gave her ticket to the waiting hand.

As they strode down the Jetway, she said, "It's still fritzing. Can I use your phone to call Matt's father back?"

"No service here, sorry," Abel said in a tone of earnest regret. "Our phones are not international, and the trip was so sudden, I didn't have time to check out one that works everywhere. We'll be able to call everyone you need to when we stop in Panama. Now, we're going to need a list of Matthew's bank accounts and credit cards, plus any of yours that he might have cards for. We'll put a flag on the accounts, and if anything is accessed, we can trace it. You have this information?"

"Some, yes, but I doubt I know of all of them."

They found their seats, and Abel gave her a small pad and pen to write down the information.

"Also, does he have any devices with him we can trace besides his phone? Portable gaming device, tablet, laptop?"

"Yeah," she said, fishing a pen out of her handbag. "I'll resurrect what I can.

THIRTEEN

A tli rolled his filthy thumb across the jutting surface again. Was that a jeweler's cut? A gift from the wise god Njoror, he thought, his eyes widening at the multicolored stone. He wedged his hand in and wrested the sword from the heap of still-warm Saracen warriors. It looked like an opal, a stone that some women wore in their hair, though he had never before seen one cut with facets. The gem had been set in the pommel, enhancing an already beautiful sword. He turned the grip around and observed the many other gemstones embedded within. A quick glance at the blade itself, and his smile widened. A Damascus sword! The wearer was a wealthy man, for certain. It would be a shame to leave such a masterpiece in a pile of corpses.

His scabbard didn't accommodate the blade's curve, so he sunk his hand deep into the sludge and found the belt. His fingers traced it to its clasp and unhooked it. He inhaled sharply and smiled, for the scabbard, too, bore a wealth of gems large and small.

I could buy a farm with this alone!

The sound of the battle raging at the northern wall returned to his ears. Had it been silent until now, or had his ears been shut for a few moments? Suddenly, he could hear the distant clamor of a thousand pieces of metal striking a thousand more. There were shrieks and trampling and foreign commands shouted from above, the frenzied cries of a thousand insects from the treeline behind, and the sound of his own breath and the scritch of his armor against that of the dead beneath him.

He peered up the towering wall and then left and right. He could hear some of his men chuckling among themselves a few yards away.

87

"*Tcht!*" Atli commanded, and the men fell silent. The Saracen warriors inside this fortress knew not of their presence and had shifted all defenses to another wall—a foolish maneuver, and the one he and his men had been waiting for.

"*Tchk, tchk!*" Atli sounded off his command to raise their arms and be counted. To his left he found thirteen hands, to his right twenty-five. Either he had twenty-one dead or they were fighting with the main army—likely half and half. From his position, he searched for several specific faces and found them all—his lieutenants and friends. They, too, lay among the piles of dead soldiers, awaiting his order to advance.

He pulled back his long brown hair, wringing out some of the accumulated sweat and blood, and then tucked it back into the shirt under his armor. He buckled the new scabbard at his waist, sheathed the Saracen blade, and replaced his helm. He heard his men quietly follow suit as they prepared. Atli signaled to them and hissed, "*Shwt!*" And they began their quiet ascent up the wall.

★ ★ ★

"On the horse, Atli," Endrid warned his friend and captain.

Atli turned only his eyes down the path and spotted the commander, Grim, approaching atop a muscular roan horse. Grim was the worst sort of leader: arrogant, greedy, heartless. He had connived at his role with the Norwegian royals, betraying whomever he must so that he could gain power.

They continued walking the path toward shore as if they hadn't noticed the commander's presence. The four of them had just taken turns dunking themselves in the imam's freshwater bath basin, washing away two weeks of desert grime and the dried blood of three battles. Knowing Grim, this was proof they hadn't fought at all, let alone won this fortress for him.

Atli stopped in front of the horse. Grim was knitting his bushy eyebrows toward the still-smoking fort, feigning ignorance of their arrival.

"A report, Grim?" Atli offered.

"What? Who are you?" Grim replied with odd feigned dismay.

Atli sighed and raised his brow as if to say, "Truly?"

"Oh . . . what? Is that Atli? Where have you been?"

Endrid and the other two warriors averted their eyes from the debasement that was surely coming. But Atli sought to defuse this ass before he could begin kicking and braying.

"If the general is wondering why my men and I are not coated in our enemies' blood, it's because—"

"I'm not interested in excuses, Atli. And don't presume to know what I'm going to say, until it's said."

The two men were silent for a moment as Grim appeared to ponder Atli's thoughts and Atli fought to control his breathing and expression.

"Tell me, Atli," Grim finally said, "Are there any young women about, or did they all escape with that initial swarm of flee-ers?"

Atli knew where this would go. He had been hiding the women from the keep in an underground storage room so they might escape after the army moved on to the next fortress. He wondered whether the general was honestly inquiring or whether someone had reported back to him about the women.

"I'm not certain, but have a look at this." Stepping beside the commander's horse, he pulled the Damascus blade and scabbard from his waist and held it out flat on his two palms for Grim to see.

The transparent diversion had clearly worked. Grim's eyes were fairly popping from his hairy face. Atli slid the sword partially from its sheath, and Grim turned his attention to the blade itself.

"What is that pattern?" he asked, referring to the light and dark swirls in the steel.

"It's called Damascus. Some sort of special forging skill by the Saracen blacksmiths. If you like it, I shall try to find one for you."

You already have, Atli thought.

"You already have," Grim said with a haughty smile, and snatched it from Atli's hands.

Grim watched with thorough pleasure as Atli's face warped into an expression of shock and anger, clearly struggling to restrain himself.

"I'll tell you what," Grim continued. "I'll need twenty men to stay behind here as a garrison. For such a fine gift, Atli, I shall let you lead them." He chuckled as he tugged his horse's reins left and kicked it to return down the hill.

Keep that one far from you, Grim thought.

THE OPAL

*** ✦ ✦ ✦ ***

Matt handed his ticket to the Colombian gate attendant and noticed her double take on seeing him. He must have looked as haggard as he felt. The plane was smaller than those on the transpacific flights—long and skinny with a single row of seats down each side of the aisle. Well, that was *something*—he'd get to sit alone this time.

After going through his usual drill of covering up, he took his seat, with Rheese behind him, Fando in front, and Garza across the aisle. He had already given his account of the sword and the battle, to which Rheese had replied with a shrug, "Did you somehow find this information relevant to the task at hand?"

Matt prepped the timer, and Rheese handed him the opal in its velvet pouch.

✦ ✦ ✦

Nine-year-old Haeming Grimsson ducked his head against the fierce wind and stinging sleet. With his free hand, he tugged his hood down as he plodded through the snow toward the house. Reaching the covered doorway, he glanced over at the goat shelter. If any died overnight, Pa would be furious. Haeming was supposed to have completed a second wall on the new shelter before another storm hit. Clearly too late now, he watched them huddle against the far end of their solitary wall. The rain and sleet were coming in from the northwest, so the goats on the outside of the group were unprotected. He could hear their bleating over the wind and the dull patter of the sleet hitting the turf roof. Pa had built the old shelter by himself, and it hadn't stood through last winter. Either intentionally or purely out of sloth or imprudence, Pa hadn't built a new one in the spring but simply told Haeming to do it by himself—after the first snow had already come. Haeming didn't know how he should go about such a daunting feat, but he knew better than to ask. Some offenses were forgivable, but questions had never been.

He pulled the rope to unlatch the door, and the wind flung it open. Rain and flecks of ice flew in as he hurried inside to the sound of his father's curses. As Haeming pitted his frail strength against the door, Grim shouted at him to hurry. The boy finally managed, and slid in the plank to hold it shut. The room hushed but for the crackle of the struggling fire and the howl of the gusts outside.

"Where is the ax?" Grim asked him in that familiar ominous tone.

Haeming hesitated for a second, but then his face brightened—a technique that sometimes defused or distracted his father's brewing rage.

"I . . . I couldn't find it, Pa, but look!" Haeming opened his coat and pulled the sword from where he had it clenched under his armpit. "It was on top of the shelf over the picks and shovels!"

Grim gazed at it from the table. He was thinking—scary thoughts, perhaps, but maybe nothing at all. Either way, Haeming wished the sword were an ax.

"We could cut the wood with this, yes?" Haeming persisted with his best smile, but immediately rued his ill-chosen wording. *We could cut the wood with this,* he should have said. Grim didn't allow questions. They were a sort of burden, invariably intended to stump him, to expose him for a fool.

The clay cup flew across the room, shattering against Haeming's head and sending him reeling to the floor. The sound stayed in his ears, and he wondered whether his skull, too, had been smashed.

"I'll teach you to keep your greedy hands off a man's property!" Grim shouted. He rose from the bench and lumbered over to the cowering boy. He raised a thick hand and then stopped, seeing Haeming's eye peeping up at him from between his arms.

"What, you've nothing to beg this time?" he growled.

Haeming's mind raced. His father was accustomed to hearing him plead for his punishments to exclude certain things. He might beg, "Please, not the face," or "No more burns, Pa." But Haeming had observed that Grim's preference tended toward whatever he was imploring against, so better to be silent and let the elder's whim take him where it would.

The last thing Haeming wanted his father to know right now was that any beating was preferable to what he most feared: the sentence of sleeping outside again. That cruel punishment had become a frequent favorite of Grim's since the last wave of biting cold swept over the Reykjavik hillside. Haeming had recently begun to wonder if his father truly wanted him dead. It didn't appear to be on his mind at present, but Haeming could see the thoughts churning away as the fist hovered above him. Should he say something? A quick "Please, Pa, not in the head," to guide him toward a more bearable punishment?

The threatening arm dropped to his side, and Grim turned to go back to the table. Was that it, then?

"Outside," he said quietly, his back still turned.

Haeming could see in his mind the satisfied smile that came with speaking the word, but all he could feel was desperation and dread. He could hold his tongue no more.

"No, please, Pa, no! Please no, not tonight! Tomorrow night, I will . . . for two nights! Please, Pa, it's too bad outside!" The tears poured from his eyes as he ran to his father and pulled at his clothes. "No, please no, please no, please no . . ."

✶ ✶ ✶

Haeming nudged his way into the tight knot of protesting goats and wedged himself between the shelter wall and their warm bodies. He had first run to the toolhouse to retrieve some coarse flax-thread sacks after Grim had refused him so much as a blanket. Though Grim told him to put the sword back where he found it, he had kept it with him. There were thieves all across Iceland, and if they should find him among the goats they had come to steal, well . . . He had heard of boys being taken for slaves on ships or in faraway lands.

As he curled up with the sacks amid the goats, clutching the sheathed sword to his chest, Haeming held out hope for a reprieve from his father. Maybe an exasperated "Get in here boy!" shouted from the door, or nodding off for a moment, only to wake in Pa's burly arms as he was carried inside. He knew better than to expect any such reprieve tonight, though, as he gripped the rope collar of the nearest goat. Snorts and groans. Noses warmed by slithering tongues.

The sole buck in the herd was Big Dad. He had one normal horn, the other misshapen and curving in on itself. He disliked Haeming and had more than once butted the boy off his feet or bitten him. Whenever Pa left the boy to the elements, Haeming would huddle in with the goats to keep warm. But if Big Dad noticed the intruder's presence, rather than bite the boy, he would instead nip at the other goats and push them away, leaving Haeming alone and cold. The buck would then stare at him from the new huddle, as if to flaunt his power and warmth.

Haeming reached a hand out into the driving sleet and felt around for another collar. If Big Dad awoke or noticed his presence, he would at least have two goats with him.

But where was Big Dad? He popped his head out from under the sack covering his upper body, and as his head rose above the wiry coat of the doe beside him, he saw the gnarled horn poking up like a broken, wind-scoured branch, just beyond the doe. Big Dad's head emerged only a second later, and a single eye locked its gaze on Haeming. The boy despised those speckled yellow eyes with the demonic black stripe across the middle. When Big Dad harassed him, Haeming sometimes fantasized about carving them out with a spoon.

The adversaries stared at each other for a moment—the goat's nostrils encrusted with frozen snot, its expression of understated irritation the same as always. A series of strong gusts buffeted the shelter, and both tucked their heads back down. The goat didn't appear interested in moving the herd away from the trespasser anytime soon.

Haeming released the collars of the nearby goats and pressed his hands to his frigid ears.

✶ ✶ ✶

Matt knew what Rheese would say. Though he was slowly discovering the sword's chain of possession, he still had nothing solid to offer concerning a treasure hunt in Cuba. With envy, he noted that Garza was asleep beside him. *He gets to sleep . . .*

He decided to do one more half-hour session before trying to get some rest.

✶ ✶ ✶

THE OPAL

The smell of smoke and cooking meat reached them well before they summited the ridge. It was surely past midnight—an unusual time to be cooking in a remote Sicilian village. But the nineteen-year-old commander, Haeming, well knew that abnormal mealtimes were almost routine for a traveling force. He sent back an order for quiet and a slower pace, and the units complied in succession down the line. When the crest was within sight, but before the cover of small, leafy trees thinned, Haeming signaled a full stop as he and his second, Ragnarr, shed their loads and hiked the rest of the way up.

Down in the broad river valley, another village lay before them. Haeming's eyes were fixed, not on the many buildings but on the people, featureless silhouettes lit by staked torches and a large bonfire. Some walked about the clearing while others sat on rocks or wooden chairs. He couldn't tell whether the bodies lying about were dead or merely sleeping. Some men were shouting, others laughing. Another sound—a woman's screams—carried above the rest. Between her throaty screams, they could hear some of the words of the shouting men, and they were Norse.

"Just bring it to me, you lazy ass!" floated up from near the fire. It could have come from any of seven or eight men.

"Someone needs to shut that bitch's mouth," a different voice said.

The large bonfire, encircled by a low wall of mortared stone in the middle of the clearing, lay beneath a makeshift rack supported by two latticework stands. Atop the rack, Haeming spotted the source of the enticing meat smell. He leaned and whispered in Ragnarr's ear.

"Look . . . There."

It took Ragnarr a moment to see what it was, but he eventually caught on. A man in a chair near the fire pit sat tearing meat from a large bone. The bone was a human arm. Above the fire, two or more bodies lay on the wide rack, and the scent of their roasting flesh was wafting right up the hill. The reality of it must have hit Ragnarr, for he gagged and choked, so that Haeming was obliged to clap his hand over the young lieutenant's mouth as they ducked behind the ridge.

The wind turned for a moment, and they each inhaled a lungful of fresh air, which seemed to help Ragnarr recover. Haeming waited patiently for him to wipe away the tears and take in another deep breath. Ragnarr swallowed and looked up at him. His eyes wandered over Haeming's face, his mouth, his nose . . .

He was doing it again. Neither had ever spoken a word of it, but Haeming had known for years that Ragnarr's obvious admiration for him went beyond

94

simple respect and veneration. Haeming frowned and turned away to look down into the canyon again. Ragnarr was an outstanding thinker, a strong warrior, but he needed to find a wife to set him right.

Ragnarr slid back up, a bit further from Haeming this time, and peered down as well.

"I count eleven outside," Haeming whispered. "Two on the ground I haven't seen move, though they appear just to be sleeping. It's your guess how many are inside the structures."

"No more than two per," Ragnarr replied. "Depends how many are sharing the screamer, though."

"As many as forty—more likely twenty-five to thirty."

Someone below shouted "Atli!" followed by slurred words that Haeming couldn't catch. He caught Ragnarr's glance. They were surely thinking the same thing: Atli? The general whose army they had come to reinforce against the Arab conquerors? *This* was the "most formidable fighting force" King Harald had ever seen?

A dark figure on a stump near one of the huts sat up and replied to the call.

Haeming gazed out over the village, deep in thought, weighing options and calculating outcomes.

"What would have brought them to this?" Ragnarr said. "Inhuman . . . Monsters . . ."

"My guess is large losses and starvation. The village didn't have enough food, and plenty of wine."

Haeming slid down from the moonlit ridge, and Ragnarr followed.

"Our strongest archers at distance," Haeming said when they were halfway back down to the woods.

It was a question. Haeming's habit confused others, but Ragnarr knew his way. The commander never asked questions in the usual manner—that had been beaten out of him long ago.

"Bondi, Hedinn Ingisson, Brandulf, and the woman, Vigdis. How many do you need?"

"I thought Vigdis a doctor like the others. She is many-skilled."

"She is, yes."

"And a thing of beauty, as well, if I recall."

Ragnarr ignored this last statement. They arrived back at the woods, where the faces of the soldiers in the front lines were alight with anticipation. Haeming gulped down some water from his bag, grabbed an extra dagger from his pack, and tightened up his straps. His fighters had no idea what he had planned, but that would have to do for now.

"Fetch those you mentioned and four more of the best at distance. Split them up: four up here and four on the far side. The latter group must make haste and no sound."

Ragnarr walked down the line to post the archers. When he was out of sight, Haeming gave a nod to the gawking men at the front and strode off down the path that led to the village.

Coming into view of the huts, he slowed his pace. No one had yet noticed him, but this would quickly change. The one eating in the chair actually glanced directly at him, then went back to his meat, likely thinking Haeming was one of his own, back after a piss. Haeming now stood less than forty feet from the nearest warrior, a man breaking branches for the fire. Haeming checked his periphery, careful not to pass beyond the first two huts, though he still needed them to see him before he proceeded. No one should be able to get around behind him without his seeing them first. He stood there for what seemed a long time before the seated man looked at him again.

"Who's that?" he said around a mouthful of meat.

"Who's what?" someone else answered.

"Is that Arni?" the eater called out.

"I'm right here, Randvér," the man snapping branches said. "Seems you aren't yet drunk enough."

This man Arni sounded sober and clearheaded.

"Then who's *that*?" The one called Randvér tried to block the firelight with the ragged cooked arm, holding it by the exposed bone as if it were a giant goose leg.

Heads turned, laughing and talking ceased, and a large figure stood up from the stump beyond the bonfire. The pop and crack of the fire seemed to grow louder, as did the sizzle of the ghastly cadavers roasting above it. The far house, the one with the screaming woman, was the last to go silent. Haeming hoped that on the ridge above him, bows were now being bent by well-practiced archers, their breath falling into the slow rhythm of that perfect pre-shot calm that he himself had never mastered.

The figure from the stump staggered as he walked past the fire to get a better look at the silent intruder. He stopped several paces from Haeming and rubbed his eyes before tilting his head to the side. He looked old, finished with life. His long brown beard hung to his navel, and his face was decorated with two decades of battle scars.

"Who are you?" he finally asked.

"I am Haeming. You are Atli."

Several heads shared questioning glances. Atli seemed to ponder for a moment. "How many are with you?" he asked with no sign of concern.

Haeming said quietly, "I wish to speak with you alone for a moment, if you would."

"That means not many."

"Atli . . ." one of his men began.

"Arni," Atli interrupted. "Handle this little boy and then gather the men to hunt down the rest of his group. They surely have food."

Haeming stood quietly with his right hand still resting on his sword hilt.

No arrows had yet flown—perfect. They knew that either Haeming would signal them or the need to fire would become clear. As long as they were in position. Surely they were already in position . . .

"Atli," Haeming said again. "As I said, I only wish to speak with you alone for a moment. There's no need for a fight."

The only way this could work was if Haeming allowed Atli to save face. Their conversation couldn't happen in front of his men.

Atli shot a look behind him and barked, "Arni, I said to handle him. Go!"

Arni hesitated for another second and then picked up a sword from the dirt beside the fire. Hefting it with confidence, he walked toward Haeming, not slowly but certainly not with brash imprudence.

Haeming said to the man walking toward him, "You are following orders, so I apologize." With a whisper, the Saracen blade left its sheath, and with a continuing whisper, it opened the man's throat.

Atli yelled "Arni!" as the second strike stabbed down through Arni's shoulder and deep into his chest.

Arni went from one knee to facedown on the ground just as the man eating by the fire staggered to his feet. Someone else yelled "Arni!" and a clamor ensued as men ran about in search of weapons or, perhaps, simply in panic.

"Calm them, Atli!" Haeming yelled. "We can still talk!" Though the man didn't seem to be hearing his words at all at this point. The giant Norwegian didn't even bother finding a weapon. He stomped toward Haeming as Randvér, the arm-eater, followed clumsily, wielding a large battle-ax. Haeming raised a forestalling hand to the ridge just as one of the archers released the first shot. It struck Randvér in the chest, and he grunted, looking down at the protruding arrow without comprehension. He shuffled to a stop, but by then at least twenty Norwegians were charging toward Haeming and the body on the ground beside him.

With Atli nearly on him, Haeming held his sword before him in a passive guard stance. He still hoped that they might talk like civilized men, but perhaps not.

Atli suddenly stopped with a jolt and bounced back, as if striking an unseen wall, and for a moment Haeming had to wonder whether God, or maybe the old gods in whom he had ceased to believe, were intervening. The towering Norseman's head craned down and twisted, reminding Haeming of a snake examining a nest of bird eggs.

Atli threw a hand behind him to stop the charging throng of Norwegians. They flung their arms out to their sides to stop themselves and each other, and their shouts died down to silence.

Atli's voice, suddenly sober, seemed to come from somewhere deeper within him than before: "Are you . . . are you the son of Grim?"

"Yes, I am the son of Grim, for whom you fought many years ago." Haeming hoped this declaration might pacify the older man—until it was half-said. Atli's chest heaved as he looked down at the body of Arni, then up to the sword in Haeming's grip, and finally at Haeming's face. He released a sudden, explosive growl, and his whole body seemed to expand like a great bird puffing up. Haeming flicked open his palm to signal the watching eyes on the ridge.

Arrows whizzed as Atli charged at him. Haeming dodged the clumsy attack and sprinted toward the foot of the hill, out of the way of the archers. Atli rose from the dirt, turned his head toward Haeming. Atli was a large man, and Haeming wasn't interested in feeling one of his charges actually connect. Instead, he lowered his body, swung his sword around behind him, and dashed at the larger man's midsection. As Haeming and Atli struck the dirt, the Damascus sword fell to the ground beside them.

✳ ✳ ✳

"I'll not touch it again," Atli said and again glanced around the corner of the building, toward Norway's grandest church.

Solva looked at her husband. He was small and weak, frightened of everything. She took a deep breath, shoved the Saracen sword and scabbard against his chest, and said with teeth bared, "You will carry it to the foot of those steps, get down on a knee before him, and put it in his hands. When you stand again, you will stand tall and proud like a man. It is not for him, my love, it is for you."

He clutched the sword before it fell and looked back at her with despair.

"You don't understand. It's an insult. He gave it to me . . . as recompense for Arni . . . and for peace."

"It has never been that, only a reminder. It is the worst sort of punishment. And if he is the good man you always claim, then you will not keep for one more day the weapon used to slay your brother. Go now or I leave. Neither the boys or I will live our lives with half a man for husband, half a man for father." She spun and trot down the alley.

Atli watched her go and grumbled. Haeming and King Harald were both seen entering the church. Atli knew the risk. Haeming or one of his men could see him coming and think it an attack. He looked down at the sword and scabbard, Arni's wise young face flashed through his mind. Atli took the hanging belt and wrapped it tightly around the scabbard and over the guard, around the grip, tying the end tightly. It was now clearly inaccessible as a weapon, and he had nothing else on his person. He closed his eyes for a moment, then rounded the corner toward Nidaros's church.

After only a few minutes, Haeming and King Harald walked down the tall, wide staircase, Haeming's eyes spotting Atli at once. Unafraid, he walked directly to Atli, down to the same level stair as he. King Harald hung back with his men, a keen eye on Atli.

"Well met, Atli," Haeming said. His tone and posture were gracious, friendly even. It was disarming. Only 21 years old and he looked like a wise old sage with his short-trimmed black beard, knowing eyes, and humble clothing.

Atli dropped to a knee, bowed his head, and held out the Saracen sword on both palms. "Haeming, with all honor, respect, and appreciation . . . I wish for you to have and keep this."

Haeming was silent. Atli looked up to his face. It appeared concerned, unsure.

"You know that I returned it to you in the same vein . . ." Haeming said.

"I do," Atli said, his arms still outstretched. After a beat, he felt the weight of the sword lift from his palms.

"I think I understand," Haeming said. "But I want you to know that it is yours at any time you wish. You need only ask. I will have not a single thought."

Atli nodded, rose to his feet, gave the king a respectful bow, and turned to walk away.

"Atli," Haeming called. Atli halted and looked back. "I have a proposal for you and your family."

★ ★ ★

The Reykjavik Emporium was Iceland's biggest social gathering place. Haeming and Atli leaned against the rails of the horse corral and watched fishermen and traders from all over the country come and go. With no moon, and an invisible shroud of cloud cover, the darkness was near-absolute. The Emporium had a lit torch on each side of its great barn doors, but even the light from these seemed unable to reach more than a few feet.

"Look at that lot," Atli snorted. "Plenty of mead money on them tonight, I'd say. Where are Olaf and Finn with our so-called navigator?"

"Olaf's fond of mead, as well," Haeming replied in jest. "Perhaps he was thirsty."

"I don't think your friend Finn would allow that."

Haeming nodded in agreement.

"You know him from around here?" Atli asked.

"No. We met a few years ago . . . in Sicily." Haeming caught himself too late. He tried to avoid mention of Sicily around Atli. "He taught me everything I know about Christianity. He owns a real Bible—practically a priest. You should talk to him sometime, away from your men. Be warned, though: his words will outlast your ears."

Hearing slow footsteps in the corral behind them, Haeming elbowed Atli. Thieving was rampant this winter, and a corral full of unattended horses was an obvious target. Haeming kept his hand on the pommel of his sword, but Atli seemed uncharacteristically opposed to a fight. He turned around suddenly and called out to the nothingness, "I'm not in a face-smashing mood tonight, but that doesn't mean the hankering won't strike at any moment."

The footsteps paused, then reversed at the same slow pace with which they had approached. Atli and Haeming chuckled.

Haeming felt Atli's eyes on him and peered right to catch him gazing at the tiny glint from the Damascus sword's pommel. While Atli had always insisted he bore no more ill will toward him about the Saracen blade, Haeming knew it could not be so simple.

Haeming looked back at the lit doorway and said, "I told you, it's yours to take back whenever you wish it."

"No, no, I wasn't . . . it wasn't that. It's yours forever. I could never . . . forget it."

Haeming knew that Atli would never be free of the blade's history, but he wouldn't ever speak of it. Atli cocked his chin toward the raucous scene within the building. Olaf appeared in the doorway, his beefy hand around the neck of a slightly built man, well into his forties and with a pronounced hunch. Finn emerged a second later, leaning on his walking stick. Olaf nodded at the dark figures of Atli and Haeming, barely illuminated by the torches. Olaf escorted the little man, and Finn followed behind, tucking his gray beard against his throat for warmth.

"Got 'im," Olaf said as he approached. "Tried to gut me with this."

He held up something, and Haeming leaned close to see what it was: a wooden spoon with a broken handle.

Finn rested on his walking stick and chuckled. "Look at the point—not sharp enough to split an ant."

Haeming smiled, then addressed the scowling man before him. "I'm Haeming Grimsson. You're Skamkell, of Borg."

The man's suspicious eyes examined Haeming and Atli for a beat. He sighed and dejectedly answered, "Aye, Skamkell. Aye, from Borg."

"You've been to Vinland," Haeming said.

Skamkell's expression changed to one of surprise and relief. He surely had thought they had come to kill him, but Haeming needed the old man to join their crew and guide them across the Atlantic, to Vinland.

FOURTEEN

essup Canter—Jess to everyone but his mother—got the call from Roger while wrapping up some business at the Essex County Morgue in Newark. With surprisingly little traffic on the interstate, he made it to the Turner house in Secaucus in less than twenty minutes. While his old partner, Roger Turner, had retired as detective sergeant, Jess had stayed on the force and was now detective lieutenant, running his own special task force in the Major Crimes Division.

He let himself in the door and called out, "Guys?" The house smelled of coffee and dryer sheets.

Beth leaped up from the couch in the den and called, "In here, Jess!"

He stepped down into the sunken room and hugged her tight. "I'm so sorry," he said quietly in her ear. "We're gonna find him. Don't you worry about nothin', you hear me?"

She cried into his chest. Roger hadn't looked up from his old laptop, whose blue glow emphasized his weathered face.

"He always said it was going to happen, J," Beth said. "He knew it. He always said, someone's gonna find out and they're gonna take him and make him track something down."

"I been saying it for goddamn years," Roger grumbled. "Kid doesn't listen to a goddamn thing I say, though."

Jess squeezed Beth's shoulders and looked in her eyes, his silvered brows furrowed. "We're gonna find him," he said. "You trust me?" She nodded. "Good. Now, lemme sit down with Rog for a bit and talk over some things, yeah?"

She nodded again. "I'll go make some more coffee. You want?"

He gave her a nod and smiled, and when she left the room, he took her place next to Roger on the couch. He felt odd having Beth leave for the "man talk." His own wife would have given him a pop in the mouth for such "caveman-days chauvinism," but it had always been this way with Beth and Rog.

"What do you got so far?"

"Starting point is Bora Bora—part of Tahiti. They took his plane with his pilot."

"Matty's got a plane? *Jesus.*"

"Exactly," Roger said. "You see what I'm saying now. He ain't being smart about it at all. Two days ago, they flew to an airport in Australia. City's called . . ." He peered through his bifocals at the notepad beside him. ". . . Brisbane. It's still there. Pilot says local PD's holding him, looked for drugs, lots of questions. Anyway, guy hasn't a clue where they were going from there. If you look at this map, they could either still be there or be headed south to Sydney, north to any number of places, or God knows where else."

"You know if he has his phone with him?"

"I tried it a bunch of times. Straight to voicemail."

"Well, we can see where it last checked in. I'll call Ben at DOJ, too. See if he gets any hits on air travel or border crossings. This British guy—you know anything about him?"

Roger gave him the rundown on Garrett Rheese. Jess didn't take any notes—he never needed to. Sometimes Roger got a kick out of it; other times it annoyed him. At the moment, he seemed to appreciate the skill. He didn't have to repeat anything and could talk as fast as he needed to.

Jess stood up. "Got it. I'll go make a few calls. Hey, real quick: Matty happen to have a tablet computer? There's usually a separate tracking program on those."

Roger looked up from the screen. "Not sure. Iris would probably know . . . shit."

"What?"

"Haven't told her yet."

He picked up the cordless phone and called his daughter. She was someplace loud. She reacted as expected, and announced that she would be on the first available flight to Newark.

"Honey, do you know if Matt has one of those iPads . . . or whatever?"

She said he had a couple of them, and gave Roger a few potential passwords to try. They hung up, and he tore the page out of his notepad and handed it to Jess. Jess left the room to make his calls, and returned ten minutes later, smiling.

"One of his iPads is in his house in Raleigh. The other one connected briefly to a Wi-Fi access point at the Chateau Habana in Cuba. Two hours ago."

Roger tossed his laptop aside and launched up off the couch at the same time that Beth appeared in the kitchen doorway.

"Cuba?" Roger said to himself, trying to think. "Why the hell would you go to Australia to get to Cuba?"

"Matty?" Beth said. "He's in Cuba?"

"I've got folks contacting the Swiss embassy and the U.S. Interests Section there. We don't have our own embassy, but there are systems in place to help us out."

"What's that mean?" Roger demanded. "Help us out? As in, their law enforcement will get out an APB and search parties? Or they'll call us if my son pops up somewhere?"

"I don't know yet, Rog. Take it easy—I'm doing everything I can with a cell phone, okay?"

"Can those U.S. Interests people get Americans into the country?"

"Oh, that's not a problem at all," Jess said. "Our governments don't have formal relations, but things have apparently loosened up quite a bit in recent years as far as business and tourism travel goes. Ben says there are even direct flights to Havana from JFK now. What are you thinking? You at least wanna wait for a response from down there, or what?"

"I'm not waiting for nothing. He's there, and no one else is gonna make more of an effort than me to bring him home. There's just no way."

"I'll help you pack, hon," Beth said as they went into the hall.

"I'll find the soonest flight outta JFK," Jess said. "I'll give you a call."

"Where you going?" Roger asked.

"Home. To pack."

Roger looked ready to argue, then just compressed his lips and nodded.

Jess grinned. "Hey, Matty's my boy, too, right? Let's go bring 'im home."

★ ★ ★

Roger parked the Tahoe in long-term and hauled out his rolling duffel bag. Slung over one shoulder was a backpack with various gear he had accumulated over the years. He didn't know whether the TSA would give him trouble for any of it, or, if they did, which items would be no-go's. He had removed two knives from it before leaving home, as well as three loose .45 rounds that were rolling around in the bottom. Still in the duffel were a set of tactical night-vision goggles, a half bag of zip ties, a first-aid kit, two Meals Ready to Eat with iffy expiration dates, clothes, and a few other odds and ends that had been either left in the backpack for years or stuffed in because they might prove useful. Slung over his other shoulder was his laptop case with notepad, pens, chargers, and other essentials.

Traffic stopped at the light, and he hustled over the crosswalk to Departures. His cell phone rang in his pocket, and he cursed under his breath as he put down his gear. The screen read "JC Mobile."

"You here yet?" Roger said.

"Look to your right."

He looked left for some reason, felt dumb, then looked right. Jess was waving at him from the sidewalk, four entrances down. He had three other people with him. Roger hung up and wrestled his bags back onto his shoulders before hiking over to join them.

"We have forty-five minutes," Jess said. "Let me introduce you to your team."

Roger was dumbstruck. "You got these . . . you all are, uh . . ."

"We're going to help you bring him home, sir," replied a young woman with big eyes and a military tone and demeanor. She wore a black down vest over an orange-patterned flannel. Her shiny black hair hung at shoulder length. "I'm Núñez, sir."

"Sorry, Rog," Jess said. "Let's do intros. Everyone, you know this is my old partner, Sergeant Roger Turner, retired."

"Just 'Roger,' please," he said, holding his hands up as if in surrender.

"And, Rog, this is everyone. The unfortunately named Chuck Kohl—'Chuckles' to those with no respect." Jess winked as the tall, stout, mustachioed thirty-something to his right rolled his eyes and reached out to shake hands. "He's on my task force. Real hard-ass—sorry, I mean *bad*-ass. Seriously, though, I brought him over from SWAT—he's good."

"Good to meet you, sir," Kohl said, shaking hands.

"And this is Paul, with DOJ. You may not remember this, but you met him when he was about this high and still pissing himself."

Paul said in a deep voice, without a hint of a smile, "I still piss myself."

"Ben Kleindorf's boy?" Roger said, shaking the 24-year-old's hand.

"Ben couldn't come himself," Jess explained, "so he arranged for the next best thing. He got Paul off a shit detail in Brooklyn, so everyone wins. Lastly, I got . . . Miss? What is it, Núñez? You gotta rank? First name?"

"Just Núñez, sir."

Jess shrugged. "Ben said he'd get us a field-trained fluent Spanish-speaker to translate as needed." He leaned close and cocked his head toward Núñez. "Not sure what her story is. Just met a few minutes before you showed up."

"Well, I just want to thank all of you," Roger said. "It's really . . . well, just unbelievable what you're all doing for my family. I, uh, thought I was going this alone, but I'm real glad I'm not."

As they all walked into the terminal together, Kohl turned to Paul Kleindorf, who was sporting what appeared to be a few days' worth of facial hair. "You Justice guys don't have to shave, huh?"

Paul continued walking without looking at him. "Not our *faces*, anyway."

FIFTEEN

"**A**gain, it's nonsense," Rheese said as he transferred gear from a duffel bag into a backpack: flashlight, headlamp, bug repellent, huge point-and-shoot digital camera that Matt thought must be the first model ever produced. Rheese continued moving items as he went on. "I'm not saying the opal or Sayf Allah *couldn't,* at some point, have fallen into the hands of the Norse people. That is to say, they spent time in North Africa and the Middle East, fought for the Byzantines, but the timing would be all wrong, and they certainly wouldn't have been in Cuba that far back."

"I've spent hours with this thing, Doctor," Matt said. "I'm telling you exactly what happened, from hand to hand. The imprints may not have presented themselves in chronological order, but each time, I know the date right off the bat. It's a snap to put them in line: from North Africa to Iceland, to Sicily and back to Iceland, the whole story's coming together. There were a few Egypt blips in there, but those obviously don't help here. The one thing I can tell you after spending this much time with it is, no pirates—an imprint would have popped up by now."

Rheese regarded him for a moment, as if trying to sort out whether it was all a lie, and, if so, to what end.

"What do you know about the so-called Vikings?" Rheese asked him.

"Is this a pop quiz?"

"Yes. What do you know?"

"The usual public knowledge stuff. The museum never had me work with any of their artifacts, so I guess just the raping-and-pillaging stuff."

Rheese chuckled and shook his head in condescension.

Matt said, "Beyond that, I thought I learned in junior high that they discovered America before Columbus."

"'Discovered'—ha ha, right. They did indeed discover progressively that there was more land to the east of them. They settled in Iceland; then Erik the Red established a colony on Greenland. His son, Leif Eriksson, then set out to find more land and eventually found Newfoundland in Canada. There are theories that he or others made it farther south, perhaps as far as the state of Rhode Island, but there's not a bit of evidence suggesting further progress."

"This Haeming guy said the land he was looking for was called *Vinland*. Do you know of any place being called that?"

"Yes, that's what Leif Eriksson called the land he found. Supposedly, they came upon wild grapes. It's irrelevant, though. Let's say this Icelandic fellow did find his way across the Atlantic . . ."

"Bringing Sayf Allah with him."

"Sure, fine. It's one thing to set up camp a week or two from Greenland, and another thing entirely to have ventured down the entire east coast of North America—*and* then to decide to hazard another hundred miles to reach an island they didn't know existed. You don't understand: these people didn't risk the open sea. Some other sailor got caught in a storm and spotted Canada. He made it back, and word got around. Only *then* did someone decide to attempt a crossing."

Matt sighed. "And yet an Egyptian opal ends up inside a tree on Cuba . . ."

Rheese harrumphed and stood up as Matt sat down on the curb outside the small café where they had eaten lunch. Rheese began slathering sunblock onto his arms and nose.

"Haeming, you say."

A-ha, not so certain after all. "Yeah, kind of like 'lemming' with an accent."

"You'll need to find out more. Give me something substantive. Garza, where the hell is—"

"Here he comes," Garza said, gnawing on a toothpick.

Fernando "Fando" Solorzano pulled up in the silver van he had just rented.

Rheese said, "Hopefully, whatever you lads cook out in the field will be better than that rubbish was."

Matt watched Garza's expression when he glanced back.

"Everything will be handled, Doctor."

I'll tolerate you only so far, Garza's face told him, but only Matt seemed to notice.

The van's side door slid open from the inside, and out stepped Fando. He and Garza grabbed duffels from the curb and began loading into the back. Matt took the cue and grabbed his own small suitcase while Rheese scrunched his nose to read the ingredients on the sunblock.

He mumbled to himself, "Blasted cream's supposed to *prevent* burning . . . nose is on bloody fire."

"I'll just grab this for you, then, Doctor," Fando said peevishly, picking up Rheese's knockoff Samsonite case to load it. At the back of the van, he grabbed Garza, and Matt pricked up his ears. "Raúl hasn't checked in since yesterday. I've gotten nothin', and he hasn't responded to my texting, neither."

"You get texts from anyone else? Maybe it's your service."

Fando said, "Yeah, I got some from Lorenzo."

"He ready for us? We should get moving."

"Yeah, he said he got permits and everything. Everything else'll be there by the time we are. But what about Raúl? Something had to happen, homes. I can't even think straight right now."

"Just chill," Garza said, patting his shoulder. "I'll get a hold of Tessa—she's still on the island—and have her check in and call me back, *sí*?"

"Yeah, yeah, all right."

Garza climbed into the rearmost seat of the van, behind Matt. Rheese got in the passenger seat up front, and Fando drove off. Matt could hear Garza's thumbs tapping away on the screen of his phone.

Rheese shifted around in his seat. "The problem with your story, lad, is that if the Norse had settled on Cuba, there would be an archeological record. The island has been thoroughly explored for centuries, with not a hint of unexplained artifacts."

"So if I could show you something, then what?" Sleeping on the plane and the large meal had him feeling a bit better, or at least better able to think, interpret, and plan.

Rheese's eyebrows shot up. "Such as?"

"I don't know yet. Gimme back the opal and I'll see if I can find something."

Matt didn't know what he was looking for, but the Norse guys were about to head out for this Vinland place, and he knew that somehow, in the end, they had reached the island of Cuba. The next imprint could be more of Egypt, more quality time with goats in a winter storm, or even the Cuban sawmill worker who found the opal. He maintained hope that figuring it all out would lead to Tuni's freedom—and, perhaps, even his own.

As Rheese dug around in his backpack, Garza spoke up from the back of the van. "How, exactly, does this help us find what we're looking for, Doctor? I mean, why does it matter if the thing got here with Spaniards, or Vikings, or the goddam Sinaloa cartel?"

"The conditions under which the artifact arrived mean everything," Rheese sniffed. "You wouldn't understand. Here, Turner."

Matt took the stone in his gloved hand and placed it in his lap, then rolled up his left sleeve and fished the armband timer out of his pocket. As he slid it on, he could feel the two cold metal contacts slide against the skin of his forearm. He powered it on, and the LCD screen lit up, reading "00:00." He pressed the up arrow until it read "00:10." That would be enough time to delve deeper. When the countdown was up, the device would send an intermittent shock into Matt's arm until he turned it off. It had been his father's idea when Matt was 14—a way to leave a reading session on his own. During the session, he was always unaware of his own body, but the shocks brought back the sensation of his arms. They had practiced with it for months, tuning the amperage and rhythm, until it became a reflex action to open his hands and pull them to his body when the pulses began.

Matt slid off his left glove, pressed START on his timer, and rested his flat hand on the gem.

Immediately, he felt the familiar rushing sound, light-headedness, blurry vision, the shock of changing body positions and motion. In this case, seated in a moving car, then instantly standing, running. Different climate, clothes, anatomy—breasts, in this case—smells, sounds, time of day. Consciousness always followed physical sensation. Someone else's voice in his head. He had grown accustomed to the transition, and after first "experiencing" an artifact, each repeat session grew easier as he familiarized himself with its personality or, rather, the personalities of those presented within.

The opal's first imprint belonged to Tadinanefer. Her emotional stamp being the most powerful, it would always be that way. But Matt had learned to fast-forward through events he had already seen. To him, it looked like skipping through scenes on a DVD in ten-second, one-minute, sometimes ten-minute intervals. He just said things like "Seen it" or "Yes, yes" as the story progressed, until he came to dark space or some new place he had yet to see. The fast-forward had also been his dad's idea, after Matt discovered that he could rewind and repeat moments.

"If you can rewind, you can fast-forward, and we don't have time for you to sit through this whole thing again."

"I can't, Dad . . ."

"That's what you always say."

As Matt fast-forwarded through Tadinanefer's imprint, he felt the same old mix of appreciation and resentment he had always had for his father. He reached her dark space, then continued past the rest of the parts he had already seen.

I am male. My name is Haeming Grimsson. I'm at the stern of the ship, cleaning the salt from my sword while speaking with Finn. The Epistle of Paul to the Galatians again—one of my mentor's favorites. I wish to discuss Jesus himself, and for Finn to finally acknowledge the remarkable timing of my birth. I've hinted at it before—this fact that my birth and the death of Jesus imply an undeniable significance. But every time, he politely accepts it, concedes that it may actually mean something, and moves on. I cannot simply say it myself. Someone else must.

Someone calls from behind me, from the mast: "Look! The cliff!"

Everyone stands. I see it . . . close my eyes. It can't be real. Open again. No! Finn touches my arm—an attempt to console or an involuntary reflex from the shock of the sight.

A knarr, much like the one we are now sailing, sits high atop a cliff before a backdrop of the strange, green, southern trees. It has no sail, but the mast stands high. As we draw closer to shore, we see the words carved into the cliff below it. My stomach twists into sour knots. The runic letters read "Kingdom of Southland."

Now, that's something to find!

Matt paused with a perfect view of the tropical landscape, mountain features, a cove or inlet or whatever they were called. *A bay?* Above the carved runes, he could see the giant ship, perched like Noah's ark on the high slopes of Ararat. It was maybe a hundred feet above the beach. *How the hell do you get a ship on top of a cliff? Haeming is furious, too. They came all this way . . . almost a full year since Iceland. He thought he'd be a legend like Leif Eriksson himself. But no, like Vinland and everywhere else they stopped along the way, this land belonged to others . . .*

Matt tried to commit the scene to memory. *Two peaks on left side, bigger one in the distance, cut off at the top by clouds.* The cliff was the essential location, though. He imagined that either remnants of the ship or the carvings in the rocky cliff face could have survived this long.

Dark space. How long have I been in this? Gotta be close to ten minutes.

Still wanting to keep his dark space exit opportunities a secret, Matt decided to wait for his timer.

Oh, here we go again . . . Haeming again . . .

This place is called Southland—so named by another. At my feet, my friend and mentor sits, dying. I press the pommel of my sword into a break in this tree's bark. Work it in tight. I hold the sword steady while I carefully pry the stone free with a dagger. I step back. The gem shines at me from its new home, as if the tree had opened a secret eye. Finn leans against the trunk. Slumped, bleeding, he looks up at me weakly. "Outside," he says, but his mouth doesn't move right. "What's she saying, man? What happened? Tell me what happened, goddamn it!" *What the hell is that? Something happening in the van . . . How am I hearing this?*

I run my fingers over the gem a final time and touch Finn's head. He clutches my wrist, but not aggressively. It's as if to say, "It had to happen this way . . . Just calm the hell down and pull over!"

There it is again! That's Garza shouting! Fando before that . . .

Tzzzzz . . . tzzzzz . . . tzzzzz . . .

Finally.

Matt's hands popped up and snapped to his chest as his hearing came back. His stomach turned a little, and he figured it was from the physical transition. But then he felt the van swerve, and his brain began processing his environment and its sounds. Yelling, among other noises.

"Just tell me, I swear to God!" Fando shouted from the front.

Rheese reached over and tried to take the wheel.

"Get your fucking hands away from me, asshole!" He slapped Rheese's hand away and looked in the rearview mirror.

Garza continued talking from behind Matt: "Fando, man, I'm telling you to pull over the goddamn car and talk to me outside. You're going to kill us all—WATCH OUT!"

Everyone snapped their attention forward to see a small car up ahead in the van's lane, stopped at a red light. In front of it, cars were crossing the intersection. Fando slammed on the brakes and swerved. Loose objects inside the van flew. Matt slammed up against the window beside him, and a stinging pain shot through his cheekbone.

"Stop the bloody car, you idiot!" Rheese shouted, but it was too late.

They missed the stopped car, but the van's brakes weren't going to stop them before the intersection. An enormous old Buick crossed in front of them, and everyone yelled. The driver's eyes bugged out, and he slammed his foot down—fortunately, on the gas and not the brake. Fando cut left and missed the Buick's chrome bumper by less than a foot. At the sound of a squawking horn, all eyes shot left. A huge shipping truck barreled toward them, and Fando was still braking. The truck's brakes squealed.

"Go, go, go, go!" Garza and Matt roared in unison.

Fando gunned it, and the van cleared the intersection as the truck howled past behind them. Fando pulled onto the dirt shoulder and stopped. Everyone sat silent but for the sound of their heavy breathing.

"Well, that was bloody brilliant!" Rheese shouted.

"Shut up, Doctor!" Garza yelled. "Fando! Outside, now!"

Garza climbed past Matt and slid open the door while Fando got out on the driver's side. Both men closed their doors and walked around in front of the car. Matt and Rheese watched them, trying to read their lips, but they were speaking Spanish. Fando's face twisted in horror as Garza appeared to speak soothing words and reached out consolingly. Fando swatted his hands away and screamed an expletive that Matt recognized. Then he reached into his waistband and pulled out a semiautomatic pistol. He yelled in Garza's face while pointing the gun at the van. Rheese yelped and took cover behind the dash. Matt ducked a little, too, but he quickly saw that Fando wasn't pointing the pistol, just gesturing angrily with it. His finger wasn't even inside the trigger guard. Garza motioned for him to put the gun away and glanced around worriedly, afraid someone would see.

Fando screamed some more and began to pace. He was shaking his head and shouting, "No . . . no . . . no," over and over. Matt tried to guess what was happening. He had somehow heard them shouting while he was reading the imprint; the voices had worked their way into the reading. This had never happened before that he could recall, but then, things had always been relatively calm and quiet around him while he read.

Garza had been on the phone with someone, and that someone had told him something he didn't want to tell Fando while he was driving. He wanted Fando to pull over before he told him. And he had been clearly right to worry. Fando was rolling around in the gravel and dirt in front of the van.

Someone died.

Matt looked around the van. In all the violent veering and braking, things had been tossed about. He looked behind him at Garza's bench seat. Nothing. Another glance out the windshield. Garza was still consoling Fando.

"Is he coming?" Rheese whimpered.

"Yeah," Matt hissed. "Stay down!"

Ducking down, Matt looked to the floor at his feet, then under the seat. *Yes!* Garza's cell phone lay on the floor beneath him. Matt slid it to the space between his feet and ticked his timer to one minute. *I gotta get a new one that can do seconds,* he thought as he risked one more look outside. Fando was up now, wiping his eyes. Garza was patting him on the back. The gun was still in his hand, but it looked as though the blind fury was gone and only sorrow remained.

Hurry up!

Matt put his hand on the phone's screen.

I am a thirty-one-year-old male. My name is Danny Garza. I was born in Amarillo, Texas. I'm in a van, on the phone with Tessa. She tells me that one of our men, Raúl Solorzano, is dead—shot in a hotel room. Police everywhere. She can't get to the room to see if the woman is there, too, but she's watched a long time and hasn't seen her. I grew up with both Raúl and Fando. I see Raúl as a young teenager when we'd pass a football back and forth across our street. Fando is going to flip. He'll forget he's driving.

Fando yells from the front, "What is it, man? Who is that? Tessa? What's she saying?"

I can't say everything is fine—it isn't.

Everything has gone to shit. I just wanted to pay off my upside-down mortgage and be able to get my wife and daughter the things they want. Never to have to say, "Not this time, baby." I remember telling Fando, "No mortgage, bro—can you imagine that shit?"

"Find out who did this," I say to Tessa.

"Will do," she says. "I'll call you back."

I put the phone down and say, "Pull over, Fando."

Tzzzzz . . . tzzzzz . . . tzzzzz . . .

"Get up, Doctor," Garza said from the open side door. "And keep your mouth shut for the next couple hours."

"I beg your pardon? What happened?" Rheese sputtered. "You *will not* tell me—"

"I *am* telling you, and it's for your own good." He peered out at the roadside weeds, where Fando was walking randomly, shaking his head. "He's calming himself down, but anything could set him off, especially if you start bitching about his driving. Just keep your mouth shut."

"Get up, Turner," Garza said. "No one's going to shoot you—at least not right now."

Matt pulled on his glove and did one more thing, knowing that Garza couldn't see his hands or the phone between his shoes. Then he slid the phone back under his seat and slowly sat up, blinking nervously.

"Did he . . . did he put that gun away?" Matt said.

"Yes. Now, sit back and shut up. He's coming back."

In the front passenger seat, Rheese huffed and puffed and muttered under his breath. Fando walked past the hood. His sunglasses were back on, and he acted as if everything were normal. He opened the door and climbed into the driver's seat. Garza slid the side door shut and made his way to the backseat as Fando shifted into drive.

Rheese didn't keep his mouth shut. Apparently, he couldn't help himself. "If you *ever* point a gun at me again, or so much as—"

Without warning, Fando's fist shot across the cab and caught Rheese in the jaw. It was a powerful blow from a monstrously big and strong arm, and it knocked him into his door. He spat a gout of blood and a couple of teeth onto the floor.

"I said to keep your goddamn mouth shut!" Garza barked. "Don't say one more thing!"

Fando hit the gas, and the van bounced back onto the road. Matt heard the phone beneath him slide backward. Garza's seat springs creaked, and Matt could feel him lean over behind him. He wanted to glance back, to see if Garza was giving him any odd looks. He could feel an accusing stare. He heard thumbs tapping the glass screen, then silence. To look back would look suspicious. He just hoped that the person on the other end of the message he sent would be smart enough not to reply.

SIXTEEN

"I don't have anything definitive," Tessa said. Garza watched the waves crash on shore as Fando drove the highway.

Garza pretended the call was unrelated to Raúl to keep Fando focused on the road. "Yeah, sounds good. What else is going on?"

Tessa rolled with it, "Well, the FBI has had a lot of chatter around a flagged guy they think came to the U.S. We're talking about a major worldwide player, and he apparently did business with Dr. Rheese in the past couple years."

"Mm-hmm . . ."

"His name's Jivu Absko. Nicknamed 'the Gray.' Birthplace unknown to authorities, as is current base of operations. Alleged criminal activities run the gamut from arms dealing to political assassinations, providing mercenaries for civil wars, fixing elections. They've got a list of more than three thousand people who've disappeared entirely or been found dead; law in numerous nations believe him involved, though no firm links have been made to his organization. He's been known to operate in Nigeria, South Africa, Kenya, Spain, Oman, Egypt, and Jordan. Both FBI and CIA have large files, his name is apparently found alongside certain dictators and organized-crime heads."

"Right, well, maybe it's something for us to look into at some point down the road. Let's get some pics and whatever else is out there."

"There're actually three photos associated with him . . . I've got them right in front of me. Each is clearly of a different man. One's older, maybe in his fifties when the shot was taken. Shaved head, prominent cheekbones, dark skin tone of central Africa." Garza heard papers shift on the other end of the line. "Second one looks like maybe North African or Middle Eastern.

Mid-thirties to forties, eyes almost Asian, long neck, square jaw, smiling. The third shows a younger man, also dark skin but with a medium-length Afro, long face, impressive build, wearing aviator sunglasses. That last one looks like it was taken from afar . . . telephoto lens, for sure."

"Yeah, yeah, what else? I gotta go."

"Let's see . . . guy runs some high-profile charities." Tessa spoke faster. "Have you heard of VEC? Value Every Child? Employs some twenty-three hundred people in eighteen countries. Website says their intervention in numerous humanitarian crises has saved a hundred and eighty thousand children . . . blah blah blah . . . more numbers . . . says VEC's latest endeavor has been the establishment of Protect the Women, a subsidiary that builds fortified safe havens in war-torn areas where women and girls are targeted by militias . . . They house medical, education, food service staff."

"Got it. So the Feds want him, but he's probably got some powerful friends."

"Yeah, the file says his charities have made investigations difficult and accusations politically imprudent. Last year, it was suspected that millions in currency looted from African nations by their political elites was being funneled through VEC. But VEC and Absko have been unofficially deemed untouchable by the United Nations. The message to the world's law enforcement community: 'Return with proof of criminal activities when said activities' detriments outweigh VEC's ongoing benefits to humanity.'"

"Not sure if that helps or hurts us," Garza said, chewing a fingernail. "Keep on it. Find out how this might . . . *relate* to things."

✶ ✶ ✶

Jivu Absko rolled around a balled-up gum wrapper between his fingers and thumb as he held the telephone receiver between his shoulder and ear. He chewed slowly as he listened and made affirmative "Mmm-hmm" noises every few seconds.

"They need to be waiting there one hour after signaled," he said in a thick Kenyan accent. "But don't let them congregate like idiots—they will stand out too much. Tell one of them to bring a football or the like. Understand? And to leave any armaments at home . . . mmm-hmm, good. Yes. Oh, and tell them to dress like soldiers, as best they can. Good . . . Have you ever been? . . . Ah, no, me, either. I would love to sometime, though. Their cigars are magnificent . . . Very well, I'll let you get to that. Good-b—oh, no, please don't call me that . . . No, no, it's okay, you didn't know . . . It is okay, really. Stop talking about it now. Thank you again. Good-bye."

He hung up the phone and looked at the small paper ball between his fingers. She was new. Sounded as though she was going to have a heart attack or kill herself. *Someone should have told her.* No one called him "the Gray"—not to his face, anyway. It had begun as a child. They'd call him *"kijivu"*—the Swahili word for the color gray—as a nickname. As he rose in eminence, it became a title of reverence, like "the King." He had enjoyed it for a while, but then it began to feel self-righteous and pretentious, so he told people to stop calling him that. That act had made him seem more humble and, therefore, an even greater man. *Let them say it amongst themselves, and in the news.*

But now he had other things on his plate: loose ends to clean up and funds to recover. He had seen the early profit and loss statements for the second quarter, and on paper it would look like a first-time dip in revenues. Accounting said it wouldn't be a significant issue, but he wasn't going to accept it. Though Dr. Rheese's expedition was unlikely to assist with that, Absko maintained optimism that he could potentially kill two birds with one stone. At least one, of that he would make certain. The second, this thinly-veiled mercenary company, SecureElite, with whom Rheese now worked, had crossed paths with Absko before without conflict. But now their interests and his were at odds, and he had no qualms about making an example of them.

SEVENTEEN

Tuni stuffed her face with a premade deli sandwich. It was airport food and revolting, but she just wanted something in her stomach. The two men with her, Isaiah and Oliver, ate enormous single slices of cheese pizza. Isaiah had pronounced cheekbones and ever-lazy eyelids that made him look like a stoner. Oliver, the silent one, had a round, cherubic face. Both were tallish, with dark brown skin and short-cropped hair. Abel Turay reappeared from the newsstand with a newspaper under his arm and a plastic bag dangling from his hand.

He held out his hand to her. "Gum?"

She nodded gratefully as she balled up the paper sandwich wrapper and threw it in the trash beside them before pulling out a stick. "Thank you. Were you able to get hold of anyone? The pay phones wouldn't accept any of my credit cards to make an international call."

"Ah, yes," Abel said. "I spoke with my superiors to give them an update, and they told me some things as well. More importantly, I reached my contact at the FBI and they have been in contact with Matthew's parents. They know you are okay now and that we have people working on his situation."

Tuni sighed with relief and sat down on the food court bench seat behind her. "Thank God. Roger was a policeman, too. He can probably help."

"Yes, yes, I'm sure. Now, we must get to our next plane, miss."

"Hold on," Tuni said. "Before I go any further with you, I want more answers. I know you're not telling me everything."

Abel took a deep breath, and his eyelids fell.

"Sit with me," she said, and he complied. "Tell me again what your department's interest is in all this. And where are you even *from*? And why are you taking me to Cuba, which I appreciate, don't get me wrong, I want to, but typically I would imagine the police sending me home while they went on with their business. Aren't you endangering me by bringing me to where these kidnappers are?"

Abel smiled thinly and raised his eyebrows. "Is that all?"

"For the moment, yes. Start with those."

"Very well, Ms. St. James." He flashed a blank look up to Isaiah and Oliver, who immediately turned and walked away. "You are too smart for me. As I'm sure you suspect, we are not with Interpol."

Tuni nodded and glanced around. There was an airport security station within forty feet of her, if she needed them.

"But our mission is the truth. We will free Matthew and send him home with you, capture Garrett Rheese, and return with him to our superiors."

"And who are your superiors?"

"The government of Kenya."

"Did you break my phone so I couldn't call anyone? Cancel my credit cards?"

Abel sighed, scratched the back of his neck, and smiled like a child caught stealing candy.

"As I said, we have no jurisdiction. This could turn into some sort of public—"

"I want to talk to my mother," Tuni said firmly. "Myself. On the phone. Now."

"Will you still accompany us to Cuba? Help us to recover Matthew and Rheese?"

"Yes."

"Will she keep quiet?"

"Yes."

"Then yes. Use my phone."

"No international plan, huh?" She glared at him and he shrugged innocently. Phone in hand, she punched in the number.

Four rings. "I'm not home now. Leave a message after the beeping."

"Mom, it's me. Matthew's been kidnapped by Dr. Rheese and taken to Cuba to help him find something. I am with three men from the Kenyan government, Abel Turay and two others named Oliver and Isaiah, who want to arrest Rheese. They broke my phone so I can't get calls or messages, but I will call you again. This is Abel's phone I'm calling from. Note the number. Don't tell anyone about this for now. I'll be in Cuba in a few hours. Love you."

She handed the phone back to him.

"You didn't mention the part about us saving you from kidnappers."

Tuni smiled. "I didn't want to worry her."

Abel blinked and sighed. "Can we go?"

"Let's." She stood up and strode toward the gate.

Abel's eyes lingered on her long legs and shapely figure as he shook his head. "Beautiful women," he murmured to himself, and grabbed his bags.

EIGHTEEN

The van pulled into the parking lot, and Fando shifted into park.

"This doesn't look like it, either," Matt said cautiously, scanning the terrain. It was their third stop along the coast and Garza was on edge since his last phone call. He seemed distracted and more irritable than usual.

Garza climbed forward and opened the door. "Giant bay with a cliff on west side—that's what you said! Those same mountains we saw before should be at about the same angle as that other inlet. Look over there."

Garza was pointing to a hill rising over a palm tree-lined resort. Atop the hill was a beige structure.

"Well, is this it or not?" Rheese demanded. He winced when he spoke. His left cheek was purple and red, though the bleeding in his two empty tooth sockets seemed finally to have clotted.

Garza said, "I mean, we can drive up and down looking at all hundred bays along the northern coastline, but this is the most well-known. Big tourist area."

"'Most well-known' is now meaningless," Rheese snarled as he walked around the van, nursing his tender cheek. "We're talking about a thousand years ago. I say we get on to the mountains. I'm dubious of this entire notion."

Matt did his best to ignore him. Slowly circling, he took in all the shapes of the distant landscape. The mountains seemed to look like the ones he had seen from Haeming's ship, but the angle still didn't seem right. He wished he were on an actual boat.

Fando stood away from them, leaning on the hood of the van and staring off at nothing.

127

"Well, should we go up that hill, or what?" Garza asked. "If you don't think it's it, then let's not waste any more fucking time."

Matt shrugged. "Yeah, let's check it out." He could see that Rheese was about to protest. *Best to stroke his ego.* "Doctor, in terms of land change and erosion, is a thousand years enough time for a whole landscape to change? You're the expert on this stuff."

It worked almost comically. Rheese's posture stiffened, and he walked with one hand behind his back, gesturing with the other. "Indeed. There are several factors to watch for, and an equal number to ignore. Ignore trees, shrubs, roads, footpaths, and even the absence of lesser terrain features . . "

He went on as they walked. Garza noticed Fando still at the van and whistled for him to come. He turned, looking almost startled, and jogged to catch up. They walked the bike path along the shore. Seagulls swarmed around a pelican with a full bill pouch.

". . . Man can remove mountains, but he can't truly create them. It's always more important what *is* there than what isn't. Landslides, too, can irrevocably alter a landscape . . ."

Reaching the small resort, they walked the garden path between the buildings. Other tourists took no notice of them, and Matt made no effort to signal anyone. It would be futile. He was pretty sure that Tuni was free, though he wasn't positive. He also didn't know whether he could outrun both Garza and Fando if he should try to bolt away.

". . . desert climate versus tropical, coastal versus inland, riverside versus hillside—it's the nuances of each that combine to sculpt the landscape. Rivers can go from massive to nonexistent in under a century, not to mention . . ."

They came to a well-worn footpath that branched off and led up the bay side of the hill. There was also a cracked concrete road that appeared to wind around to the opposite side. A small sign read "Suites de Colina 30 – 42," with an arrow pointing left, to the road. Matt turned onto the dirt path and headed up. He reached the summit, and it still didn't look familiar. But then he saw something that struck him: a guardrail lining the cliff—presumably to keep people from blundering off the edge to their deaths. Its steel posts were sunk into the bedrock.

Rheese said, "This plateau was clearly machine-planed. Might have risen another ten, fifteen meters, perhaps more."

Garza and Fando stood and gazed out over the blue Gulf of Mexico while Matt poked around. He leaned over the rail and peered down the cliff. Then, without a word, he put his gloved hands on it and vaulted over, disappearing over the edge.

Garza said, "What the f—"

"Did . . . did he just . . . ?" Rheese stammered.

"Little shit's dead for sure," Fando said.

Matt walked along the hidden second cliff, pulling apart the hanging foliage in an effort to expose the rock behind it. This was definitely the spot, but maybe the carving had worn away by now. A thousand years of tropical sun and rain and hurricanes was a lot of weathering. The epiphytes, aerial roots, and other hanging flora were too thick and heavy, and a layer of wet, crunchy vines behind them moistened his gloves as he reached in. He was elbow-deep in vegetation when he felt rock.

"Rheese, get down here!" he yelled.

"No shit!" Fando muttered.

"Where the bloody hell are you?"

Rheese squatted under the guardrail, holding firmly on to an anchor post as he craned his neck out over the edge. Matt waved to him from scarcely a body length down. Behind Turner, just a couple of feet back, a sheer cliff dropped away to the crashing surf and wave-polished boulders.

"The ledge is wide enough to stand on," Matt said. "Just hold on to the plants and shimmy down if you're afraid to drop."

"Did you find it? Is it carved?"

"The plants are too thick, but come here—you can feel a whole symbol."

Rheese crept carefully down until he stood on the ledge and sidled over to Matt. As Garza and Fando held on to the fence above and watched, Matt pulled aside a curtain of vines, and Rheese reached in, his face screwed up in an expression of concentration. Then his eyes widened.

"I'm no expert in runic script, but this feels like an enormous asterisk. I know I've seen that symbol before." He pulled his arm out. "Is there more?"

"I haven't felt any other spots. Here . . . try over here."

Matt pulled aside another sheaf of hanging plants as Rheese reached in.

"Ow, damn!" Rheese howled. "Bloody wall is right here—nearly broke my fingers!"

He pulled a thin layer of roots out of the way and wiped away clumps of dark soil. Before them, engraved into the rock, was a vertical line with a short line jutting out from it at a downward angle. They both looked at it in wonder.

"I remember seeing this," Matt said. "I could probably draw out on paper what the whole thing looks like."

Rheese looked at him with a toothy grin, and in that instant, Matt could see why the man had gotten into archaeology in the first place. It clearly thrilled him.

"Turner, do you realize what this means?"

"That Vikings were in Cuba a long goddamn time before Columbus?"

"Well, yes, that. But, as an aside to that, no one in the *world* knows this. . . except us." Rheese ran his fingers down the carving. "This would be a career maker for someone. Published the world over, name forever associated with the find. Like Carter and King Tut's tomb!"

"Yeah." Matt nodded. It was interesting—even a little disarming—to see Rheese in this mode. "You should do it. Hell, find out where they dumped the top of this hill here, and you'll probably find whatever's left of a thousand-year-old Viking ship."

Rheese clapped the dirt from his hands and sighed. "Ten years ago, perhaps. The damage has already been done to my former career. There's no going back, no, no. I need to load up my new bank account and go where no one knows or cares who I am."

"You don't think this is big enough to make people forget all that?"

"Attempted murder? Kidnapping? Fraud? Now *this*? I've gone international, lad. Probably considered a terrorist of some sort in *your* bloody country. No, no."

"So what now?" Matt said. "There's obviously no pirate treasure buried where you thought—you must see that now."

Rheese frowned. "Hmm, yes. A valid point."

Matt found a high clump of dirt and root clusters that provided an easy way back up to the lookout point. Crawling up under the guardrail, he wondered, could Rheese actually let him go now? He seemed to have softened a bit. Perhaps getting his teeth knocked out had brought him down to earth a little. But would Garza even let that happen? Fando still appeared to be in shock—no doubt, after losing his brother, he could think of little else.

Crawling up after Matt, Rheese said, "I don't know what to tell you two. It doesn't look like this is going where we anticipated. I made no promises, though." He chuckled nervously. "Probably best to part ways."

"*Part ways?*" Garza said.

"Indeed. Call it a day. Move on before we dig ourselves in too deep, and all that."

"What about that sword you were talking about?" Garza said as he stretched his fingers, curled them into fists, then stretched them out straight again.

"Sayf Allah? There's really no telling where it could have gone—or even if it still exists today…"

"You're planning to flip that opal for a profit . . . or find that sword on your own. There's less payoff now, and you don't want to share."

Rheese gave him a wounded look. "That is ridiculous! The thought hadn't even occurred to me! Think about it! The thing walked off with its owner, *separated* from the stone that we have. Turner can't trace where it went after that. Tell him."

"Yeah, it's true. I can only read what happened before the opal got put in that tree. I would need another artifact that went on with the sword and stayed with it. Make sense?"

Garza's nostrils flared as he paced. Matt's father had told him once what that could mean. *"He's oxygenating his muscles. Perp could be getting ready to run or else to fight. It's subconscious. Know what that means, boy?"*

"Screw that," Garza barked. "We're going up that goddamn mountain and finding what we can find. I don't buy that there's suddenly nothing up there."

Rheese said, "But there's no—"

"You don't know that! Shit, that sword could be buried right by where the tree was! You don't know!"

Matt took a subtle step back. He didn't really want to be seen as *with* Rheese. Better to let Garza's anger focus on Rheese alone.

"And you propose what exactly?" Rheese said in his usual snooty tone. "We take shovels up there and just start digging up the mountainside until we find something? We don't even know where that tree was."

Garza pointed at Matt, "*He* does. He'll lead us right to it. Won't you?"

"Uh, well . . . actually, I don't know. There were just a bunch of trees around us that apparently are gone now. Really no way to identify where that was."

Garza was breathing deeper, heavier, his big shoulders rising and falling.

"I ain't stupid, Turner. You found this hill; you can find where the damned tree was. If you can't, well, in that case, we'll already have the shovels and a perfect spot to bury you. Your job is to give us a reason not to. Let's go." Garza shoved both of them forward and snapped his fingers in front of Fando's face. "Wake up, man. Let's go!"

Fando blinked. "My mom, man," he said. "How'm I gonna . . ."

Garza slapped him on the back and said, "Come on. We can at least make it easier on her by bringing her his cut."

"Garza, I think we need to have a word," Rheese said. "I think you may have grown a bit confused over who is in bloody charge here."

Matt winced inside. As much as he despised Rheese, it was painful to see him so clueless. Maybe he was in charge once, but not any longer. This was Garza's show. In fact, Matt could think of no good reason why they needed to keep Rheese around any longer. If they really were killers—a strong possibility, from what he had seen so far—they probably planned to get rid of both of them the moment they had what they wanted. Fortunately, they hadn't yet decided the opal was enough for just the two of them.

Garza turned around suddenly, his mouth an inch away from Rheese's eyes. "I ain't confused, Doc. We're just continuing our business, as planned." He turned and walked to the van. "We have to make a stop before we go."

Rheese seemed to get it, or maybe he was just intimidated enough not to argue. Fando threw Garza the keys and took the backseat. Rheese sat on the middle bench, beside Matt, which Matt found ironically appropriate.

"We got two hours back to Havana, Matthew," Garza said. "Maybe you want to spend your time wisely."

NINETEEN

Matt fast-forwarded past everything he had already experienced, until the next imprint forced him to halt. In the past, he'd tried several times to push past an unread imprint, but it had always been beyond his control. It was as if the story—even the person's dreams—demanded to be known. This he had learned as a child sleeping in other people's beds. The worst part of it was that it seemed that the only things anyone imprinted while asleep were nightmares. These could be fascinating when not one's own, but these days, the abstract, herky-jerky nature of dreams tended to irritate him more often than frighten him. It was one thing to have a nightmare, and quite another to relive someone else's without being in an actual dream state. The imprints streamed by at dizzying speed and jumped chaotically from subject to subject.

As the new imprint came into focus, Matt was pleased to find that it was still Haeming's.

He is not in the place he called "Southland," nor does he yet seem to be aware of such a place. He has successfully crossed the Atlantic to "Helluland," "Markland," and now looks on with wonder at Leif Eriksson's houses in "Vinland." Beyond the crowns of trees, five or more smoke plumes rise separately in the distance. The land is beautiful, warm, and beckons him in a way he has not felt of other places. But it belongs to others, and he would not become a conqueror. They would sleep here the night, gather water and supplies, and continue south. His new land, the one he promised to his people and their families, would be home to nothing but the trees and the wild.

TWENTY

J ess Canter threw his duffel to the floor and flopped down on the motel
bed. He had been on the phone for eight of the past nine hours. The group
had filled out piles of paperwork at the U.S. Interests Section office.
Formerly the U.S. embassy building, USINT was situated on prime real estate
on the northern coastal edge of Havana. They'd planted that building as close
to D.C. as possible without getting wet. Jess had met with Hernán Conserrate,
a short, balding man whose face and head seemed to have a perpetual shine. He
had been the management officer at USINT for the past decade. After a quick
briefing, Hernán had taken Jess outside to a small private courtyard, where he
jotted down a name and phone number.

"You can get whatever supplies you need from this man," he said. "I don't
know where he's doing business these days, but call that number and tell him
you were referred by Julio Iglesias. He is shamelessly expensive, but it is
because there are no other options in country, and he knows it. If he asks, don't
tell him anything about what you're doing—he's nosy and not to be trusted.
I haven't heard of it happening before, but he could very easily report your
group if he thought there was a reward in it for him."

Each of the two motel rooms had two twin beds and a couch. They all
squeezed into one room for a few minutes, and Jess told everyone they were
going to stay in the area until they had intel directing them elsewhere. As it
was, Matt's iPad had yet to connect to any more Wi-Fi access points, and they
had already checked out the hotel where it linked up before. Their motel was
nearby, though, so Roger, Núñez, and Chuck Kohl were to canvass the area,
show pictures to passersby and shop owners, and pass out cards with a phone

number to call. Paul would stay with Jess and go through the phone book, calling hotels.

"Got it?" Jess asked the group.

Paul said, "*No hablo español.*"

Núñez said, "Just tell 'em you speak English, and if they don't, they'll put someone on who does."

"*Sí, comprendo,*" Paul replied.

"Whose number do we give people to call if they see or hear something?" Chuck asked.

"Mine," Roger blurted. "Sorry—mine, *please*. It should work here. I had international roaming added. Let me just make sure it works." He pulled his phone from his backpack and saw a big "SOS" where the signal strength bars belonged. "Crap."

Paul peered over his shoulder. "If you just had your plan changed, you might have to reboot it for it to take or whatever."

Roger turned the phone off, waited a few seconds, then turned it back on. After a minute, the signal bars began to flash and change colors.

"That looks promising," he said, and then a big envelope appeared in the middle of the screen, and the phone chirped at him. "Hang on, I have some messages here . . ."

Ears in the room perked up. He tapped the SELECT button, and two messages were listed: one from Beth's phone, the other from a number he didn't recognize. He turned the phone to the side as he opened the message from his wife.

Let me know when you are there safe. Bring our baby home.

He clicked back and went to the second message.

Havna silvr van 2 guys guns + rheese

"Oh, my God, it's from Matt!" he shouted. He reread it aloud. "Call in this number! Where's five-one-two?"

"That's Austin," Paul said.

Roger read off the whole number to Jess, who repeated it into his own phone.

"Silver van," Chuck said. "Would have to be a rental, right? Núñez, can you call up all the rental car places around here? Start with the airport ones."

She nodded and grabbed the phone directory.

"Good boy," Roger said, smiling. "Son of a gun, that's good. He knew what information was most valuable that he could text out quickly."

"You gonna text back?" Chuck asked. "Ask him where he is now?"

This brought groans and snickers.

Without looking up from his phone, Paul said, "Logical."

Chuck realized the stupidity of the question and shut up without another word, but socked Paul in the shoulder for good measure.

✶ ✶ ✶

A half hour later, they had gathered some solid leads. Only two silver vans had been rented in the past twenty-four hours: one to a large family of Italian nationals, the other to a local named Ernesto Guevara. Mr. Guevara prepaid with cash for two days, though he still had to provide a credit card to guarantee the vehicle. The Visa card belonged to one Fernando Solorzano, a U.S. citizen and former Marine, honorably discharged two years ago. Since then, he had no employer on record, nor any paycheck from which taxes were withheld. But he had somehow received $112,000 in total income during that time and paid the appropriate taxes.

"Mercenary work," Jess theorized.

"Do they have any kind of tracking devices in their vehicles?" Roger asked Núñez.

"I asked. Sorry, no."

"I've got this Solorzano's credit and debit cards all tagged now," said Jess. "If he uses any of them, we'll know within minutes. Also waiting on a call back from Customs to find out who else he flew here with, but at a glance they couldn't find any record of him traveling under his own name in the past year, or Ernesto Guevara, for that matter."

"Well, if we get a call on a credit card hit, what do we do?" Roger asked. "Call the Cuban police? We have no weapons, and Matt's text says they do."

Paul offered, "I can throw rocks like a motherf—"

"I have a contact," Jess interrupted. "Could be sketchy, though, so I say we all go. Just need to make a call. Núñez, would you do the honors?" He handed her the note from Hernán Conserrate. "Tell him you were referred by Julio Iglesias."

She stared at him, unamused. "Seriously?"

THE OPAL

"He sings that song 'Hero,'" Paul said.

"Seriously, yes," Jess confirmed.

She pulled out her phone, then thought better of it and grabbed the hotel phone. As she dialed, Jess and Roger huddled close to listen.

A man answered. *"¿Mande?"*

Núñez softened her voice, suddenly sounding very ladylike and pleasant—a dramatic change from her usual harsh monotone. *"Nos derivó Julio Iglesias. ¿Nos puede usted conseguir equipo para investigación?"*

She listened and cupped the receiver. "How many and how big? Ten—half-and-half?"

The men nodded. She resumed the voice: *"Diez . . . la mitad grandes y la mitad pequeños, más las pilas."*

She pointed at her watch and held up a hand inquiringly. Jess mouthed, *Now.* *"Hoy, al mediodía."*

She grabbed a notepad and jotted down an address.

"Gracias, señor." She waited to hang up the phone completely before speaking. Her strictly-business tone returned. "We need ten thousand dollars," she said. "And we have forty-five minutes."

"Did he say there was any problem?" Roger asked.

She shook her head.

Roger turned to Jess. "I've got the money in my accounts, but I doubt a foreign bank will let me do a wire transfer for that much, that quickly."

"I can answer this one, Lieutenant Canter," Paul Kleindorf said. "The Department of Justice has released funds for this operation."

Roger looked at Jess, who shrugged.

"First I've heard of it. How much, Paul?"

"In the grand scheme of government spending, chicken feed. One hundred thousand plus a special account in case ransom enters into it."

He produced an all-black Visa card with a tiny U.S. flag in the corner.

Roger appeared to be holding back emotion. "You'll have to thank your dad for me, son. This is just . . . there's just no words."

"Souvenirs," Paul said, flicking the card between his fingers.

"Can we get cash out of that thing?" Chuck asked.

"Pretty sure," Paul replied.

★ ★ ★

138

After loading up the rental SUV, they went to the Banco Central, the largest bank in Havana, where they spent two hours obtaining the requisite approvals from what seemed like every employee in the building. At last, they walked out with twelve thousand Cuban pesos, which, apparently, had roughly the same value as U.S. dollars.

Núñez found the supplier's address on a map and navigated while Chuck drove. They found the house: a small duplex with crackled white paint and wide-open windows. They passed it without slowing and turned right at the next street, then right again into a dirt alley. The house looked about the same in the back but with a low chain-link fence enclosing a yard full of weeds, some old cinder blocks, and an ancient wringer washing machine.

Chuck parked and turned around in his seat. "How do we want to do this?"

Jess looked at Roger, who had done his share of undercover drug and weapons buys in the past. "What do you think, Rog?"

"Núñez and me at the door, you at the gate, and everyone else in the car. Doors unlocked and windows open so you can hear anything that goes down."

"You're not going inside, are you?" Chuck asked. "Looks dodgy . . ."

"Not if we can help it, but he might not accept cash out in the open like this. We'll play it by ear. Núñez, I take it you can be counted on if the situation should get physical?"

She shrugged modestly. "Yes, sir."

A wiry, dark man in a white tank top and cut-off denim shorts opened the security screen before they made it to the steps.

"*Hola, hola. ¡Bienvenidos, mis amigos!*" he called out, smiling. Most of his teeth were capped with silver. "Call me Larry!"

Jess watched from the gate as Núñez shook Larry's hand. He grimaced and made a show of acting as though her grip had hurt his hand, then laughed uproariously. Then, leaning out, he waved to Jess, gazed at the SUV, and waved to Chuck, beaming the same sunshiny smile. He gestured for Núñez and Roger to come inside, but they stayed on the porch. Larry made a melodramatic pout and then laughed again, holding his belly with one hand as he laughed.

He disappeared inside as Roger held the security-screen door open. Núñez and Larry spoke back and forth, and Larry could be heard laughing from inside the house. He returned to the front door with two large duffel bags and set them down on the floor, just inside. There was a rapping on the security screen at the front of the house.

"Un momento, un momento . . . Don't go anywhere, okay?" he said as
Núñez inspected the contents of the duffels.

Roger leaned into the doorway. The front door was exactly opposite the
back, with no walls obstructing the view. He could see Larry conversing with
a tall, muscular man in sunglasses, jeans, and a tight gray T-shirt. They shook
hands, and Larry did his wincing-with-pain-and-buckling-at-the-knees routine. Laughter. He pointed a thumb behind him and motioned out front, as if to
tell the man that he was busy and to wait outside. Muscles gazed past Larry to
Núñez and Roger, said *"No problema,"* and walked down the steps and went
away.

"So sorry," Larry said as he came back. "The money, *por favor.* Let's finish this up. Busy day today."

"Are they good?" Roger asked Núñez.

"I opened up two of the forty-fives; they're good. This shotgun needs oil,
but it appears to be solid. Who knows about the two bolt-actions, but otherwise I think we're good." She looked up at Larry. "You don't have buckshot?
Preferably, double-ought."

Larry smiled and shrugged and shook his head.

Roger signaled to Paul, who appeared from the backseat of the SUV.

"Another one!" Larry said, and laughed. "This is like a Cuban family
reunion!"

Paul handed the envelope to Jess, who then walked it to Roger, who handed
it to Larry. Larry fingered through the tops of the notes, then looked up and
said, *"Gracias,* come again! Bring the whole family next time!" and closed the
screen door. It locked with a metallic *thunk* as Núñez and Roger each lugged
a duffel back to the SUV.

Inside the car, they pulled out everything and laid it on the third-row seat
to begin inventorying.

"I'd like the Mossberg," Chuck said. "That's a police edition."

"What's with the museum pieces?" Paul asked, referring to the two aging
rifles.

"Those are American M-fourteens," Núñez said. "Good for long range."

"How much ammo we got?" Roger asked.

"Looks like a hundred shells . . . birdshot, though. Fifty rounds for the
fourteens," Núñez replied. "Three of the pistols are forty-fives. We have one
. . . two . . . three . . . four—two hundred rounds for those. The other two are
nine-millimeters—a hundred rounds of nine."

"That should do us, right?" Chuck asked from the driver's seat.

"I don't think we'll be getting into any prolonged firefights," Jess said. "We have two targets that are actually dangerous, and as long as Matty's with them, we shouldn't be shooting anyway. These are really more of a show of strength—"

A gunshot rang out, and the SUV shook.

"What the fu . . . ?" yelled Chuck.

"Who's shooting?" Roger barked.

Another three shots, rapid-fire.

"Everybody down!" Jess yelled. "Load up, load up!"

"Anyone see the shooter?" said Núñez. "Is it from the house?"

Roger poked his head up and took a fast glance around. At the end of the alley, he spotted a muscular man in a tight gray T-shirt, aiming a scoped rifle at them from behind a utility pole.

"Oh, shit, stay down!"

Automatic fire riddled the front of the SUV, sending windshield fragments flying everywhere and blasting the eardrums of those inside.

"Shoot back, somebody!" Jess shouted. "Let 'em know we're armed!"

"I'm trying to load this thing, hang on," Núñez said. "Five seconds."

She slammed a magazine into a Colt Government model .45, chambered a round, and fired three shots out through a ten-inch hole in the windshield. She handed the pistol to Paul, in front of her, and started thumbing rounds into another .45 mag. No more shots had been fired at them for several seconds, but they couldn't see through the shattered glass of the windshield.

"How many are there?" Paul shouted.

"Someone kick that goddamn window out!" yelled Roger. "We can't see jack!"

Chuck kicked twice with his boot, and the shattered glass fell out in big sections. Núñez handed Roger one of the .45's, and he poked his head up just in time to see Muscles walking away with rifle in hand. A silver van screeched to a stop beside him, and he climbed in, sliding the door shut as the van sped away.

"Silver van! Silver van!" Roger shouted. "Go, go! Follow 'em!"

"I saw it, too," Jess said. "Let's go!"

Chuck turned the engine over, and horrible clanking sounds emanated from under the hood. He put it in gear anyway, and the SUV lurched forward. The steering wheel vibrated erratically in his hands, and he realized he had no control over their direction.

"I think the tires are all blown, guys. God damn it."

Roger screamed a curse and slammed a fist against his door. "Right there in front of us! He was right there!"

They sat there stunned for a moment until Roger got out and looked around. Faces stared from the surrounding houses. All four tires were indeed shot out. Those were probably the first four shots, he guessed.

Jess stepped out, then Núñez and Paul.

Roger had a look of despair; then his face suddenly lit up, and he slapped Jess on the arm.

"Larry!"

"Wha—?" Jess began, but Núñez was already following Roger back to the gate.

Larry met them at his screen door with an AR-15 assault rifle. For once, he was not smiling.

Roger had his gun up before Larry's, and snapped, "Drop the gun, God damn it! Put it down!"

¡Suéltelo!" Núñez barked.

But Larry swung the screen shut, then slammed a door behind it. Roger pointed her right, then ran left around the house, toward the front. The rest of the team made it to the gate just in time to see Núñez jump up and dive through a high open window.

"Holy crap! You see that?" Chuck gasped.

Two gunshots rang out inside, and those outside could hear a screen door swing shut in the front. Jess tried the back door but found it had automatically locked. Chuck and Paul took positions at the windows, Chuck with the shotgun. Inside, Roger barked, "On the ground!" Núñez called, "All clear in here!"

The rest of the team ran around and entered through the front door. Roger had a foot on Larry's back, and a .45 pointed at his head. Núñez was covering a frightened woman in a very messy kitchen. At their feet, a pool of blood was spreading from the head of a young man with a revolver still clutched in his dead hand.

Larry was moaning, "Rolando . . . he never did nothing."

Roger motioned Núñez over.

"Tell him he has two minutes to tell us everything or he joins Rolando in hell."

"I am not going to say that, sir," Núñez said. "But I'll get him to tell us what he knows."

TWENTY-ONE

Abel Turay stepped out of the hotel bathroom with only a towel wrapped around his waist. Drying his ear with a hand towel, he said, "Your turn if you like, miss."

Tuni looked up from the map Oliver was showing her, and her eyes widened in surprise. Abel had the physique of an Olympic decathlete. The suit he had been wearing did nothing for him. She looked away too quickly, and Isaiah elbowed Oliver and snickered.

"Sure—thanks," she said, and grabbed her suitcase, dragging it quickly into the suite's luxurious bathroom. The resort was obviously a pricey one. From behind the locked door, she said, "Are we going anywhere tonight?"

"I don't believe so," Abel called back. "I'm waiting on some information from headquarters. Besides, not a good idea to leave tourist areas after dark."

"Very well, I'm just throwing on some PJ's, then," she said.

Isaiah raised his eyebrows, smiled, and made an "Mmm" sound. Abel, in sweatpants now, strode right up to him and grabbed his face by the chin, as one might a misbehaving child.

"Respectful," Abel hissed.

Isaiah gave a sharp nod and tried to say "Sorry, sah," but it came out garbled. Abel released him and smiled gently. He turned to Oliver.

"Would you please empty the closet safe? The code is one-nine-seven-three."

Oliver hopped up and went to the large wall safe and punched in the code. The door popped open a little. He swung the door wide and found six black Sig Sauer pistols. Three were full-size .40-calibers; the other three were little

143

backup-size nine-millimeters with two-inch barrels and clip-on holsters. He grabbed one of each and brought them out to Abel.

"In my pack for now, please," Abel said. "And be discreet with yours, as well."

Abel pulled on a tight white T-shirt, grabbed his cell phone, and went to the attached bedroom, where he dropped onto one of the two queen-size beds. The room had been decorated in elegant, bright whites, contrasted with cobalt blues. He shoved the throw pillows aside and shifted into a casual pose, one hand behind his head.

The shower shut off, and a hair dryer blew. Then came toothbrushing sounds. The bathroom door swung open, and Tuni walked out in thin pajama pants and a big T-shirt with elephants on it. As she stuffed her clothes into her suitcase, she looked up at Oliver and Isaiah, intent on their game of Kalah.

"Where'd Abel go?" she asked.

Oliver nodded toward the bedroom without looking at her. She stepped into the doorway and saw Abel on top of his still-made bed, staring off at nothing as he listened to someone on his phone.

"Yes sir," he said. "We're all checked in and just waiting for word . . . Yes." He glanced at Tuni, smiled absently, and then returned his gaze to the wall. "Are we certain of their numbers? . . . And do we know if the subject is safe? . . . Good. And we have a support team on standby? . . . Good, thank you. I'm going to sleep now but will have my phone close if there are any changes. Thank you, sir."

He hung up and plugged in his phone before setting it on the nightstand beside him. Tuni had already climbed into her bed and had her back to him.

"They say Matthew is still all right?" she asked.

"That is the information we have, yes. We just received word on where they are headed: a town called Viñales. We will get on the road first thing tomorrow morning.

"What is this support team you mentioned?"

"It's never wise to meet your opponents with equal numbers, if avoidable. In our case, tomorrow, it's avoidable. We'll meet them on the way."

Tuni was silent.

"Will you be able to sleep, miss?"

"I don't know. This all sounds exceedingly dangerous. I'm glad someone like you is handling it, that's all I've to say. Tell me a bloody story or something. Where are you from, exactly? You're obviously not ethnically Kenyan."

Abel chuckled. "I was born in Nairobi, my mother Kenyan, but my father was Lebanese."

"Ah, that makes sense. And why is your English so good? You hardly have any accent."

"Well, thank you. I suppose, though, if you heard me talking to my mother, you would not say the same. I attended a boarding school in Leicester for a few years and later spent two semesters at Cornell in New York."

"And you still returned to Africa. Very noble—that's typically a one-way trip."

"It's my home. And there's so much work to be done. If all the good people leave, how will it ever be fixed?"

She twisted her head around to look at him. "Sorry all the selfish ones like me keep abandoning ship."

"That isn't what I meant, Tuni."

"Of course it is. And it's true." She turned away again, and silence filled the room for a moment. "You having much success fixing things over there?"

He laughed quietly and said, "It's a work in progress." He looked pensive for a moment. "Do you mind a personal question? Off the topic."

"Not at all," she said, gazing out the window at the darkening Havana sky. Thinly-spread clouds stretched infinitely out toward the horizon.

"What is it you see in this Matthew?"

She turned over in her bed and faced him. "That wasn't quite what I expected. But, um . . . well, sure, I can answer that. He's bloody hilarious, and he's smart—very smart. I think he speaks somewhere around eighteen languages that I know of. And he's not exactly a disaster to look at, and . . ."

"Ah, okay, good," Abel said, and flicked off the light.

"What do you mean by that?" she said. "What did you think it was?"

"No, nothing, I didn't think anything. Was just wondering."

"That's a bloody lie. You said, 'Ah, okay, good,' as in 'Phew, that's a relief!' Tell me what you thought. Don't be a coward."

She heard him sigh in the dark.

"Sorry. I didn't mean for anything . . . I just thought perhaps, you know, with his vulnerability and his previous victimization by Dr. Rheese . . . the hospitals and everything . . ."

"Yeah, what about them?"

"I don't know . . . that it would be some sort of maternal thing." Talking faster now. "There's nothing wrong with it, mind you. It was just a thought.

As in, I could see that happening, what with him being so much younger than you."

"*So much younger?* He's twenty-six! I'm only thirty-two."

"Eh . . . never mind. Forget I mentioned it, please! Go to sleep. We'll rescue your practically-same-aged boyfriend tomorrow, all right?"

Tuni huffed and flipped back over in her bed. *Maternal!* she thought, then muttered it aloud. She tried to push it out of her head, but the word stuck, and she actually found herself wondering whether there might be some element of nurturing going on there. And if so, it would have nothing to do with their age difference. The only thing *that* really affected was the old "settling down" notion. She needed to get cracking on kids, and Matthew had always seemed to deflate at the very mention. In that sense, she supposed, a thirty-two year old woman was in a somewhat different place than a twenty-six year old man who saw years of freedom ahead of him. But who the hell was Abel to judge or question, anyway? Her mind flipped through recent interactions with Matthew, all of them healthy and equal. *Besides,* she thought, *he needs me.* And she needed him, tooBut as she tried to sleep, her head remained busy with thoughts and memories of Matthew. Her feelings for him were more intense than ever, but was she idealizing their relationship due to the circumstances, as one can often do in such situations or after being dumped? No. She listed his wonderful qualities and looked back on all the joyous times they'd shared. But what about the negatives? There were plenty, but why did she need to think about those right now? To be fair? Fair to whom? It was Abel's fault, getting her spinning like this. The man probably wasn't used to women showing no interest in him, that's all. For all his confidence and charm and good looks, how could she *possibly* still be thinking about her kidnapped boyfriend? Arsehole.

She looked at the nightstand clock and yawned, forcing her mind elsewhere. Mr. Pups, her cat, chasing the red dot of a laser as she streaked it across her apartment floor.

TWENTY-TWO

Haeming worked his way up the steep hill, his small scouting patrol following close behind. He had come this far yesterday, though not on the path and not in view of the sentries. On this trip, they intentionally walked through the small village of Tainos at the base of the mountain to see how the natives would react to their presence. Haeming's group received only silent stares.

Yesterday, he and Ulfr had avoided the village, instead negotiating the dense tropical forest to find the mountain people's town. They discovered the entire hilltop was encircled with a sturdy wood fence. It was by no means an impenetrable barrier, but its builders had strung twine along the inside, attaching shards of broken pots that would ring out should anyone attempt to break through or sneak in. Haeming knew he could easily have disabled the crude warning system if he wanted, but his mission yesterday had not been to infiltrate or attack. Nor was it today. He just wanted to meet these mountain people.

As he walked, his head hurt. His jaw had been clenched most of the past two days, since meeting a white man living with the Taino—an inexplicable presence until the man spoke to them in Norse, told them of the mountain people. Haeming tried to remain aware of his mouth and relax it, but each time, his thoughts snaked inevitably back to the intolerable, to this place, to *losing*. And without realizing it, he would again clamp his jaw. Despite his serene outward expression, he burned with rage inside.

They neared the tall gate, and the guards posted in the two towers above simply watched as Haeming stopped a few feet away and smiled up at them. The towers infuriated him. The gate infuriated him.

"Hello, there," he said.

"Welcome, strangers," the one on the right replied in Norse. He was a gaunt fellow with a short, wispy brown beard. He wore no shirt, and his necklace hung down as he leaned over the platform's edge. His skin was bronzed by years of sun. "Please leave your weapons there. You will have no need of them inside these walls."

"We are a peaceful people," the blond young man in the left tower said. He was perhaps fifteen and also shirtless.

Haeming turned around and made eye contact with each of his men. He gave them a tiny nod and they began disarming. Haeming kept the Damascus sword, in its jewel-encrusted sheath, strapped around his waist. A dagger remained concealed in the small of his back. He hadn't gone completely unarmed in half a decade, and he wouldn't start now by entering this loathsome village without a weapon.

"Very well, my friends," he said. "We have put aside our arms. We come in peace."

Haeming watched the bearded man's eyes, which were riveted on the bejeweled pommel of the Damascus.

"Ah . . ." the bearded man stammered, "I'm afraid you *all* must leave your weapons."

"We have," Haeming said, smiling earnestly. "If you mean this decorative trifle here, it is purely ceremonial, like a crown or chest piece—nothing to worry about, I assure you."

The man turned around and spoke in low tones with an unseen woman beyond the gate. His face returned a moment later.

"We extend our deepest regrets, good sir . . ." His nervousness amused Haeming. ". . . but I'm afraid there can be no exceptions. If you prefer not to leave it, we can keep it for you."

Behind his back, Haeming gave one of his men a hidden signal with his left hand.

"Outrageous!" his man, Ulfr, bellowed. "Sir, let us leave this vulgar place at once! I told you they would be uncivilized Norwegians."

"Open the gates!" a deep voice called out. "Stop this nonsense. They are guests!"

Ulfr grinned and whispered to Haeming, "The day will come when you are wrong."

Haeming replied softly, "That day has already passed. It was horrible." He said it as a joke, but inside, he knew it to be true. He had been very wrong—and not only once.

Michael Siemsen

The gates parted to reveal a stout old man with a bushy gray beard. He had the demeanor of someone exhausted by life yet trudging on. Already walking away, he glanced at Haeming's group with mild interest before disappearing from view behind the fence.

"You may enter Bodvarrston," the man on the right tower said.

A middle-aged woman leaned cautiously into view and smiled politely to Haeming. "Welcome," she said.

Haeming bowed his head to her and returned the smile. Crossing the threshold into the village, he looked around as if he had never seen it, and, indeed, spotted structures and people not visible from his earlier scouting mission.

The townspeople seemed to be busying themselves with fruitless tasks, no one aware of Haeming's group walking into their village. A man took baskets one by one from a stack and restacked them a few feet away. Two children "washed" garments in an empty bucket. Haeming peered to his left and saw the old man, now seated in a tall stone chair. A throne. Beyond him, several strong-looking men hammered rocks into smaller rocks. He counted people in his head: twenty-seven that he could see.

The town enclosed by the fence was bean shaped: elongated, with rounded ends, and bent in the middle. Haeming wondered how many people were inside the houses, which looked like a blend of traditional Norse design—log walls, turf roof—and the round palm-thatched huts favored by the native people. The mountain people had kept the log walls, but opted for thatch roofs—likely better for the heat, but he wondered how they held up to prolonged rain.

The old man waved impatiently for Haeming and his men to approach. "Step lively, if you don't mind, son. This is a busy day, as you can see . . ." He gestured around him as if this were obvious.

Haeming walked up and halted a few steps away. He noticed that the throne was tall enough for the seated occupant to look down on anyone standing before him. The old man wore a threadbare woolen shirt with no sleeves. Between his spread legs hung a tattered green tunic. *They have no sheep—no new wool.* Haeming stood and waited.

"I am King Bodvarr," the old man said, looking Haeming over. "Welcome to my island, Southland, and my city, Bodvarrston."

My island . . . The words repeated in Haeming's mind. This was supposed to be Haeming's island. Unoccupied, lush, perfect.

"Who are you, and what brings you so far from home?" Bodvarr said. Then he muttered, "As if I need ask."

THE OPAL

"I am Haeming Grimsson of Reykjavik. We come as explorers."

Bodvarr snorted, and Haeming could detect the smile beneath the gray beard. The man's eyes alit on the Saracen sword at Haeming's waist, though they did not linger there.

"Lovely. And I congratulate you on your journey. When do you plan to leave?"

Haeming had expected this.

"We are not sure," he said. "It appears to be a fruitful land."

Bodvarr peered past Haeming, to the men standing behind him. "The rest of your party are camped somewhere along my north shore, I take it?"

Haeming ignored the question, surveying the village as if assessing it for a good fit. "You must house close to a hundred here."

Bodvarr's smile disappeared.

"Well beyond that, Icelander. Did you say Grimsson?"

"I did."

"I wonder if I knew your father."

"Not likely." Haeming brushed it off. He wished to control this conversation. "I find it strange that you live on this island so clearly dominated by its native owners, and yet you possess no armaments. Seems quite a vulnerable position to be in."

Bodvarr's eyes turned cold, but his smile returned. The disinterested front he had put on turned to defiance as his eyes locked on Haeming's. They held their gaze in silence for an uncomfortable length of time. In his peripheral vision, Haeming noticed that the two men previously breaking rocks had ceased their toil and stepped closer to their king, though not closer than Haeming.

Bodvarr finally broke the silence. "Are you Christian?"

"Yes," Haeming said.

"Interesting. I studied this Jesus back in Norway. A very modern outlook, as I recall. His stories lack intrigue—no tradition."

"Your studies mustn't have—"

"What's more, he seemed a bit of a weakling," Bodvarr interrupted. "Such a passive participant in his own life. Certainly not a religion for a strong country to take on or dictate to its citizens. Very Icelandic."

Now Haeming smiled, satisfied with his decision to come here. Bodvarr was making it easy for him.

"Norway, too, is Christian now," Haeming said. "You must have been gone a while."

Bodvarr's face twitched as he tried not to react. Reaching over the armrest of his stone throne, he picked up a cup and gulped its contents noisily, then wiped his beard across his hairy arm.

150

"I am almost certain I knew your father," Bodvarr began again, wagging a knowing finger at Haeming. "Grim the Black, or something of the like?"

Haeming remained silent. *Grim Blackface,* he corrected in his head.

"Most assuredly not a Christian, this man I recall." Bodvarr spoke dreamily, studying the clouds above. "Truly a vile man. Hated by all. May I ask—I don't wish to offend—was your mother a slave?"

"It was a pleasure to meet you, Your Majesty," Haeming said with a nod, and began to turn. *Do nothing now—not enough men. Walk away.*

"Oh, well," Bodvarr continued, feigning surprise at the sudden departure, "just wished to be sure. When were you born, exactly?"

Haeming stopped and turned his head toward the self-declared king. "One thousand years after the death of Jesus Christ on the cross. Good day."

"I meant in what month, my friend!" Bodvarr called after him. "Was it in a harsh winter?"

Haeming and his men walked out of the village and heard the gates close behind them as a woman chastised Bodvarr.

"Are you *trying* to incite them?" she shrilled. "Do you not think for a moment of the *children?*"

Haeming's men retrieved their weapons and buckled them on. Haeming continued walking down the hill, taking in the beautiful view of the lower hilltops and, beyond them, the uneven blues of the ocean. *This was supposed to be mine. Everything we went through . . .*

Footsteps trotted up from behind, and he turned as Ulfr approached.

"Do you think he *wanted* you to kill him?" Ulfr asked.

"I believe he thought I would try but that others would then have grounds to kill me in my clumsy haste. He thought it a good opportunity to decapitate the invaders in his land while most of us were unarmed, and with so few of us present. Now he knows what happens next."

"And what happens next?" Ulfr asked. "Finn won't allow a full-scale unprovoked attack—there are women and children up there."

"Finn is not in charge," Haeming said as they continued down the wide path toward the Taino village.

"Yes, we know this, but . . . I just don't see how . . ."

"You don't need to see how yet," Haeming interrupted. "But there is only one path forward."

TWENTY-THREE

"Why are we stopping here?" Rheese asked, peering about at the quiet, seemingly impoverished neighborhood.

"We need to get some things," Garza answered, grabbing his cell phone from the center console. "Just stay in your seat."

Rheese glanced behind him to where Fando sat, arms spread across the back of the bench seat, eyes looking dead behind the semiopaque sunglasses. Rheese wished he could find a way to cut these two criminals loose.

Fando said softly, "Turn your fuckin' ugly-ass face around."

Rheese turned around, in the process catching a glimpse of Turner beside him. The fingers of his left hand, resting on the opal on his lap, quivered ever so slightly. The timer read "00:16." Outside the van, Garza was shaking hands with a skinny Cuban in cutoff jeans and a white tank top. The Cuban winced and acted as if Garza had squeezed his hand too tightly. Rheese thought he looked like a clown. Garza turned around and walked to the patchy front yard and paced for a few minutes before returning to the front door. The Cuban handed him a black backpack and two long, black cases. At that point, Garza turned and gave a quick nod toward the van.

Fando leaped up and climbed past Rheese to the driver's seat. "Stay put, asshole!" he growled. "Something's goin' down!"

As Fando started the engine Garza slid open the door and sent one of the big hard-shell cases whizzing past Rheese's head to the backseat, then opened up the other case on the floor.

"What's going on?" Rheese asked.

THE OPAL

"Shut up and sit tight," Garza said as he lifted from the case the biggest rifle Rheese had ever seen. He shoved in a loaded magazine, grabbed another one from the case, and slipped that into his hip pocket.

"Flip a bitch, slow," Garza said to Fando. "Meet me on the alley west end in two." Then he slammed the door and ran off down the block. Fando checked his watch and brought the van around to the other side of the street. A moment later, gunshots rang out.

"He's shooting!" Rheese gasped. "He's bloody shooting!"

Fando ignored him as more shots were fired. Then Fando took off, made a left at the end of the block—sending Turner's limp head against his window—and stopped the van.

"Open the door—now!" Fando shouted. Rheese jumped and fumbled with the handle until it finally slid open. Now he heard bursts of automatic fire. It sounded like an all-out war to him, and he ducked for cover. The van lurched forward, tires screeching, and Garza jumped in and slid the door shut.

"Who was that, bro?" Fando asked.

Garza ejected the magazine from the rifle and began reloading it with rounds. "American law. I think I only took out the vehicle, though. We need to get out of town," he said, reinserting the loaded magazine.

Rheese turned on his charming voice. "I . . . I think we've had a bit of a breakdown in communication amongst us, gentlemen. How can we better work together—you know, moving forward?"

Neither man bothered to answer.

★ ★ ★

Tzzzzz . . . tzzzzz . . . tzzzzz.

Matt inhaled sharply and his left hand jerked up off the gem, while his right went to the timer and stopped the pulses. He grabbed his other glove from the seat beside him and slipped it on. His eyes darted around nervously as he continued the heavy breaths, as though he'd been fully aware of the gunfight. He looked at Rheese, who seemed even more troubled than before.

"What happened?" Matt asked. "Did something happen?" He twisted around to see Garza in the backseat, a huge black rifle lying across his lap.

154

Matt knew that smell. It had to have been fired pretty recently. But who was Garza shooting at?

"Nothing to worry about," Garza replied while busily texting someone on his cell phone.

Matt peered past him, out the rear window. Something big had clearly happened, but no cars appeared to be following them. No massive plume of smoke rose from an exploded building. No plume of smoke . . . rising up into the clouds . . .

That piece-of-shit king—he just doomed his people. Matt was still shaken from Haeming's encounter in the village. He felt angry and eager to hurt someone or break something. The pure rage in Haeming's head . . . the plan that was percolating as he walked away . . . so many details all at once. He was thinking of women and children, but not how to keep them safe. No, he was orchestrating their inclusion in the coming mayhem. *What happened to protecting children?* Matt's stomach was churning, and he felt the bile in his throat. Fando's driving didn't help—he was taking corners too fast and making the van lurch violently as he accelerated and braked.

Matt thought back to his encounter with Atli, over an hour ago. *It's Haeming's encounter, damn it!* he reminded himself. *Gotta stop doing that.* Longer reading sessions could sometimes cause blurring, his own identity subordinating itself to the imprinted persona. It reminded him of something his father had tried to explain before Matt could grasp the concept.

"We *are* our memories," his dad had said. "But you need to distinguish between your memories and theirs." Looking back on those words while in his angst-ridden teens, Matt had wondered whether his father worried that by living inside the minds of depraved murderers and other criminals, he would somehow become one. He later learned that his father did indeed have this fear, caused in part by Matt's sudden change, at age 10, from being right-handed to fully ambidextrous. A serial arsonist Matt helped put behind bars had been left-handed. If Matt's imprint experiences left behind traits as important as hand dominance, what else was staying with him? This concept of imprints imprinting on *him* was one of the main reasons he avoided prolonged sessions.

What Matt thought his dad really meant was, *We are our memories, but I want you to ignore the bad ones I subject you to.*

Matt wondered whether he could kill a person. In self-defense, perhaps? He didn't think so, and he prayed he would never be put in a situation in which he had to decide.

He thought of being back home in Raleigh, close to his sister. He thought of his Xbox, just sitting there, lonely. The boxes he still had to unpack. His twelve-thousand-dollar mattress, the most comfortable thing upon which he had ever lain. He remembered Tuni's iron resolve never to touch it, for fear of imprinting on it. It made him regret ever telling her about the couch incident. She had asked, "Did you get *another* bloody new sofa?" "Yes," he told her. "It was quite disturbing to lie down on it and find myself kissing myself. It had to go." With that, he had inadvertently injected a heaping dose of his neurosis into her, and there was no going back. She saw the world through his eyes a little more each week, and it made him feel guilty. He could have lied to her to spare her such a burden, but he didn't. Maybe he had *wanted* her to feel guilty. For all her kind understanding of his quirks and rules and need for special handling, he had often suspected she was growing tired of it . . . or at least frustrated by their constant presence. There were no breaks when it came to a relationship with Matt. But this was probably all simply fear-based thinking, borne of his prior record with girlfriends, he consoled himself.

The van bashed into a particularly nasty pothole, jarring him out of his daze. He just hoped Tuni was safe. He believed he could handle the danger and distress better than she could. This in itself was a character change, he realized, for he had always been the weak one.

They drove in silence for another twenty minutes before Rheese asked Matt whether he had learned anything new.

"I did, yeah. There was a whole town here full of people from Norway, on top of a mountain. And not at all related to Haeming's group."

Rheese's tired, defeated eyes flashed with that old glint of excitement. "Indeed! An entire settlement? How long were they here?"

"Not sure. Must have been a while, though. They were pretty well settled in—had some sort of partnership with a native tribe nearby—houses and such."

"Could you find it, Turner?"

"Well, maybe. I'm not exactly sure what happens to it next. There might have been an incident. Some destruction. Hell, for all I know, the whole thing could have been destroyed."

Rheese frowned, "Is that so? 'La la la, Norse settlement in the bloody Caribbean . . . archeological gold . . . but, um, Doctor, I'm afraid there's zero evidence it was ever here.' Most convenient, don't you think?"

Matt bristled. "I don't know, Rheese. I tell you what I see, and you doubt it till I show you. I just don't know what, if anything, there'd be to show in this case."

"Wars and fires have destroyed the mightiest of history's cities, lad. There's always something to show."

"So you do believe me or you don't? Make up your damned mind."

Garza chuckled. "You tell him, Turner."

"In the absence of anything else concrete, I say we make it our next target after the opal tree site. Solorzano, might we soon find an eatery on our present course? I don't know about anyone else, but I'm bloody famished."

Fando's shades appeared in the mirror.

Garza said to Fando, "Yeah, let's find something in Pinar del Río before we head north."

✳ ✳ ✳

"Are we still headed to Viñales?" Rheese asked, not expecting a reply.

The farther they drove from Havana, the more anxious he felt. He suspected that his hired help were beginning to see just how little use they had for him. And now that Turner had quashed all their hopes of a big payoff, they had likely calculated that splitting a smaller reward two ways would pencil out a lot better. He had to keep them doubting Turner and, at the same time, hype his own worth as historian and fact-checker—at least until an opportunity for escape presented itself. He would make an effort to free Turner as well, but not if it meant being a hero. He had finally come to appreciate the greater potential the lad had for unlocking the deepest mysteries of human history—truths long lost to modern-day scholars—but if Turner didn't make it out of this predicament, the world would be no more unenlightened than it was today.

"Any idea where that sword is?" Garza asked Matt.

"Not really, no. Same as before. The imprints end when he puts the opal in that tree. In all honesty, he could have thrown the sword down next to it, or taken it back to Iceland with him. He cherished it, though, so I doubt he'd leave it willingly."

"How do you do this shit, anyway?" Garza said. "Just by touching stuff."

"Born with it, I guess. I don't know."

"Could you, like, touch me and read my mind?"

"No. It doesn't work on living things. They have their own . . . I don't know, energy, I guess."

"The doctor here told us he knocked you out for months by sticking something into your skin. What happens if you *swallow* something that has a story?"

"I don't know," Matt said. This line of questioning was beginning to worry him.

"What about water? Can water get a story in it? Then you get wet and you're stuck until it dries?"

"No, I don't think it works with water . . . or any liquid for that matter."

"You ever been a chick before?" Fando asked.

Matt sighed, though he much preferred this sort of juvenile question to Garza's worrisome exploration of his vulnerabilities. "Yes, many times." *Here it comes . . .*

"You ever get *banged* as a chick?" Fando smirked in the mirror, and his head moved as if to disco music.

Play it up. Be ashamed. "I . . . I don't remember."

Garza and Fando both burst out in gales of laughter.

"Ah, shit, homes, you got *nailed*!" Fando howled, and the van swerved a little. "Probably liked it, too."

Matt's expression said, *Real mature, guys*.

"Wait," Fando continued. "You ever been a gay dude?"

"*Basta*, Fando," Garza said. "*Hay un café*. Up there on the left."

Fando pulled off the road and into the dirt parking lot, leaving a plume of dust behind them. As they got out of the van, Fando's cell phone sounded a hip-hop ringtone.

"Bro, you still got signal?" Garza said.

Fando glanced at the screen, "Shit, man, it's Celia. What should I do?"

"You pick it up, tell her you miss her, how boring these things are, and that you're gonna be home soon. Hurry up, get it! We're going in."

＊ ＊ ＊

"Hey, baby," Fando said into the phone. "Whoa, whoa, slow down. I can't understand a word if you talk like that. What? Slow the hell down! Now, start over. Is Papo okay? Okay, so what's on the house? . . . uh-huh . . . uh-huh . . . Did you see who put it there? . . . Okay, calm down. Calm down and listen to me, baby, yeah? You go outside. Okay, good. You lookin' at that paper? I need you to walk right up to it and tear that shit off the garage door. You hear me? Tear that shit off right now. Nobody's takin' *shit* from us, yeah? . . . Good. Now, ball it up. Get the tape, too. Yeah, don't leave nuthin' . . . Nah, it don't matter if Little Man sees. He needs to see Mommy and Daddy don't get punked like that, ha ha ha . . . Okay, yeah, I'm gonna be home soon—like, a few days, all right? Stop cryin'. I gotta finish this thing up." Garza mouthed *bo-o-oring* to him through the café window. "These things are so damned borin', you know? Yeah, I will. Love you, too . . . Huh? *Who* called? He give a name? What'd he say?" Fando's teeth clenched and he swallowed hard. "Nah, that's a wrong number, baby. You were right. Hang up if someone like that calls again. It's bullshit. What? . . . God damn it baby, I gotta go! Ay—which card? You tried every single card and every single one doesn't . . . Well, how much were you tryin' to spend? Okay, well, it's a mistake, obviously. We have money. Yes! We have fuckin' money! Shut up with that shit! I gotta go."

He hung up. He could hear Junior starting to wail in the background. It was because his mom was crying, though. He was sensitive that way. Sees her freaking out about shit he doesn't understand, so he freaks out, too. And she was too selfish and unconscious to calm herself down to not scare the baby. That was why he didn't want to marry her high-drama ass.

Now the bank said they were taking the house? He knew fools who had been in their homes for over a year without making even half a payment. He skipped three to save up and they said they're foreclosing? Bullshit. That wasn't real. That was a tactic to make you pay when you didn't really have to. Regardless, it didn't matter. He was going to come home with a pile of cash. Screw that house, anyway. He'd get a better one. By the time Junior was old enough, all this bullshit would be in the past and he would be growing up as a spoiled-assed rich kid.

★ ★ ★

THE OPAL

Fando opened the glass door of the café, and an old cowbell hanging from a braid of pink yarn clanked.

"What's up?" Garza asked.

Fando shook his head and grabbed a takeout menu, mumbling to himself. "Goddamn bloodsuckers."

"How do I order just plain meat?" Rheese asked. "Without any sauce or soup or fur?"

"Tell her you want *flan con mojo*," Garza said. "If she argues, just say it again. Insist. Only way to get what you're looking for. *Flan . . . con . . . mojo.*"

Garza winked at Fando, but his friend's sense of humor had run dry.

Matt leaned in front of Rheese and put his finger down on the laminated menu taped to the counter, pointing at the number 11 meal. His eyes met Rheese's, and Rheese caught on. *Interesting gesture on the part of a hostage,* Rheese thought, imagining how annoyed he would have been to get whatever prank meal Garza was suggesting.

They were sitting at a table in the far corner of the room, which was empty of other patrons. They sat in awkward silence until the food came out, and then, a few minutes into the meal, Fando finally spoke.

"Yo, man, I think we're wastin' our time up on that hill."

Rheese nodded. "I concur fully with Mr. Solorzano."

"Shut up," Garza said, and turned back to Fando. "You think we should go straight to this mountain instead?"

"We should do whatever the punk thinks is gonna make money."

They both turned to Turner, who swallowed his half-chewed mouthful of black beans.

"Yeah?" he said after wiping his mouth with a napkin.

Garza asked, "You think there's money to be made on this mountain?"

Turner glanced at Rheese as if for backup, and Rheese gave a mildly optimistic shrug.

"It was a pretty big place," Turner told them. "Lots of people, buildings, and stuff. I'd definitely pick that over a logged and scraped hilltop."

"Not to say the hill is a lost cause," Rheese put in.

This time, Garza had only to look at him to shut him up.

They paid with cash and got back onto the paved road.

Rheese said, "I was just thinking—"

"Shut up," said Garza.

160

TWENTY-FOUR

Jivu Absko picked up the phone, saw that the call was from Spain, and answered in Spanish. *"¿Mande?"*

"Mr. Absko, we have a hit on the subject," the woman on the other end said.

"So I presumed. Please go ahead."

"Phone call from one of the spouses. They stopped in a small town called Pinar del Río, southwest of Havana. We called petrol stations and eating establishments in town and found the café where they ate. Would you like the address?"

"Pinar del Río, you say?" He brought up a detailed atlas of Cuba on a computer. "Ah, yes, I have it. Please inform our closest team of the address. Was the phone call regarding financial issues?"

"It was."

"Good. Have the accounts of the other two been handled as well?"

"They have."

"Very good. And what is your name?"

"Talena Ferrer, sir."

"Ah, Catalán?"

"Well . . . yes, sir."

"Talena Ferrer. Very nice, I like it. The people at the café who provided the information—were they forthcoming?"

"They were. And there is more."

"Good. Please have them rewarded appropriately, and do the same for yourself. What is the 'more'?"

"Thank you, sir. She stated that she overheard a bit of conversation between the two contractors and your acquaintance."

"Yes?"

"They argued about their destination. Viñales was mentioned."

"I already know about Viñales. Anything else?"

"They seemed to debate between 'the hill' and 'the mountain' as their destination, if that makes any sense."

"Hmm . . . interesting," he said. "I do not know what that means just yet, but please send that to the team, as well. Anything else?"

"That is all, sir."

"Thank you, Miss Ferrer."

He hung up and took a deep breath. This would end up a very lucrative day for Talena Ferrer and the lucky owner of a dirt-poor Cuban café. These little surprise benefactions made the nasty tasks more bearable. His other phone vibrated in his pocket, and he pulled it out. The screen bore a text message from another Spanish number. He replaced the phone in his pocket, then returned to the first phone. Scrolling through the recent call history, he found the contact he sought, and tapped it.

Two rings, and a voice said, "*Priviet?*"

Absko said in English, "Markus, may I speak with Vitaliy again?"

"Ah, of course, Mr. Absko, just one moment. He is swimming."

A moment later, "What can I do for you now, Jivu?"

"No, no, nothing like that," Absko said. "I wanted to let you know that everything is working out thanks to your cooperation. Please let me know when I can return the favor."

"Yes, sure, okay. That friend of yours—is he finished yet?"

"Not just yet, no. Anyway, thank you again."

"Yes, yes . . ."

Absko hung up and checked the call off his mental to-do list.

The mountain or the hill, he thought. *Mr. Turner must be learning much from the opal.*

TWENTY-FIVE

The helicopter, an old Soviet Mi-8, flew high over the forested hills. The cabin had been converted for civilian use but remained essentially spartan and painfully loud. Jess was strapped into one of the frontmost seats, across from Roger, staring at his cell phone. He grabbed the coil-corded transceiver from the partition in front of him and yelled into it.

"Will we have cellular service again?" He pressed it to his ear while plugging a finger into his other ear. Putting the handpiece to his mouth again, he said, "Cellular. Cell service. *Teléfono celular,*" then quickly put it back to his ear again. Nodding, he hung it on its clip.

Roger leaned across the open aisle. "What'd she say?"

"I think she said there's a tower a couple kilometers from our LZ, but that she doesn't know if it reaches that far."

Chuck and Núñez poked their heads forward. "What's the plan, boss?" Chuck shouted. "We gonna take out the two preemptively, or we gotta wait for provocation?"

Jess cocked his head sideways. "We're not authorized to so much as wipe our asses preemptively, but I tell you what: we get both of them in our sights at the same time, chances are we'll suddenly come under fire and have to take defensive measures."

"Defensive measures . . . gotcha," Chuck said, grinning.

"What about Dr. Rheese?" Núñez said.

Jess started to say something, but Roger interrupted. "We need him alive if at all possible, but he could be just as dangerous as the other two. We can't assume."

Paul appeared in the aisle between Núñez and Chuck. He yelled over the engine's whine, "I feel like I'm back at the kids' table at Thanksgiving."

Núñez ignored him. "Who's on sniper duty?"

"You requesting it?" Jess asked her.

She lifted her chin as if to say, *You got someone better?*

"You got it, then. Chuck, we both know you're for shit with anything other than a handgun. Rog, how's your marksmanship these days?"

Roger shook his head. "If it wasn't my kid's life on the line, I'd be a lot more confident about it. You always were a better shot than me, anyway."

Paul leaned farther forward. "I can shoot a dog out from under a flea's ass."

"Good to know," Jess said. "I'll do it, Rog. But that means you're down there with the ground team."

"That's where I want to be."

"Looks like we're landing," Núñez said.

It looked as though the bird was descending straight into dense jungle canopy, but as they moved along, a clearing appeared. Most of the ground was covered in gravel, and heavy equipment littered the area. No people were visible. A construction site trailer sat at the far edge of the clearing, and beside it was a half-loaded log truck. The helicopter touched down.

Jess grabbed the transceiver and said, "If your dispatch doesn't hear from us in twenty-four hours, can you come back here to this spot?" He listened but didn't hear anything.

The pilot appeared in the doorway and spoke to Núñez. "*¿Qué quiere decir?*"

Núñez replied in Spanish, and the pilot nodded, smiled curtly at Jess and Roger, and returned to her cockpit.

"You tell her twenty-four hours?" Jess asked as they stepped down to the ground.

"Yes, and she understands."

They unloaded their gear and watched with half-guarded eyes as the helicopter took off.

"You think anyone's in that trailer?" Chuck asked.

"No," Roger said. "They would have come out when they heard a damned chopper landing outside."

"Oh, yeah, duh."

The site was essentially what Larry had described: a logging base. To the north, a small road for the Cats, skidders, loaders, and log trucks; to the south, the only access road into the site. A steep hill rose up to the west, patterned evenly with young plantation redwoods. Eastward was more forest, though obscured by two tall cranelike vehicles.

Núñez scanned it all, then said, "Do we want to use one of the cranes for a sniping position, sir?"

Jess gazed up at the two towering arms. "If you want to climb your ass up one of 'em, be my guest. I sure as hell ain't."

"It's a prime spot, sir," she said. "Also provides quick access to the ground, if needed."

"How much time do we think we have?" Roger asked Jess.

Jess looked at his watch. "It's almost five p.m. Anywhere from four hours, if they sped the whole way without even pulling over to piss, up to eighteen hours, if they stopped to sleep and are taking their time. Either option is equally likely, I suppose. But either way, it's doubtful they'd be planning to hike it outta here before daylight. If they show up tonight, they probably plan to camp here or somewhere near. If they arrive in the morning, they'll probably march right through this place and down the hill Larry spoke of."

"How do we know he wasn't lying?" Chuck asked.

Roger and Núñez shared a glance, and Núñez said, "He wasn't lying."

TWENTY-SIX

Machine-crushed rocks popped and crackled beneath the van's tires as it crept slowly over the rugged fire road. Garza had his window down as he drove, letting the cool, moist air swirl in along with the sounds of the jungle. Matt couldn't see anything beyond the tree trunks that lined the road, glowing faintly red as the van's taillights passed. Behind Matt, Fando had his eyes fixed on a paper map illuminated by a penlight in his hovering fist.

"There should be a big turnout about two hundred yards up," he said.

Garza had the brights on and leaned forward over the steering wheel as he drove. Sure enough, a minute later the headlights shone across a broad clearing. The bare ground was scarred with deep trenches and three-foot-high walls of sunbaked mud. It was clear that vehicles much larger than the van had driven all over this ground during or after a big storm, rendering it essentially unnavigable to a passenger van.

"Are we supposed to stop *here*?" Garza asked as they passed the clearing.

"Well, you could take the road to the end if you want, but it just curves left in another hundred yards and then dead-ends."

"I don't like a dead end," Garza replied.

"Exactly."

Matt said, "There was a flat area back there—not too big, but enough to park off the road."

Garza stopped the van, threw an arm over the passenger headrest, and said to Matt, "Don't try to be helpful to an enemy. It doesn't endear you to them—just reveals weakness."

Matt swallowed and said, "I'll remember that for next time."

Garza backed into the flat space.

"Hmph," Fando murmured. "Next time . . ."

Matt had to wonder whether they were up here not just to find potential riches but also to execute him, and ditch the body where no one would ever find it. Garza had said as much, but at the time, it had come off as an empty threat.

Garza killed the engine and lights, and they all stepped out into the brisk mountain air. Matt felt farther away from civilization than ever before. There was no sound of distant cars passing, no airplanes overhead, no one to wonder about the echoing crack of a gunshot. He laughed halfheartedly inside at the fact that the closest thing he had to a friend up here was the loathsome Dr. Rheese. As his eyes adjusted to the starlight he looked around. The treetops silhouetted against the sky told him where the woods began and the truck-turnaround clearing ended. Garza read his mind.

"We're both faster than you, and a bullet beats everyone."

"If I was going to run, I would have done it when there was actually somewhere to go," Matt replied.

Garza chuckled. "You say that now 'cause you wish you had."

Matt hated to think that someone like Garza could be smarter than him. He preferred to think of both Garza and Fando as mindless thugs, but that wouldn't be honest—or wise.

They pulled out duffels and a big rolled-up tarp. Fando opened a molded plastic case and pulled out a rattling helmet contraption with two scopelike cylinders protruding from the front. They had to be night-vision goggles.

Fando put one on, clicked a switch, and scanned the area. "Nothing moving on the ground," he said.

"Let's camp away from the road," Garza said.

Matt reached for his suitcase, but Garza pulled the hatch down and slammed it shut.

"You don't need anything from there," he said. Then, turning to Rheese, he paused for a few seconds before saying, "You need anything, Doctor?"

"Well, if it's to be a campout, we should have our sleeping bags. We did bring one for Turner as well."

Garza thought for another moment, then reopened the hatch. Rheese shuffled in and grabbed the two sleeping bags, tossing one to Matt. Matt wondered, was Garza growing progressively colder with him? Perhaps dehumanizing him to make killing him easier?

Garza said, "Let's go."

Everyone followed Fando as he dropped into a long, waist-deep trench. The dry mud had kept the mold of the tracked vehicles that first pressed the path into being. He reached a double X where four tracks crossed, and continued where the channel resumed. The track curved right before the treeline, and everyone climbed out and headed into the forest. The duff beneath them squished a little as they walked—nothing like the dry, crackling twigs and pine straw of the drier temperate woods back home. As they walked, Matt could smell Fando's scent trail of sour sweat and futile deodorant. A few minutes later, Fando spotted a moderately flat location surrounded by thick tree trunks.

"You two have a seat," Garza said, tossing his bags down.

"Men gotta set shit up," Fando muttered.

The ground was mossy and wet and quickly seeped into Matt's jeans and gloves. He took off a glove and slid a hand into the soft mush of decaying leaves, pine needles, soil, and who knew what else. He was at once fascinated and mildly horrified, imagining the kinds of creatures and fungi and slime molds he was touching. He closed his eyes, inhaled deeply, and held it in. It was a rare gift when he could touch things in the outside world without worry. He pushed out the creeping idea that this could be his last moment of genuine pleasure in the world, and wiggled his fingers around. He enjoyed the smell, too. The scent of fertility, he imagined this must be. And then he realized that he recognized that same earthy smell. Haeming the Icelander had been in this area, maybe a thousand years ago, and inhaled precisely this rich scent.

He slid his hand out of the compost and tried to dig the bits out from under his fingernails as he watched Garza and Fando straighten out a large tarp on the ground.

"Should we stake it, bro?" Fando said.

"Yeah, but we need a rock. I'm the dumbass that forgot a mallet."

The gunshot came from Matt and Rheese's left. Garza's blood, brain tissue, and skull fragments sprayed to their right.

✱ ✱ ✱

Oliver handed Tuni a headset with a boom mic and pointed out the pinch-activated buttons at the base of the boom. They were riding in a large, bouncing military-type truck with a canvas-covered bed. Before her and to her right sat twelve gun-wielding Cuban men with nothing more interesting than her to look at—and, apparently, no conditioning that prompted them to look away when glared at. At first glance, the men appeared to be soldiers, but their haphazard garb—some with camouflage khakis or T-shirts, others with cargo pants of various colors—struck Tuni as the attire of mere hired guns.

"Is Abel on this?" Tuni said to Oliver, sitting across from her. He nodded and redemonstrated the pinch method on his own boom mic. She squeezed it and heard the click. "Abel, are you there?" She let go.

"I hear you, Tuni. Everything all right?" He was in the cab of the truck in front of theirs, with Isaiah behind the wheel, and another fifteen men in back.

"Yes. Are we almost there?"

"That's what I was going to tell you, yes. We have information that they are in one of two locations. You'll go with Oliver's team to one, and I will go to the other with mine. We will meet up when they are sighted."

Tuni looked around at the men, then turned toward the wall, hunching over and cupping the mic. "I don't know about this," she whispered. "How can we know that this won't end up a big gunfight with Matt getting hit by one of these . . . *guys*?"

"Because their weapons aren't loaded," Abel replied. "Only mine, Isaiah's, and Oliver's. These men are a show of strength only. I would not trust them in so sensitive a situation, either. Now, my men, I trust—they will not fire unless the outcome is certain."

Tuni nodded and wiped away a tear before it fell, "Okay, Abel, thank you," she said. "I mean it."

"Of course, Tuni. But know that you're assisting here, too. Oliver has seen photos of Rheese and Matthew, but he doesn't make a move until you approve. Good?"

Oliver smiled kindly, and Tuni realized that his headset received everything they were saying. She liked Oliver and couldn't imagine him actually shooting someone. He was the gentle sort, and being essentially mute, he relied largely on exaggerated facial expressions to communicate. When needed, he spoke with his breath, in a whisper that further enhanced his kindly image.

"Good, yes," Tuni said. "I trust he will do his job, with Matthew's safety as his highest priority."

170

Oliver nodded to her.

"We are turning off the road now," Abel said. "Your truck will continue for a few minutes before turning right up the hill. I'll see you soon."

The radio crackled off, and she heard Abel's diesel truck shifting gears as it slowed, turned off the main road, and began bouncing and clanking behind her truck. *If they're up here, they're going to hear us coming a mile away*, she thought. A moment later, she was pushed backward as her truck swung right onto an even rougher surface. In the sliver between the canvas cover and the beating rear flap, she could see that the trees were still green in the light of the sunset.

A few minutes later, the truck slowed and the men with her stiffened, readying themselves for action. Oliver stood up, walked carefully to the back, and peered outside. Reaching up to his mic, he clicked it twice, and Tuni heard the two bursts of static in her headset. He grasped a metal upright beside him one second before the truck lurched forward again.

They parked a couple of minutes later, and everyone piled out. They were at a dead end and had nowhere to hide the truck. Tuni glanced at her watch: 8:18 p.m.

✳ ✳ ✳

Núñez looked at her watch: 8:18 p.m. From her vantage point at the top of the crane's boom, she could see the sun sinking into the ocean. Her left boot sat cradled in the loop of a thick steel cable, her right knee tucked tight against her breast, while her right shin sat nestled in the channel of a huge pulley. It was the best she could do to stabilize herself. The crane was outfitted for winching logs up hills, not carrying people in comfort. The cramped position meant that every ten minutes or so, she must balance the rifle in front of her and switch legs. Now she felt the impending need to pee.

MARSOC was testing her, she used to suspect—bouncing her from team to team, mission to mission. Just two months ago, she had been in a burka in an Afghan market; last year, on an aborted infiltration of North Korea— aborted once she and four others had already reached the shore. That one, she had decided, was a poke test of the North Koreans' coastal surveillance and

defenses. And now this civilian thing. It meant that her real goal was finally presenting itself, as her original guidance officer had told her it would. The CIA was now testing, and—for a while, at least—maybe even watching.

She took a deep breath and gazed across the site to the adjacent hill, where Jess had concealed himself somewhere among the scrubby foliage. She knew roughly where he was, but not precisely.

She caught the whine of an approaching diesel engine.

"Hear that?" she said into her walkie-talkie.

Jess's voice said, "Yeah. Visual? Sounds like a construction vehicle."

"What is that?" Roger's voice cut in.

Headlights swept across the trees as a truck came into view on the road's final approach.

"Military," Núñez said.

"Shit!" Jess muttered. "Stay out of sight."

The truck squealed to a stop, blocking the road right at the exit. The driver shut off the engine, stepped out, and looked around. Others began streaming from the back of the truck, rifles in hand.

"What do you suppose they're looking for?" Roger said.

"Maybe just some routine check?" Jess said.

The driver made a megaphone of his hands and called out in a strange accent, "Rosher Tuhner!"

"What the . . . ?" Jess said.

"I'm going," Roger replied.

Núñez popped in. "I don't know if that's a good idea, sir."

"It's okay," Roger replied. "I'm bringing Chuck with me. You guys just cover us."

Núñez said to herself, *Cover against about twenty soldiers—right . . .*

Jess watched through his scope as Roger appeared from the woods beside the truck. He said into his walkie, "Paul, you got visual?"

"Yeah, but this is stupid."

Roger walked out with his hands in front of him, Chuck right behind him with a shotgun pointed toward the ground.

"Who are you?" Roger said as he approached.

The driver peered at him a moment, then glanced back at the windshield of the truck. Roger looked, too, but made out only the vague outline of a passenger still sitting inside.

"We are looking for your son, too."

Chuck repeated the man's message into his radio for the others.

"Izzat so?" Roger said.

"Yes. Workers spot a silver van enter base camp north of here." He pointed beyond Roger, where the recently logged hill dropped off.

Roger glanced back, then said, "So why would you come up here if they're down there?"

"Our other team went that way. We are make perimeter. Cut off escape routes. If you want, you stay up here to aid us."

Chuck echoed this for the rest of the team. Jess's voice said, "Screw that!"

Roger said, "Yeah. Thanks, and all that, but I think we'll head down where my son is before there's a goddamn shoot-out. You guys even trained for hostage rescue?"

The man shrugged. "Some. We are having many skilled soldier."

Roger raised his eyebrows in a pantomime of being impressed. "I bet. You just tell your people to keep their fingers off the triggers, hear me?"

"Do they have a precise location?" Jess asked.

Hearing the question, the man shook his head apologetically and simply pointed toward the hill again.

"Come on down, Núñez," Jess said. "Meet up at the north end of the site, everyone."

Strapping the rifle across her back, Núñez slid down the crane's vertical beam, feeling the friction heat up her leather gloves as she descended. Then she slipped into the bushes to pee before going to the designated spot.

They all gazed downhill. The steep decline studded with tree stumps reminded Núñez of a gigantic stubbled chin.

"Looks like a giant Plinko game," Paul said. "You know . . . if *Chuck* slips."

"This is an unfavorable change, sir," Núñez said. "The advantage is now theirs."

"Not if they still don't know we're coming," Jess said.

"I don't care about any of that," Roger said, starting down the hill. "We need to get down there before these morons get my son killed."

The others spread out and followed him down the slope.

★ ★ ★

Isaiah watched the last American head disappear down the slope and opened the driver's-side door of the truck. Abel was talking on the radio.

". . . positions down the road. If they spot the truck, they should already be past you. Good."

Isaiah said, "What now for us?"

"We wait here until the Americans figure out they went the wrong way. We set up a position facing north."

"And when they come back . . . ?"

"We play dumb. They won't question it."

"And Oliver?"

"He has his instructions."

✳ ✳ ✳

Tiny needles of light pierced the trees from up the road. Oliver lowered his head, and Tuni followed suit. Her eyes shifted left across the road, where the other half of the men hid in the undergrowth. Just as the van came into view it stopped, well before its lights landed on the parked truck around the bend. She could hear a man's voice but couldn't make out the words. Then the van reversed.

"Did they spot us?" she whispered in Oliver's ear, but he shushed her and peered through his binoculars.

The headlights suddenly shined right on them, and Tuni jumped. Oliver put a hand on her back and a finger to his lips as first the lights turned off, then the engine, and four men got out of the van. Their voices carried, but still she couldn't catch the words. Oliver handed her the binoculars, and she peered through them. And there, standing at the back of the van, she saw Matthew. She couldn't make out his face or the color of his clothes, but she recognized his shape and the way he wore his beanie low, covering his neck, with the turtleneck layered over it. How many times had she rearranged that overlap for him when it came apart and exposed his bare skin? Then the liftgate swung open, and a light came on and there he was. She could even see his expression of defeated irritation. Swallowing, she fought back the tears. This was not the time.

Oliver put out his hand, and she gave the binoculars back. A moment later, Matt and his captors had walked out of view. Oliver had his men wait in silence for several minutes. It made Tuni crazy to have Matt practically within spitting distance and then watch him walk away.

Oliver finally sat up, picked up the scoped rifle from the log beside him, rechecked the breech, and signaled the men to move out. They crossed the road, and Oliver tapped six men to go right, the other six left. As the Cubans melted into the woods with scarcely a sound, Oliver looked at Tuni for a second, then pulled a small black handgun from his waistband and handed it to her. She held it up close to her face to make out its details. A small lever above the trigger guard pointed to a red dot at twelve o'clock, not to the white one at nine.

Gently, Oliver pulled her hand away from her face, pointed the weapon at a downward angle, and pulled her forefinger away from the trigger, repositioning it straight out along the barrel. She took a deep breath and nodded apologetically, and he gave her another comforting smile before setting off into the woods again, staying low. She followed in the same fashion.

Soon they could hear talking, and Oliver squatted down and duckwalked forward. Tuni got on all fours and felt the wet moss and duff soak through her pant knees. They stopped again. Oliver pointed, and she craned her neck sideways to see around a tree. Flashlight beams zipped around ahead of them, and she saw and heard two men shaking out a large tarp. Matt and Rheese were sitting with their backs against the buttress roots of an enormous tree.

Oliver eased down onto his bum in the dirt and crossed his legs, placing his elbows on his knees to aim the rifle. It had a very narrow scope on the top—nothing like what Tuni had seen in the movies. She hoped he knew what he was doing.

The rifle went off with an ear-shattering roar. Through the ringing in her head, Tuni heard, as if underwater, someone shout "Danny!"

Oliver pulled back a knob on the rifle and aimed again. The same voice shrieked a howling curse, and gunshots came back at them in quick succession.

Oliver pushed Tuni's head down. She could hear more yelling and swearing, but the return fire had stopped. Oliver cracked off another shot, and the forest seemed to go silent.

Tuni cautiously raised her head, spitting dirt and bits of dead leaf and who knew what else.

"Did you get them?" she whispered.

Oliver looked solemnly at her. She stood up and looked at the site. A dropped flashlight lit the base of a tree and some of the ground where Matt and Rheese had sat. They were gone, and all was quiet but the high-pitched ringing in Tuni's ears.

"We have to go after them!" she hissed to Oliver. "Does Abel know? Where are the others? Why are we just sitting here?" She squeezed the buttons on her headset. "Abel . . . Abel, Oliver got one of them, but Rheese and the other one ran off with Matthew!" She waited for him to reply. "Abel, are you there? Can you hear me?"

Oliver looked around helplessly. Tuni grabbed him by the forearm and said, "C'mon!" They ran up to the little campsite, and Tuni saw the dead man's shoulder holster. After picking up the flashlight, she pushed the body over, trying not to look at the partially destroyed head, and yanked the handgun until it came out.

"Will this . . . *work* . . . if I need it to?" she said.

Oliver took it, checked a few things, then handed it back to her with a nod. She gave Oliver his own pistol back and, with the new one in hand, took off running in the direction she thought they had gone.

* * *

"What the f . . . ?" Chuck gasped when a shot rang out behind them.

The group stopped. They had scrambled down to the base of the hill, crossed a low stream, and were rounding the base of another stump-speckled hill. A quick burst of semi-automatic gunfire followed, then another rifle shot.

"That's way past the logging site," Núñez said.

"Lying sons of bitches!" Roger roared, and began pounding back up the clear-cut hill.

Jess looked confused for a second until Paul ran past him, saying, "They either lied or were stupid. Either way, they suck."

* * *

Abel's headset crackled, and Tuni came on, telling him Oliver had shot one of them. Isaiah heard it, too, and looked at Abel.

"Abel, are you there? Can you hear me?"

Abel waved his finger at Isaiah and then pressed it to lips.

∗ ∗ ∗

"Move, Rheese, God damn it," Fando growled. "If you can't double that speed, I'm better off blowing yer bald-ass head off."

Rheese was struggling. Matt tried to help by pushing him along, but Rheese kept swatting his hands away, saying, "I'm fine, blast it!"

"Go right," Fando ordered. "Hard right. Harder!"

The course he had taken them, beginning downhill and away from the shooter, had changed several times. Fando was cursing in Spanish and wailing "Danny!" every now and then as they crashed through the woods, tripping over each other, lungs burning, legs cramping. Matt felt himself overheating under the knit cap, turtleneck, and undershirt. He pulled off the hat and stuffed it in his pocket, untucked his undershirt, and held it up to let the cool air in.

"Faster!" Fando barked. "Hard left!"

Matt couldn't keep track, but as far as he could tell, they had gone perhaps a mile east of the site and two miles south, gradually ascending the slope at a diagonal angle. The turns seemed random, yet consistently moving away from the campsite.

"Stop!" Fando ordered. "Sit down!"

Matt and Rheese dropped immediately. They had stopped in a small clearing where moonlight shone between two distant treetops. Fando didn't seem all that tired, as if his heavy breathing was more emotional than physical. He surveyed the area behind them as he reloaded the magazine to his pistol.

Matt watched, counting the rounds as they went in. He didn't know why, but he remembered the good guy in cheesy movies telling the bad guy that the bad guy was all out. The villain would laugh knowingly and pull the trigger, then hear the click as the gun dry-fired, whereupon the hero would take him out, one way or another.

Fando slapped the magazine back in, released the slide, and thrust the gun just under Matt's jaw. *Please don't touch,* Matt prayed. *That's gotta have an imprint.*

"Did you see 'em, you little punk? You see 'em comin' and not say nothin'?"

Matt looked him dead in the eyes and shook his head. He swallowed and felt his Adam's apple graze the gun's muzzle. A quick dizzy spell came and went—the imprint, letting him know it was in there, waiting for him. Fando pressed his sweaty forehead against Matt's, and his hot, rancid breath filled Matt's nostrils.

"You little bastard, you know you wouldn't have said shit."

He slammed the butt of the gun into Matt's nose, and something crunched. Blood flowed both ways: down into his throat, and out over his lips and chin.

"We didn't see anything, Solorzano," Rheese said. "Leave him alone! He's the bloody victim in this, for Christ's sake. Anyway, who the hell would be up here? And bloody shooting at us?"

Matt forced an eye open and watched Fando's head turn. He pushed off Matt, stepped calmly over to Rheese, and smacked him across the side of the head with the gun. It went off, and for an instant all three of them thought Rheese had been shot. Then, after a strange pause, Fando hit Rheese again with the gun, then again, harder, faster, kicking, beating. Rheese curled up into a ball, groaning, as Matt looked on in horror. Unless someone or something intervened, Fando was going to beat him to death, right here and now, simply because he had told Fando to leave Matt alone.

Matt looked around for a branch or rock big enough to do damage with a single blow, because he might not get the chance for a second. He saw a grapefruit-size rock, half buried in the roots of a big fern.

Fando was swinging away with the pistol again. Matt heard a rib crack and imagined other things bursting. Rheese wasn't moaning or pleading anymore. Matt looked back down at the rock and realized that it was now or never. His fingers scrabbled into the soil, curled under the rock, and pried it out, and with Fando's back to him, he raised it over his head and lunged. As he brought it down, he yelled, "Get off him!" It hit hard, though not on the head, where Matt had hoped, but between the shoulders. Fando cried out as he went sprawling on top of Rheese. Swearing, he got to his feet and turned toward Matt.

"I honestly didn't think you had an ounce of fight in you, punk," he said, wiping Rheese's blood from his face with his shirtsleeve. Behind him, Rheese coughed and let out a wheezing moan. "Now what? I bet that's what yer thinkin'. Hadn't thought past swingin' the stupid rock."

"Yeah, not really," Matt replied.

Fando just stood there, eyes locked on Matt. Matt supposed this was better than simply shifting the beating to him, but then, maybe the guy was just thinking of a creative way to kill him.

"Hey, where's the jewel?" Fando suddenly asked.

"I think Rheese still has it."

Fando stepped over to Rheese and pried him out of his fetal pose, then started digging through his pockets. Rheese moaned and coughed blood.

"Where is it, you old bastard?"

Rheese coughed and spat. "Sin m-m ba-a-ag . . ."

"In yer bag?" Fando looked around. "Where the hell's yer bag?"

Rheese choked again and made a sound that may have been laughter, though it quickly deteriorated into more groaning.

"It's back with Gar—. . ." Matt began. "Back where we were going to, uh . . ."

Fando's hands went up to his face, and he pulled at his cheeks as a stifled scream erupted inside his throat.

"Strip!" Fando shouted.

"What?"

"Strip, you little piece of shit! Yer clothes! Off, all of 'em!"

Matt pulled his turtleneck off, then the white undershirt. He hesitated for a second.

"Keep going, God damn it!"

Sitting down on a fallen tree, Matt took off his shoes and stuffed his socks inside before shucking off his jeans. He stood there in his navy boxer briefs with a white waistband.

"You ain't done, punk."

"Whah yuh gonna d'now? Rape 'im?"

There stood Rheese, one eye open. Somehow, he had gotten to his feet and shambled over to them.

Fando cackled, then squatted down in front of Rheese.

"I can't wait to kill you, old man. I would do it right fuckin' now if it wasn't gonna put yer fat ass outa yer misery. How 'bout this, though, for a taste o' what's to come?" Fando pulled the long knife from his belt and plunged it through Rheese's calf so that it poked out the other side. As Rheese let out a raspy cry, Fando said to Matt, "Now strip *him*."

"I'll need my gloves back on."

Fando gave him an annoyed wave of consent, then went back to scanning around them nervously. Matt slipped his gloves back on and went to Rheese, who was gasping for air and gawking at his calf with disbelief.

After another minute Rheese seemed to calm a little. Matt crouched down beside him, and Rheese panted, "Crehfurry, lad."

Matt nodded. "Oh, I'll be careful."

He started with Rheese's plaid button-down, meticulously avoiding touching any of Rheese's clothes with his bare skin. Then he peeled off the sweat-soaked white undershirt. As Matt moved to the trousers, Rheese forced himself onto his back with a pained grunt. He had only his left eye open, out of Fando's sight. Matt caught it, and Rheese gave a quick leftward glance before locking eyes with Matt again. Matt looked and spotted it, all but covered in soil and pine needles. The opal.

"Hurry the fuck up!" Fando shouted. "Yer not tryin' to seduce the old bastard!"

Matt moved to Rheese's feet and pulled the slacks off by the cuffs as Rheese struggled to lift his bum off the ground. Then came the socks. Matt stood back up, silently refusing to remove the remaining white briefs.

As Rheese curled back up on the ground Fando shrugged and gathered up all the clothes into a big pile. He peered up at Matt, who just stood there watching.

"Take the gloves off and sit yer ass back down." He looked at Rheese and said, "Guess we know where all yer hair went. Damn."

Matt tossed his gloves onto the pile of clothes and sat back down, wondering what Fando had planned. Would he make them strip just to shoot them? He watched as Fando picked through the clothes and pulled out Rheese's rank-smelling socks. Their eyes met for a second; then Fando tossed one of the socks at Matt's face. Matt didn't duck fast enough, and he slumped back onto the ground and lay there, limp, with the sock across his face.

★ ★ ★

Fando made a "hmph" sound and seemed to congratulate himself. He looked at Rheese, then stepped over to him and kicked him hard in the back. Rheese hardly responded. Taking the other sock, he tied it around Rheese's head, effectively gagging him. Then he looked at his watch, grabbed the little pile of clothes, and took off running, back the way they had come.

TWENTY-SEVEN

"We're bloody lost," Tuni said. "Abel, can you hear me now? Abel, are you there?"

Still no answer. They began hiking back, Oliver's eyes fixed to the ground in search of their previous steps. Up the hill, perhaps a mile away, a gunshot echoed. They looked at each other, turned, and ran straight toward it.

Tuni's headset crackled. "Tuni, are you there?" It was Abel. "Are you all right?"

She slowed to a fast walk and replied with great relief, "Yes, I'm here! Been trying to reach you. Oliver and I got separated from the rest of the group after he shot one of the guards. Rheese and the other one got away with Matthew, and we chased but can't find them. But we just heard a shot."

"Yes, yes. Was it anywhere near you?"

They stopped walking, "It sounded fairly close. I don't know, maybe a . . ." She made an inquiring face to Oliver. He whispered, "About a mile south," and she relayed.

"Understood," Abel said. "I've pushed my team east, following your initial gunfire, and we have slowly moved toward you in a line. If anyone comes this way, we will capture them. Your men have been waiting at your truck. I'm sending half of them to rendezvous with you, so watch for their flashlights. Do not attempt to rescue Matthew by yourselves, understood? Stay away from that gunfire."

"Understood."

"That last gunshot made me worry."

"Me, too," she said, but then realized Abel's concern at the moment was for her, not Matthew. "We'll wait for the men."

She turned toward Oliver, the whites of his eyes and a shine on his forehead reflecting the moonlight. He glanced at his watch. As she stood there in the dark with only the sounds of insects and her heartbeat in her ears, she found her fear for Matthew's safety spreading to her own vulnerability. The adrenaline of the past hour had shielded her from such realities, but no more. The night appeared darker, the air colder, and she couldn't be farther from civilization.

✶ ✶ ✶

"There's another one," Roger wheezed, hands on his knees.

They had just made it back up to the logging site. No sign of Cuban troops anywhere.

"You want me to keep moving, sir?" Núñez said. Her sweaty brow shone in the moonlight, but she didn't sound the least bit winded.

"I can go with her," Paul added, breathing heavily. "I'll last."

Roger nodded, and the two jogged across the site to where the steep hill resumed southward.

Jess knelt beside Roger while Chuck drank from his canteen.

"What do you wanna do, Rog?" Jess asked. "I can't have you killing your heart out here."

"Just need . . . catch my . . . just gimme a . . ."

"C'mon, bud, hunched over isn't a good position. Put your arms up, hands behind your head. Feel better?"

"Feel like I'm being arrested."

They could see the dim shapes of Paul and Núñez working their way up the next slope, moving through shadows and behind trees. The gibbous moon behind them improved the visibility, but that meant that their quarry could see equally well.

"Just one more minute," Roger said. "Jess, you don't think that single shot . . . you know, just one shot out of nowhere—"

"Nah, Rog, I don't think that. There's no future thinking that."

"Yeah, all right."

Jess glanced nervously up at the tree-covered slope.

"Go catch up with them," Roger said. "Chuck and I'll be right behind you guys in a minute."

"You sure?" Jess said, though he didn't want the only son of another friend, Ben Kleindorf, to be out there without him. Sure, Núñez was supremely capable, but Paul was *his* responsibility.

Roger smiled and waved him off. "Go on. I'll say it again: this whole thing goes so far beyond any kind of favor I could ever return."

Jess winked as he trotted off. "Brewskis for life, my friend, that's all I ask."

* * *

Abel was looking at the almost-campsite where Rheese had clearly been. A dead man with part of his head missing lay sprawled on a blood-drenched tarp. A duffel bag contained survival food, digging equipment, and weapons. On the ground lay still-rolled sleeping bags, and a pack clearly owned by Dr. Garrett Rheese. The pack held clothing, a tablet computer, maps, pens, compass—pretty standard stuff—but no opal. He had the men comb through the area for it, but it wasn't here. They had also searched the silver van parked off the road, but it wasn't there either, which meant that it had probably gone with the three when they fled.

"Did you check Mr. Garza?" Abel asked Isaiah. Isaiah nodded.

He was furious with Oliver for letting Tuni go after them. She was only supposed to observe from afar—see Matthew, see their efforts to rescue him. But now she was in real danger. He wished he had kept her with him, but then, that would have complicated other aspects of the plan. He needed to make some calls, but he had no cellular signal.

TWENTY-EIGHT

Ears ringing, head in agony. Bleeding. Warm where it's coming out; cold where it's spread. He's going to kill me . . . no way to stop this! Oh, God, no, it isn't right! I don't bloody deserve this! My side . . . something broke . . . won't stop . . . This will never stop! Turner could do something, but why should he? Dear God, he's going to get this next. Ow. Oh, God no! He stopped . . . Why did he stop? Why can't I hear? Whole body hot. Am I even alive? There is only pain—no smell, no sound, no sight, only pain. This could be it . . . no, it can't be.

"Tuhner"

My own voice . . . No, Rheese's voice. My clothes are being taken off now. Rheese's clothes. I'm taking Rheese's clothes off.

"Tuhner, can you hear *Hurry the fuck up!* Just hold *seduce the old bastard!*"

Matt felt his pants sliding down, and pain all over his body—Rheese's body, Rheese's pants sliding down. Through one eye—Rheese's eye from the imprint—Matt could see his nearly-naked self, undressing Rheese. *I look terrible,* he observed. *And completely vulnerable.* "Hang on, almuss there, lad." *Rheese talking, but not me—Rheese, not the imprint of Rheese. I hear real Rheese, outside the imprint! Can I move my body? Open my eyes?*

Matt felt the first sock peel off Rheese's foot. He tried to open his eyes but couldn't feel them. It was as though they didn't exist. But then he became aware of Rheese's closed right eye. It hurt and had stinging sweat and blood in it. He imagined that he could somehow control Rheese's right eye in the imprint. In his head, he said, *Open up, eye!*

THE OPAL

And it happened. Impossible, but it happened. *No, wait, wrong eye. That must have been when Rheese opened his left eye. I didn't have anything to do with that.*

Through the left eye, he watched himself pulling off Rheese's other sock. But then he suddenly realized something. With his *own* right eye he could see the darkness of the sock on his face, and a bit of light from the side. And he could smell it! Ripe and disgusting.

Left eye: view of Matt standing up . . . fading. The imprint was sliding into dark space.

Right eye: the sock sliding off to the right. He could even feel it on his face. This was unprecedented. That was at least four senses of his own body that he was able to use while still reading an imprint. His body returned to him completely, and he turned to see Rheese, dirty, battered, and exhausted, right beside him with the sock in hand.

"Fando ran off, lad. We need to get out of here before he returns."

Matt glanced around—their clothes were gone. "Can you even walk?"

"It bloody hurts, not sure what works. I . . . I might be bleeding inside . . . and I think bad things happened to these back ribs . . ." He reached around under his arm and winced from some tentative probing. "And this bleeding—I don't know . . . I need a hospital." He poked beside the knife's exit wound on the inside of his calf, then pulled his knee inward to see the other side.

"Tie that sock around it for now," Matt said, and Rheese complied without hesitation. When he was done, he reached behind him. His hand reappeared with the opal cradled in the palm. "At least you kept that."

Rheese looked at it. "It's something, I suppose, for all this."

"You're probably imprinting on it right now, just so you know."

"Ack, the historical record! And me in my skivvies. No, thank you." He picked up the other sock and dropped the opal inside. "Let's go. No idea when that psychopath will be back."

Matt stood up and was helping Rheese to his feet when a voice right behind Rheese made him jump.

"Yeah, who knows? It could be any fuckin' second."

It was Fando. He apparently hadn't gone far—perhaps just circled back and waited. He walked a few steps downhill toward them. He wore a smug grin on his face, his gun in hand.

"Hand me that nasty-ass sock," he said.

Rheese paused, perhaps debating whether hurling the thing off into the dark would help them in any way. Apparently deciding against it, he lobbed it into Fando's free hand.

"Lots of people out here lookin' for you, Turner. They had to have heard that shot earlier. Could run up on us any second." He stuffed the sock into his pocket. "So here I am, thinkin', do I just book it outta here? Go home? But people are lookin' for me back home. And then I think how yer gonna go home to yer big-ass house, thinkin' how lucky you are to be alive, and how I'm off in Bumfuck, East Nowhere, tryin' to keep from gettin' caught, or maybe I already been caught and I'm rottin' in some jail, with my kid thinkin' Daddy's a piece-of-shit loser, and my woman gettin' banged by some new punk-ass fool. And I start gettin' all these, like, visuals in my head of her with some other dude sweatin' on her and her doin' stuff to him, and she *likes* it, even, and thinks this dude ain't a loser like that other son of a bitch—what was his name . . . Fernando? Oh, yeah! And I think now, no, screw that shit! That ain't a life! I ain't got no brother." His voice cracked on this last word. "My best friend just got killed 'cause of both you *pinches pendejos*. So then I ask myself—just now I asked myself—'Self, how you get outa this goddamn shit pot?' And you know what the answer was?"

Matt said, "Let us go?"

Fando's mouth flashed a humorless smile. "Please shoot me in the face."

"What . . . ?" Matt said, and Rheese echoed him.

"That's all I hear," Fando went on. "Every time shit comes out of yer mouth, that's all I hear: 'Please, sir, shoot me in the face.'"

"I didn't mean . . ."

"Yeah, whatever—shut up. The answer was, there might be no goddamn way out of this. You gotta take yer chances. But if both of you are dead, I at least feel better about being a piece-of-shit loser somewhere, knowin' there ain't no witnesses sayin' I did this or I did that. And hopefully, if I get my way, that never even happens. I'll eat a bullet if I'm about to get cau—"

A gunshot rang out from the darkness behind Matt, blowing bark off a tree behind Fando. All three jumped. Matt and Rheese hit the ground while Fando crouched down, shooting blindly into the woods as he ran backward. He tripped on a root and fell back.

Someone yelled, "*¡Nadie se mueva!*" and another shot resounded. Fando regained his footing and took off down the hill, disappearing.

Matt heard many footsteps approaching behind him and stood up cautiously, hands high.

"Matthew! Oh, my God!" Tuni cried, stepping out of the shadows.

"Tuni!" Matt said in bewildered joy.

A black man with a slung rifle and with a pistol in his hand appeared behind her, eyes locked on Rheese. Other men streamed out of the forest, surrounding them, while still more ran past in pursuit of Fando. They all had rifles, too, and those who stayed had theirs pointed at Rheese.

Tuni rushed to Matt, arms wide to hug him, but he stepped back, panic on his face. "Wait!" he yelled. "Wait . . . you can't!"

She stopped in her tracks, realizing that he was in only his underwear. "Oh . . . of course—right! Where are your clothes?" Then she looked at his face and chest, seeing the horrorshow of blood Matt himself had forgotten was there. "Oh my dear Matthew. Your face . . ."

Matt peered down at his chest. "Oh, right, the blood. He got me good in the nose . . . head, too, but I'm okay—just a little stuffed up. Could probably use something stronger than ibuprofen, too. My clothes, well, they're somewhere in this forest, I guess. But I—I can't believe you're here! You actually came all the way here! I'm . . . oh, my God, you don't even know . . . . I'm just so glad you're okay. You have no idea . . . no idea."

Tears welled up in her eyes and streamed down her cheeks. "*You* have no idea!"

Matt reached up toward her face to touch her cheek when two of the "soldiers" began grabbing Rheese and picking him up roughly. Matt stepped back from her and hurried to Rheese, patting one of the men on the shoulder "Easy," he said, smiling. *"Con cariño, por favor. Él es un víctima también. Como yo, ¿no?"*

The men backed off a little, confused. They turned to the black man with Tuni, looking for instructions or clarification. Rheese quietly thanked Matt and stepped forward from the crowd. Tuni stood there, bewildered.

"What's this, Matthew?" she said.

"I'll explain it all," Matt said. "But for now, just know that the two of us were in the same boat all this time."

Tuni looked confused, blinked, shook her head. "That's not . . . that *man* . . ." She could hardly look at Rheese. She inhaled a quick breath, held her hands out before her, flat, and focused on Matt. "It doesn't matter. Let them handle it. Just come with me. It's all over now, baby." She slid off the two rings she wore on her right hand and stuffed them in her pocket, then reached out to Matt. "It's all over. Oliver, tell them they can take this trash back."

The black man, Oliver, gestured to the men near Rheese and they grabbed hold of him again. But Matt pushed the Cubans back once more, "No, no . . ." receiving increasingly annoyed and perplexed faces in return.

"Matthew, forget about him!" Tuni's chest began to heave and her face turned. Oliver whispered in her ear.

Matt saw the anguish and frustration, but she just didn't understand yet.

"Exactly, yes!" she said to Oliver. To Matt, she said, "He bloody kidnapped you, regardless! Left *me* with some psycho to hold me hostage. Whatever else has happened is irrelevant! They're taking him to bloody jail! Hell, he could stay here by himself and starve to death for all I care."

Matt needed to explain but she had suddenly dropped deep into her dreaded stubborn mode, an often unreachable state that he'd typically walk away from until she cooled down. But this was a higher stakes situation than their comparatively meaningless arguments of the past. He realized he needed to appeal to her humanity.

"Tuni, listen! This is a human being, and *we* . . . you and me . . . are good people, right? He saved my life today. How it started . . . yeah, that sucked, but you're okay, I'm okay, and, trust me, everything changed here. It's hard to explain—kind of embarrassing, actually—but I've *been* him, if you know what I mean. I know where he's coming from." Matt turned to address the soldiers and Tuni's whispering friend. "Listen. You guys know English . . . *¿Entienden inglés? ¿No? Este hombre fue secostrado junto conmigo.* The other two men took *both* of us hostage. *Los dos estamos víctimas. Ambos. No es justo detenerlo.* Understand? *Favor de no detenerlo.*"

The soldiers nodded and lowered their weapons, then ran off down the hill in pursuit of Fando. Two of the men stayed back.

"Thank you, lad," Rheese said. "Honestly, I . . . I can't say enough."

"This is unbelievable, Matthew!" Tuni gasped. She was beyond hearing reason from Matt. "I can't abide it. *Think* for a second who this man is! What he's done to both of us. You're standing *by* him? Is this that psychological rubbish where the victims feel sorry for their captors and relate to them?"

Rheese murmured, "Stockholm syndrome."

Matt growled with frustration but tried to keep it together. *Sweet talk her, maybe.* "No, it's nothing like that, baby . . ."

"Don't call me that!" she yelled. "Not right now! I can't believe you. I am . . . I'm just . . ." Her angry face suddenly turned stoic. Her voice went quiet. ". . . *disappointed*. Utterly, completely, beyond disappointed. You . . . you can just set aside *everything*? Everything he's done to you? For God's sake, to *me*? Think about the life we've been building, our *plans*! Things he doesn't give a shit about destroying. I can't believe you're on *his* side in this."

"I'm sorry, ba—Tuni. But there's no *side* in this. I get where you're coming from, I do, of course! But I'm fine. I'm here, alive. And you're fine. Right?"

Her chin and voice lowered as anger began to brew again. "I am alive. I am physically unhurt, yes. But that in no way excuses this . . . this *monster*. An attempted murderer on trial does not get to simply go home when the judge verifies that all the victims pulled through."

"Yeah, I know what you're saying," Matt said, shaking his head. "He's real sorry. I know that personally. Tell her, Doctor."

"Truly, I am."

Tuni's eyes glanced at Rheese, she glowered for a second, then returned to Matt.

"Oh, then everything's just bloody dandy! Let's all go out to a pub and have a good laugh on it." She closed her eyes and sighed. "Can we just go?"

"Yeah, I think that's the best idea," Matt said. "Let's get the hell out of here." Matt looked at Rheese, who cocked his head up the hill.

"Oh, right." Matt said with hesitation. He turned to Tuni with the uneasy air of a child about to ask Mom something that may not go over well. He spoke quickly and matter-of-factly, knowing it would sound ridiculous, but that being cute would win out. "Hey, um, would you be opposed to us taking a detour on the way out? There's an undiscovered Viking town just up the hill from here. It's, like, a thousand years old." He smiled apologetically.

"Un-fucking-believable. That man is still out there somewhere," Tuni said through her teeth. "You would keep me in a life-threatening situation so that you and *him* can go play archeologists? It's true! You care nothing about me, our plans, our future . . ."

"They're *your* plans," Matt said quietly.

Tuni looked like she had been slapped. "Excuse me? You're going to speak to *me*—"

Oh, now the high and mighty . . . Matt couldn't hold it in anymore. "Yes, I *will* speak to you that way, princess!" Tuni was stunned. "I almost *died* today. That fucking psychopath out there was going to kill Rheese and me, not you. You have no clue what's been going on out here and you start coming at me with your 'big plans' and our 'future.' I want to go five minutes up a fuck-ing mountain . . . *five* minutes out of your way, and you're going to throw a goddamn tantrum because I don't immediately bow to every one of your demands, and without question. Perfect example of Princess Tuni in action."

Tuni just stared at him, astonished.

"Turner . . ." Rheese began.

"Shut the fuck up, Rheese! And plans? What fucking plans are you referring to, exactly? When you say plans, I know exactly what you mean: children. Did you ever really, *really* think that one through? *Me* as a father? Out of your mind! It'll *never* happen. 'Future?' You say future and I see a big fat question mark at the end of a sentence. 'When will Tuni leave me?' because I was *never* good enough for you. No one is good enough for you, let alone the highest-maintenance freak on the planet."

Silence. Tuni tried to find words, then just shook her head in defeat.

"I don't know who you are," she said. Tears fell from both eyes.

"No," Matt said. "You don't. You can't see past your *plans*."

"Come on, Oliver," she snapped. "We're leaving."

"Yeah, go! If not now, a month from now . . . a year from now! Only a matter of fucking time!" She continued stalking away with Oliver and the two remaining soldiers close behind, their flashlights bobbing to and fro.

Unbelievable, Matt thought. He opened his fingers, realizing they had been balled into tight fists.

"We should probably follow them, Turner," Rheese said softly. "They have flashlights—and guns."

"Fuck!" Matt shouted. "Can you believe how fucking selfish she is? I'm standing here practically naked . . ." He heard Tuni scream and sob from somewhere off in the darkness, but he was still angry and her outbursts were only to bait him to go after her. He was supposed to come running and beg forgiveness.

Rheese tried to push him along. "Yes, yes, fine all that. You can sort it out later—not while our only protection disappears into the night."

"Protection from what? Garza's dead and Fando is about to be caught by twenty armed and trained troops, if they haven't got him already. No, screw that! I'm going up this damned hill while I'm here, 'cause I sure as hell won't be coming back. Hell, you're the one that brought up the village in the first place!"

"I'm severely injured, lad. Honestly, I don't even know why I brought it up. It's my fault she's upset . . . eh . . . on many levels . . . And we're in our skivvies."

"Yeah, I noticed that, Rheese. Maybe you don't mind leaving this place with only your bruises and broken bones, but it has to have been worth

something for me. We'll catch up to them when we've seen it. Listen . . ."
Matt inhaled deep and shook out his arms, trying to clear Tuni out of his mind.
"Haeming was walking up this wide path. There was a massive gate with two
sort-of tower things. Should be right up here."

Matt started uphill, grumbling.

"Now hold on there," Rheese said after him. "You do realize that you're
not thinking bloody clearly, lad . . . Do you even know which way she's going?
How will we . . . blast it!" When Matt didn't answer, Rheese limped after him.
"Slow down, lad! I've only just been beaten half to death."

TWENTY-NINE

"**A**bel, are you there? It's Tuni." Treading cautiously over a patch of crumbled limestone, she slowed to grow some distance between her and Oliver, ahead of her. Her eyes stung; vision blurred, the tears streamed like they were flowing from two faucets. Her chest burned. She felt as though her heart had literally been ripped from her.

"I'm here. What's happening?"

"We're on our way out. Heading to the truck. It's over." She glanced back, half hoping to see Matthew running to catch up. But the other half was much louder, stronger.

"You have Matthew? Oliver says we're not arresting Rheese. What's going on exactly?"

"Matthew told them that he and Rheese were *both* victims. That Rheese committed no crimes or has somehow redeemed himself. It's bloody nonsense. I just want to go home."

"Regardless of Matthew's claims about the current scenario, Rheese has multiple arrest warrants from numerous countries. He's coming back with us. Where are you now? Are they still with you?"

"I don't know where we are—just going to where we parked . . . I think. As for them, we left them . . . out there. Oliver can tell you. I don't care anymore." Another look behind. "Where are you?"

"My team is intercepting the other mercenary. With Oliver's men coming down from above and us moving up, we should be closing on him any minute now. You stay with Oliver at the truck until I get there, all right? I need to know you're safe."

"Okay." The tears gushed anew and she couldn't keep her eyes open. Oliver appeared beside her and helped her along. She clutched his shirt as they stumbled after his flashlight's oval beam.

✴ ✴ ✴

Abel sat in the passenger seat of Oliver's team's truck. The three Cubans who had accompanied him up the hill sat outside on a termite-pocked log, drawing in the dirt and discussing whose improvised outfit looked the most authentic. Abel switched to Isaiah's frequency.

"Here, sir,"

"Send all your men south, up the hill."

"What to say to them?"

"Be on the lookout for anything unusual. Meet at the upper clearing whether they find anything or not. You drive up here when they go. Meet me at the end of the road."

"Understood."

Outside the truck, three people were approaching from the woods to the right, where the body of Daniel Garza still lay. For a second, Abel thought that somehow Tuni and Oliver had already made it all the way back, but their sizes and shapes and the way they walked were all wrong. It was the Americans. Abel undid the top two buttons of his shirt and grabbed an old baseball cap from the footwell and put it on. He watched the three Americans walk toward the lounging Cubans, who, of course, were unaware of anyone approaching from behind. *They're going to point right at me,* he predicted.

A tall white man with silver hair and goatee—clearly the leader—got their attention, and they jumped. A Latina with a cradled rifle spoke for him. *Aaand . . . here's the point.* As if on cue, all three Cubans pointed toward the parked truck.

The Americans walked out of the shrubs and into the road, and Abel rolled down the window the rest of the way.

"You speak English?" the leader asked.

Abel observed the Latina. She had the incisive look of someone too sharp to fool with his Castilian Spanish or his unpracticed Cuban accent.

"Enough I speak," Abel said in broken English.

"Are you in charge of these men?"

"Not really, no. Only when boss in jungle, yeah?"

"Let's go, Jess," Paul said to the leader. "He doesn't know squat."

Abel studied the stocky, unshaven young man, "You need help, yeah?"

Jess said, "We saw the body over there. Any idea which way the other three went?"

Abel put on his best confused face, smiling at the Latina. "Oh . . . dead man. Yeah, he dead. I check."

"See?" Paul said. "Can we go?"

They began to turn, and Núñez said, *"Puedo preguntarle de qué parte es usted?"*

Where am I from? Deciding that he had perhaps played it a little too stupid, Abel switched gears. "Heaven, baby, like you," he said with a lecherous smirk. "You like *this* body?"

Success.

Núñez glared and spat on the ground, and they walked off, back toward the tall eastern woods, perhaps to recheck the area around Daniel Garza.

✴ ✴ ✴

Roger and Chuck slogged their way uphill. Their thighs and calves burned with each step. They were so out of breath that they had stopped even trying to speak to each other. As they hiked up, the woods become more and more dense, the size of the tree trunks tripling in diameter. Behind them, the moon was all but eclipsed by the forest canopy, and the sound at ground level had become eerily quiet. No detectable wind sounds, no insects—only the crunching beneath their boots and each other's heavy breathing.

Roger spotted it before Chuck: a pile of clothes. He drew his .45 and scanned around, holding his little underpowered flashlight alongside the barrel. Chuck followed suit, though without a light.

Roger holstered his gun and crouched down, his calves and quads screaming. Then, looking around him, he found a fallen branch the thickness of his thumb and used it to lift a plaid shirt with a button-down collar off the pile. It was a detective's habit, not touching the evidence. A spider the size of his hand and dense with hairs, suddenly laid bare, scuttled out of the light.

Roger didn't recognize the jeans or other clothes as specifically Matt's—they didn't really see each other these days—but soon there was no question of what belonged to his son: turtleneck, knit cap, knee socks, a flesh-colored leather glove. The rest of the clothes obviously belonged to someone else.

"Matt's?" Chuck asked.

"Yeah," Roger said solemnly.

"What do you think that means? Why would they strip him?"

"And not just him. There's someone else being held—forty-two waistline, XL shirt."

Their walkie-talkies beeped simultaneously.

"Jess to Rog."

"Go ahead, Jess."

"Looks like the Cubans took out one of the perps. Head shot—very dead. No sign of Matty."

Roger said, "I've got a pile of clothes here: one set Matt's, the other unknown."

A pause. "We talking a full two outfits?"

"Affirmative. Minus the shorts. Listen, we're going to move on. Radio silence unless you find something or someone, yeah?"

"Ten-four. Watch your back."

Roger stuffed all the clothes into his pack as his mind wandered to a memory of Matty in swim trunks, 8-years old, skinny, running around the pool, laughing. He cinched the pack closed.

They walked on, weapons drawn, through a surprisingly dense growth of ferns and bracken. The moon shone through the open spaces between the trees, casting a thin, silvery light that made the dark areas seem even darker, and suddenly the rhythmic clicks of katydids and tree frogs seemed to turn on.

✳ ✳ ✳

Rosalío Valdes y Rodríguez trod softly through dense timber, with men he didn't know walking on either side of him. Yesterday, his cousin Pepe had

Michael Siemsen

told him there was easy money to be made. All he had to do was get himself to the baseball field in Guanajay the following morning—*this* morning. It wouldn't necessarily be clean work, and it could even get him into trouble, but a thousand American dollars for a single day's work was not something he could easily turn down. In Cuba, opportunities for extra income were all but nonexistent.

He had arrived early in case spots were limited, but even so, when his uncle dropped him off at the field, many men were already waiting. Some kicked a soccer ball around, while others spent their time asking everyone else if they knew what the job was, who heard what and from whom, and whether the whole thing was perhaps bogus. Worse, a rumor was afoot that it was a government setup meant to expose those disloyal to *la revolución*. Apparently, some had believed this nonsense and left, but by the time two old military trucks pulled up, twenty-five men were still present. All were hired; no one even did a head count. Rosalío had to wonder, what if fifty had shown up? Would they have taken them all? And did they really have twenty-five thousand dollars to pay out at the end of the day?

Now, marching through the jungle, hungry and with a useless empty rifle, in search of a man with at least one demonstrably loaded gun, he wished he had followed his instincts. Too good to be true always proved untrue. Fortunately, he and his new colleagues had silently agreed that they would pursue the man at the slowest speed possible. Let him get away, and let them return home alive with money in their pockets.

Oh, but of course, that, also, would be too good to be true.

The men were spread out in a line, walking three to six meters apart. When someone three men to his right stopped, the rest of them stopped, too. "What is it?" the man to Rosalío's right whispered down the line.

"I heard something . . ."

"Probably a deer, man. Or a wild pig. Keep walking."

Two or three steps later, something popped out from behind a tree and charged down the hill. When it crossed into a bar of moonlight they saw him: a big man in a T-shirt, with a shoulder holster crisscrossing his back.

After the initial flinch, Rosalío shared glances with his neighbors. No one seemed eager to give chase. It was one thing to take their time, never find anything, and go back up to report the disappointing news. But for at least eight of them to see their target—apparently, a dangerous criminal—and ignore him? That seemed another matter entirely. Someone down the line shouted, "There he is!" and, just that easily, the choice had been taken from them. Empty rifles held across their chests, they dashed after the sound of breaking branches and snapping twigs.

As they went, they converged into a pack, split up, and came together as trees and other obstacles necessitated. Many fell behind—perhaps those still inclined to avoid danger, Rosalío thought as he ran.

Someone shouted, "There!"

Slivers of the roadway appeared through the fifty or so meters of forest. The trees were thinning out, with skinny palms and banyans taking the place of pines. They spotted him sprinting toward the road, and they sped up on the easier terrain. Seeing him run gave them all a sense of dominance, despite their lack of ammunition.

"Stop or we'll shoot!" someone shouted. "Your only warning!"

Rosalío and three others were gaining on him as the approaching road became clearer, gleaming in the moonlight. The runner glanced back, saw them, and cursed as he slowed to a stop on the road's dividing line.

"Okay, okay, okay," he said. "Don't shoot!"

They quickly had him surrounded. Their eyes darted from the runner to each other and back, posing the common question: *what now?*

The big man, hands in the air, took a closer look at his captors. While some wore camouflage or khaki cargo pants, there was no uniformity among them. And Rosalío became keenly aware of how unofficial they came off. He looked around at his cohorts and observed that they were all staring at the butt of the black handgun protruding from under the man's armpit. He asked the question for them.

"So, what now?" He had a little smirk that made Rosalío nervous.

"Put . . . put the gun on the ground!" stammered the dark, scrawny one who had so notably shouted, "There he is!" thus sealing their fates.

The big man's smile widened a little, and he said, "You really want me to take my gun out? With my hand? And then what? *I* put it on the ground? *Myself?*"

The scrawny one said, "Yeah—no, give it to me! In my hand!" He took a few steps forward and held his hand out insistently. He kept the rifle in his left hand, barrel to their captive, finger on the trigger.

The big man said, "You mind not pointin' that thing at me with that death grip on the trigger?"

"Oh . . . sorry," he said as he pointed the muzzle upward.

The big man chuckled a little and looked around him. "Real pros, huh? I have to tell you guys, I'm lookin' at you and thinkin' how I could take out half of you—probably more—before one of you gets a single shot off. And would that shot even be close to hittin' anything? Doubt it. I got this knife, too—could do a lotta damage. But . . ." He held up a warning finger for himself. ". . . with eleven of you, it gets pretty tight. Pretty risky, know what I'm sayin'? I mean, chances are, I pull out my gun that has a full magazine of sixteen rounds, and start blastin' chests, those that ain't dead are gonna have their first reflex be to beat feet runnin', as opposed to shootin' those antiques. Plus, why would you bother pullin' the trigger on a rifle if you ain't got no ammo?"

He scanned their guilty faces for a moment. No one said a word. Some even took an admissive step back. The big man dropped his hands to his sides and shook his head.

"Put them back up, sir!" the scrawny one shouted, and took a step forward, lowering his rifle to train it on the man's chest. "We have bullets! All of us! Give me the gun or we will shoot you!"

"'Sir'? Wow, so formal! Look, we're all about to be real close, so I want you to call me Fando, okay? Now, listen. There's another problem here, my friend. You guys are in this little circle here around me, and I'm just thinkin' you start shootin', fillin' my poor body with those bullets, but some go through me, some miss, it's gonna be a big, crazy shootout! And yer gonna end up shootin' each other. Maybe you should make a half circle or somethin'."

No one moved.

Rosalío swallowed. This man was going to kill them all and enjoy it. The sweat from his forehead was stinging his eyes, and he squeezed them shut to try to push it out. He didn't want to wipe it, didn't want to move a muscle.

"Tell you what, *sirs,*" Fando said, pulling out the large knife from the sheath on his belt. "I'll make this a little more fair. And *you*"—he pointed the knife at the scrawny one—"are *last.* My gift to you, 'cause yer the only one of these idiots with any balls."

He spun around and leaped at a man in a black T-shirt and dungarees, who held up his rifle as a guard, only to receive the full length of the blade in his gut. It sounded like a punch, and the man made a horrible retching sound.

A few men immediately dropped their rifles and ran, while most stood fixed, unsure what to do. They held their rifles before them as cudgels. A chubby fellow with a beard actually jumped forward and jabbed with his rifle butt. Fando spun around, slashed his arm, twisted him halfway around, and cut his throat. Two down. Scrawny tentatively rushed Fando and fetched only a punch in the jaw.

"I told you, yer last, Big Balls! Stay the fuck back for a minute—I'll get to you!"

Rosalío saw Fando's eyes fix on him, and he swallowed. Fando frowned and came toward him. This was it. Rosalío closed his eyes. *Holiest Jesus Christ, my savior, please forgive my sins, protect my family* . . . But he felt himself get pushed sideways and heard another stab and another choking scream. He heard men running away down the road, begging for mercy. Opening his eyes, he saw three bodies on the ground, and one trying to drag himself off the road. Scrawny was trying to help the wounded man.

Rosalío turned back and saw Fando chasing another man down the road. Unable to catch him, Fando threw his knife but missed. Stopping, he turned and walked back toward Rosalío.

"Help me with him!" the scrawny guy yelled, and Rosalío snapped out of his daze, grabbed an arm, and helped drag the bleeding man toward the woods.

"He's coming!" Rosalío hissed.

The injured man moaned and said, "I . . . I have a pocket knife."

Rosalío stole a glance back to see Fando just a few seconds from them, pistol out. They made it past a palmetto thicket before Scrawny tripped. The man they were carrying fell hard and cried out when he hit the ground.

"Not so fast, gentlemen," Fando said, rounding the thicket.

Rosalío rummaged through the injured man's pocket and found the knife. It was a tiny thing with a two-inch blade, but it was *something*. Opening it with shaking hands, he stood up, concealing it at his side. Fando raised the gun in front of him and fired. Rosalío's eyes slammed shut reflexively, but he didn't feel anything, so he opened a cautious eye and lunged forward with the little knife in his fist. Fando grabbed his arm and rolled him over his leg, dropping him to the ground with lung-emptying force. Another gunshot echoed.

Rosalío lay in the thicket of spiny palmetto fronds, trying to catch his breath. He opened his eyes but couldn't see past the leaves around him. He rolled out and saw the scrawny guy lying over the man they had dragged. Each had a bullet hole in his head. A booted foot stepped in front of him, and he looked up.

"You married?" the big man asked calmly, quietly.

Truth or lie? He could have killed you twice now. What's the right answer? Truth!

Rosalío shook his head.

"You look like my brother. He wasn't married, either. You go home, find a hot little bitch that doesn't mouth off or spend too much, and you marry her . . . an' bang her every fucking night. Understand?"

He nodded.

The feet walked slowly away.

Rosalío lay in the palmettos, ants crawling all over him, spines jabbing his legs and side, sweat dripping in sideways streams across his chest, and a cramp forming in his calf. And he lay there and cried.

THIRTY

The wooded slope decreased to a more manageable pitch. Matt peered behind him. Rheese was struggling forward, a hand on each knee, one miserable step at a time.

"We're almost there," Matt said. "I think I recognize this . . . maybe."

Rheese responded with a wheeze and a dismissive wave, so Matt slogged on. Thirty feet later, he was at the summit. It was almost entirely flat as far as he could see, and covered mostly in palms and ferns. The ground lit up faintly red for a couple of seconds, then went dark. Red again. Looking up, he spotted some kind of utility tower another hundred feet away. It had a blinking red light on it—to warn aircraft, he supposed. Along its steel lattice, he could see drum-shaped cylinders and numerous antennas jutting out and up. Power cables disappeared in both directions behind the fanning crowns of massive palm trees.

Matt turned slowly around in search of familiar ground features but could not get a bearing. The environment was right, and so was the size of the mountain, but there wasn't a single detail he could pick out.

Rheese finally appeared, puffing like a steam train, and hobbled over to a low rock. He sat down on it with a melodramatic sigh.

"Great idea, Turner. Walk it off, eh?"

"Hey, you're the one dead-set on finding fortunes in fucking jungles."

"Cute, son. But you've got things a bit easier than I, these days. I can't even hock the bloody opal and go back into hiding."

"So what are you going to do?"

"Care to foot a loan?"

Matt laughed weakly. "Not a bloody chance, as you'd say."

Rheese peered around. "Now what?"

"I don't know. You tell me. I can't tell if this is the spot."

"Brilliant." Rheese squinted around the area, glancing briefly at the red-flashing electrical tower. "Well, is it or isn't it? If there's nothing to see, I'd much prefer a shower, fresh clothes, and a stomach full of food—oh, and maybe a nice Bordeaux . . . that is, *after* my extensive abdominal surgery." Rheese spat. "Look—all blood!" He scooped a finger into the pool and squinted at the fluid. "Hmm—perhaps just the light."

"In the imprints, I came up a mountain. I just don't know if this is the one."

Matt began walking around, looking for signs of any kind that this had once been a bustling town. The intermittent flashes of red light didn't seem to help.

"Turner, we really should be going. What if they actually leave this area entirely? Ms. St. James did seem put out enough to consider it. We'll be stranded."

Matt was standing upright, shoulders back, taking in the area around him. He didn't want to think about Tuni. The air was still warm on his bare skin. It was the strangest feeling, being so exposed, soft soil between his toes. The relief of knowing that his ordeal was essentially over. *Well . . . and a new one with her . . .* He closed his eyes and tilted his head back, breathing in the smell of this place. It had almost a moldiness, though not in an unpleasant way. Rheese was talking, but Matt wasn't listening. Rheese wasn't in charge of his life anymore. Nor were Garza and Fando. Or Tuni . . .

He opened his eyes just as the light flashed on. In front of him, about thirty paces away, was a dark area beneath a large tree with draping aerial roots. He walked toward it.

". . . if we had a bloody flashlight, but the . . . Turner? What is it, lad? You see something?"

Matt ducked under the vines, took one more step into the tree-domed area, and smacked his toes against something. With a yelp, he dropped onto his backside, massaging his smarting toes. He had kicked a rock that jutted up from the ground. And he smiled. Because right next to it was another rock, sticking up at the same height, and of roughly the same pointed shape. After it, another, and another. He felt around behind him and found another row of rocks. They seemed to mark a path leading deeper into the darkness.

"Rheese! Come here!"

Michael Siemsen

Matt walked, hunched over, vines dragging up his chest and over his shoulders. The little bit of flashing red that penetrated through the leaves was illuminating something—something out of place beneath a tree on a mountaintop.

"Where are you?" Rheese called.

"In here—the viney tree!"

Behind him, Matt heard Rheese pushing vegetation out of his way.

"Did you actually find something?"

Matt reached out and felt it: hard, cool to the touch.

"Hang on. Stay right there," Matt said. "Can you pull an armful of those vines away to let that light shine in?"

"Er . . . well, let me see . . ."

Rheese grunted and strained as he gathered and pushed vines.

"Good . . . yeah, a little more!"

Rheese muttered and swore to himself as he pressed on, swatted and scratched by the hanging growth. "These things aren't exactly light, boy!"

"No, no, that's perfect!"

Matt pulled away a layer of ivy, broke off a branch, and swept away dead leaves and moist soil. What remained was a massive rock—but a rock that had been chiseled and shaped by men.

"Do you see it?" Matt asked.

Rheese fought to free his head from the swatch of vines. Then the tower flashed, and he gasped aloud, and Matt knew that he could see it: a giant rock shaped like a chair. It had a high back, and armrests of equal height. It was leaning forward, for the giant roots of the tree behind it had tilted it over time and might one day push it over entirely, obscuring its familiar shape.

"A throne!" Rheese breathed. Matt continued brushing debris off the surface.

"Exactly!"

"Remarkable . . . Say, careful there, lad. Couldn't the thing—"

But the warning came too late. Matt's fingers and palm brushed away the last layer of accumulated soil and leaf litter and touched the actual stone beneath. His head buzzed, and his legs gave out.

I am King Bodvarr of Norway. This is my land, Southland. I hold in my lap my second child, my firstborn son.

". . . now, lad. There you go. Can you hear me?"

Matt felt his face. A new scratch, bleeding. "Well that was stupid," he said.

They were in almost complete darkness. Rheese had dragged him away from the throne.

"What was it?" Rheese asked. "Or, rather, who?"

"It was just a real quick snippet, but it was him, the king of Southland. He had a baby in his hands. I could sort of make out the village in his peripheral vision. It was this whole area."

Rheese ran his hand over the smooth surface. "I'm pleased you found this, lad, but I really must insist we go. Much as I've enjoyed our late-night stroll in our unmentionables . . ."

The unexpected imprint had left Matt a bit shaken. He planned to avoid reading anything for at least a month. "And this place isn't quite as exciting as I'd hoped," he muttered.

Rheese helped him up, and they burrowed out from under the canopy.

"It's archeology, lad. This is what it looks like."

"Looks like nothing much."

"Precisely. Typical, really, before excavation begins. Hell, that bloody throne, up and out of the ground and intact after a millennium, is a fluke. No, this place would begin to take shape after a few weeks' work." He took a wistful last glance around. "Probably make a pretty penny off these trees that need clearing. A not-insignificant perk of the trade, if you know how to work the locals."

"That's super." Matt said. "Which way, do you suppose?"

"Always go the way you came, Turner—best way to avoid getting lost."

"Matty?" A man's voice called from the far side of the hilltop.

"Good God! Who's that?" Rheese whispered.

"Holy shit, it's my dad!" Matt said, rushing toward the voice. "Dad?"

Rheese muttered, "Anyone else you're meeting up here?"

They spotted each other at the same time. Behind his father, Matt saw a big guy he didn't know, carrying a shotgun. They stopped a few paces from each other, and Roger gaped at his dirty, bloody, nearly naked son.

"Jesus Christ, son! Are you okay?"

But before he could answer, both Roger and Chuck noticed someone behind Matt, limping toward them. Chuck raised the shotgun, and Roger drew his pistol.

"No, no, it's fine!" Matt said. "Rheese isn't a part of this . . . uh, anymore."

Matt could see the fury in his father's eyes, and his friend's wariness.

"Please," Rheese said, his face cocked sideways and his hands before him as if they could block oncoming bullets. "Listen to the boy. We've already gone over this with the Cubans and were just about to head back to civilization."

"Shut up!" Roger said, keeping the gun trained on Rheese. "What do you mean he's not part of it?"

"Well, I guess he was in the beginning, but we've both pretty much been hostages of these other two guys since we got to Cuba. Everything's changed. Just put the guns down—please."

"Obviously, I'm not armed, gentlemen," Rheese said gently.

Roger shined his flashlight over Rheese's battered body.

Chuck lowered the shotgun but kept it at the ready. "Looks like he got thrown in a clothes dryer with some bricks."

Roger lowered his pistol, too. "What happened to the other guy?" he asked. "We heard one of 'em was killed by the Cubans."

"Yeah, Fando ran off down the hill, and a whole bunch of soldiers chased after him. We heard gunshots a little while after that, so I'm guessing he's probably joined his buddy, Garza. Hey, so how'd you even find me? Are you here with Tuni?"

Roger frowned. "Tuni . . . what? She's here, too? I came with Uncle J and Chuck here and a couple others. Must have been less than fifty yards from you when we went to that house outside Havana. Almost got shot by one of your pals."

Roger holstered his gun and shrugged the backpack off.

Matt turned to Rheese. "What's he talking about? They were shooting at my dad? You didn't tell me that!"

Rheese stammered, "I-I didn't know! Garza ran off with one of the guns he'd just bought! Said he was shooting at American police. I had no idea who it was, and you were, um, indisposed."

"I'm radioing Jess," Chuck said, turning his volume back up. "Chuck to Jess."

"Here," Roger said, tossing Matt's pants in front of his feet. "See if they're imprinted."

Matt crouched down and tapped the pants lightly with one fingertip, as if checking to see whether a pan was still hot. They were clear, so he picked them up and began putting them on.

"Listen, Matty," Roger said as he threw Rheese his clothes, "whatever you think about this man, and however it happened that his mercenaries turned the tables on him, it doesn't undo his crimes. We're taking him to the Cuban police. Don't try and argue."

Chuck's radio beeped, and Jess's voice said, "Go ahead, Chuck."

Rheese sighed and put on his khakis but did not protest.

"Well, if there's some kind of trial, I'll be a witness," Matt said defiantly. "I know what he did and what he didn't do."

"Jess, we found the kid and Dr. Rheese."

"Turner," Rheese said quietly, "I appreciate this, I do, but you don't know me. I'll get mine while you go off back to your vacation. You don't need to worry about what happens to me."

"Well, that is just about the sweetest shit I've heard all day," Fando said, and fired a single shot through Chuck's back.

The radio fell to the ground. "Outstanding, Chuck! What's your location?"

Matt and Rheese dropped their shirts and jumped aside, diving to the ground as Roger spun to return fire. Fando swatted the gun from Roger's hand, smiled, and put the muzzle of his own pistol against Roger's sternum.

"Dad!" Matt cried.

"Can you hear me, Chuck? What's your location?"

The red light above flashed, illuminating the wild eyes, the blood-spattered face and shirt.

"Spittin' image, eh?" Fando said, and pulled the trigger.

THIRTY-ONE

Jess, Paul, and Núñez walked along the center of the road, shining their flashlights through the wall of trees on either side. The most recent gunshots had come from this area. They hadn't encountered any more Cubans since leaving the little campsite where one of the perps was killed. Paul had a rifle slung over his shoulder, and a pistol in his hand. Núñez still held the bolt-action rifle.

Jess's and Núñez's radios beeped in sync, and Chuck's voice said in stereo, "Chuck to Jess."

They paused on the road as Jess unclipped the walkie-talkie from his shoulder strap.

"Go ahead, Chuck."

"Jess, we found the kid and Dr. Rheese."

Núñez and Paul snapped their faces toward the radio. Jess tilted his head back, closed his eyes, and inhaled a deep breath of relief.

"Outstanding, Chuck! What's your location?"

Núñez cocked her head toward a faint rumble in the distance. "Hear that?"

Paul said, "Yeah. Thunder, or was that another gunshot? Jess was talking . . ."

"I didn't hear anything," Jess said, holding his radio away from him to listen. He pressed the button again, "Can you hear me, Chuck? What's your location?"

Núñez shined her light down the road in front of them. A single figure was approaching.

"Contact!" she yelled, and aimed the rifle.

Jess and Paul followed her lead, pointing guns and lights.

"Stop right there!" Jess shouted. Another rumble echoed in the distance, but he ignored it. "Let me see your hands!"

The man stopped and raised his head slowly.

"*¡Arriba las manos!*" Núñez repeated.

The hands went up. Jess shined his light on both hands, verifying that they were empty, and all three moved forward with their guns trained on the man. He was about six feet tall, wearing camouflage pants and a T-shirt, both stained with blood, though he did not appear to be bleeding.

"This has gotta be our guy," Paul said.

They stopped several feet in front of him. He squinted at the lights, but his face appeared more dreamy than frightened.

"Get on the ground!" Jess shouted, but the man didn't move.

"*¡Echarse en el suelo!*"Núñez said.

The man finally spoke. *"Yo no hice nada. Me llamo Rosalío."*

"He says he didn't do anything," Núñez said.

"Oh, phew," Paul said.

"I don't give a shit what he says," Jess said. "Tell him to get on the ground before I shoot him in the leg."

Núñez conveyed the threat, and the man sighed as he went to his knees, then sprawled out facedown. Paul walked over, dropped a knee on his back, and cinched his wrists together with two zip ties.

Jess got back on the radio. "Chuck, Jess. Can you hear me? What is your location?"

"It's coming through on mine," Núñez remarked. "Chuck, this is Núñez. Can you hear me?"

The man on the ground moaned and murmured in Spanish that he just wanted to go home.

"Ascoos me," said a cautious voice from the woods to their left.

Instantly, all three guns and lights were on a middle-aged man in dark jeans and a flannel shirt. He had his empty palms out before him, and an apologetic smile on his face.

"What now?" Jess groaned.

"I no bad man," he said. "No bad man him, too." Pointing at the man on the ground. "We run from . . ." He gestured farther down the road.

Núñez asked him for details, and he told of the big man stabbing or shooting most of his group, and of the few who got away. He had been hiding in these bushes for a half hour and hadn't seen anyone else come this way, so he figured the big man had gone a different direction.

Núñez interpreted for the others.

"So he knows for certain this guy is clean?" Jess asked.

"*¿Está seguro de él?*" Núñez asked, gesturing to the one on the ground.

"*Claro que sí.*"

Paul said, "Ask him if we can expect anybody else to come creeping out of the bushes."

"This means the other perp is still out there," Jess said. "Chuck said they only had Matty and Rheese. The fact we can't get them on the radio when they were just talking to us makes me awful nervous."

Núñez said, "Sir, we've got bodies on the road up ahead, and possibly some injured still alive."

"Right, I caught that. Shit! If we had the damned channel the Cubans were on . . ."

Núñez pressed buttons on her walkie-talkie until it began beeping every couple of seconds, pausing on each frequency. After a minute, it stopped back at their channel. "Nothing."

Jess pulled out his cell phone to check signal strength. A single bar. It jumped to two for an instant, then back to one.

"I have a little signal. I'm going to try to get a text out to USINT. Let's go check out the folks down the road. Not to be a heartless asshole, but I'm hoping they're all dead, so we can go find out what the hell is going on with Rog. I don't want us splitting up into any smaller group than this while some psycho's running around."

Paul cut their captive's zip ties, and they left both men and double-timed it down the road. Ten minutes later, they arrived at the scene of the bloodbath and found no survivors.

Núñez picked up one of the rifles from the ground and worked the bolt.

"Empty," she said. She sniffed the open breach. "Hasn't been fired recently, either."

They checked some of the other rifles strewn across the road. None loaded.

"So what the hell does this mean?" Jess demanded. "They send their men out into a hostile situation with no way to protect themselves or take out an enemy?"

"Well, *someone* had ammo," Paul said. "Just ask the guy up at the campsite who's missing half his brains."

"They're obviously hired hands, sir," Núñez said, "and untrained. Whoever's paying them either didn't want them armed or didn't want to pay for ammo. Seems a minor expense, though. I don't get it."

"Maybe they didn't trust 'em," Paul said. "Just wanted the numbers, like for appearances."

Jess stood and thought for a minute. He turned and peered off back up the road, where they had been.

"This is a setup," he said. "We gotta go."

Núñez dropped the empty rifle, and all three of them began running back up the road.

"That guy sent us down the hill," Jess shouted. "Knew there was nothing down there. He just wanted us out of the way. Núñez, was that black guy even Cuban? The one that talked to Rog?"

"I didn't hear him talk, sir. Could be Afro-Cuban."

"He knew Rog's name," Jess continued as they rounded a curve. "Said they came to save Matty. How would they even know about him? If it was government, they wouldn't have sent amateurs with useless weapons. Which means it's someone else who knows Matty's situation." He unclipped his radio again and held it to his mouth. Panting from the exertion, he tried again. "Rog or Chuck, please reply if you can hear this!"

"Maybe he never turned up his sound," Paul said. "Just radioed that they found them and thought you didn't get it."

"Maybe, but with the slasher from back there running around, I'm assuming the worst."

They caught up with the two Cubans, who almost sprinted away when they heard someone running up behind them. But Núñez called out to them and they stopped.

Jess said to Núñez, "Ask 'em why they're here and who hired them."

"And keep your bullshit detector on," Paul said.

THIRTY-TWO

Abel watched Tuni emerge from the woods out onto the road. Oliver was behind her, trying to keep up. She looked as though she was still upset since last radioing. He was just relieved to see her, knowing that Fernando Solorzano had not yet been caught. He climbed down from the truck, and she surprised him with a hug around the neck.

"We have to leave, Abel," she sobbed. "I can't be here a moment longer."

He made soft shushing sounds. He could smell her hair, feel her breasts against his chest. He had to wonder about anyone who would let this woman walk away from him.

"Sorry," she said. She let go and pulled away from him, wiping her tears on her arm and sniffling. "Can we just go?"

"It's all right, my dear," Abel said. "You need not apologize. Sometimes we just need a hug. It's not as though you could embrace Matthew when you finally saw him, right?"

"What?" she said. "Oh, right. No, I couldn't. I don't want to talk about him, though. I'm just sick . . . he's *not* who I thought he was. I . . . I don't know how I didn't see it. He's like a ch—" She didn't finish the last word, but Abel knew what she was going to say. "And I am *not* that person . . ."

"I'm so sorry, Tuni," Abel said kindly.

Tuni blotted her eyes and wiped her nose. "Oh, hell, are we leaving or not?"

"Well, we need to retrieve Dr. Rheese and Matthew. We cannot leave either of them out here alone. The other kidnapper has yet to be apprehended, too. So I must stay here. But I do not wish for you to have to remain for another moment, so I'm willing to send you back to the city with Isaiah, if that's what you wish. Oliver and I will fetch Matthew and apprehend Dr. Rheese and his accomplice. Is that what you want?"

She glanced back at the woods. The sky was starting to lighten in the east. She clearly didn't want to see Matthew, but she didn't want him out there in danger, even if he hadn't felt the same concern for her.

"Yes," she finally answered. "Please get him out of there. I want to be in a bed."

Abel snapped his fingers for Isaiah to come. "Take Miss Tuni back to the hotel."

"What about the men here?" Isaiah asked of the eager-faced Cubans congregating near the truck. "They were told few hours, and they no like all the shooting."

Abel glanced at the ten or more men standing around the back of the second truck and trying to ascertain whether the present conversation involved them, their return home, or the promised money.

"Climb into the truck, Tuni," Abel said. "I'll see you in the morning. Everything will be all right, you hear?"

She attempted a smile. "Thanks," she said.

Abel closed the door and walked to the rear of the truck. In Spanish, he told the men that the truck was heading back to town now and that anyone who wished could get on and receive their pay upon arrival. Or they could stay with him for a few more hours and double their money.

Five of the men were game; the other six didn't want to stay another minute, no matter what he was paying. They climbed into the back of the truck, Tuni got in the cab, and Isaiah backed down the hill to where the silver van was parked. Then he swung the truck forward onto the dirt road and headed back toward Havana. Abel waved Oliver over and gathered his five remaining recruits. "We're going to go out there and end this," he said. "How would you gentlemen like some ammunition in those rifles of yours?"

THIRTY-THREE

On the flat-topped mountain, the highest peak in the area, Chuck Kohl lay with his face half buried in the dark soil and leaf litter, mouth open, unblinking eyes gazing at the walkie-talkie. A few feet from Chuck's body, Roger Turner lay on his back on the ground. The hole in his blue polo shirt, an inch below the placket, still smoked. A purple flower blossomed across his chest as he labored to inhale.

Matt sat on his knees, watching his dad struggle to breathe, wishing he could do something. As he watched, a hand moved. It seemed to be pointing at something. Matt caught on, grabbed the half-buried rock out of the dirt, and put it in his dad's hand, closing his fingers around it. Roger smiled faintly and closed his eyes, his breath growing shallower with each rise and fall. With what little strength remained, he squeezed the rock.

* * *

Fernando Solorzano rummaged through the second backpack, discovering an MRE and nodded his pleasure. He had burned off too many calories during the night and needed fuel. He tore open the brown plastic and found the main course: tuna and noodles. *Ugh.* Side of applesauce, oatmeal brick, giant cracker, peanut-butter packet. He ripped open the oatmeal cookie and stuffed the whole thing in his mouth.

As Fando chewed he glanced up at Turner, handing a rock to his dying father. No appreciable threat in that, so he let them be. Then he had a sudden thought and glanced around. Shotgun on the ground, three feet away from Turner. Pistol in the bushes, where he had smacked it out of the dad's hand. Pistol on the hip of the dead dude with the shotgun.

He turned his eyes to the tree that Rheese had run behind. He could still see the dumb shit's elbow poking out the left side. If Rheese weren't such a useless coward, he could have gone for one of those guns. And Turner? Making him strip down was brilliant. Danny would have been impressed with that one. Turner couldn't touch anything around the site, not even the clothes in which his own father was dying in. Fando snorted, amused at the father and son's plight, but he needed to figure out what to do next. They couldn't go back to the car, for others would surely be there—maybe more American cops.

What do you want? Fando thought. *Turner and Rheese dead, especially Rheese. So kill them now. Just do it, homes. What the hell are you waiting for?*

He couldn't quite sort out the answers in his head, not in any clear, rational form—only that he didn't want to be alone, and he didn't want it to be over. If he killed the two of them now, he would be on his own, the only survivor, and he couldn't be that. Raúl, Danny, him. He couldn't go home. No, when this thing was over, he would put a gun in his mouth, aim high, and pull the trigger. But he wasn't ready for that yet. That was why Turner and Rheese—or at least Turner—got to live for now. He could control Turner. Rheese, though—he was feeling just about done with that fat, useless, stuck-up piece of shit.

✳ ✳ ✳

Matthew Turner, wearing only his jeans, knelt in the dirt, hunched over his father with his hands shaking before him. He needed to get pressure on the wound, but his dad's shirt would be imprinted for sure. He needed something between them, something *clean*. One of his gloves sat nestled in the ball of clothes behind him, but he couldn't think. He looked up at Fando, digging through the backpacks. That man needed to die. Matt's mind raced. Even if he stopped the bleeding from the chest wound, could anyone even survive an injury like that? It was in the middle of the chest, and he obviously couldn't breathe right. He could see his father looking up at him, trying to move his lips, shape them into words, but they just quivered and contorted, and he finally gave up. His chest expanded a little less with each breath.

"Get up," Fando said coldly. "We're moving out."

Matt didn't even look up. "Fuck off."

Fando cackled, as if both shocked and delighted by such bold defiance. "Oh, you wanna join yer daddy there on the ground? Get yer ass up before I put one through yer head."

Matt glared up at him, wishing him dead. He scanned around him as best he could without moving his head. There was the shotgun on the ground near his dad's dead friend. But he needed a way to grab it without touching it, and fast enough to get a shot off before Fando could react.

Roger gargled up some blood.

"You're going to be all right, Dad," he said.

Fando laughed again. "Really? You got some kind of big-ass Band-Aid on you, gonna fix up his boo-boo? He's done. Let's go."

"I'm not leaving him like this," Matt said.

"Oh, right," Fando said gently. "Shit yeah, I don't know what I was thinkin', bro. No way you could just leave him lyin' here dyin'. Dude, what kinda asshole am I?"

Fando stepped forward, knelt on the other side of Roger, and put his pistol muzzle to Roger's forehead. Matt screamed and leaped up to tackle him, but Fando pulled the trigger, and blood sprayed over all three of them.

Matt's shoulder bashed into Fando's neck, and they crashed to the ground. Matt felt a flash of Fando's consciousness enter his brain, but he rolled aside before it could knock him out. Fando clutched at his own throat, choking, as Matt hopped to his feet, blind with rage. Yanking the gun out of Fando's hand, he felt his legs give out as the imprint came on, but he flung the weapon out into the woods as hard as he could, and his body was his own again.

Fando coughed, swore, and turned on his side to get up. Frantic, Matt looked around and spotted a rock about the size and shape of a Frisbee. He lurched over, and picked it up.

Fando was on his hands and knees, about to rise. He said, "Now I'm really gonna tear yer punk ass apart."

Matt brought the rock down on the back of Fando's head, the rock breaking into two pieces. Fando crumpled to the ground and was still.

"Rheese!" Matt shouted.

"I'm here, lad. Is the bastard dead?"

"I don't know, but he's out. He . . . he killed my dad."

"I am so sorry, son."

Matt turned around and picked his long undershirt out of the pile of clothes and, walking over to his dad, laid it over his face. Blood seeped up into it at once from the head wound. Matt returned to the clothes and shook out his turtleneck, and a glove fell out of it. He put it on his right hand and looked around for its mate.

"We need to get out of here, Turner," Rheese said. "I know you don't want to leave him—"

Matt cut him off. "It's fine. We're leaving. I'll have someone come back for them. Just one thing first . . ."

Matt pulled one of his socks over his exposed left hand, then bent down to pick up the shotgun. He slid the bolt back halfway, revealing a fresh shell in the ejection port, then slid the bolt shut again and walked over to Fando's limp body.

"Are you really going to do it, lad?" Rheese seemed shocked and a bit frightened at the thought.

"Yup. He dies right here."

Rheese stepped beside him and nudged Fando's leg with his foot. No response. His face was planted in the dirt, facing away from them.

"Go ahead, Rheese," Matt said.

"Go what? What do you—"

"The opal . . . his pocket. Just get it. I know that's what you're thinking."

"Well, I'd bloody well forgotten about it, but since you mention it, I suppose it'd be a right waste just to leave it." He crouched down and dug under Fando's hip for a moment. "A-ha!" He pulled his sock out from Fando's pocket. The end snapped up at his hand, empty. "Must have come out in his pocket," Rheese said, shoving his hand back under.

"Hurry up," Matt said.

"I'm trying, Turner. The man's not exactly a featherweight."

"Flip him over."

Rheese paused and peered up at Matt with an expression of incredulity. "How about *I* hold the gun, and *you* turn him over?"

Matt had waited long enough. He let go of the shotgun's barrel, leaned over, and pulled Rheese's shoulder back. "Out of the way. I need to get this over with."

"Just hang on, Turner . . . I think I feel it."

"Move, Rheese. I'm not joking. You can root through his pockets after he's dead. I'm not risking him coming to, like the end of a bad horror movie."

Fando's leg spasmed.

Rheese flinched and fell back toward Matt, and Matt shifted to the left, out of Rheese's path. The shotgun muzzle dipped just as Fando rolled right and swung his free arm blindly out. His hand caught the shotgun barrel.

Matt tried to pull back, but Fando twisted the barrel in one sharp motion, breaking Matt's trigger finger and forcing him to let go.

It all happened in a second or two. Now Matt was standing, nursing his gloved hand. Rheese was on the ground, trying to shuffle away. Fando was sitting with one knee up, the other on the ground, the shotgun aimed at Matt.

"You two are funny as hell," Fando said. "Can't do nothin' right! Yer like those cops that bungle around fallin' over each other in the old movies!"

Rheese muttered, "Keystone Cops."

Fando's smile evaporated. "So let me show you how this shit is done. I just decide I'm killin' one of you. So now I just do it!"

He moved the muzzle from Matt to Rheese, and Matt jumped in front of it.

"Wait!" Matt said. "Just . . . wait."

"I can't believe you, kid! This is yer goddamn homeboy now? This son of a bitch would throw yer ass in front of a bullet without a second thought! You gotta be the dumbest fuck I ever met. 'Get off him!'" Mocking Matt's earlier plea. "Let me tell you somethin' about yer buddy that maybe you didn't catch. That rich Russian dude? Rheese wasn't tryin' to sell him no Bible. That was just the icing or whatever. That was just to make the real shit look shinier. He was sellin' *you*."

Matt looked at Rheese, sitting on the ground, his head hung low, not saying anything.

"You woulda spent the rest of yer life in a damned dungeon or somethin'. Who knows what the hell that dude was gonna do with you? But he was gonna pay twenty-five mil to do it." Fando laughed. "And you screwed the whole thing up! I don't know what the hell you said, but I guess he was like, 'Screw this shit; you can keep his punk ass!'" He giggled. "So what you think of yer buddy now, eh? You still wanna take a shot for him? Or maybe—ha ha—maybe you wanna take him out yerself. No one would know—just you and me, homes."

Fando held the shotgun with his right hand, ready to fire should someone move. With his left hand he dragged over one half of the flat rock that Matt had hit him with. He positioned the rock on the ground before him, and now he had the opal in his hand. He placed the gem on top of the rock, in a little concave dip in the middle. Then he stood up.

"Get up, Rheese," he said. "I ain't gonna shoot yer fat ass."

Rheese tentatively rose, as if suspecting a trick, but he must have decided he was no more at risk of being killed standing up than lying in the dirt.

"I want both of you to pay attention to this for a second," Fando said, taking a step back. "This shit is gonna be crazy, all right? Trust me."

Matt looked at Fando and at the shotgun pointed toward the rock on the ground. The opal was sitting on the rock. Matt's eyes suddenly widened, and he shot a look up at Fando, who smiled and said, "Yup." Then, putting the muzzle of the shotgun a couple of inches from the opal, he fired.

The opal exploded into thousands of tiny bits, ricocheting off the rock and into Matt and Rheese.

Matt hit the ground hard, his arms and legs flailing as if he was being electrocuted. He tried to scramble off his back but kept flopping down again. He mumbled strange words in a high-pitched voice, with intermittent outbursts of garbled nonsense, and made snappy flinching movements like someone possessed.

THIRTY-FOUR

The rising sun lit up the highest trees on the mountain, steadily descending to those of lower elevation. Jess, Paul, and Núñez veered off the paved road to climb the hill toward the campsite and the silver van. A deep gunshot rang out from over the mountain and echoed all around them. They stopped.

"You got a mark on that, Núñez?" Jess asked.

"Yes sir. I'd say one to two clicks south." She surveyed the sky and landmarks around them. "I can get us close."

"Then let's move. But we're still talking to our buddies at that truck."

Núñez had been trying to raise Chuck or Roger on her radio every few minutes. A few steps farther up the hill, they heard the distant sound of a diesel engine drifting away.

"Bastards are leaving!" Jess said.

They kicked up their pace.

The two Cubans had told them about the job offer that had spread by word of mouth, and about the three men and one woman—"*muy guapa, muy sexy*"—who had picked them up at the baseball field in Guanajay. They mentioned the offered pay, and the only information describing the job: to help find a missing young man. Jess had asked who was in charge, and the older of the two told him of the tall, well-built man who spoke Spanish with the vocabulary and accent of a Spaniard. The two black men clearly worked for him, he had said. And the beautiful woman seemed to be just the boss's girlfriend.

When they made it to the hilltop where the remaining truck was parked, not a soul was around. Paul found the tracks of the departed second truck behind the one still parked.

"Maybe they all left in the one truck we heard," Paul said. "Obviously, a much smaller load for the way back . . ."

Jess checked the door on the remaining truck and found it unlocked, so he climbed inside the cab and poked around for anything of interest. Nothing in the glove box, nothing in the door compartments. He turned around and noticed a storage space between the back of the cab and the seat back. Clicking on the overhead lamp, he peered into the space and found some duffel bags. Crammed behind the driver's seat was a nice suitcase.

"Anything, sir?" Núñez asked.

"Yeah, we got some luggage here."

Climbing down, he lifted the release lever, and the seat back sprang forward and down. He grabbed the first duffel and threw it to the ground. "Here, root through this."

After heaving another duffel bag down, he wrestled the heavy suitcase from where it lay wedged, and opened it on the seat. In a zippered pocket, he found airline tickets, all for Tuni St. James.

Matty's girlfriend? It didn't make sense at first, but then he recalled that she had phoned the Turner house to let them know that Matt had been taken and that she was with people claiming to be law enforcement. She had to be Ms. *"muy sexy."* Something was starting to come together in his head, but he was missing pieces. Unless these men she was with were part of Rheese's group, how would they have known that Rheese and company were going to Cuba? Especially if they didn't really have access to law enforcement data. And why would they want Tuni here? Was it a double kidnapping? Two completely separate perp groups competing for the same goal? And what was that goal . . . besides just Matty?

"I've got clothes and some men's toiletries here," Núñez said.

Jess opened the suitcase's main compartment and found neatly folded and organized women's clothes, along with a toiletry bag that matched the suitcase.

"No photo IDs?" Jess asked rhetorically, and Núñez shook her head. "We gotta piece this thing together, folks. I feel like everyone on this goddamn mountain knows what the hell's going on except for us. We got no clue where Matty and Rheese are, or Roger and Chuck, or our maybe-Cuban buddies that are sending us off on wild-goose chases. Not to mention, we got us a bloodthirsty murderer out here. At least we got the damned sun, though. That's something."

"Chuck or Roger, this is Núñez. Please respond."

A few seconds later, a strange voice came on: "They're dead, bitch," it said. "You can shut up now."

Paul, Jess, and Núñez looked at each other. Jess swallowed and closed his eyes, but a second later they were open again. "Let's go get this fuck," he said.

Núñez led them down the dirt road, across the turnaround area, and into the woods, heading south toward the flat-topped mountain. Whereas last night they could only imagine a wooded slope that went on indefinitely, they could now see the peak in the sunlight.

The voice from the radio kept repeating in Jess's head. *They're dead, bitch.* But *who* was dead? Roger and Chuck? Everyone? Or maybe it was a lie. He hoped to God it was.

THIRTY-FIVE

Matt saw the muzzle flash from the shotgun, and his eyes slammed shut out of reflex. He felt a million things strike his body, and he fell backward, certain he was dead.

I am Tadinanefer, daughter of Bes of Swenet. I run between the West End houses. The path hits the wide outer road that follows the city wall in both directions. I turn and keep running.

I'm Matt Turner. I am me. I feel my body burning all over. Fando shot me. Pieces of the opal are inside me. Probably the little pellets from the shotgun are in me, too. Am I bleeding internally? I can feel my arms and legs. I hear Fando laughing, Rheese moaning. But I can see only a road outside an Egyptian city ahead of me as I run—no, as Tadinanefer runs. She's making my legs run, too! And making my arms move. I need to get up. If I'm not dying, I need to get up and run. But I can't see.

Matt opened his eyes, and the image before him was still a bouncing road, but now with the backdrop of an early-morning sky behind a foreground of treetops. He tried to turn his head left, but Tadinanefer snapped it forward again. He tried to put his hand down beside him to sit up, but the girl wanted to run.

How am I conscious through this? It must be the searing pain. It's all over my body—I guess, reminding my brain that my body is still there. This has happened before. I've seen this double vision before!

Between snippets of Tadinanefer's rolling internal dialogue, Matt recalled flashes of pain from when he was ten years old. Someone had thrown a bottle at their house. The brother of someone his dad had busted. He'd been threatening the family. He threw the bottle, and it shattered on the stucco next to their front door. His dad had called up some uniforms to come over, and the guy had been arrested at his home later that night.

A week or two later, Matt had been running around in his sock feet in the front yard. Hidden in the grass was a shard of green glass, which jabbed into Matt's foot. He had fallen down on the lawn, screaming in pain, but he had also sworn, shouting out bad words he didn't even know. And as his mom and dad came running, he was seeing double. He could see the bright sky with cotton-puff clouds cruising by, V's of migrating geese, the contrail of an invisible jet. But he also saw his house—the view from the street, where they put the garbage cans on Tuesdays. It was nighttime, and the porch light was on. He could see the bench and the potted tree, the rain gutter, the front door. He saw and felt himself chug down the last of the Heineken beer he had brought with him.

"Got it!" Dad had said triumphantly. He held the bloodied shard of glass between thumb and index finger, and Matt cried. But it was done—no more double vision, no more yelling out someone else's curses.

That's gotta be it, Matt thought. *It's the pain lighting up my nerves.*

Tadinanefer hurdled a bush and crouched down between a tree and the city wall. Her chest heaved.

Now, she's sitting still. See if you can get up!

Matt felt as if he now had more control over his body, though her breathing was out of rhythm with his own, and her endless, fear-filled train of thought terribly distracting. He managed to roll onto his side and get a foot under him. He had his eyes wide open, trying to differentiate the ground around him from that around the girl. Both views were equally real.

He heard the radio on the ground beep, and the same woman's voice from before said, "Chuck or Roger, this is Núñez. Please respond."

Fando sighed, "*Hijo de la chingada,* lady, get a damned clue." He walked over, picked up the walkie-talkie, and said, "They're dead, bitch. You can shut up now," and clipped the radio to his pants pocket.

Matt made it to his feet, though he found himself falling to one side. Tadinanefer was leaning against a wall that Matt didn't have, throwing off his balance.

"And where're *you* goin'?" Fando said, laughing.

Tadinanefer got up, stretching a leg over a bush, and Matt lifted his foot over an invisible obstacle. As he moved, he could feel his jeans rub against tiny shards protruding from the skin of his legs, tearing each little cut ever so slightly. The girl began to run again.

Every step Matt took gave him the jarring surprise of having climbed the final stair and thinking there was one more, only to step down hard on the landing. His arms and legs trembled with small convulsions, and he felt the girl's desperate thirst. He sped up his own body to try to match hers. The wide, house-lined road ahead of Tadinanefer was clear. She glanced back to be sure she wasn't being followed. Matt's head turned as well. He could see Rheese, lying on the ground and holding his hands over one eye . . . his dad's dead body . . . the body of his dad's friend. *This is all my fault. They would still be alive if I'd gone with Tuni.* Tadinanefer head turned forward again, and a giant tree smashed into Matt's face and chest. He bounced back and crashed to the ground, screaming and flailing as if he were having a seizure.

"Holy shit!" Fando yelled, laughing uproariously. "Did you see that, Rheese? Funniest shit I ever seen in my life! Look at him—oh, shit! Ha, ha!"

Matt tried desperately to right himself, feeling like a bug trapped on his back, and the agony renewed all over his body. His nose was definitely broken now if it hadn't been before. Blood poured down his throat, gagging and choking him. He rolled over and planted his hands on the ground as he pulled his knees under him.

✳ ✳ ✳

Fando watched, still giggling at Matt's quaking, constant humming, and unintelligible outbursts. He was like a street racer revving in front of a red light. And then he took off.

"Whoa, green light!" Fando cheered.

Matt disappeared behind the tree he had hit, reappeared beyond it a second later, and then was gone, down the hill. The crunching of leaves, branches, and fallen palm fronds marked his path until the sound faded into the din of the waking jungle birds.

Fando sighed out the last bit of laughter, rubbed his eyes, and turned to Rheese, still whimpering on the ground. "That was the shit, eh?"

"Just bloody kill me, you sick bastard," Rheese said, with his hands still covering his ruined eye.

"Yeah, that'd be the decent thing to do, right? Turner's gonna go run his ass off a cliff, so you oughta get off that easy, too, yeah?" Fando scratched his cheek with the shotgun muzzle and chewed his lip. He took a deep breath. His posture sank, and his eyelids drooped with his exhalation, as if he had breathed out all the high of the moment. Thoughts of reality returned: flashes of his son's grinning face, his woman's gleaming curly hair, Raúl's rare laugh, Danny always calming him down when he got too wound up, his mom. His mom eclipsed the others—her eyes so disappointed, her mouth pursed. She would blame him for Raúl. For Danny, too. She always liked "Daniel," as she called him, accent on the "e," and told Fando he'd finally picked the right kind of friend—now he just had to start learning from him. She didn't know that Danny did some stupid shit, too. He was the one who, at 15, stole the neighbor's Suburban for a joyride and then picked up Fando and Raúl to cruise with him. But Fando was the one driving when they got busted, so he took the fall, which was fine, but it didn't make his mom's words sting any less when she said, "You're gonna drag Daniel down with you! *He* would never have been involved in something like that if he didn't know you!"

He had always followed Danny. Signed up for the Marines after him, requested Afghanistan when Danny's unit got deployed there, and when they got out he applied to SecureElite after they hired Danny. Some of the jobs were shit, and Fando would have quit, but Danny said they had to bide their time for a "big-payoff op." That was what Rheese was supposed to be. All this was Rheese's fault. If not for him, they would be bouncing at a Saudi prince's party or delivering the ransom for some company's kidnapped VP in Colombia.

Fando looked down at Rheese. "You wanna die, huh?"

Rheese looked small and defeated. "Just bloody do it," he said.

Fando nodded and looked around him with the bewildered air of someone walking out of a serious car accident. *I gotta . . . gotta do somethin'. We gotta go or . . . I don't know. We gotta go . . .*

"Get up." He had no plan, but he knew he wanted to get off this mountaintop *now*.

Rheese whimpered, "I can't."

Fando used his calm, menacing voice. "Get up or I'll make it worse. You don't get to die yet."

★ ★ ★

Rheese began to cry. He sobbed into his hands, and his belly trembled. He hadn't actually cried since he was 15, after being dumped by the girl he thought he would marry. He had later written her off as a whore who wanted only to shag his footballer friends or anyone else who caught her fancy. He had not thought of her name, her face, or her very existence for at least thirty years, but at this moment, she had come back to his consciousness. Judith Marwick. Strawberry blonde, pale blue eyes, upturned nose. Big lips he'd kissed more than once, large breasts he'd never gotten to touch. If she could only see him now: fat, bald, one eye knocked out by a piece of flying gemstone—a wanted criminal, a coward begging for a merciful death, blubbering just as he had in the library when she'd told him it was off . . . *I am a repulsive, vile wretch.*

"One more second, and I'm takin' a finger," Fando said, suddenly close to Rheese's ear.

Rheese flinched and rolled his remaining eye over to Fando's looming mug. He wished the man would just put the shotgun to his head and take away his pain, but that was clearly not in the cards. There was more suffering to be had. *This is bloody karma,* he decided. *All of it. Be a man, Garrett Rheese. Be a gentleman, an Englishman, until your time is up. Don't give him the bloody satisfaction.*

He inhaled a deep breath, pulled his hands away from his face, and stared defiantly at Fando's curious eyes.

"Very well," Rheese said, sitting up. "Let's be off, then."

Apparently not expecting such sudden compliance, Fando nodded and said, "Yeah, right, we're goin' . . ." He scanned the sky. "Southeast. But put somethin' over that nasty-ass eye before I fuckin' puke."

Rheese found the clothes pile again and tied his undershirt around his head to cover up. He also found his button-down shirt and pulled it over his shoulders.

Fando picked up Roger Turner's backpack and slung it over his shoulder. "Walk," he said. "That way."

Rheese stood up with all the dignity he could manage: shoulders back, chin up, as he limped forward with an arm cradling his ribs.

THIRTY-SIX

Just keep going, Matt thought as he leaned against Tadinanefer's direct path. There was another tree in front of him, a cluster of palmettos ringing its base. It worked. As he continued down the hill, he found with each step that he still had some degree of influence over his body. But the double vision remained an insufferable hindrance. They were moving too fast for him to quickly distinguish the objects and terrain in his own reality from those in hers. And then her imprint ended and dropped into dark space. His body and senses were his again, if only for the moment.

He stopped and turned around, surveyed the scene, listened. The birds in the canopy above were in full riotous song, and he couldn't hear anyone coming. If Fando had decided to follow him, he would have had to leave Rheese behind. Who was more important to him?

Matt looked down at his perforated body. He could see where the shards of opal had shot into his chest and stomach. There seemed to be a hundred little spots, some with tiny trickles of congealed blood, others with thicker clots. Some of the larger pieces still showed above the skin. He needed these fragments out of his body, and he started by plucking the biggest ones first. One shard in his left pectoral muscle was long; it seemed to keep coming far after he expected it to be out. He winced as the end finally left his body. The long spicule looked like a little bobby pin, flat but with a few wiggles. He flicked it away into the jungle and began pulling out every piece he could get his fingernails around.

The Atli imprint from the Arab fortress would begin any second. Could he even *get* them all out? There had to be some buried deep beneath his skin.

Again he thought about all the shotgun pellets that could be in him, and wondered whether this all was a waste of time. For all he knew, he could be bleeding out internally, his organs well on their way to failing.

Atli's hand curled around the buried sword's jutting hilt as he lay on the pile of slaughtered bodies.

Great . . . here we go.

Atli's thoughts streamed into Matt's head: visions of wealth, the woman who (he hoped) awaited him back home, the farm he would buy, the sons he would raise (seven seemed a good number), his brother and whoever *his* wife turned out to be. They would buy neighboring farms and pool their livestock.

Matt's wide eyes blinked, and his arms hung in the air as if he were balancing on a tightrope in the dark. He hesitated to take a step, because the darker overlay of Atli's world eclipsed the jungle before him. It sounded as if a battle were raging up the hill, where he had just been, but he knew that the sounds came from the past, on the other side of a fortress in North Africa.

Though Atli remained indifferent to the mutilated flesh around him, Matt found himself reminded of his father. Gone forever. No inevitable reconciliation to put on hold for just a few more years. Dad had been trying so hard. *I was such an asshole. Why did I always have to be such an asshole?* The transgressions that had once seemed so unforgiveable shrank to triviality in Matt's head. *A decade ago—no, further back than that, even. How long did Dad have to pay?*

Atli stood and began climbing the wall. Matt lost his balance and fell backward—fortunately, onto soft soil. He remained there, his leg, arm, and chest muscles tensing rhythmically as Atli continued climbing. He tried to get up, but Atli said no, we're running down stairs now.

Now, after the battle . . . the Grim encounter. Matt didn't bother trying to stand while Atli was in motion.

Atli and his lieutenants walked toward Grim. Atli chanted the words in his head. They weren't the exact words his father had said, but they still came together, and in his voice: "Bear up, son. Tomorrow is always better, though tomorrow may not come tomorrow."

Atli stopped in front of the black-bearded commander on his horse. The sun was behind Grim.

Matt took the opportunity to try to stand, finding a semi-sturdy sapling beside him. He pulled himself upright, but suddenly felt a new pain on his wrist. Another!

"Ow, sonofa—!" he shouted as he spotted the sources of his pain: frantic army ants scurrying around his hand and wrist and some on their way up his arm. He violently brushed his arm with his other hand and said aloud, "A report, Grim?" One more bite on the inside of his wrist. He flicked the perpetrator then got rid of two more strays. He checked the rest of his arm, his shoulder, torso, and then the ground. Hoping he was now *clean* of ants, he took a few cautious steps away from the infested sapling.

"It's called Damascus," Matt said. "Some sort of special forging skill of the Saracen blacksmiths. If you like it, I shall try to find one for you."

A few moments later, Matt's legs flexed and he struggled to maintain balance as Grim rode off on his horse. The sensation of horseback riding had Matt tripping forward in tiny skips. He found a giant leaf in his face and smacked it away, actually growling at it. He felt overcome with anger and frustration. The imprints needed to stop. And he needed to be out of this godforsaken jungle. Fando was going to pay for this. Dark space.

What's next? Little kid Haeming in the cold . . .

He stepped away from the bushes and brushed away the dirt and leaves stuck to his sweaty skin, in the process grazing several tiny jutting shards of opal. He could very well have hundreds, thousands, of these bits in him. How could he ever find and remove them all?

It was time to get moving again. If he continued in the same direction, he would eventually hit the road they had taken here. And then . . . well, he didn't know what then. Flag a passing car, perhaps, or maybe he'd find Uncle J or that woman with the drill sergeant voice on his dad's friend's radio.

He began trotting downhill, weaving in and out of trees and thickets, when his bare torso began to chill. *Iceland . . .* Little Haeming running through the snow from the toolhouse. Here the double vision wasn't as hard to sort out, what with all the white in Haeming's view. Matt felt his legs tripping up again, so he tried to shorten his strides to move in sync with the boy's. It happened quickly and, to his surprise, naturally. It felt like how his legs *wanted* to move. They were at the door to the log-walled house in no time, and Haeming was wrestling with the door. Matt's body couldn't reconcile the disparity in motion, so he halted and leaned against some sort of fig tree. He felt feverish, alternating hot and cold chills surging and ebbing over him like ocean waves on a beach.

Haeming stepped inside to face his father's perpetual wrath.

A thought struck Matt—one he was shocked to have missed up to this point: might it be possible to pause this? He closed his eyes and commanded the imprint to halt. Amazingly, it did, with a freeze-frame view of Haeming's hands closing the door. Matt opened his eyes and peered warily around. The still shot of the door and hands remained, filtering the view of endless green and shafts of sunlight. Matt smiled for the first time in a long while.

He took a cautious step forward.

"Where's the ax?" Grim growled.

Damn it, pause!

The vision stopped again, this time with a candlelit view of Grim's fearsome profile. Seated at the table, he had his eyes turned only halfway to the boy. Matt could see the terracotta cup on the table before him—the same cup that very soon would come flying across the room to break against his head.

Matt ventured another step, concentrating hard to keep the imprint paused. The image of his own father popped back into his head, his dead face turning toward Matt and saying, "We have to practice this, boy! Enough with the whining!"

"I . . . I couldn't find it, Pa, but look!" Matt and Haeming said, pulling the sword from their cloak.

Shit! Focus!

Matt closed his eyes again and stood still. He inhaled a deep, calming breath and let it out slowly. *Pause,* he said in his head. It came out in a serene voice, like a hypnotist's. This time, the frozen image was of the plank floor: dark and fairly uniform. Matt opened his eyes slowly and continued to repeat the tranquil *"Pause"* command in his mind. He took a step as if balancing books on his head. The imprint remained still. Another step. *Good . . . very good . . . pause . . . yes . . .*

Using this self-encouraging method, he coached himself downhill for a good half hour, and the view of the jungle changed. Below, a horizontal bar of gray came into view in the spaces between trees. The closer he approached, the more certain he became that it was the road he sought. *Keep going . . . still doing good . . . pause . . . don't get distracted . . .*

Matt emerged from beneath the forest canopy and glanced right. The poorly maintained road curved out of sight a short distance away. To his left, about fifty yards away, it looked as if a truck had dropped its load all over the asphalt. He maintained the soothing chant in his head, in time with his steps as he walked toward the mess. But this wasn't abandoned cargo—it was the scene of a massacre, and the spilled parcels were dead men.

Some of the bodies had fallen in disturbing, contorted positions, and most were surrounded by a glaze of dried blood. A few still clung to old rifles, staring up at the sky through buzzing clouds of flies. The ones whose faces he could see all wore the same astonished expression. It reminded him of the piles of bodies where Atli and his men had lain in ambush.

The clay cup struck Haeming in the head and shattered.

Matt's head shot back, slammed by an invisible force, and he collapsed to the ground. He and Haeming held their head, and their eyes teared. *Pause!* But it wouldn't stop. Grim was over him, beefy fist clenched. *Come on, pause!* Haeming's rambling, desperate thoughts overwhelmed any effort by Matt to regain clarity. *Let it play out . . . get to the goats. Get to Big Dad's gnarly horn . . .*

Grim said, "What, you've nothing to beg this time?"

Matt lay on the hard pavement, looking into the gawking eyes of a Cuban kid of about eighteen. He had a wispy beard and an overbite and was floating like a ghost in the air between Haeming and Grim.

"Outside," Grim said.

Overcome with Haeming's emotions, and recalling his own father arching over him like this, scalpel in hand, Matt begged along with the boy. "No. Please, no . . ."

Just a few more minutes, Matty. You need to be tougher than this, though. Lotta people depending on you . . .

Grim grunted and went back to his chair as Haeming gave up. There would be no reversal. To persist would only make it worse. He and Matt stood and dried their eyes and nose on Haeming's cloak sleeves so they wouldn't freeze on their face, and opened the door to the relentless, mocking wind.

Pause? No chance. Matt tried to calm himself again—clear his mind, relax. He wanted to get one of the rifles off the ground, but he was stuck here, standing, juddering with each of Haeming's steps through the snow. When Haeming finally reached the goat shelter and nestled in with the wretched animals, Matt regained control of his legs and gradually calmed down along with the boy. *Deep breath . . . Pause.*

The scene froze on a split image: the lower half dark (the curved horizon of a fat doe's belly) and the top half white with snow. Matt resumed his measured breathing and peered around at the carnage. It had to be Fando's doing. The ragtag soldiers who had come with Tuni—they had chased Fando down, but he had somehow taken them out. *Calm . . . still pausing . . .*

Matt tried to imagine what Fando and Rheese might be up to at this point. He knew that Rheese, too, had been injured from the shotgun blast. And now

Fando had only one victim to torture. If Rheese was still living, it was living hell.

As Matt's eyes drifted over the murdered men, a new idea began to take shape. *Don't lose focus . . . maintain the pause . . .* His body was still working. The immediate pain from the opal shrapnel had mostly subsided, and the aching from the smashed nose and broken finger, though both throbbing, were bearable. Would the imprint soon fully incapacitate him as they always had, or had he developed a new control over his ability? In the car, he had been able to hear during an imprint. That was new. And he had felt the motion of the vehicle even though he had been in someone else's body; the same had occurred in the jungle when Rheese's sock was on his face. Perhaps the shock and the pain simply brought this ability fully out. It wasn't practical, by any stretch, to be walking around—or, for that matter, doing anything with his own body—while reading an imprint. But if he could continue this simultaneous awareness and vision in the future, he wouldn't need the timer, and the whole problem of vulnerability would be behind him. This could be the next step that his father had always insisted was there.

Pausing . . . doing good . . . keep going . . . Rheese . . .

Rheese the coward, Rheese the selfish bastard, Rheese the man who, apparently, had tried to sell Matt—a *living person!*—to a Ukrainian billionaire. Rheese, who had stood up for Matt and even took a beating for him. Rheese, who, deep down, had wanted Matt to go free, even if it meant paying with his own life. He tried to push the thoughts away, to focus on his meditation, but he only accomplished the opposite. Images filled his head: Rheese being slowly eviscerated by a maniacally laughing Fando. Fando pissing on him, making him eat dirt, beating his already battered ribs.

And out of nowhere, an idea arose—a what-if that he knew he must test.

THIRTY-SEVEN

Abel and Oliver worked their way upslope with their five Cuban recruits, each carrying a loaded rifle. They hadn't heard any more gunfire in the past hour, not since that single deep blast just before dawn. Nearing the summit, they could see a steel electrical or cellular tower between the branches and palm crowns. Abel drew his pistol, and Oliver followed his lead. Abel slowed his pace and trod carefully, aware that the man he hunted was well trained and lethal.

Though things hadn't gone *exactly* according to plan, they had fallen into place closely enough to work. Now it was time to let it play out, and see what would happen. The one complicating factor that now dominated his outlook was the addition of Tuni. What he did today would undoubtedly affect any future they might have together. It was exhilarating to have one's plans disrupted in such a way. Exhilarating and head-buzzing, for all its presumptuousness. He pulled his shirt collar up to his nose and inhaled. Her scent was still there.

Oliver stepped ahead of him and put an arm out. Abel stopped, and so did the Cubans behind him. Oliver pointed at the ground, tracing a line of tracks that crossed their path up to the summit. The tracks were deep and erratic, and Oliver gestured that whoever made them had been barefoot and heading downhill. Abel surmised that it had to be Matthew. Certainly, Rheese would not be bounding about so energetically, and Solorzano wouldn't have removed his boots.

So Matthew was free, and Rheese and Solorzano were likely trying to make an escape. Abel knew that Solorzano was unstable; his military record

239

had revealed as much. That was why he had been allowed to live. Garza had been the thinker, the level head. Oliver had taken him out, as ordered, and let the others flee. The unhinged Solorzano at large was quite a big bull in a china shop, but any actions he took from here on out would be in line with the acceptable outcomes for the mission. Oliver's only mistake had been in allowing Tuni to drag him off in pursuit of Solorzano, Turner, and Rheese. Normally, Oliver would have been relieved of his duty—perhaps his life—for such a blunder, but in the end, there could have been no better outcome. Tuni had been able to face Matthew herself, on her own terms. And Matthew—remarkably, beautifully—had sealed his own fate with her in only a couple of minutes. In Tuni's most vulnerable moment, Matthew had confirmed and crystallized every doubt in her head. Sad, but perfect.

Now the job was to clean up the mess and get the opal. A beautiful but not quite complete sword was sitting on a pedestal in a quiet study in Muscat, Oman, and the Absko mansion would not be whole again until Sayf Allah was whole again.

The small group moved slow and low as they reached the plateau. Two bodies were immediately visible on the ground. Abel and Oliver examined the area from the concealment of thick foliage. They could see debris, mainly clothing, strewn about.

Abel turned and gestured for two of the Cubans to advance. He was met with apprehensive stares, but his face must have warned them, and a second later the two men crept past, rifles at the ready.

Oliver and Abel watched the men survey the scene, then Abel stood up and strode into the clearing. He recognized both bodies on the ground. One of them was the American who had stood with Matthew's father back at the logging camp, when they were speaking with Isaiah. The other was Matthew's father. He hadn't needed to die. In fact, Abel had taken steps to distract the Americans away from the area so they would not interfere and not be killed or injured.

He continued examining the scene as he wondered whether the elder Turner's death would complicate anything in the future. It took him only a moment to decide: probably not. The man's death was Rheese's collateral damage, not Abel's, and as far as the Americans were concerned, the incompetent Cubans merited no suspicion.

Oliver clicked twice with the side of his mouth. Abel turned and saw him crouched and peering up at him with raised eyebrows and a solemn expression.

"What is it?" Abel said.

Oliver nodded at a piece of flat rock the size of a small frying pan. Abel stepped closer. At first, he couldn't see what he was supposed to see. There was blood on the rock, no doubt from the . . .

"Are those . . . ?" Abel dropped to his knees and pinched up a few tiny fragments of iridescent stone. "*No . . . Why would anyone—? . . .NO!*"

Oliver picked a larger piece out of the dirt and handed it to Abel. It was a lenticular shard the size of a dime cut in half. Its shimmering nacreous hues quashed any further doubt—the opal had been destroyed. Noticing the black residue on the rock, Abel leaned close and sniffed. Indeed, it was burnt gunpowder. Someone had actually *shot* the opal. He wiped his face and massaged his temples with his fingertips. He swallowed and felt himself begin to sweat from his head and back. His face felt like it was burning.

Abel looked up at Oliver's still woeful—perhaps even apologetic—expression. Was this Oliver's fault somehow? Abel tried to think how it might be. He *wanted* it to be, because whoever had done this was not in front of him at the moment and, therefore, could not be properly "compensated." But Oliver had been *told* to keep Matthew free out here with Rheese and Solorzano. And his mistake in letting Tuni go after them couldn't be reasonably seen as leading to this.

Abel stood up and stretched. "Find the tracks out," he said. "Solorzano needs to be put down. Take them with you. Go quickly, and bring Rheese back to me!"

Oliver nodded and strode away, no doubt relieved to put some distance between himself and Abel. The five Cubans hurried to keep up.

Abel stared at the shimmering bit of stone that Oliver had found. He had never in his darkest nightmare fantasies considered this as even a remote possibility. But he immediately called himself out as a liar, for it had been the very *first* risk he had thought of. But like anyone who desperately wanted something, he had swiftly convinced himself otherwise. Of course the stone would be safe in the hands of anyone who knew its value, he'd thought. They would safeguard it as their own. Throw in the mostly-true story of its origins, and they would be doubly careful! Merely adjust the timing of its discovery, he had suggested.

If Rheese knew that the opal had been found back in 2003, he would have asked the logical questions: *Why haven't I heard of it? Why sell it now? Why hasn't anyone torn the site apart?* No, it had to be freshly discovered, straight from the hands of novices—men looking to make a quick buck. Of course,

THE OPAL

Abel didn't necessarily trust the men hired to do the exchange, and so he had one of his own monitor the transaction. How foolish, though, to have felt such relief upon receiving word that the opal was safely in Rheese's hands! He wanted to scream out, beat something, shoot something, *hurt* someone . . .

"Drop the gun on the ground, amigo," an American voice said from behind him. "Don't think about it; don't hesitate, don't turn around. Just drop the goddamn gun *now*."

A woman's voice barked, *"¡Suelta el arma! ¡Rápido!"*

So the Americans—the ones still alive—had found their way to the summit. And here was Abel, standing over the dead bodies of two of their friends, gun in hand. He didn't bother turning or attempting to explain. He slowly moved his hand away from his body and let the pistol fall to the ground. Both hands wide open and held out at his sides, he wondered whether Oliver was yet aware of the new arrivals.

"My friends," Abel said in the same broken English he had used earlier, "these are not from me. I just get here, believe me you."

"Check 'em, Paul," the silver-haired American said. The tremor in his voice told Abel that the men on the ground were more than mere acquaintances to him.

"Shit, shit, *shit!*" this Paul chanted as he passed Abel, picking up the pistol on his way to inspect the bodies.

"¿Está usted aquí solo?" the woman asked.

"Sí . . . alone."

She lowered her voice, but Abel could easily hear her. "That's bullshit, sir. No way he'd come up here alone."

"Just stay sharp. Paul?"

"Yeah . . . um . . ." Paul was kneeling over Roger. He seemed unable to say it. "Yeah."

Abel caught the slightest movement in the corner of his right eye. This could end badly, he realized.

He moved his hands a little farther out from his sides—as nonthreatening a position as he could imagine—and called out in Swahili, *"Je, si kuwaua!"* The Americans would have no idea he had ordered Oliver *not* to kill anyone; in fact, they would surely assume the opposite. But no matter—Oliver's training was matchless.

Startled, Paul spun around, pointing his handgun. Abel heard the two behind him spring into action, as well.

242

"What the hell was that? What'd he say?" The American leader was rattled.

"Not Spanish, sir! Watch left!"

"Paul, you got anything?"

"Only a bad smell in my pants! What do I do with the guy?"

"Get 'im on the ground! No, scratch that! Just watch your side!"

From his left, Abel heard the quick, sequential cracks of something falling through a tree and hitting several branches on the way down. A low whistle from behind. It sounded unnatural at first, but then the pitch went high and pulsed, like some sort of bird-call.

"Izzat a bird, Núñez? What the hell?"

"Diversionary, sir. Never look where you think the sound is."

"Hey, amigo!" the leader shouted to Abel. "You tell your goddamn men to stand down, you hear me? Tell you what: with my best friend dead on the ground over there, any shit goes down right now, I'll just start by shooting you in the fucking head."

In that moment, the first shot rang out, and the woman, Núñez, let out a short, agonized chirp of a scream.

THIRTY-EIGHT

F ando whipped the long, stiff switch against Rheese's ankle and told him for the umpteenth time to speed up. Rheese didn't bother moaning; indeed, he seemed beyond recognizing new pain. His feet shuffled faster for a few steps before falling back into the same slow, dragging stride. Fando briefly suspected it was a passive-aggressive act of rebelliousness, but remembered how badly damaged the man was, not to mention fat and old.

"How'd you get that fat and live so long, Rheese?"

"Apologies," Rheese replied.

Fando wanted him to say something smart so he could smack him around some more. He wanted him to say something about Danny or Raúl or his mom—give him a reason to go completely off on him, maybe even bash in his head or ram a stick down his screaming throat. The final blow. But then it would be over. He would be alone with his thoughts and the reality he had created. And reality right now was a boiling pot of pig shit. He needed Rheese. He snorted softly and thought, *Yeah, Rheese, my only friend in the world. Let's let bygones be bygones, whaddya say, homes?* That's what he would say before he ended him. Say some shit to make him think everything was going to be all right. Shake hands, pat him on the shoulder. Then shoot him through the other eye. And when would that be, exactly? Fando asked himself. *Soon, man, soon.* And then what? *I'll see, you know . . . I don't know . . . figure it out.* You know you just gotta turn that piece on yourself, right? Soon as you take out Rheese . . . you can't wait. *Yeah, I know. Shut the hell up, I know.* Just sayin'.

"Which way?" Rheese asked.

Fando peered past him to a fork in the path. One route led downhill into a valley, where the weathered roof of a house rose through a clearing in the treetops. To the left, a ridge appeared to join this hill to an adjacent peak. They stood there as Fando thought through the options.

The hill next door was as thickly forested as the one they had been on. No one would ever find them there without dogs. How long was he planning to stay out in the woods, though? When would he end it for them both? Could they go on for another day? He turned back down toward the clearing with the roof. There might be people in the house. More people, not just Fando and Rheese anymore. Fresh food. Maybe a woman for one last turn in the sack before his exit. The house began to look very attractive.

"Go right," Fando finally said.

"Downhill," Rheese sighed with relief. "I'll take it."

Fando had hoped Rheese would move faster on a downslope, but his careful, limping steps ended up slowing their progress further still. Just push him, bro. *Nah, that'll kill him for sure.* Fuck it. *What if there's no one in the house?* You know what you gotta do. Push his fat, stank old high-and-mighty ass.

✳ ✳ ✳

The terrain was too different. It wouldn't work if it wasn't at least roughly the same. With a groan, Matt paused the imprint. His throat and mouth felt as though he had guzzled a glass of sand. He needed water. The Norse guys had collected rainwater water from their sails. On beaches and in jungles, they had drunk the water that pooled in certain plants. Looking around, he spotted some broad, bowl-shaped leaves.

Pausing . . . doing good . . . keep it up . . .

The first one contained a surprisingly large reservoir of water, but he drank too fast and choked, spilling half of it. The next one he tilted more carefully, keeping the sides of the leaves bent up like a taco.

Slowly . . . take it easy. Still pausing . . .

Quenched for the time being, Matt surveyed the terrain again. He knew he couldn't predict where Fando would be when the time came, but if he could

246

practice this successfully and figure out what didn't work, he would at least know when *not* to strike.

His visual overlay was mostly the dark silhouette of a tree and the fire-lit ground between Haeming and Atli, a volley of arrows frozen in the air above their heads. The gentle slope to the scene, the surrounding bushes and lack of obstacles, the nearby trees—they were probably the best analog to the terrain around him now: the quick approach, the tackle. And the subsequent fight, too, would be essential. Fando wasn't just going to lie there after Matt took him down. Matt had to get him locked and pinned.

Or maybe all this was just crazy. From his experience of the past few hours, the idea seemed sound, at least conceptually. But put into practice, it could be an epic failure and simply another opportunity for Fando to laugh at him before blowing his brains out.

He wondered how quickly he could rewind or fast-forward to another scene while in the midst of a physical struggle, if need be. So many things would be happening at once, and he was nowhere near used to this *condition*. Maybe in a few years, he could have the whole thing perfected—if he was still able to maintain consciousness while reading, and more crucially, survive his planned encounter with Fando.

The thought repeated in his head, and he cringed. Would he be stuck with the opal for the rest of his life? Or would medical imaging systems be able to find every minuscule piece? And what about other objects? He couldn't read two things at once. The opal was monopolizing his ability.

If he could pause dark space, that wouldn't be so bad—the opal would then be a shield from the rest of the world. *"All it takes is practice, boy . . ."* His dad's words interrupted his train of thought. *Yeah, I got it, Dad. Can I get back to this?*

Matt closed his eyes let the imprint resume to the point just before Haeming set off at Atli. He began to move. His body fell into rhythm with Haeming's: hunched over low, taking soft, measured steps. The sickening sound of arrows piercing flesh. Shrieks and war cries.

Matt turned forward again, saw Atli's towering figure before him. The wrong kinds of trees lay beyond him, unlike those on this mountain: curved trunks, wide crowns, gnarled branches. Matt paused and shook his head to see what didn't move. A shrub remained static in his path, as did a small palmetto right behind Atli. Those were obstacles in Matt's reality. If he should let the imprint play out, and leap at Atli, his face or shoulder might smash into that palmetto and get skewered by the spines. He needed that little tree to be Fando, lined up just right.

Play.

Matt continued creeping forward. They sped up . . . Haeming put the sword behind him, took in a deep breath to release on impact . . . full sprint . . . *pause!* Matt stopped it just before the leap. Haeming had Atli's nice, cushy body waiting to stop him, but Matt had no such barrier to keep him from flying into whatever the jungle had in store. He slowed to a stop and peered past the spot where he would have slammed into an invisible Atli. Indeed, the rounded top of a jutting boulder rose waist high a few yards away. He would have rolled a few times before hitting it, but it still would have hurt. He had to keep his current world very much in mind before using Haeming's for this purpose.

A patch of disturbed leaves and branches beyond the outcropping caught Matt's attention. It looked like the rest of the jungle floor, but somehow, he knew it had been upset. He glanced a few feet away from it and saw a subtle depression in the layer of rotting leaves. Walking over to it, he knelt down. It looked like a footprint, though there were no sharp outlines of a boot heel or sole. Another yard to the right, he found a partially exposed section of soil. Here he found an actual boot print—horizontal bars with interspersed star-shaped lugs. Even as he studied the prints, he wondered how he had managed to notice them at all.

He stood and traced an invisible line across the three prints. Following the line, he found a path that was suddenly very obvious to him: each footprint stood out on the ground as if glowing green, heading up the hill until they were too far to see.

"If you insist," Matt said aloud.

He continued silently chanting, *pause . . .* as he followed the tracks back up the slope. Ten minutes later, a shot rang out, directly ahead. Then several more shots in quick succession.

✶ ✶ ✶

"Well, that's interesting," Fando said as they both halted. The distant echo had come from far away, most likely from the flat hilltop. "Cubans musta

broke down an' started offin' each other from the stress. Huh! No discipline."
He pushed Rheese toward the house, only another hundred yards ahead.

Fando could already see that the place had not been abandoned. Although
the small patch of grass hadn't been cut anytime recently, a well-worn path ran
from the side of the house to a large shed. Another path led to a strip of concrete, chain-link fencing surrounding it on all sides, including the top.

"Slow down," Fando said, tugging on the back of Rheese's bloody shirt.
"You live out in the boonies like this, you don't appreciate a couple strangers
comin' outa nowhere into yer backyard—know what I'm sayin'?"

"Sounds logical."

"An' if they blast yer ass, that's kinda like a travesty of justice, you know?"

Rheese turned around, the brow over his good eye cocked. "Is it, now? A
travesty, you say?"

"Yeah, you know, someone else gettin' to kill yer fat old—"

"Stinking, ugly, smug . . . yes, I got it. An injustice for certain."

They continued forward into the overgrown backyard, which was littered
with rusting car axles, an ancient refrigerator on its back, a wheelless shopping
cart. Fando held Rheese in front of him as a shield, peeking over his shoulder
toward the dark windows.

"Windows are covered," Fando said. "Always a good sign. Keep movin'."

A flight of splintery wooden steps led to a windowed side door. Fando
pressed Rheese against the wall and went carefully up the steps. Peering
into the window, he found it unobscured. It led into a small mudroom with
a water heater and a deep-basined sink. He ducked back down and pressed
his ear against the wood. There were no sounds within. Back down the
steps.

They continued around to the front, where several old tires lay in the
grass beside a rusted auto body quietly being eaten by the forest. A rocky road
curved off out of sight. On the front porch, a surprisingly new wicker swing
hung from eyebolts in a heavy beam.

"I doubt anyone's home," Fando said. "But this place ain't abandoned.
Someone's been here recently. Go knock on the door."

Rheese winced as he hobbled up the front steps. He knocked three times.

"Try the door."

Rheese looked at him skeptically.

"Don't look at me like that, you son of a bitch! We ain't friends! Try the
goddamn door!"

Rheese turned the knob, and the door creaked open. Fando moved quickly up the stairs and pushed past him.

"What a shithole," Fando said, searching through the rooms.

He checked the cupboards in the kitchen and found boxes of cereal, canned vegetables, and broths. He grabbed a box of Cheerios and set it on the dirty, dish-strewn counter. In the fridge, he found something that made him smile: a single bottle of Bucanero beer. He popped the top on the refrigerator door and chugged half the contents.

"You drink beer?" Fando asked Rheese.

"On occasion . . ."

"Tough shit, ha ha!" he replied. Gulping down the rest of the beer, he tossed the bottle into the sink. He looked around the rest of the kitchen. "Oh, shit yeah, the Cheerios, bro!" He tore into the box and scooped out a handful, crunching them in his mouth. "You eat cereal?"

Rheese regarded him stoically.

Fando frowned but quickly brightened. "Ah, I ain't screwin' with you this time, homes. Dig the hell in. A little stale, but totally edible."

Rheese crossed the room cautiously, picked up the demolished cereal box, and reached in for a handful. "So what now?"

Fando nodded, gazing thoughtfully at Rheese. Finally, he said, "Let's see what's on TV!"

THIRTY-NINE

O liver heard a woman shout, *"¡Suelta el arma! ¡Rápido!"* He gestured for the five Cubans to sit down and be silent, and they complied without hesitation. Oliver crept quietly around the back of the electrical tower, trying to distinguish Abel's dialogue with the Americans from the incessant din of the jungle. He craned his neck ever so slowly around a tree trunk to find both Americans focused entirely on Abel. Only the tip of his nose and one eye would be visible to the American man and soldier woman, but their focus seemed to hold on Abel.

The man was tall, and fit for his age—probably worked out daily and avoided America's more tempting foods. He was clearly flustered and, therefore, unable to make any effective response in the moment. But his weapon was pointed at Abel, finger on the trigger, hand trembling slightly, and that was a problem. He would need to be taken out—a shot through the ear to the brainstem, if he remained in profile.

The woman's posture was firm, semiauto pistol at the ready, but with the trigger finger held straight along the slide, outside the guard. She, apparently, perceived no immediate threat. Her baggy cargo pants and loose-fitting shirt revealed nothing of her physique, so he looked at her neck. It was thin, and the clavicle sharply defined. He needed to see her move, though, to make any proper assessment.

Oliver slid back and peered around the other side of the tree trunk to see Abel and the third American. That was when Abel shouted, *"Je, si kuwaua!"* Oliver sighed. Back to the drawing board, as the English said—he hadn't come equipped for nonlethal conflict.

THE OPAL

Crouching down, he picked up a plum-size rock and peeked around for another look at the woman. She had taken a step or two forward, but her position was the same. Oliver lobbed the rock over their heads, to the trees beyond, and refocused on the woman. The rock whooshed through leaves before striking a thick branch. She flinched, but her head snapped straight toward Oliver instead of toward the rock. He didn't move. She scanned the area as her superior started shouting at Abel.

Oliver backed away, below the horizon of the Americans' view. He cupped his mouth and whistled toward a dense stand of trees behind them. Stopping in a new position, he could now see all three of his targets. He would shoot the woman first—wound her to use the males' instincts to draw their focus to her instead of to the attack's source, while eliminating the most formidable opponent. Then the leader, whose unstable state required him to be dropped as soon as possible. The third may fire blindly in response, but his proximity to Abel meant that he would likely be handled without need for Oliver's help.

A light breeze moved the broad leaves hiding Oliver, so that every few seconds a three-inch-tall window gave him a full view of the scene.

The tall American shouted to Abel again. His regional English was difficult to follow, but Oliver caught the last part loud and clear: ". . . shooting you in the back of the head." *Say no more,* Oliver thought as he used the tree trunk to steady his aim. Above the glowing white tip of his front sight, the woman's right hand, middle knuckle. Her steady aiming position only helped him. He squeezed the trigger, then immediately shifted his aim to the leader's foot, which was already rising and pivoting into a nice, wide profile. He fired again, striking the bulging base of the fibula, and the man crumpled to the ground.

Oliver swung back to the woman. Ignoring her devastated right hand, she was squatting to pick up the dropped gun with her left. Beyond the two wounded subjects, the third American was rushing to the female. Abel stuck out a foot, tripping the younger man, then grabbed him and twisted him to the ground. This distracted the woman enough that she failed to follow through with her previous intent: to spin around toward the source of the gunfire. That was Oliver's cue.

He holstered the pistol and sprang from the bush, sprinting to the woman's back. His eyes flashed around the scene, inventorying weapons. The leader's pistol lay on the ground beside him as he clutched his ankle and watched Abel toss away the other man's gun. That was a good thing for all three Americans to see—it brought their estimation of their own strength down, confused their instincts, made them think.

Oliver closed the distance between himself and the woman in only a couple of seconds, coming at a dead run. He launched at her middle but saw her shoulders flinch. She knew he was coming, and now had an instant to respond. She pivoted out of his path, the pistol in her left hand. It tracked his flight as he soared helplessly past, tucking for a soft landing. But he was dead before he landed, the bullet passing through his right eye, temporal lobe, and occipital lobe before peeling apart against the inside back of his skull. The lead bullet continued out the back of his head while most of its copper jacket remained inside, bouncing around and turning brain tissue to slurry.

* * *

Núñez readied another shot as the body slid to a stop. Jess, too, had retrieved his weapon, and was trying to reassess the situation despite the agonizing ankle wound.

"Shit—other dude's gone," Paul said.

Jess and Núñez looked up and around, and indeed, there was no sign of their detainee.

"How's your hand, Núñez?" Jess asked as he turned back to his ankle.

Núñez held her right hand close to her face, grimacing with pain as she took in the extent of the damage. It looked as though the middle knuckle of the second finger was gone, the rest of the finger hanging uselessly by a strand of sinew. Bright arterial blood pumped rhythmically from the stub.

"It's screwed, sir. Artery looks completely severed in there. I can slow the bleeding, but I'm going to lose my other fingers, too, if this isn't fixed quick. Can you walk on that?"

Paul opened up a first-aid kit and tore into some gauze wrap packages.

"I don't know," Jess said. "That son of a bitch either had horrible aim or perfect aim. Gimme one of those."

Paul tossed him a wrap and began trying to help Núñez slow the bleeding from her hand.

"He hit was he was aiming for, sir. I didn't have valid cause to kill him."

THE OPAL

"Bullshit" Jess snorted. You had valid goddamn cause the second he shot
you. What would've happened if you didn't? What was these guys' plan, huh?
You don't know, and I don't know. Paul, you know?"

"I'm just happy not to be bleeding."

"Núñez, you think that guy's gonna come back here? He could be watching us right now, eh? We're sittin' goddamn ducks."

"I think his purpose was to escape from us, sir. I don't believe he'd hang
around. Looks like he did recover his gun, though."

Jess's eyes drifted to Roger's and Chuck's dead bodies. He tried weighting
his ankle and gasped in pain. "Nope."

"We need to make you a crutch, sir," Núñez said.

He looked at her hand, which Paul had bound as tightly as he could, but
she was still bleeding badly. She started toward the edge of the clearing, her
steps weaving drunkenly.

"Hang on, Núñez," Jess said. "Better sit down. Paul, can you find something that'll pass for a crutch?"

As Paul jogged to the treeline to find a suitably thick branch, Núñez sat
down next to Jess and checked his wound. She called out after Paul, "Not
there—beneath the pines to your right." To Jess she said, "You need a mede-
vac, sir. Paul and I can carry on to find Matthew."

"No, you cannot. I may not be able to walk, but you're losing blood a hell
of a lot faster than me. If we're callin' time-out, we're sticking together and
coming back with more people—*trained* people. Not like those jokers that got
slaughtered on the road, God rest their souls."

Paul returned, slicing the twigs from a thick branch with a right angle at
one end. He handed the crutch to Jess.

Núñez said, "If Roger's son is still alive, he's on a countdown, sir. We
can't leave him if we have a chance to save him. Roger—"

"You don't need to tell me what my best friend would've wanted, if that's
where you're going."

Núñez narrowed her eyes at him. "I was just going to say that Roger died
for his son. I'm willing to take the risk to honor that act. Sir."

"Well, you won't. I appreciate it, but no. We're going across that ridge,
back toward the road where the pilot said we might get cell signal, and we're
calling in to U.S. Interests. Americans have been killed, so they're not gonna
drag their asses on this. Paul, gather up any . . ." He looked around for Paul,
and Núñez did the same. He was nowhere to be found. Jess shouted his name,
waited a breath, and repeated, louder.

"He went off on his own, sir," she said.

"God damn it! You just watched him leave? Paul!"

"No, I didn't. I think it's obvious, though, given the situation. He knows he's the only one physically capable."

The radio clipped to Jess's lapel crackled, and Paul's voice said, "You should stop yelling—bad guys'll hear you."

Jess pressed the button. "God damn it Paul, you get your ass back here this second! Your dad's not gonna stand for this bullshit. I made him a promise, you understand? This isn't just about you."

"No, it isn't. Back soon, Jess."

Jess was about to yell into the walkie-talkie when Núñez put her hands up. "Easy!" she said.

He ran his fingers through his sweaty silver hair, then looked at her with glassy, confounded eyes. She nodded with empathy.

"Let's go," he said. "Help me up onto this stick. We need cell signal."

* * *

Paul jogged at a quick clip, eyes on the tracks of several people—at least four of them, walking east in a single file.

His fiancée, Belinda, would no doubt tell him this was another of those quick decisions that could have benefited from a couple of seconds' deliberation, to which he would reply, *"Like when I proposed to you?"* And she would punch him.

This Solorzano guy was a trained killer, and although Paul had been through all the standard Justice Department training, he couldn't recall any specifics they had taught about one-on-one engagement. Sure, there was hand-to-hand combat, takedowns, combat shooting, and all that, but all the building-entry scenarios and pursuit-and-capture tactics revolved around teams. How, exactly, was he going to surround this guy? They had spent a couple of days on hostage incidents, but that was pretty early on, and because it was unrelated to his job, he had pretty much learned what he needed to know to pass the test, then promptly deleted it from his active memory files. There just weren't a lot of physical hazards in accounting-fraud cases. The Sarbanes-Oxley

Accounting Reform Act, on the other hand, he could recite verbatim, and had done so at more than one party—until being politely asked to shut up.

Fortunately for Paul, the trail he was following was an actual trail, worn into semipermanence by frequent hikers. And while he didn't catch the subtle clues that distinguished a fresh track from an old one, the prints before him were the same ones that came from the hilltop. One thing he could tell from the distance between steps was that they were walking, not running. So what to do when he caught up to them? And what made him think they would lead him to Roger's son? Well, it did seem that the Cubans knew something more than his crew. And he had no other leads to follow. And then the tracks abruptly stopped.

Paul overran the endpoint by a few strides before noticing. He stopped and went back to see where they had turned off, but there was no turn, no split in the bushes through which they would have slid. At his feet, four or five sets of footprints came up to an invisible line and just stopped.

He looked up, then immediately felt silly. They hadn't climbed a tree or been evacuated via helicopter. Crouching down, he noticed that a few of the prints were incomplete—cut off mid foot or showing only a heel. Someone had erased the tracks, walking backward while sweeping a leafy bough side to side. Or maybe they just dragged something behind them. Either way, it was scary. They could be anywhere . . . maybe only a few feet ahead, hiding in the undergrowth. Paul kept his hand on his holstered pistol as he continued—walking now—down the trail.

"Paul, you there?"

He flinched, jumping in a way that would have embarrassed him if anyone had seen. He grabbed the walkie-talkie from his waist.

"Yeah, go ahead," he replied.

"We got signal over that ridge," Jess said. "Backup on the way. You need to come back now, you hear? Wait for reinforcements."

Paul stood and thought for a moment. If an ally's voice on a radio had made him almost jump out of his skin, how would he react when it actually came time to act against an enemy? He had been essentially useless on the mountain when the shooting started. He was just relieved that neither of his remaining team had called him out on it. *"Say, what were you doing when we were getting shot?"* would have been a reasonable question. *"Duh, well, I guess I was busy being tripped, like a kid on the playground, by the disarmed guy I should have taken down. Oh, yeah, and maybe holding on to the guy's gun would have been a good idea, too."*

Wait for reinforcements? Was he contemplating this out of cowardice or practicality?

Branches crunched in the woods to his left, maybe thirty yards off. He dropped to his knees and turned the volume on the radio all the way down. The crackling and rustling continued at a quick pace, growing louder. Definitely human steps, walking toward the trail. They would probably pop out about ten yards ahead of Paul.

Gingerly setting the walkie-talkie on the ground, he wiped the stinging sweat out of his eyes with his sleeve and slid the pistol out of its holster. The rustling continued, and a bare foot poked out from behind a palm tree, stepping over some unseen obstacle. A white male, aged 20 to 30, jeans, no shirt, no socks. The man glanced right toward Paul, then left, then inspected the dirt on the trail. His face and chest were flecked with blood, and his arms were a mess, too. He seemed not to have noticed Paul, who was only partially obscured by foliage hanging over the trail.

Paul had seen enough photos to know that this was Matthew Turner standing before him, but for reasons he couldn't name, Paul remained silent and motionless, pistol still aimed at the subject. *Say something . . . say something . . .*

"You come here with my dad?" Matthew said without turning toward him.

Paul cleared his throat, quickly lowered the gun, and swallowed. Did he already know Roger was dead? He must—they were all together.

"Yeah . . . I'm, uh, Paul Kleindorf. DOJ."

Matthew turned his head, his eyes seeming to wander before finding and settling on Paul.

"Kleindorf," Matthew began. "I feel like I know that name . . ."

Paul rose and brushed himself off, reclipping the walkie-talkie to his waist. "Yeah, my dad and your dad worked together a long time ago, before mine went off to Justice. Don't know if you ever met him . . . Ben?"

Matthew looked the other way, down the path. He looked as if he were sleepwalking—not fully here.

"My dad's dead."

"Yeah, I know. Awful sorry, man."

Matthew turned back to him, frowning, "Where were you going? Did you see someone on this trail?"

Paul walked toward him. "I came looking for you, but yeah, there's these Cuban guys that went this way. Shot Jess and this woman we came with.

They're alive but gotta get to a hospital. I'll radio them that we're on our way, so they can hold the chopper for us."

"Jess . . . Uncle J? *He's* shot, too?"

"Yeah. Took one in the ankle. Come on, let's go track him down." Paul put the radio to his mouth. "Jess, this is Paul; I've found Matthew. Bringing him to your position. You'll have to guide us in after we reach the plateau."

"I'm not leaving yet," Matthew said.

Jess's voice said, "Outstanding, Paul. Is he okay?"

"Uh . . . what do you mean you're not leaving? We are absolutely leaving." To the radio, he said, "Um . . . physically, yes. Mentally, not so sure. Hang on."

Matthew began walking away. "We have one more person coming with us," he said.

"Who?" Paul called after him.

"Dr. Rheese," Matthew shouted back.

Paul stood baffled, watched him leave. "Jess, he says he's going to bring Dr. Rheese, too. He's walking away from me, heading southeast."

Jess's shouting voice crackled over the walkie-talkie. "No, he goddamn sure isn't! You do what you need to, to turn his ass around—now! Cuff him if you have to!"

"Ten-four." *Shit.*

Paul chased after him and quickly caught up. Matthew had an odd walk, hands held slightly out to his sides as if he were balancing or walking in the dark. Each step forward looked somewhat robotic, with a measured pace.

"Hey, buddy," Paul said with a smile. "I think we're going to have to come back for Mr. Rheese later . . ."

"Doctor."

"Yeah, okay, sure—*Doctor* Rheese. Throwing out big respect. Anyway, that psycho killer guy is still out there, and we've got this awesome helicopter . . ."

"Rheese is *with* that 'psycho killer guy'—pausing, still pausing—that's why I have to get him. If you want to come with me and help, fine. Otherwise, I'll be back up to that lot where the van is, in just a bit."

Pausing? Paul thought. He was just being funny when he questioned Matthew's mental health earlier, but it looked as though it might actually be an issue. *Cuffs it is . . .*

Paul kept pace behind him as he unclipped the pouch at the small of his back, pinched the links to keep them quiet, and readied the handcuffs for a

258

quick hookup. He doubled his steps to Matthew's back, seized an out-held wrist, and pulled it back, slapping a cuff against it. The single strand flipped around and clicked into place, but Matthew suddenly spun around, twisting his wrist out of Paul's grip, grabbed Paul's wrist in return, and wrenched it around behind Paul's back, also capturing his other arm.

"Whoa, whoa, hey!" Paul shouted as Matthew tightened his grip and bent Paul backward into an awkward arch with only one foot on the ground.

"Where's the key?"

"Look, hey, easy, man! Let me go. I'm just following orders to get you out of here! Let me go, damn it!"

"Key!"

"Shit . . . front right pocket. The little one."

As Matthew reached around to the pocket Paul felt his knuckles pop and his hand bones squeeze together painfully.

"Easy, man! I told you, I'm here to *help* you!"

Matthew gave him a sharp knee to the back to push him away as he unlocked the cuff.

"Christ . . . guess your dad taught you some stuff, huh?"

Matthew didn't answer. He tossed the handcuffs out into the jungle, the key along with them, and continued down the path, mumbling. Paul followed after him, contemplating just how to frame his next message to Jess.

He ultimately chose pleasant exuberance: "Hey, Jess. Paul again. Smidgen of resistance here. Go ahead and take care of yourselves when help arrives. I'll be up there with our friend in two or three shakes."

The static-filled, obscenity-laced response faded to a whisper as Paul twisted the volume knob down to 1.

FORTY

Matthew and Paul passed without noticing them. Abel watched the faces of his Cuban aides. They were hunched down in the bushes, confused, sweaty, exhausted. Oliver had been a serious loss. These men were useless, though they had provided him an air of legitimacy when required earlier.

Only twenty feet from where Matthew had emerged from the jungle, Abel had heard the entire exchange between him and the other young man. Fascinating that Matthew was intent on rescuing Dr. Rheese. Abel couldn't comprehend the reason, but if it led him to his target so that he might finally conclude this miserable trip, then so be it.

He craned his neck up from behind the clump of bushes and, satisfied that they were out of sight, climbed out of hiding.

"*¿Cuánto tiempo más?*" one of the increasingly reluctant Cubans asked.

Abel glared back with a look that said, "*As long as it takes.*"

He set them off down the trail at a slow pace. He wasn't interested in catching up. There was still a murderer on the loose, after all.

★ ★ ★

Two helicopters approached the deforested ridgeline where Jess sat. Núñez had been unconscious for a little over ten minutes but still had a pulse. He stroked her clammy forehead in his lap, his other hand shielding her face from the flying debris churned up by the rotor. The choppers landed, and out of one climbed two men in jumpsuits with a stretcher.

The medics tried to ask Jess questions as they moved Núñez, but he could pick up only every tenth word, and they didn't speak a lick of English. After strapping her in, they carried her back to the helicopter. One climbed in after her while the other returned to Jess and helped him to the chopper.

Inside, the medic was putting an IV into Núñez's arm. The other one felt around her neck, found a chain, and pulled her dog tags out from under her shirt. The chopper began to rise and pitched right, sending Jess sliding. He grabbed the hanging straps and belted himself in. Below, he could see a swarm of men in green uniforms streaming out of the large second chopper. Someone in charge was shouting commands. He prayed that someone was competent, that someone cared about their duty.

Jess turned back to the two working on Núñez and saw a packet of blood marked "O+" joining the clear packet on the IV hook. The medics spoke back and forth in rapid fire, one getting the blood flowing into her, the other cleaning away the mushed flesh from her hand. It all felt a bit like being in a dream. He wasn't the boss anymore; he was a casualty awaiting triage. His bleeding had stopped, of that much he was certain, but every time he shifted his leg, he felt as if someone were stabbing his ankle with an ice pick.

One of the medics cheered and high-fived his partner. Good news, apparently. Jess leaned forward and spotted two surgical clamps sticking up out of Núñez's hand. He guessed they had stopped the bleeding. The cheering one shouted to Jess and gave him a thumbs-up and a smile. Jess returned the gesture and slumped back into his seat, peering out the window at the rolling hills in the distance. Streaming by beneath them were busy roads and apartment buildings, gas station signs and a baseball field, a small airport, a highway, a flock of birds. A different world.

His cell phone vibrated repeatedly in his pocket, and he pulled it out. It had full signal now and was receiving data. The vibrations continued as he unlocked it and scrolled through the list of text messages: two from Ben, four from his wife, thirteen from Beth Turner. He stuffed it back in his pocket and let his head loll back against the cushion. What to do?

The medics were dabbing Núñez's forehead with a wet cloth and lightly smacking her cheek. Her closed eyes began fluttering as the helicopter descended to an unseen landing spot.

Michael Siemsen

When they touched down, medical personnel were waiting on the ground outside a large single-storied glass building. They rushed Núñez onto a rolling stretcher and eased Jess into a wheelchair. The medics walked with them, rattling off information.

Inside the building, Jess's ankle was washed and examined, and an English-speaker informed him he would be going into surgery within the hour. He asked for some privacy and pulled out his cell phone. It was time.

"Jess?" Beth answered.

"Hey, Beth . . ."

"Oh, God, oh, dear God . . ." The phone fell away from her face for a moment, then returned. "Dear God, Jess, tell me. Just say it, just tell me."

"Beth, ah—"

She shouted, "Which one? Dear God, not both! Don't you dare say—"

"No, no . . . I, uh, listen, Beth—"

She screamed, "WHICH ONE!"

He could speak only in a whisper. "Roger. He's, uh . . . he's gone."

The phone on the other end dropped onto something soft—the couch, he supposed. For a few moments, there was no noise, until it clicked and sound returned very close to the receiver, so that her quiet sniff seemed to happen inside his ear. She spoke softly, but the sound was loud, close. He could hear her shallow breath, even the noises of her tongue and lips moving.

"Jess, tell me about Matty now."

"He's okay." As far as Jess knew, Matt *was* fine. It wasn't really a lie . . . "He's not with me right now, but he's with one of my guys and he's fine."

He heard her sigh and sniff away from the phone again. When she came back again she said, "Bring them both home to me, okay? Will you do that? Jess?"

"Yeah, I'll bring 'em. I'm so sorry, Beth. This is all . . ." But she had hung up. He consoled himself with the belief that she wouldn't do anything crazy as long as she thought Matty was coming home. If that changed, he wouldn't tell her over the phone. He'd need to be there—and with Iris and Beth's sister. He flushed the idea from his mind. Paul was with Matty. Paul was smart. They'd get out.

263

FORTY-ONE

Down a thin trail, the prints of Fando's boots and Rheese's bare feet continued. The small valley was shaped like a boat: narrow at the top and wide at the far end. Matt and Paul crouched in the bow, peering down at a single house nestled in the woods.

"So sketchy," Paul said. "We should go back."

But Matt stood up and resumed downhill, so Paul drew his pistol, checked the magazine and chamber, and kept the weapon at the ready. Matt slowed down as they approached an unkempt yard. A dangling branch hung in the way of a small side trail that angled off left of the house. That side of the yard was shaded, while the opposite side sat in full sunlight. Matt ducked under the low-hanging branch, and Paul followed him onto the smaller trail while scoping out the yard. The back windows of the house were obscured by black shades, or maybe the panes had been painted black on the inside.

More trees and shrubs blocked the view of the house as the trail continued around the perimeter. Matt halted and put a hand up. They stood and listened: only the drone of cicadas. A large airplane was passing in the distance.

Matt looked down and spotted a narrow space beneath the bushes, leading into the side yard. He got on his belly and had started to crawl forward, when Paul tapped him on the back. Matt looked back to Paul's shaking head.

Paul mouthed, "*You're staying here. I'll check it out.*"

Matt nodded and crawled out of the way, and Paul took his place, lying down in the bed of dead leaves, and slithering forward through the gap. On the other side, he could see the three unobscured windows on the dark side of the house. The area was shaded by mature, vibrantly green soursop trees, leaving the grass patchy and much of the ground muddy. Paul pressed his elbows down into the sludge to stand up, got his feet under him, and wiped the mud off on his jeans with his free hand.

He crept to the first window and rose onto his toes to peep in. It was a kitchen. No one was visible through either of the doorways he could see. He went to the next window and peeked in: a bathroom with a pink toilet and one of those cushioned seats that stuck to your butt when you got up.

The next window looked into a living room, but this one Paul approached slowly because he could hear a TV. It sounded like an old Western movie, judging from the music and the distinct inflections of the characters' dialogue.

Paul stood beside the window frame and moved his eye ever so carefully to the corner of the glass. From his angle, he could see the TV—the old tube type—sitting atop a stand away from the wall. The screen was pointed away from him, toward a couch that someone had probably found dumped on the side of a road. Beside it was a recliner covered with a yellowed sheet. No one appeared to be in the room, but he could see the flickering light of the TV reflecting off the brass-colored coffee table.

Suddenly hearing the slap of running feet in the mud behind him, Paul spun around to see Matt charging toward him, his face twisted in fury.

✶ ✶ ✶

Matt lay prone in the dark, leafy tunnel and watched with detached guilt as Paul crept along the side of the old house, unaware that he was, in fact, bait. Fando was watching, and Matt knew it. He couldn't see him, but he felt him.

From his position near the house's back corner, he could see across the yard to the fenced-in dog run and the ivy-covered wall beyond. There was a space of about ten feet from the back of the house to the start of the dog fence, and this was where Matt's eyes focused. He had taken to cocking his head to the left in quick twitches to differentiate the "read" images before him from those of here and now. The real world remained level while the paused view from the past tilted counterclockwise with him.

Haeming was frozen in a hunched stance, one hand planted on the ground in front of him, one knee barely kissing the soft soil. Ten paces in front of him were the silhouettes of bushes, tree trunks, and an infuriated, drunken Atli.

Matt had the imprint queued and primed—in his mind, it was like a cocked gun that he could fire when needed.

Across the yard, a boot and then a leg emerged from behind the curtain of ivy. A second later, the familiar square jaw and goatee, the buzz-cut head with deep-set eyes and pockmarked cheeks. Fando waited there a beat, glancing at the trailhead at the back of the yard, then turned straight past Matt toward the front of the house. He didn't suspect Matt's presence at all. *Perfect.* Fando came out the rest of the way and was now fully exposed in the sunlight. He pulled his shades from his shirt's collar and put them on, quietly checked his pistol's chamber, and tiptoed out of sight around the house.

Matt looked left and saw Paul peeking into the second window, oblivious of the killer about to intercept him. Paul moved on to the next window as Matt snaked his way forward, out of his hiding spot. *Pause . . . still pausing . . . almost there . . .* Pulling his feet beneath him, he shifted his stance to match Haeming's.

Beyond Paul, Matt could see a front corner of the house, and the edge of the raised porch with its white lattice border along the side and front. Through the diamond-shaped holes in the lattices, Matt could see the sunlit front yard and then, as Paul rose up on his toes to peer in the third window, a shadow moving across the holes, blocking the light. Matt inhaled a deep breath and unpaused the imprint.

Haeming continued forward, gradually accelerating as he closed the distance between himself and Atli. Matt positioned Atli's semiopaque outline in the emptiness at the corner of the front porch. His instinct told him Fando would *step* out to shoot Paul, rather than poke his head out for a peek first. As his bare feet padded across the cool mud, he hoped his instincts were correct. If they were wrong, at the very least he was giving Paul a warning, and perhaps a fighting chance if Fando should react in time to kill Matt.

Matt saw Paul spin and aim at him as he passed. He sped up, his legs driven forward by Haeming. Atli's surprised face drew near as Matt reached the end of the house. Fando's thick arm appeared, gun in hand, followed by his leg, torso, and head. Matt's footfalls were now deadened by the moist grass. Fando stepped out into the open, right where Matt had predicted. Haeming leaped, with his sword tucked behind him.

Fando turned to see Matt in the air, hurtling toward him. Putting his arms up, he let his legs fold beneath him and rocked backward. Matt's forward momentum, redirected by Fando's drop-and-roll, sent him flying over Fando, who rolled up onto his feet. Matt's body curled into a ball, and his head swung back and to the side as Haeming bashed into Atli. Matt landed on his shoulder and face, legs cartwheeling awkwardly over him before he slid to a stop in the tall grass. His arms and legs spasmed as Haeming struggled to pin Atli.

He tried to pause the imprint again, but it kept rolling, and then Fando was all over him. A kick to the head, another to the neck. Fando dropped a knee onto Matt's diaphragm, knocking the air from his lungs. The gun came down hard on Matt's forehead, and Matt's gyrating body fell limp.

"Don't move, asshole!" Paul shouted. "Throw the gun to your right, hands up, and get off him!"

✳ ✳ ✳

Fando smiled. This was just what he had wanted—more players, situations, keeping busy.

Without turning, he said, "Isn't that, like, a cliché or whatever? Where the cop says don't move but then tells you to do a bunch of shit that requires you to move? And I'm supposed to say 'but you told me not to move,' and then you say the same shit again but louder, and you leave out the 'don't move' part?"

"Or I could just shoot you in the back of the head and call it a day."

Fando laughed. "That's true! Shit, if dumbass cops did that in the movies instead of talking to the bad guys, they'd save themselves a lot of trouble! And not as many of 'em would get dead."

"Great. Now throw the gun to your right."

"Uh-oh, now yer repeatin' the same shit, bro! Why haven't you shot me in the back of the head yet? You a rookie? You gonna cock yer gun to show me yer serious?"

"It's already cocked, Bane. Last time, then I shoot. Throw the gun and get off him."

"Wait—who the hell's Bane?" Fando said as he turned his head to the left, making eye contact with Paul.

Michael Siemsen

"Big-ass villain from Bat—"

Fando sprang up and spun, firing before the gun's muzzle had made it around to his target. It was intentional, causing Paul to cringe and shrink back, losing his aim.

Paul squeezed off two panicked rounds as he tripped back behind the porch's meager cover. Fando fired again, hitting the corner of the house and sending splinters flying at Paul's face.

Fando glanced back at Matt's motionless body to be sure he was down for the count—or maybe even dead, finally. No change, and his only weapon, apparently, had been his own scrawny body, flying through the air at his enemy. Fando snorted "Dumb shit," and continued toward the young cop who was afraid to shoot his own gun. He poked his head quickly around the corner before popping it back. The side yard was empty. Fando hurried after him before he could get too far, before he had time to think or grow a pair of *huevos*.

* * *

Paul sprinted across the back of the house, panting. *Shit shit shit! Why didn't you shoot him? Just shoot him! Him or you, him or you, him or you . . .* He rounded the corner and put his back to the cracked and peeling white paint. He checked his pistol: fourteen rounds left, two more full magazines in holster pouches. He tried to calm his breath so he could hear. There was no sound from the backyard. Was the guy coming back around the front? He had played this game before as a kid, only right now he didn't have the length of the whole house to run before the boy that was "it" caught up with him. A bullet could cover the distance in an eyeblink. *"You're on the defensive. Get on the offensive!"* Some sergeant at the academy had said that.

A noise to his left made him jump. It came from the front of the house. He snapped his head toward it but saw nothing. There it was again—a muffled voice.

"Rrm-m-m-m!"

He looked down and saw a square, concrete-lined pit beside the house. It was the well leading to the crawlspace, and inside it was a bloody bald man, bound and gagged. This must be Rheese . . . Paul poked his head around the corner to the backyard. Nothing. *Shit! Where the hell is he?* Fando must be thinking the same thing he was—the chase-around-the-house game—and had decided to come back around the front. With guns involved, the only way to win this game was to stop the back-and-forth and get away from the house. He shot a final look around the corner, then to the front of the house. All clear for the moment. Holstering his gun, he squatted down and grabbed Rheese by the armpits.

Without another backward glance, he shoved Rheese to the ivy curtain, and after a few encounters with a prickly, unyielding bush, the two disappeared from sight.

★ ★ ★

Fando watched the cop's face poke out from the opposite corner of the house. His face was soaked with sweat and panic. A moment later, he dared another look, probably wondering which side Fando was coming from. *Neither, idiot. You're coming to me.*

Lying beneath the dense shrubbery surrounding the house, Fando held his .45 in front of him, elbows resting in the dirt. The cop hadn't shown his scared-shitless face for a minute—must be daring a walk around the house. That was fine; he'd be back in front of Fando's .45's muzzle in a few, thinking they both had sneaked around the house at the same time. Or he'd start thinking Fando was *in* the house. Either way, he wasn't going to expect a big, scary son of a bitch like Fando to be hiding in the bushes.

A noise in the distance, to the left, prompted Fando to peer through the leaves toward the front of the house. Humming and pops and clanks—it was a vehicle, driving on the rocky dirt road to the house. The engine revved as it turned the final curve into the front yard. He had to wonder if they had run over Turner. *Ha ha! That'd be the shit!*

Voices, male and female. The woman was talking shit—telling the guy he needed to slow the hell down before the truck fell apart. Dude says, "Yeah, yeah." The screen door swung open, the spring squeaking, and they went inside, the screen slamming behind them. Well, this was going to get even more interesting, Fando thought. Cops always had to warn civilians that they were in danger, but the dumbasses never learned—just always assumed that the bad shit would happen to "other people." Fando felt warm inside. Again, this was just the thing: keeping busy, more players, situations. He had heard somewhere that dictators and criminals of all sorts—bad guys, essentially— never thought they were the bad guy; they always justified themselves somehow so that they came out righteous in the end. But as Fando pulled himself out of hiding, he mused, *No, I'm the bad guy now.* And he was perfectly fine with that.

From the other side of the house, Fando heard the woman screaming at someone to get off her property. *"¡Fuera de mi vivienda, que pedazo de mierda!"* Chuckling to himself, he bent over and shuffled along the side of the house, back toward the porch. He peeped around the corner and spotted the woman hanging out the doorway, double-barrel shotgun aimed at the cop on the other side of the porch. He had his hands up and was pointing and whispering in hilariously awful Spanish, *"Me policía . . . Peligro hombre . . . pistola . . . su casa . . . um . . . el trucko you go . . . ¿rápido?"* Fando held back from laughing aloud.

She screamed at him again and fired a shot to his left. Fando peeked again and saw that the cop had run off. Inside, the woman's meek companion was trying his best to calm her down, to no avail. Fando leaned forward, away from the house, to check the front yard. He could still see Turner's toes sticking up in the grass. Apparently, the truck hadn't run him over, after all.

Fando ducked back down and ran in a crouch alongside the house to the back corner, where he lay down and elbow-crawled the rest of the way. No one in sight. He put an elbow on the ground in front of him, aimed his pistol, and waited. *Come on, pig. You know you only got one way to go now . . .*

A sharp crack came from near the fenced-in dog cage, then angry, hissing whispers. Fando turned his attention to the bushes where he had originally hidden, before Turner and the cop showed up. He had almost forgotten about fat-ass Rheese, and now he could see him through a small gap in the curtain of ivy, rustling the bushes, slowly crawling beyond the fence. Fando smirked and took aim. Rheese's ass disappeared into the foliage, and the cop's face appeared. They were still arguing—probably the cop telling Rheese to hurry the hell up, just as Fando had till he wanted to kill the guy. The cop moved a little and waited again, his torso now framed in the gap. Perfect. Through the lung, the heart . . . at least a lung. Fando closed one eye, lined up the shot, and gently squeezed the trigger.

FORTY-TWO

Haeming held his sword as he walked again into Southland's warm mountain city. He scanned the townspeople for potential threats. Many had retreated into their houses, while others simply averted their eyes, busying themselves with tasks real or feigned. Behind Haeming walked his elite fighters, adorned in their iron plate armor, with weapons drawn. The last time they had worn their armor was in Markland, seven months ago, as they stood against an army of outraged Skraelings. Haeming's second visit to the mountain felt a bit more like being on the Skraeling side of things this time—wronged, and with only one motive in mind.

He spotted Bodvarr, the "king" of the land, shuffling half-dressed to his stone throne.

We're unexpected, Haeming mused. *Excellent.*

"Welcome back, friends," Bodvarr announced in his booming voice. "Welcome . . . ah, so many this time . . ."

Haeming walked up to him and stared him in the eye. "You know why we have returned," he said.

Bodvarr's disingenuous smile slowly melted as he gazed up through bushy white eyebrows. Haeming watched him scratch feverishly at his groin. *Truly, a revolting individual.*

"I can't say that I do know why, son of the vile Grim," Bodvarr finally said. "But your intentions look less than peaceful."

"You've a keen tactical eye," Haeming said, and leaned close so that only Bodvarr could hear him. "I'm going to take off your head and burn down your pitiful excuse for a city."

Bodvarr appeared unshaken and even chuckled a little, his great belly bouncing. But Haeming could see the fear behind his eyes, and watched where those eyes looked first: to a house at the far west end of town.

Haeming turned to Olaf and Atli. "That house, there! Empty it and bring anyone inside to me."

They ran off. Behind him, he heard Finn, his mentor, say, "Haeming, don't lose sight of your stated goal here. There is but one task. Complete it, and let us be off."

"Quiet!" Haeming growled. *One task,* he thought. There was never only one task. He hadn't expected Finn to make it up the mountain. He wasn't supposed to be here. Haeming could hear his men behind him, murmuring among themselves.

"Now, that is a beautiful piece," Bodvarr said, indicating Haeming's sword. "It certainly doesn't look Norse, though."

"It isn't," Haeming said. "You'd first like to see it."

Bodvarr looked up at his eyes. Haeming observed that he'd caught his meaning. *Would you like a closer look at the blade that will soon kill you?* Atli and Olaf returned with three children: a girl of perhaps 12, and two boys between 7 and 10, their skin tanned dark, almost like the Skraeling boy he had saved.

Bodvarr shifted on his throne. "May I?" he said, and held out his palm.

Haeming gave a bow and held out the jewel-encrusted sword.

"A wonder," Bodvarr said. "Truly a wonder." *I could break it at least,* Bodvarr thought. *That would be something. He's going to kill my children before my eyes . . . all for greed and envy.* "Unique in the world, I would imagine." *I could attempt a thrust at his neck. Ha, old fool. He wouldn't have handed it to you if that was a possibility. It's too late. Everyone is dead—the mountain is over.* He looked back at his three youngest. *They are so frightened. End this.*

"You may hand it back now," Haeming said, and Bodvarr complied.

"Tell me something, son of Grim," Bodvarr said. "Your Jesus Christ— what would he think of this visit. Of your intentions?"

Haeming smiled. "You still fail to grasp. It matters not . . ." He spread his legs into a new stance, changed his grip on the sword.

"Finn!" Bodvarr shouted, holding up a hand. "My fellow old-timer. Come . . . please."

Haeming glanced back, saw Finn shrug and shake his head. "I . . . I have nothing to say to you."

"No, no, of course not, my friend. But come here . . . come close."

Finn reluctantly approached and stood at Bodvarr's side.

"Careful," Haeming said.

Bodvarr gestured at Finn to lean closer, then gently pulled at his shoulder until he could whisper in his ear. Haeming watched, intrigued. Was he going to try to stab him? Take out the easiest target? Even with Finn in the way, Haeming knew he could hack off Bodvarr's arm should he reach for a weapon. But he made no provocative moves. Instead, he let go of Finn's shoulder and leaned back in his great stone chair. Finn straightened, with a strange, confused expression on his face. His eyes fell on Haeming's, and he frowned as he slowly shook his head.

"Is it . . . is it true?" Finn said in a tone of quiet desperation.

"What . . ." Haeming said. "Tell me what he said."

"You see, young man, I grasp perfectly," Bodvarr whispered as he leaned forward. "I know what you *believe*. Of yourself. And your friend here knows it, too. Tell him, Finn. You know it is so."

Haeming froze. His face changed, and his lip quivered subtly. *How . . . ?*

"It's an insanity you have," Bodvarr continued. "Not unlike my old friend Othormir over there. He thinks he's a young boy some days; other days, a squirrel. Gets into baskets, snatches food with his teeth from the children. It's the same sort of thing."

Haeming swallowed and took a deep breath. His men were hearing this. Finn stared at him with shame, disappointment, incredulity.

"You know what I believe?" Bodvarr continued. "I believe that it vexes you. You find you want to do wrong—what you *know* to be wrong—but can't quite figure out how to make it work. I'll tell you, though. I can settle it right here. If this Jesus were indeed a real person on earth, with the powers of your one God—sent by your one God—he would *not* be so conflicted. Look at you, working away at it in there right now! It is at once humorous and tragic." He raised his voice to a shout. "Kill me now! Kill my helpless people! Take all that is ours! The work of the Christian God!"

Haeming's thoughts screamed in a jumble of colors and words, and the image of Bodvarr's face, twisting, elongating, warping into impossible shapes as it laughed. It flashed between images of his father, Grim, with the same strange contortions and laughter, and back to Bodvarr. Haeming's arm darted out, effortlessly, the last few inches of the Damascus blade flicking through Bodvarr's throat as if it were not even there. His beard fell free and drifted to the ground. Blood welled up from the gash, and Bodvarr's eyes rolled back as his body convulsed there on the throne.

"Kill them all!" Haeming roared as he darted for the three nearby children. Bodvarr's children. Each one stood agape, horrified by the sight and sounds of their dying father. They made soft sounds of being punched in the stomach as Haeming pushed his sword through the center of each in turn. They fell one at a time but ended up together in a small huddle, quietly consoling each other as they bled out.

The rest of Haeming's men had branched out to attack the townspeople. Few offered any resistance, and none had any weapon more substantial than a thick branch. Haeming watched Finn take a fierce blow to the arm from a stave and answer with a slash to his attacker's neck that cut through to the spine. The man dropped instantly, and Finn glared across the courtyard at Haeming as if to say, *You made me do that.*

"Burn it down!" Haeming shouted. "Everything burns!"

Flames rose up from dozens of blazing structures, generating an unbearable heat.

Finn found Haeming and grabbed his arms. "We must go! Now!"

Haeming glanced around in a daze. *Erased,* he thought. *This place is erased.* He saw his men, splattered with blood, some finishing off writhing villagers on the ground, others throwing baskets, chairs, and barrels into burning houses.

Atli suddenly appeared in front of him and said, "Are we done with this?"

Haeming nodded.

"Out the gate!" Atli yelled. "Everyone out! We're leaving!"

Haeming walked out last. As they marched down the hill, the pops and crackles of the burning mountain town receded behind them, and a slanted column of smoke rose up to the clouds.

As Haeming and his men walked silently down the wide path, some men poured water over their faces while others drank. A short time later, they reached the Taino village. The first natives who saw them shouted warnings to others, and by the time the bloodied group reached the village clearing, not a soul remained. Haeming and the others walked through without noticing.

Haeming sheathed his sword.

✶ ✶ ✶

A short time later, the sword was in his hand again. He pressed the pommel into a break in the tree's bark and worked it in tight. He held the sword steady while prying the stone from its housing with his bloody dagger. It was Finn's blood. At his knees, Finn bled steadily from his belly. Haeming wept and thought of when they first met. Sicily.

"You're not him," Finn said between coughs. "Not Jesus."

Haeming closed his eyes and squeezed them tighter. *Hurry up and die. Stop talking.* He raised his fingers to the gem—a gift to the old gods. Payment, perhaps, for Finn to go where he should. An old ritual, a carryover.

Finn grabbed Haeming's wrist, clutched it with enough strength for Haeming to pay attention. Sad eyes peered up, like those of a horse with a broken leg. Finn must have known that it had to happen this way. He was in many ways the conscience for all the men, and they didn't need a conscience now. Quite the opposite. His grip on Haeming relaxed, and his eyes closed.

Haeming used his thumb to mark a cross on Finn's forehead, then stood up and touched the opal one last time before returning to the trail where Atli and the men awaited. Finn must have succumbed to his earlier wound, he would say. And the men would be sad, but deep inside, Haeming knew, they would be relieved. They could all return to their families in Iceland, in Norway, in Denmark, without a thick, black soup drowning their souls.

FORTY-THREE

Amid the high-pitched whine, gloved hands guided the smaller logs onto the next conveyer. Álvaro Ovéquiz was well into his shift at the lumber mill outside Alamar, Cuba. In his hand, he held something that didn't belong. He had thought it some strange sap deposit at first. But when he brought it close to his face, turning it over, he could see that it was a massive jewel, cut with facets like a diamond, but with the colors of tropical water at sunset.

"What's the holdup, Ovéquiz?" the foreman shouted.

Álvaro closed his fingers over the gemstone.

"Nothing, boss! Keep them coming!"

He dropped the prize into his apron's large front pocket and pushed the gnarled fig log through toward the chipper.

"What have you got there?"

Álvaro closed his eyes and swallowed.

Matt opened his eyes, feeling the mill's itchy sawdust stuck to his neck and along his waistband. *Not the mill. Pause.* The imprint halted with Alvaro's hand outstretched before the foreman, presenting the opal. *Where am I?*

His memory caught up with him, and he remembered leaping at Fando, missing him entirely. He wondered what had possessed him to think it could work. In fact, he had known for certain it would work; there had been not a doubt in his mind. *Because Haeming has no doubts. But I'm not Haeming.*

He tilted his head back and tried to see between the blades of grass and weeds in the front yard. There was no one on the front porch, but he could hear a man and a woman talking. Well, the man was talking, and the woman was yelling. He tried to make out the words. Spanish. "So *he* said! I say fuck Americans, and fuck police! He came for my crop!"

Matt's head throbbed. He raised his eyebrows and felt a massive lump across his forehead. Where was Paul? Was he in there with them? And Fando? And Rheese? *Keep pausing . . .*

He rolled onto his stomach and parted the grass in front of him. He could see along the shaded side of the house, where Paul had peeped in the windows and where Matt had made his ill-fated sprint. No one was there—except . . . there! On the ground at the back corner of the house, he could see someone lying on the ground, legs sticking out toward him, head facing the backyard. Matt raised his head a little to get a better view. He saw the shape of the shoulders and back. It was Fando . . . waiting for someone.

Matt quickly rolled to his left, out of sight of Fando if he should take a backward look, and stood up. *Paused . . . good pause . . . Now what?* He tried to think of any possible way that he could sneak up on Fando. No, there was nothing. Another bum-rush was out of the question—for one thing, he was far too dizzy to handle any kind of physical altercation. His only hope was the Cuban couple in the house. They apparently had a gun, from what the woman was saying.

Matt quietly walked up the steps and across the squeaking porch to the screen door. Inside, he could hear the male voice murmuring to himself as a woman sang in Spanish.

"Seguir adelante y odiarás a tu vecino . . . Seguir adelante y engañar a un amigo . . ."

Matt's eyes slowly adjusted as he peered through the screen and saw the man leaning against a wall, facing into another room. Matt definitely didn't want to knock, or in any way alert Fando that he was up and about. After a sideways glance to the edge of the porch, half-expecting to see Fando with a gun pointed at him, he turned back to the door and saw the man looking straight at him.

"*Ai, mierda,*" the man said, and threw his head back in exasperation.

The woman stopped singing. "What now?" she yelled in Spanish.

"Someone else at the door. Just be calm. Don't shoot anyone else, please, my love . . ."

Anyone else? Oh God . . .

As Matt watched, the man was shoved out of the way, and a terrifying woman in a burgundy dress with white flowers stood in his place. In her hands was a submachine gun with a curved magazine. She rushed toward Matt, screaming curses and pointing the rifle at him. Matt put his hands up and tried to gesture for her to be quiet.

"You want some, too, you piece of shit? I will blow your pale gringo ass into a thousand pieces!"

"Shh!" Matt hissed, putting a finger to his lips as he glanced nervously to the right. He whispered in Spanish, "A killer out here, ma'am. He has a gun, too. Please. He killed my father . . . many others."

Her face turned from fury to suspicion. "That piece-of-shit muscle man killed your father?"

He kept his eyes fixed to the right as he continued to whisper, "Yes. Just last night. His body is on the mountain back there. With others. The killer is just around the corner . . . or he *was* . . . He might have heard you and moved."

Her face softened, and a hint of a smile appeared. "Oh, he isn't going to move. I already killed that fucker."

A moment later, they were standing over Fando's dead body. A dotted stripe of bloody bullet holes ran diagonally across his T-shirt. Broken glass littered his back and the ground around the body. A flurry of emotions ran through Matt's head. His arms and face twitched as the imprint paused and unpaused, while he struggled to keep focused.

"See?" she said, leaning the AK-47 on her shoulder. "Dead like a dog in the road. I got him through this window." She nodded to the shattered window frame beside them.

Matt leaned over to look at Fando's face. The eyes and mouth were open in an expression of surprise. Matt liked that. He imagined Fando wondering as he died, *How did someone actually get me?* But perhaps he didn't consider himself as invincible as Matt had come to think of him. He took a mental picture of the astonished face. He wanted to keep that.

Matt turned to the woman. "Thank you for killing this man. I feel a small amount of peace for my father." She nodded and shrugged. "Do you happen to know where my friends are? There were two more of us down here. An older man with a bald head and—"

"I have them inside. I thought they were with this pile of shit. The one said he was a cop."

"He is, yes. He came here with my father."

"Come inside."

She led him just outside a cracked bathroom door. He could see only a sliver of a grimy toilet and sink.

"They're in there?"

She merely pointed again, then looked away, remorse in her eyes. Matt's previous sense of relief suddenly fell away, replaced by a new dread. She had said, *"The one said he was a cop." Was.* She had thought they were with Fando. *Oh, God . . .*

He pushed the door aside and peered in, bracing for the worst. To the right was a half-papered wall; in front of him, the stained sink and lime-encrusted toilet. A yellow plastic shower curtain hid the tub. He shook his head and stepped in, tugging the curtain toward him.

Inside lay Rheese and Paul, stacked nude with Rheese on top. Rheese was facing down, his wrists bound with a thick zip tie. The gag around his head looked like an old T-shirt. Matt stepped in further and saw Paul's face, also gagged, looking up at him. His eyes pleaded for help.

"Here," the man of the house said from behind Matt, and handed him a pair of wire cutters. He turned to the woman. "I told you."

"You told me nothing, faggot! Don't tell me you told me when you don't tell me nothing!"

Matt leaned over and cut the zip ties off Rheese. Rheese flexed his wrists and strained to get up. Matt helped, and Paul moaned as elbows and knees pressed into him. Matt pulled off his gag.

"This is so unsanitary," Paul said.

The two of them dressed hurriedly as the woman lectured Matt that there was no reason for any of them to talk about this house. She was keeping all the guns and ammo, and God damn it, no one had better complain about it, either. She would get rid of Fando's body, and if anyone came knocking on her door asking questions, she would track Matt down, dead father or not.

As the three walked out the door, Paul muttered, "Thank you for the hospitality."

They waited until they had cleared the yard before anyone spoke again.

"Is he definitely dead?" Rheese asked. "Did you see him dead?"

Matt replied, "Yeah, I saw him. He's right back there; see for yourself."

Rheese squinted back toward the house, then said, "That's fine. I'll take you at your word."

✳ ✳ ✳

Michael Siemsen

As they hiked on in silence, Rheese pondered what was next for him. Turner would go back to his life, likely somewhat the worse for wear. He had some difficult conversations ahead of him around the violent passing of his father. The fellow with whom Rheese had just shared an intimate time in the bathtub would return to whatever law enforcement life he had interrupted to come here. Probably not too shaken up, no long-term damage. As for himself, well, he would surely end up in prison, although he hoped it would be a British one. Somewhere he would be fed three meals a day, have access to a library, hopefully a solitary cell, though not a cell *in* solitary. If he must have a cell mate, he would rather he be a timid, passive sort, though not opposed to good conversation. Rheese would go mad if he couldn't share the occasional stimulating dialogue.

Farther up the path, Turner broke the uncomfortable silence again, "We need to bring my father's body back, Paul. I'm not leaving him up there. His friend, too."

"Jess had people coming," the officer, Paul, said. "Must be up there by now."

Just around a bend, Turner stopped. Rheese halted and looked up to see that Paul, in the lead, was standing transfixed by something up ahead, and slowly raising his hands.

"What's up?" Turner said, looking over Paul's shoulder.

Standing in the path were five or six men, the one in front dressed in a tight shirt with a shoulder holster. He had a pistol trained on them. Rheese looked past the muzzle and saw the man's face. It was a face that, more than any other, he had hoped never to see again.

"Bollocks," he said.

"What now?" Turner groaned.

Paul said, "We're unarmed."

"Hello, Dr. Rheese," The Gray said with a smile. "Would you mind a quick word?"

Rheese's shoulders fell. With frustrated and confused expressions, Turner and Paul stepped aside for him, and he hobbled forward.

"My goodness!" The Gray said. "You've looked better, Professor."

Rheese stopped several paces away. He scanned the other men with guns. They looked like Cubans and wore a ragtag combination of military and civilian clothing. Would he kill Rheese in front of them? In front of Turner and the American policeman?

The Gray cleared his throat. "Step a little to your left, please."

Rheese complied.

"Good."

There was a flash and a thunderclap, and the back of Rheese's head burst. His lifeless body crumpled to the ground.

* * *

Matt and Paul dived into the bushes on either side of the trail.

"Run the other way if you can!" Paul shouted.

Matt was on his back, looking up through thick foliage, but all he could see was a flight of metal stairs. César, the foreman, was climbing them on his way to the office, with the opal in his hand. He was trying to work out a way he could get away with keeping it himself. Perhaps if he fired Ovéquiz, the mill worker, or even paid him off . . .

Pause . . . c'mon, pause!

"Matthew Turner," said the man who had just shot Rheese. "I see you in there. Can you hear me?"

"I hear you."

"Do you know who I am?"

"Uh, lemme see—a murderer?"

"My name is Jivu Absko. I am a businessman. Now, listen closely. I need you to know a few things, and then I will leave you. First, Tuni is safe. I will be taking care of her now."

"What?" Matt blurted. "Where is she? What do you mean, take care—"

"As I said, she is safe. If she is not already, soon she will be on a flight back home to New York. She has no interest in speaking with you at this time—apparently, you, um, weren't all she'd hoped you were. She is actually quite cross with you. Give her some time, though. Maybe there is forgiveness in her heart. But for now you should tend to your own life and your family. Which brings me to the second item. I'm very sorry for the loss of your father. I had nothing to do with that, as I'm certain you are aware."

"Yeah, I'm aware," Matt said, struggling to right himself in the thicket.

"Good. My third and final item is actually a question. My opal . . . did you *experience* it?"

"I don't know what you're talking about. Rheese had an opal. Fando blew it to shit."

"Solorzano, yes. I was pleased to watch the woman dispatch him. But I am speaking of your psychometry—that supernatural ability to extract the unknown histories of objects via physical contact. Dr. Rheese told me all about it when he attempted to settle his debt with me by selling you to me at a 'greatly discounted price.' I didn't accept the offer, obviously. I do not trade in people. After that, he tried to blackmail me. Now, he has finally paid the price for that. So, with that said, back to my query: did you experience my opal?"

"A little. Why?"

"Were you ever in Egypt?"

"Maybe." Matt righted himself and stood up.

"What about Babylon?"

"I don't think so."

"Hmm. I should very much like to speak with you again someday . . . now that my opal is . . . gone."

"You shouldn't think of it as being yours," Matt said. He now faced Absko over the top of the bushes.

"Oh?"

"Yeah, you may have held on to it for a little while, but nothing ever really belongs to a person. Except, maybe, if they made it. Land, animals, jewelry, money, *people*—they're not ours. I'm guessing you probably have a lot of money, and you probably think you're pretty important. And maybe you are, right this second. But your perspective is off. People are here for an instant, and they're lucky if they matter to someone else. A few leave a little mark, like a carving in a tree trunk. But those inevitably disappear, too. Most people, though, are like a match: they're conceived, flare into life, burn out, and get forgotten within two or three generations. You probably think you're one of the ones who leave a mark, but in my experience with people like you—no offense—I'd say you're a match."

Absko nodded for a beat, gazing at Matt. Then he smiled and put on his sunglasses.

"Look me up when you're in a better place, Matthew," he said. "I have a sword you may wish to see, and I'd still like to chat."

Absko turned and walked back up the trail, his men in tow.

"Harsh," Paul said, climbing out of the bushes and brushing off his clothes.

Matt and Paul found several large palm fronds and used them to cover Rheese's body. Paul picked up a long, tapering branch, tied a strip of red fabric to the top, and propped it up near Rheese for others to later find him. Not wanting to run into Absko again, they waited there on the trail for several minutes. Paul looked over Matt's wounds and cleaned and dressed the worst ones, using swabs and antiseptic from his first-aid kit. In the process, he found several slivers of opal, which he pulled out with tweezers and deposited in a little plastic bag.

With each piece extracted, Matt waited for the frozen overlay of a fluorescent-lit Cuban lumber mill office to disappear. But there it remained, as if he were wearing glasses with painted lenses.

After hiking up out of the valley, they kept right on going until, an hour later, they were back at the mountaintop. Roger's body was exactly as Matt had left it. The other man, Paul told him, was Chuck Kohl, the detective who had filled Roger's position at the Newark Police Department.

Matt found his shirt and pulled it on, then got down on his knees next to his dad. Paul left them alone without being asked.

"I'm not going to tell you that I was wrong and you were right, or that you were the best father I could have ever wanted, or any of that other bullshit," Matt said. He wiped a tear on his shirt. "But I did hold on to it for too long. I couldn't let it go. I saw you as selfish, and that I *do* regret. I know you were the opposite of that, the whole time. It was always about other people. After that . . . well, I think I was right to be angry after that."

Matt dried his face again and glanced around. Paul was well out of earshot, trying to reach someone on his walkie-talkie.

"I don't remember the last time I said it . . . probably around thirteen, fourteen. But I love you, Dad. I really hope you can hear that. Sorry I . . . well, you know why I'm sorry."

Matt looked his father's body over one last time, then got up to go. He traveled a single step away and stopped, remembering the stone. Dropping back to his knees, he drew his father's hand to him and pulled open the fingers. Picking up the smooth little rock, he almost expected it to throw him into the imprint, but, of course, it didn't—one César González Machado held that honor at present. Matt dropped the rock into his pocket.

Paul called out, "Hey, we got guys coming up the hill."

Matt sprang up. "What kind of guys?"

"Look like military. Real ones. Might want to put your hands up . . . they've got guns at the ready."

FORTY-FOUR

Tuni took the cat from her neighbor's hands, thanked him profusely, and turned the key and went inside. Then, letting the cat escape her grasp, she checked the place out from top to bottom. Satisfied, she wheeled in her bags from the hall and locked the door behind her. The familiar scent of old wood was comforting, but it didn't fill the empty space or soothe her as she had anticipated.

She went down the hall and flopped onto the comfy white-linen-covered couch. She had already listened to the voicemail in the cab. Hidden deep among the political and non-profit solicitors, Dr. Meier at the museum, her mum, and various friends was a message from Beth Turner.

"Hi Tuni," the voice said. "I don't know what happened between you and Matty, but I'd like you at the funeral . . ." It was set for ten-thirty Saturday morning, in Newark.

She didn't want to see Matthew yet. One cannot simply apologize for finally saying that which they had always wanted, nor could he simply take back what was said. There could be no "I didn't mean it that way" or "It was the heat of the moment, the stress." As he so coldly proclaimed, there could be no future for them.

Abel had been delicate, framed his sentences to make Matthew sound better, but it was pretty clear what had happened after Tuni had left. Matthew had snubbed his father just as he had Tuni, for he was clearly more interested in chasing treasure with the very man who had kidnapped him. So many people died as a result—his own father, for God's sake! It made her sick inside just to think of it. How blind she had been during their time together. It was crazy, the

287

things one could overlook while in the thick of a relationship. The things she had ignored, minimized, dismissed, excused.

Her phone vibrated and chirped. It was a text message from Abel: *In NYC Sat before home. Brunch?*

She plopped the phone onto her lap. The funeral was Saturday. She really should go. She didn't want to, though. Perhaps a private lunch instead—just herself and Beth on Sunday. Beth would understand. They both had been through hell, though Beth was still very much in hers. She would understand.

Tuni texted back: *Sarabeth's West. 423 Amsterdam. 11:00?*

∗ ∗ ∗

Beth and Iris Turner rode from the church to the cemetery with Jess and his wife in their car. As they pulled up alongside the grassy field, Beth saw the honor guard of men in uniform waiting beside the plot. No Matty. He had told Iris he wouldn't be at the funeral but would come to the graveside service, where he wouldn't have to talk to anyone.

"He'll be here, Mom," Iris said.

Jess grumbled, "He'd better be."

"You're not going to go at him," Beth said. "Jess? Promise me. Say it now, or so help me, I'll call him right now and tell him not to come. And you *know* how much it means to me . . ."

"Trust me, I won't even look at him."

Jess's wife put her hand over his, and they all got out of the car. With Jess on his crutches, they walked up onto the small green hill, treading carefully between rows of flat headstones. In front of the plot stood a row of black chairs. Other people got out of cars parked along the quiet lane: Beth's sister and her family, Roger's cousins, all the men and women from the precinct, including some who had never even met him. Still there was no sign of Matt.

Beth turned to Iris with pleading eyes.

Iris glanced around and said, "He texted he was leaving the hospital forty-five minutes ago."

"Is he driving?" Jess asked.

"No, he . . . can't," she replied. "He got a cab."

A taxi rolled up and double-parked, and a moment later, Matt got out, wearing a charcoal suit and sunglasses—no gloves, no cap. He hurried up the hill as the mourners began to gather around the flag-draped coffin. Jess and his wife went to join the masses as Matt walked straight to Beth and leaned over to hug her.

"Hey, Mom . . ."

She recoiled a little. "Careful, hon!"

"No," he said. "It's okay now."

He bent and put his arms around her. She was bewildered for a second, not used to her Matty being so accessible. They held each other for a long while the other guests looked on, some brought to tears by the tender moment.

Matt let go and moved on to Iris.

"Hey, Buster," she said.

"Hey."

As they walked to the chairs and sat down, Matt spotted Jess and Paul standing with a short Latina in a pantsuit. Her hand was in a cast. He hadn't met Núñez—only heard about her from Paul on their drive to Havana. All three of them wore sunglasses and stared straight ahead. Matt was fairly sure that at least Jess's hidden eyes were firing daggers at him.

The priest began speaking.

Iris leaned close to Matt's ear and whispered, "Tuni couldn't make it."

He whispered back, "I noticed. Not surprised. She probably blames me for everything that happened . . . as she should."

Iris chided him with a squeeze of his hand and a shake of her head. Beth leaned forward and glared at them, and the siblings straightened in their seats, eyes forward.

After the service concluded, Matt agreed to spend a night with his mom and Iris at the house before heading back to Raleigh. Iris would stay with Beth for as long as necessary after that. Beth had never lived alone in her life—it was going to be difficult, to say the least.

They split off on the way back to the car, and Matt rode back to the house with his Aunt Denora and her husband, Andy. As they drove, Andy told him of when he first met Roger, and how intimidated he had been by the big, burly policeman. It was only as he got to know Roger that he figured out he was just a "big ol' softy."

Andy went on, and Matt half listened, staring out the window at the passing trees and houses and cars, all a few shades darker than real life and sprinkled with tiny dots of white. The bright dots were stars on a clear night over the Atlantic. Haeming was lying on his back, head resting on his hands, watching the sky nod back and forth as the knarr rode the waves from trough to crest, to trough again. He and Atli and Finn were leading their people to a new land across the Atlantic—a promised land, where society would begin anew, with God watching over them.

EPILOGUE

Dr. Jon Meier pulled his rental car into the looping driveway at 312 Kaspar Avenue. Brown leaves lay in neat windblown mounds on the lawn. The only car parked in the driveway was an old Volkswagen Jetta that looked as though it hadn't been driven in years.

Dr. Meier parked, grabbed the bag from the passenger seat, and walked up the brick steps. The porch was piled high with local newspapers but also littered with packages, black-wicked candles, and framed photographs of people: children and adults, male and female. It looked almost like an altar that had fallen into neglect. The ornately carved door was almost completely covered in flyers, like the bulletin board of a community center. He scratched at his trim white beard and scanned the bold-printed titles, glancing at the black-and-white photos of various smiling faces.

Missing: Kylie Dunn
HAVE YOU SEEN ME?
Matthew Turner, PLEASE help find our boy!
MISSING!
WILL PAY FOR YOUR HELP
Mataji White is only 7 years old . . .

There were hundreds, small and large, tacked or taped to his door. A hundred more littered the bushes and planter areas on either side of the porch, having blown away over time. It had been three years since Matthew went "viral."

He stepped onto the porch, taking care not to tread on the sad pleas for help, and rang the doorbell. No answer came, of course, but he knew that Matthew was home. He knocked.

"Matthew, it's Jon Meier," he called, figuring that Matt had long since learned to tune out the doorbell and knocks. Still nothing.

He made his way down the cluttered steps to the first window. It was covered, but he could see in through a tiny sliver at the side, just as Matthew's parade of visitors had no doubt also tried to do. Nothing to see there. He called out again.

The side fence was locked from the inside. Dr. Meier sighed. *I'm not leaving, Matthew. I didn't fly down here for nothing.*

"What do you want, Doctor?" a hollow, scratchy voice said. It sounded like someone awakened in the middle of the night.

Dr. Meier turned and saw a head peering out the doorway, squinting with a pained expression. The ghostly figure looked plucked from a place stricken by famine: cheekbones protruding, raccoon eyes, square, pointy shoulders. He couldn't weigh more than a hundred pounds. He wore a tattered T-shirt and sagging pajama pants. Meier blinked himself out of his transfixion and put on a happy face.

"There you are! It's good to see you! I called—several times, in fact . . . Wouldn't just show up out of the blue, you know . . ."

"Okay, okay," Matt said. "Just what is it you want?" He didn't sound angry so much as exhausted.

"Well, I wanted to show you something, for one. But I also wished to sit down and just chat—hear how things are going, and all that. I'm guessing you haven't been back to the hospital in a while?"

Matthew sighed and gazed out from under drooping eyelids, but the eyes didn't quite line up with Dr. Meier's.

"The place is a mess . . ." Matthew began, but his visitor quickly waved it off. "No, it's probably worse than you can imagine. I didn't have trash service for a while, power went out, then the water. That was a few months . . . I don't know, maybe longer. Time's . . . time's sort of gone to shit . . ." He got lost in thought for a beat, then said, "My sister showed up and was pissed. She fixed all that, has the bills sent to her now, but . . . I haven't really been able to, um . . . Can we just sit out there?" He pointed to a wicker sofa in the gazebo at the far end of the yard.

"It's fine, fine—whatever you like, son."

"Let me grab some sunglasses . . ."

"Perhaps grab a small snack while you're in there."

Matthew stopped and looked back at him. "I eat, Doctor, okay? That's not my problem. I ate . . . yesterday. Once or twice. I eat."

Dr. Meier put up his hand. "Just a thought."

As they crunched through the leaves to the gazebo, Meier watched Matthew's feeble gait with some concern. They sat.

"Well, first I have some good news for you," Dr. Meier said with a smile. He tugged at his beard. "For both of us! The book's already a bestseller, a full week before its release."

Matt nodded absently.

"You're not impressed?"

"No, no, it's good, sure."

Nonplussed, Meier forged ahead "Well, that's a huge deal, so you know. It means the advance we received is already paid back and we'll have royalties coming in six months or so. I know you've had financial . . . difficulties since your return from Cuba, and this will be quite the windfall."

"Cool."

Meier sighed. "Well, on that subject, any headway on recovering the lost money?"

"No, all the accounts were drained. Transferred to some other accounts, then transferred again. They pretty much told me I was screwed and to move on."

"I know you thought that, er, that you suspected—"

"It was Tuni, yeah. She's the only one that had all the passwords and access codes used for the transfers. But whatever, I'm over it. Not going to pursue it. What else?"

As Matthew's focus drifted across the mounds of leaves Meier debated whether to tell him. Perhaps if he asked directly.

"Well, here's what I wanted to show you!" He pulled the hardcover book from the bag and handed it to Matt. Looking at it, Matt seemed a little more animated than before.

In a bold, weathered typeface, the title filled the top quarter of the matte dust jacket.

SOUTHLAND
The Stunning True Story of Cuba's
Norse Settlement

by
Jon Meier, PhD
M. Turner

The cover image was a photograph of the excavated mountain village, overlaid with the artist's rendering.

"The artist did a great job," Matt said.

"High praise, coming from you! High praise indeed! I'll let him know. You should flip through and see the interior art."

"I will, yeah. Definitely. Can I buy this one from you, or should I order it online?"

Meier scoffed. "It's yours, son! That's why I brought it to you."

A subdued smile, but Meier decided it was probably the best he could muster.

Matthew studied the cover some more, then said, "How's the Rhode Island dig going?"

"Pretty much done, actually. Construction on the visitors' center begins in a few weeks. Everything's going fantastically, thanks to you. These are all quite significant finds. Now . . . on to you. Tell me what's going on with you—physically, mentally, and otherwise."

"I'm fine."

Meier grunted and frowned.

"I'm fine as I can be. Sleeping pills keep me alive. I just don't get to dream; that's apparently the problem. Imprints keep my brain activity in a waking state all day, every day. Doctors say I should be completely whacked out by now. I think their words were more along the lines of 'long-term, persistent, debilitating neural hyperactivity inevitably degenerates function,' or something to that effect. 'You *will* go insane,' was the message. They wanted me to stay in the hospital—IVs, monitors, all that crap I'm not interested in dealing with day to day."

"What about the fragments? Any more found?"

"I told you before that the shotgun BB's were easy—those were all out in the Cuban hospital. Same Cuban docs that repaired my spleen. As for the opal, I think the total now is two hundred and thirteen pieces. Anything visible on an MRI or CT scan has been extracted. The main doctor I deal with thinks there are microscopic particles they'll never find but that might reabsorb into my body over time. He says they're nothing to worry about. Obviously, he didn't put two and two together on who I am. But *reabsorb*? Who knows what the hell that'll do? Might make no difference at all, or maybe I'll piss them out one day and suddenly be free. I'm not holding my breath."

"Well, I'm certain something can be done," Meier countered. "We just need to find you the right specialist." A car slowed to a stop in front, its occupants staring at the house. They didn't seem to notice the two figures in the gazebo, shaded by the giant maple, and after a moment they drove off. "How has *that* been for you?"

"Less of it lately, but people are still putting stuff up over there. I had my house phone disconnected after changing it a bunch of times—they always seemed to track down the new numbers. People don't understand that I couldn't help, even if I wanted to."

"Do you know who leaked?"

"Who knows? Could be the company those two mercenaries worked for; could have been someone else Rheese told about me." He paused. "Could be Tuni. Or that African guy she was seeing."

Meier took a deep breath. This was the window he had been hoping for. Now he could tell him. "Mmm . . . about that . . . have you . . . heard anything new? Say, in the past year?"

Matt looked at him dubiously.

"I'll just say it. They're . . . ah . . . still together. Tuni and Mr. Absko."

"Hah!" Matt blurted. "She has zero idea who the guy really is. He scared the shit out of me, you know."

"In Cuba?"

"No, in an imprint. Must have been a few months ago. No, probably longer—I don't know. A year? It's when I stopped trying to keep the imprints paused. I thought maybe if I let it get to the end, like with some past artifacts, that maybe it would just be *done,* you know? So I just let it roll. I'd eat and all—got food delivered, like I do now. But this thing never ended. There's so much, it just keeps going, repeating the same imprints. I don't know . . . *I* might have something to do with that. I could be willing a particular imprint to come up. Must have been through most of them thirty-plus times now. I've been Hatshepsut, Insis, Taleset, Abbrid, Minnitecet, Humehd, Ahmed, Isaac, Atli, Grim, Haeming, Finn, Bodvarr—"

"Yes, yes, I understand," Meier said.

"Álvaro, César, Manuel, Pablo, Jivu, Ricardo, Garrett, Danny, Fando. That one, Jivu—or Mr. Absko, as you so politely call him. He left a message. You know how they don't usually go in chronological order? Well, after I piece it all back together, put it in order, there's this jump from the Middle Ages to two thousand three, when the opal was found. It skips from hand to hand before being reinserted into the Damascus sword—Sayf Allah. It's handled here and there, marveled over, displayed. And then I'm looking at the opal in a pair of hands in a dark room. And a voice says, 'Hello, Matthew.' I sat up in my bed, thinking someone was in the room. Nearly shat myself. I'm just passively observing for weeks on end, and all of a sudden, this guy is talking to *me*. He says, 'Hopefully, you do not ever see this . . . experience it . . . whatever you call it. And if you do, I hope it is not too soon. Either way, here we are. You do not know me, but perhaps you soon will. No matter what happens, though, I want you to know that nothing is personal, everything is business. This is always the case. You are a rare gem, rarer still than this gem you are holding. Because of that, I appreciate you in the same way I appreciate my beautiful opal.' He goes on about how special I am, and finishes off by saying, 'I apologize in advance.' He was trying to hide from me—meaning an image of himself—as he recorded it, but like all narcissistic people, he had hundreds of pictures of himself in his head. I saw what he looked like, and I knew who he was. He was the man who shot Rheese and told me he was letting me live. He was your Mr. Absko. You know he's running for the senate or something in Kenya?

"President. Quite popular—expected to win."

Matt shook his head, smiling. "Tuni finally gets to be the princess she always was. It's appropriate, actually. Don't think I could have ever taken her *that* far." He drifted off again. "She sent me something a couple months after it was all over. This little rock. No note, so I assume the rock *was* the note. It's probably a big, long ass-chewing. I put it on my mantel, next to the one my father left for me. Maybe one day I'll get to read them both."

Dr. Meier wondered if he should bring up the last item on his list. He knew what Matthew would suspect, but it wasn't as though he would be able to reach him on the phone. And making another flight to Raleigh, just to avoid upsetting him now, seemed unreasonable.

"I've thought about suicide," Matthew said in the same even tone. "It's exhausting to be alive. All I think about is sleep."

"I've no words, Matthew. I couldn't possibly imagine your anguish. I do wish you would accept help when it's offered, though. A lot of people care about you—people who aren't just looking to get something from you."

Another car drove by, but did not slow.

"That's kind of funny, coming from you. Don't get me wrong. I believe you care, I do. But I know you want to ask me for something. Just say it. I won't be mad. I don't get mad anymore."

Dr. Meier swallowed. Matthew indeed seemed a different person. Old, and with the wisdom of a thousand years. Even with another life, another world, playing out before his eyes. Best to be forthright . . .

"I'd like us to work on a second book: the Egyptian stories. Like we did on Southland, but I could come to you. No need for you to go back to New York. Believe me when I say that the excitement for the book sitting there next to you is nothing short of *rabid,* thanks to you. You may have lost your privacy, what with the whole world knowing who you are and what you can do, but in terms of platform, we couldn't possibly do better. The skeptics blabbering about you all over the Internet only feed the fire. The fact that we have active excavations and evidence that corroborates the book—it couldn't be more perfect." He felt a little breathless and paused to inhale deeply. Matthew's stare remained impassive. "Imagine the same for this second book, as archaeologists discover new tombs or structures or . . . *cities,* even! Egypt is back in fashion, as it were. Not making any promises, but we could have a multimillion-dollar book deal before a single word is written."

Matt nodded.

"Well?" Meier blurted.

"Sorry. It sounds exciting and everything, but I'm standing in front of a crowd of a hundred thousand people right now, telling them about the weather. There are high priests on each side of me that pass the message to another set of men, who shout it to the crowds. Among the people standing on these pedestals are men whose job it is to repeat my words. It's like a human-powered PA system. The people aren't supposed to hear my voice directly, or they could die."

"Fascinating . . . I don't believe I've heard of that before. You're a pharaoh, I take it?" Matt nodded, and Meier continued. "Yes, very interesting, this is what I'm talking about! But what's your point?"

"My point is, I have enough shit going on as it is. I'm not helping you write another book, and I'm not interested in money anymore. If I was free of this thing, you know what I'd be doing?"

Meier shook his head in baffled exasperation. "What?"

Matt didn't respond. Instead, he sat and thought for a moment then plucked a dry maple leaf from the bench beside him and broke small fragments from it as he spoke. "When the ship first gets to Canada after three weeks crossing the Atlantic, Haeming tells this . . . you know who Haeming is, right?"

Meier blinked and snapped a nod as he gestured at the book sitting between them.

"Oh, right—of course, sorry . . ." Matt sighed and continued, "There were a few kids that had come with them . . . this girl, Drifa, and two boys that the men sort of bullied around without thinking. It reminded Haeming of his child-hood—the powerlessness of childhood. He wanted the abuse to stop, but he needed the men to stop *themselves*, and not for fear of punishment. So he told this story to all of them about a legendary man that everyone had heard of. I've *listened* to it more times than I can count, so I'll just say it like he said it . . . 'Thormelde of Hedeby, son of Hakar and Maemer, known as Thormelde the Strong to most Northmen. I doubt there is a man here who has not heard the story of his sunken ship, drowned crew, and his heroic two-day swim in winter water. As the story goes, he made it to a remote shore, took down a deer with his bare hands, and walked thirty miles to the nearest town.'"

Meier noticed Matthew's posture had stiffened, and he'd lowered his voice.

"'But I have heard the rest of his story. I know that Thormelde's father was a cruel man that beat his son daily, made quarrel with neighbors, and killed English priests for begging him not to burn down their church. In one instance, he stripped his son of his night-clothes and beat his cheeks until they were purple, ending with a poke from a red-hot working sword from the fire. I imagine that as Thormelde's father, Hakar, whipped his son as one whips a beast, that young Thormelde felt anger and hatred for his father. Oftentimes, the slaves would hide Thormelde in their house whilst Hakar shouted through the fields for the boy to come and get what he deserved.'"

Matt stood and began to pace before Meier, his hands gesturing as he went on, his eyes making contact with the individual eyes of an unseen audience. Meier realized that Matt was not simply quoting. This was Haeming striding across the gazebo, with Matt translating in real time.

"By the time Thormelde had grown into the legendary figure we hear of, his father had long since passed. Thormelde distinguished himself in war with the Danes, and returned to Hedeby with a pregnant wife. Two sons, he had, one year apart."

Meier watched Haeming look over the invisible group to see that all were paying attention.

"At seven and eight years of age, Thorvinn and Kollvinn were caught forg-ing a knife in their father's smithy shed. They had neither asked, nor were they using the tools to their father's liking and so, without a word to them or their mother, Thormelde beat them and then rode them on horseback far into the hills. He left them there—where the wolves and bears lived—with their blunt, bent knife, and told them to see if it would work on the predators, then to find their way home. His sons were never seen again."

Haeming was silent for a moment. Meier shifted uncomfortably.

"There is a choice to be made by every man who truly *sees* the deeds of his father. Follow the same path or walk a new one." Matt's posture relaxed and he faced Dr. Meier. "You want to know what I would do?" He asked him, and pointed toward his front door.

Meier gazed across the yard to the littered door and steps.

"I'd be finding the people in all those flyers."

END

ACKNOWLEDGEMENTS

There were a *lot* more people involved in the creation and production of this book than *THE DIG*, so I hope I haven't left anyone out. First, I must heap praise and undying gratitude to my wife, Ana—forever my first beta reader (and beta listener, before anything is ever written). I am most proud of the quality of this book, and for that I must thank my trusty editor Michael Carr, proofer Erin Griggs (the Wordslinger), my agent Alex Glass of Trident Media (both for astute editorial direction and for excellent representation), Gloria for Español help, my beta readers Vicky, Alyssa, Eric, Stacey, Angela, Darlene, and Gunilla. Everyone above contributed to the content and/or quality of this novel, so I send out my heartfelt thanks to each one of you.

Gratitude also goes to everyone else at Trident Media Group involved in this project: Lyuba, Nicole, Beth, and Michael.

An Excerpt From Michael Siemsen's Upcoming Novel, *A WARM PLACE TO CALL HOME*

1. I am a Demon

Who's ever heard of a demon named Frederick? I'm the only one that I know of. But to be honest, that statement should carry little weight as I've never actually met another demon. I have read and heard of others, and they have striking monikers like *Rashk, Xaphan,* or *Neqa'el.* Am I envious? Yes. I quite like those names. But here's the thing—*I don't believe in those characters.* I think they're all bullshit. There's no such thing as a demon, and certainly not the sort cited in the Holy Bible or discussed throughout the world's mythology. The concept of these fallen angels doing the bidding of Lucifer is laughable. It's all superstitious hokum, and anyone who subscribes to such nonsense is a moron. That said, I am a demon. And I'm self-employed.

What makes me a demon, you ask? Good question. Overall, I am not so different from you. I eat, drink, read, fornicate, text (verb form), watch TV (I'm quite fond of witty sitcoms and forensic investigator crime dramas), pore over YouTube videos like they're the zenith of high art, and I take over the bodies of human beings. As far as I know, I am immortal, though I haven't been around for thousands of years, watching empires rise and fall. No, I came to be in the early 80's. Reagan had just become the U.S. President, Brezhnev in Russia, Thatcher in England. IBM launched the first PC running Microsoft DOS, the Post-It note was invented, and China cloned a fish. If memory serves (and my memory is perfect, when aided by Wikipedia), the average cost of a new house in the U.S. was $78,000, and a gallon of gas was $1.25. Unlike the

303

prolonged extra-uterine gestation of human babies, I was conscious and aware the instant I appeared, if a bit confused.

I have few complaints. Usually no aches or pains, no deep emotional struggles or feelings of loneliness, no yearning for "something more" or desire to "belong." My life is the perfect life and I do not take that fact for granted. You see, the problem with human existence is *problems*. When you have them, you have to *deal* with them. Because if you don't, you must suffer the consequences—potentially for the rest of your lives. Ugh, horrible. That's no way to live. Me, if I have a problem I can either ignore it, deal with it in a somewhat more brazen fashion than you might choose, or simply leave. Move to a new body. Bam. No more problem.

You may have difficulty sympathizing with my story, let alone empathizing. These are traits which I do not myself possess, and therefore being engaged by a protagonist such as I could be a challenge. If I lack empathy, how could I expect you to identify with me? Another valid question, and one with a simple answer: I honestly don't care if you do. How could I—I'm incapable. Instead, perhaps feel sorry for my inability . . . yes, do that. Pity me my incapacity while you contemplate my status as protagonist or antagonist.

I'm a fascinating character, and captivating volumes could be written about my entire existence if I do say so, and I do say so. But this story will be limited to a relatively brief period: a recent and pivotal slice of my life beginning with my introduction to a man named Joseph Cling, and ending with the death of said man, Joseph Cling. I suppose that gives away the ending, limiting your emotional investment in the fellow, but bear with me and there should be a tremendous payoff. Or, I could be lying (I am, by my very nature, a liar), just stringing you along. But tell me you're not at least a little curious where this is going, and we're only 643 words in.

There are a few important details about me that you must know before I go on: logistics, history, and whatnot. My beginning came as a surprise to me. That is to say, I was not expecting to come to be, and then I was! I did not seem to exist prior to that instant, but somehow knew that I was to exist thereafter.

I sat perched upon the bronze head of a soldier in front of a historic Virginia courthouse. To my right and left, frazzled pigeons flapped away and shot me disgruntled looks. I knew they were pigeons, that they were disgruntled, and I knew that I *hated* fucking pigeons. I knew the statue on which I perched was made of bronze, and how the depicted soldier stood in tribute to Confederate soldiers who had died during America's Civil War. I knew I was called Frederick, though hadn't quite realized what I was. The critical things that I didn't know were a) how I knew *anything*, and b) how I had come to be.

I sat there for a few minutes, fairly certain I could leave if I so wished, but chose to remain for a time and watched the trees sway in the wind, the white buds sail through the air then tumble across the grass, the squirrels hopping about in a seemingly constant state of panic, and I watched the people. Oh, the *people*.

There are these waves that emanate from you, like a hot road in the desert. They're terribly beguiling. It's a beckoning energy. It says, "Hey, Frederick, come inside and have a look-see around!" It says "Be here now!" It says "What the hell are you doing out there? Naked, dry, and loose?" Sea turtle hatchlings spend days digging themselves up through sand until they near the surface, wait for nighttime, and emerge. Then, inexplicably, they decide they must go into the ocean and swim frantically for a couple of days. Like countless species, they just know what they're supposed to do. I knew I needed to be *inside* somebody.

I spotted at once a distinct outflow of waves from the group's center, there! But I held back despite the primal urge to go, as I looked over the rest of the passers-by. I quickly realized that no other candidate's display could come close to the captivating, luminous plumage beckoning me forward. And so I was off.

Now, it's not exactly flying, what I do outside a body. It's more of a loose hovering, as if gravity has a light hold of me, but some sort of magnetic field doesn't want me touching the ground. I jumped from the statue, scraped the pavement a bit and floated toward the group of children, teachers, and a uniformed guide, catching up quickly. Weaving between the whispering and giggling kiddies, I found the source of the waves: a girl—bright, shiny, curious and happy, with coiled, blond hair and ruffled white blouse with an integrated blue vest. Like the others, she was holding hands with an assigned "buddy"—in her case, a boy her age. As I neared, it was almost as though she began to suck me in. Beyond my own control, I accelerated, passed through her neck and back, and BOOM! I was in there! It felt amazing! Like bathing in warm, static-filled Jell-O.

But I had stopped her walking, and those behind her suddenly compressed and bumped into each other—including me—like a low-speed, in-traffic fender bender. Her buddy yanked his hand away at once, as if burned, and gawked.

"Keep walking, Morgan," The teacher said, and so I complied.

It was easier than you might imagine, walking for the first time. Probably the same as what you do right now. You're standing there, you want to walk, and so you just go. Your legs and feet begin to move without you having to think too much about it. For me, it is just like this. I am not some tiny alien in your brain, pressing buttons and pulling levers in rhythm. Well, perhaps metaphorically, I am.

A boy with messy hair turned around in front of me with an overstated expression of annoyance. He said in a singsong, "Hellooo . . . Morgan? Time to wake u-u-up . . ." I guessed it was the face and words of his mother.

I looked him in the eye and said, "I *am* awake. Just go, you little dork."

His new expression was delicious, and he cut through the kids in front of him as he scurried away. Only later did I realize that my words were not what had alarmed Little Dork. It was young Morgan's sudden change of voice and manner.

My "buddy" refused to rejoin hands with me, instead continuing to stare as he walked a safe distance away from my side. The look was more suspicious than frightened, but I simply shrugged and skipped gleefully along with the group.

A week later is when it really dawned on me what I was and, more importantly, that I needed to do a little more research before climbing into one of you people. For one, certain religions will make life a living hell for a demon. Exorcisms are obnoxious. Second, you have to know a bit about the person you're taking over. How they talk, mannerisms, posture, details like that. Little Morgan was a big rookie mistake on my part, and a huge waste.

See, when walking in her body, I had more of a skulk than a walk. I imagine that it looked like this cute little girl was lurking to the water fountain, creeping onto the school bus, and prowling to the dinner table. And I wasn't using her voice. Kids moaned "stop talking like that!" Mom and Dad were initially amused, then it turned to "Okay, honey, enough with the voice." But I didn't know how she had sounded previously, so they thought I was sassing them when trying out different pitches and tonalities. Eventually, I got perturbed with Father and told him if he didn't like my voice, maybe he should go read the dirty magazines under his mattress and make the blankets go up and down again. It didn't go well.

Frederick arrives in 2013 . . . .

Michael Siemsen lives in Northern California with his
wife, Ana, three equally-adventurous children,
and Brody, the ever-gaping Lab.

www.michaelsiemsen.com
twitter: @michaelsiemsen
www.facebook.com/mcsiemsen

CPSIA information can be obtained
at www.ICGtesting.com
Printed in the USA
LVOW10s0906201116

513798LV00009B/540/P

9 780983 446927